THE FABRICATION OF EDEN PRUITT

THE FABRICATION OF EDEN PRUITT

BOOK 1

K.E. GANSHERT

ALSO BY K.E. GANSHERT

THE CONTEST

TALES FROM THE HOLLOW SERIES
Wicked is the Hollow, book 1
Hungry is the Hollow, book 2

THE GIFTING SERIES
The Gifting, book 1
The Awakening, book 2
The Gathering, book 3
Luka, a book 1 companion novel

THE EDEN PRUITT SERIES
The Aberration of Eden Pruitt, book 2
The Revelation of Eden Pruitt, book 3
The Retribution of Eden Pruitt, book 4

For Becky

This story would have been kicked to the curb if not for your persistent encouragement. Thanks for saying, "Send it to me." And thanks for helping me fix Cassian, too.

FABRICATION

"Eyyyyyyye-oh-wahh." Eighteen-year-old Eden Pruitt drew out the syllables, shaping each one with the exaggerated stretching and contracting of her lips. Over the course of the past few days, she kept saying the word at random times to nobody in particular. In the dark of night, her blonde hair tangling with the ocean wind. In the car by herself on the last leg of a long journey. In the gas station bathroom while staring at her reflection in a dirty mirror. And now, on the threshold of a box-laden bedroom with another one in her arms. Perhaps if she said it enough, this new reality might feel less like a lucid dream.

Iowa.

It was an odd-sounding name, without any consonants to pin it down. A state people probably confused with Ohio or Idaho—somewhere in the middle—if their geography was bad.

"Iowa," she said again, louder this time. More matter of fact, with a slight Parisian accent. Eden Pruitt wasn't French, nor had she ever been to France. She did, however, study the language in school with the dream of living there at some point in college. Unlike many of her classmates back in San Diego, her parents were abidingly middle class. While several of her peers had spent spring breaks on the beaches of Tahiti getting tan or the snowy peaks of the Swiss Alps on a pair of skis, Eden and her best friend Erik spent theirs two hours north in Disneyland, the Happiest Place on Earth—a bold tagline when places like Paris and Tahiti existed. Eden understood that if she wanted to see the world, studying abroad was her best shot, and she absolutely wanted to see the world. Sometimes so much, she felt sick with longing for places she'd never been.

Not Iowa. But Paris? Absolutely.

She took a step inside her new *boudoir* and inhaled deeply. The comforting scent of old maps and gel pens from the box beneath her nose mingled with the newness of a room that was hers, but only just. She set the box on the plush carpet by the window and placed her palm against the white trim, taking in her second-story view. Two rows of brick houses lining an empty suburban street. And beyond that, a cornfield.

An involuntary hum sounded in the back of her throat. For the sake of her parents, she would make a fresh start in Iowa. And this time, she wouldn't mess up.

Eden watched as her mother hefted a box from the back of the U-Haul, the sun turning her ashy blonde hair lemon yellow. Could a stranger point out the sadness? Or after eighteen years of careful study, was Eden simply seeing what she knew was there? Mom passed Dad midway up the lawn, who was on his way back to the truck. She gave him a brave smile—one that made Eden's stomach twist with one part shame, two parts fortitude. Her parents said they were moving because Dad received a job offer he couldn't refuse. It was a lie. Or rather, an excuse. One Eden played along with. She didn't want to start over at the beginning of her senior year. That wasn't the kind of adventure she was looking for. Nor did she want to leave Erik one year earlier than planned. But she wasn't going to make this harder than she already had. She would be good, like her parents raised her to be. They would get through tomorrow, like they always did, and all three of them would return to normal. At least, as normal as life could be in *Iowa*.

Movement in her periphery caught her attention.

Up and to the left, a pitch-black spider dangled from an invisible web, its legs gracefully turning like an acrobat suspended in mid-air. A blood-red hourglass marked its abdomen—a clear warning. A signal to the world to stand back. Danger. Poison. But Eden Pruitt did not stand back. She didn't lurch away. Her feet stayed rooted in place, her head slightly tilted. Erik told her once that the female would paralyze its mate during sex and eat it afterward, hence the name—widows of their own making. She'd never actually seen one before, and here one was. Dangling in front of her face. A nocturnal creature doing what it wasn't supposed to do—basking in the mid-morning sun.

Slowly, she extended her hand. She held out her thumb, an invitation for the spider to climb aboard. It's eight spindly legs touched her skin like the brush of a feather. She watched it crawl across her knuckles, back and forth, back and forth.

"Eden!"

With a start, she shook the spider off.

It landed on its back, legs twisting.

She stared down at it, her pulse skittish in the hollow of her clavicle, and stomped the spider dead.

"Hey, you."

Eden turned.

Dad stood in the doorway—boyish even at fifty, his hair perpetually tousled. "Hiding in here already?"

She tucked her hands into the back pockets of her jean shorts and smiled a little too brightly, a little too guiltily. "It's a good room."

Her father smiled back—optimism shining in his eyes—then jerked his head, a handless invitation to join him. "We're going to start moving the furniture. Your brute strength is required."

There had never been anything brute about Eden's strength, but she flexed her arms and left the dead spider behind.

———

I n the kitchen, Eden's father had already connected the small flat screen and found a station that televised a constant loop of all the latest headlines. Dad was a news junkie. He'd always been that way. So much so that by the age of six, Eden could talk more intelligently about current events than most adults.

Mom plopped a box marked "crockery" on the countertop and gave Eden the same brave smile she'd given Dad. Then the three of them got to work—hardboiled to return the truck before 3 pm—making trips in and out, lugging furniture, mattresses, and bed frames while the sun reached its pinnacle in the sky and began its slow decent westward, all while Concordia News ran in the background—a highlight reel of the good and the bad, the happy and the sad, the triumph and the troubling that marked humanity.

There was a national manhunt for a missing boy named Barrett Barr—the same age as Eden. An interview with the paraplegic man who took his first unassisted steps since a car accident five years ago. Another with the neurosurgeon who made it happen. A press conference with the director of the FBI regarding the latest pipe bomb—this time in Texas—spreading fear through the country like ripples across a pond. And the approaching Prosperity Ball, an annual event going on its second year. Established and hosted by America's own self-made billionaire—CEO of SubTech, founder of SafePad, and beloved philanthropist, Oswin Brahm. A man who not only helped rebuild the country after its near collapse two decades ago but donated millions to its recovery.

At ten to three, they emptied the back of the truck.

Eden jumped into one of their two family cars to follow her

father to the nearest U-Haul location, getting her first real look at the mid-sized town of Eagle Bend while Concordia Radio played in the background.

"At this time, we are urging the public to report any package that has not been delivered via postal drone." The loud voice belonged to Kendra Cruz, America's Chairperson of the Board. "We have surveillance teams working around the clock to identify the culprit. Until then, please know—"

"Quiet," Eden said.

Chairwoman Cruz's voice turned into a whisper. Outside, the sidewalks filled with students emerging from the school day. They passed an elementary school named Truman, where a severe-looking crossing guard policed the corner and kids shouted and ran around like maniacs—making the kind of noise unique to playgrounds, the kind that could just as easily be horrified panic as unencumbered delight. They passed the one and only junior high, a large, industrial-looking building with kids practicing football in the grass. And a little further along, the high school.

A bottleneck of cars squeezed their way out of the crowded parking lot with no apparent method to the madness—just a honking, gesticulating, mostly good-natured fight for the exit. Nearby, on the expansive front lawn, a digital sign advertised Kick Off Week. A parade tomorrow evening. A football game Friday, the first of the season. Eden had seen parade signs on the drive into town on their way to their new home—tacked onto storefront windows, decorated with blue and silver balloons.

Beyond the student chaos, past a few more stoplights, Dad pulled the truck into the U-Haul parking lot, three o'clock on the nose. Eden parked while he jogged through the lot and disappeared inside the building. The quiet voice of Ms. Cruz had been replaced by that of the radio host.

"Mr. Brahm has officially confirmed that the ball will be open to fifty members of the general public via old-fashioned lottery.

Fifty tickets, folks! And of course, those of us unlucky enough to win will be able to join virtually."

"Off," Eden said, cutting the engine.

She sat for a moment in the silence, battling a strong bout of loneliness. Seeing all those students—all those cars—had done it to her. Tomorrow, she'd be in that chaos. Amongst them, but not a part of them. A stranger in their midst.

She climbed out of the car into the sunlight. She pulled her long hair into a messy topknot using the tie she always wore on her wrist. She propped the bottom of her sandaled foot against the car door, folded her arms, and leaned back. It smelled different in Iowa, with no salt on the air from the sea. She didn't like being so far from the coast. She felt closed in, claustrophobic. Something told her the Mississippi River—as large as it was— would not be the same as the Pacific. Perhaps this was what she would miss the most—the sound of waves, and the smell of brine.

Her phone dinged in her pocket.

She pulled it out and found a text from Erik.

We have a 1 in 6.5 million chance of attending.

Eden smiled. She knew exactly what he was talking about. Erik was always computing random probabilities. Today's statistic featured the recent news surrounding the Prosperity Ball and the chance that either of them would snag a ticket.

Before she could reply, a video appeared of Erik sitting on his bed playing the Ukulele next to Jeb—the one-eyed bulldog he'd rescued from a kill shelter last year. Jeb panted happily with his tongue lolling, a bowtie wrapped around his thick neck while his skinny owner sang an excessively pained rendition of *Ain't No Sunshine* by Bill Withers.

Eden snorted with laughter as a Tesla blasting loud music whipped into the parking lot. Instead of turning left toward U-Haul, they veered right, toward a squat, brick building called The Roast. A breeze danced with a strand of loose hair around her temple. She tucked it behind her ear, sent a laughing gif back to Erik, then shot her dad a text.

Caffeine withdrawal. Coffee shop next door. Pick your poison.

A scrolling ellipse appeared, and then:

Surprise me. :)

She trotted toward the storefront, which also had a sign. *Kick Off Parade. 6 pm. Starts and ends at the High School, followed by a Pep Rally. Come support the Eagles!* With a slight roll of her eyes, she pulled open the door and scooted inside, where the cool air encircled her legs and the kids from the Tesla stood at the counter. Two guys and a girl—future classmates? Eden stepped in line behind them, pretending not to notice the way they kept peeking at her over their shoulders. The door opened and shut at her back, most likely letting in more students. An after-school rush. Her skin prickled with the distinct sensation of someone's stare—so invasive, the tiny hairs on the back of her neck stood on end. She bit the inside of her cheek, her jaw jutting forward. The open stares exacerbated her loneliness.

The kids in front of her finished their orders and shuffled off to find a table. Eden smiled at the gentleman working the cash register and placed an order for two iced coffees with cream and a chai tea for Mom. She paid with a crumpled twenty-dollar bill, then turned around to wait in the back when an older lady holding a cane fumbled with her change purse.

Coins clattered to the floor.

On instinct, Eden bent to pick them up. Next to her, another good Samaritan did too. Their fingers brushed over a fallen quarter. She jerked her hand away and looked up. Into the face of a young man. They were crouched so close, she could see the black of his pupils expanding inside dark butterscotch irises. For the briefest of moments, the connection between them simmered with heat. He was attractive. Distractingly so. But then his gaze gave way to something else. Something like … animosity, as though he was angry at her for helping.

Blood rushed into Eden's cheeks as the boy surrendered the

quarter. She stood—a little dizzy, a lot confused—and poured the change into the woman's coin purse with a kind smile.

The lady was touched. Very touched. Like she didn't run into kindness often. Nobody else in line had reacted at all. Nobody else but herself and the boy. In fact, a girl at the end had groaned, making Eden feel protective of the elderly woman. She wanted to help her to the counter. Sit with her at the table. Ask her about her day. Show her the video of Erik and Jeb, who were always a hit whenever the duo joined her at the nursing home she used to visit in San Diego.

"Hey, kid."

Eden startled.

The greeting belonged to her father. He'd come inside and scooted beside her.

"What'd you order me?" he asked.

"Iced coffee with cream," she said.

On cue, a worker called her name.

The two of them collected their drinks and exited the now-crowded coffee shop. When she reached the door, she paused and glanced at the line. But the young man was no longer there. She couldn't find him anywhere. It was like he had vanished. It was like he'd never been there at all.

2

Eden was supposed to be in first period study hall, filling out college applications with Erik—the significance of today's date not lost on him. He would do his best to distract her. And if she wanted to talk, he would listen. Instead, she was here—opening her locker in this busy, unfamiliar hallway. It was a different setting, the same story. Girls and boys shoving their way up the ladder of social hierarchy, wondering where the new girl fit. The only other time she'd been in this position—when her family moved from Seattle to San Diego at the beginning of sixth grade—she'd made her disinterest in the ladder abundantly clear. On her very first day, when a group of pretty girls waved at her in invitation from the other side of the cafeteria, Eden pretended not to see. Instead, she chose a table occupied by a skinny, Filipino boy wearing a t-shirt with a black rook on the front.

When she'd plunked her tray onto the table, he'd looked up from his tattered copy of *1984* by George Orwell—a book he'd been reading under his desk during first period Health class—and gaped, as if nobody had ever sat across from him before.

"I'm Eden Pruitt," she'd said, matter-of-factly.

His cheeks had flamed red. He'd stammered for a moment or

9

two, and then finally—returned her introduction. "I'm Erik Gaviola." And then, as if she'd had a pen and wanted to write it down, he added, "That's Erik with a K."

Sitting next to Erik had been a strategic move, one that took Eden off the ladder instantaneously. It was also the best move of her sixth grade year. Because once she got past Erik's painful shyness, he was one of the wittiest, most interesting people she'd ever met. Eden should find another Erik. An ally to get her through her final year. Instead, she found herself searching for the boy from yesterday. The boy who disappeared inside the coffee shop. She couldn't stop wondering why he'd looked at her like that—his expression filled with accusation, as if she'd personally offended him by helping an old woman with her fallen change. It didn't make sense, and things that didn't make sense had a way of pestering Eden. Like a small chip on a fingernail otherwise perfectly painted. She would pick and pick until the polish was gone altogether. For whatever reason, he didn't like her. And yet, he didn't know her.

The injustice of it rankled.

His face was stuck in her mind like gum on the bottom of a shoe, and yesterday—while she helped arrange furniture and reconstruct bed frames, and smiled along with her father in a joint effort to distract Mom from her encroaching grief—Eden kept pulling it up for inspection. His was a face that lacked even the subtlest remains of boyhood. All chiseled lines and strong jaw and full lips. And those eyes. She wasn't sure she'd ever seen eyes quite like them. Not because of their color—a rich, deep gold—but because of their intensity. It was as though he had bionic vision, used every ounce of it to appraise her, and decided he didn't like what he saw. Before slipping off to sleep, she figured he was too old for high school. More than likely, he attended Eagle Bend's community college.

Even so, she couldn't help looking a little. Or wishing she had the talent to draw him from memory—make the picture as sharp on paper as it was in her mind and start showing it around. *Do you know this person? If so, does he look at everyone like they've offended him in some egregious way?* Surely the upper-classmen attended some of the same parties as the local college students. Eagle Bend wasn't so big that someone wouldn't recognize a face like his.

"Hey."

A kid stood behind her—tall and lanky with floppy hair and a straight, white smile that was a little too big for his narrow face. He glanced over his shoulder at a group of his peers off to the right, all of them watching with interest, then back at her, his smile widening. "I'm Colbie."

"Like the cheese?"

He blinked at her, like no one had ever said those particular words before.

She forced a smile, talking herself out of her irritation. Colbie No-Relation-to-Jack seemed like a nice enough fellow. At least he wasn't looking at her like he loathed her for no good reason. "Eden," she said.

He stuck out his hand. "It's nice to meet you, Eden."

She shook it.

He held on for a moment longer than necessary, then leaned casually against the locker in front of hers, his thumbs looped beneath the straps of his backpack. "So ... you're new."

"Yep."

"Where'd you move from?"

"San Diego."

"No kidding?" He gave a subtle jerk of his head, a gesture that flicked the hair from his eyes. "That's a brutal transition. Especially for someone like you."

She quirked an eyebrow. "Someone like me?"

"You look like you belong on a beach."

Eden grabbed two notebooks and a pencil. "How do you feel about pi, Colbie?"

His forehead puckered. "The dessert?"

"The ratio of a circle's circumference to its diameter." Erik had memorized the first hundred numbers. Every March Four-teenth, he insisted they go out for actual pie and when the wait-ress came to their table, he'd rattle off as many numbers as possible before the waitress could ask for their order. Last year, he reached thirty-six. The poor girl had looked from Erik to Eden like he was having some sort of seizure before finally catching on.

Colbie laughed, like Eden was being funny.

Her face remained impassive, cutting his laughter short.

"Um … I guess I don't really think about it."

"That's too bad." She shut her locker and started on her way to first period. Colbie would not be her new Erik. But he quickly followed after her, inquiring about her schedule. As he talked about Mr. Timmins—her teacher for first period Anatomy and Physiology, who apparently handed out king-size candy bars in class—she considered asking him about the acrimonious stranger from The Roast. But then, what would she say? *So Colbie, do you happen to know a guy who's a little older than us, with really intense eyes?*

"You said second period is French? That'll be right here. Ms. Bell's a little scary at first, but pretty cool once you get to know her." They passed the classroom, then walked into a stairwell, up the stairs, and back out again—into a locker bay bedecked with posters advertising the parade.

Colbie caught her looking at one. "Are you going tonight?"

"Probably not."

"You should come. Everyone goes. Literally, the whole town shows up. I'm walking during the parade part, but afterward, a bunch of us will head to The Point to have a bonfire."

"You're walking in it?"

"The whole football team does."

"Ah. The football team."

"I play wide receiver. We should be pretty good this year." He did another hair-flick without any hands, then stopped in front of a classroom at the beginning of the hallway. They'd reached Anatomy and Physiology with Mr. Timmins.

Colbie had escorted her the whole way.

She gave him a nod of thanks, then walked inside, where Mr. Timmins—a man who was almost as wide as he was tall—handed her a school-issued laptop and welcomed her to Eagle Bend. She found a seat up front and off to the side, avoiding the board, where the date was displayed in big, obnoxious print. She opened her new computer, logged in with her student ID, and opened the online material for Anatomy and Physiology. After perusing the syllabus, she scrolled through the textbook, pausing occasionally to glance at a diagram and admire the complexity of the human body until the bell rang. Class had officially begun. When there was five minutes to go, Mr. Timmins clapped his meaty paws and grabbed a King-sized Hershey bar perched on the ledge of the board Eden was avoiding.

Glazed-over expressions went sharp and attentive.

"Who's ready for a challenge?" He waggled the chocolate like a carrot. "The person who can name the most muscles in the human body wins. Computers closed. And no peeking at your phones."

Hands shot into the air.

Mr. Timmins called on a boy named Weston who was wearing a shirt one-size too small. Or maybe his muscles were one-size too big. He seemed to flex his own corresponding muscles as he recited the ones he knew aloud. "Biceps. Triceps. Abs. Traps. Pecs." He leaned back in his chair, his attention sliding to the ceiling—like there was a cheat sheet hiding in one of the fluorescent lights. "Gluteus Maximus."

The class laughed.

"Calves."

Mr. Timmins held up his hand. "Our calves are made up of two muscles, neither of which are called calves."

"Really?"

"This is anatomy class, Mr. Jones. Not Weightlifting 101."

More laughter ensued.

Weston smiled good-naturedly and shrugged.

"Does anyone happen to know which two muscles make up the calves?" Mr. Timmins asked, holding the Hershey bar aloft.

"The gastrocnemius and the soleus." The words tumbled from Eden's mouth, every bit as surprising to her as anyone.

Her classmates turned to stare.

Mr. Timmins visibly brightened. "Well done, Ms. Pruitt. Do you know any others?"

"The vastus lateralis, the vastus medialis, the vastus intermedium, the rectus femoris." Those were the four muscles that made up the quadriceps. Four muscles she had no idea existed until she saw them on a diagram in her online textbook. Somehow, it was crystal clear in her mind, like she was staring at a physical copy. She found that she could keep going. If she wanted, she could list every muscle that had been on her computer screen. It would be as easy as reading from a list. But Eden didn't keep going. Eden was too caught off guard to keep going.

Her classmates gaped.

The room had gone quiet.

"Did you study anatomy in your previous school?" Mr. Timmins finally asked.

"Uh … yeah." She smiled sheepishly. "I did."

It was a bold-faced lie. The only anatomy Eden had ever studied was forty-five minutes ago, when she scrolled through her Anatomy book. And it hadn't been more than a glance.

"Ah-ha! Well, even so, I'm impressed." He looked around the class, bouncing a little on his toes. "Does anyone think they have a better handle on the muscular system than our new student, Ms. Pruitt?"

Nobody raised their hand.

Mr. Timmins tossed Eden the bar.

It sailed across the room, and despite being cursed with butterfingers, she snagged it cleanly from the air.

3

Someone bumped Eden from behind.

"So sorry!" The apology belonged to a woman with flyaway hair and was quickly proceeded by the bark of a name. "Daniel! I told you to watch where you're going."

She tossed Eden a contrite glance over her shoulder as she ushered Daniel, along with two more boys down the otherwise deserted street. All three kids clutched small bags in their hands and talked excitedly about all the candy they were going to get.

Eden glanced around, as if awakening from a long dream.

She was standing in front of a place called Guppy's. Through her reflection in the storefront window, she could see bins of candy and an ice cream counter and an old-fashioned soda fountain. In the distance, she could hear the unmistakable sound of a marching band.

Crap!

She reached into the back pocket of her jean shorts, but all she found was the king-sized chocolate bar she caught at the end of first period. She patted her front pockets. Her phone was nowhere.

"Excuse me, ma'am?" she called.

The frazzled woman looked over her shoulder without stopping.

"What's the time?"

"Just after five!"

Oh crap.

Crap, crap, crap.

Eden stood frozen with uncertainty. She'd lost track of time—on this day, of all days. Her parents would be worried—freaking out, in fact—and she couldn't call them to let them know she was fine because she didn't have a phone to call them with.

The sun glinted off the storefront glass, too low in the sky. She shook her head, as if that might remove the fuzz inside. Ever since first period, she'd floated through the hours in a daze—spending lunchtime not in the cafeteria, but in the library on her new laptop, searching things like "sudden onset of photographic memory". She'd found nothing helpful. Mostly articles and blog posts from naysayers. It was not possible to suddenly develop a photographic memory, the experts said. And yet, when she looked up pi, glanced at it for not more than a second, then turned away, she could rattle off every number that fit on the screen. More numbers than Erik. Wicked smart, headed for Ivy League, passionate about pi Erik.

Now the parade was starting. Guppy's was closed, along with every other store along the street. Apparently, Colbie didn't lie. Everyone went to the parade—even business owners. Eden began to jog. Slow at first, then faster—guilt propelling her forward. And the urgent need to assure her parents that she was okay. Everything was okay.

The evening air was sticky. By the time she reached her new street, the cotton of her t-shirt clung to her sweat-dampened back and her white sneaker chaffed against the inside of her left foot. She fully expected to find her parents out on the lawn, waiting. She half-expected flashing lights in her driveway. But her front lawn matched all the others—empty and quiet.

She cut through the grass and flung open the door.

"Mom? Dad?" she called. "I'm home!"

Cool air clashed against her skin as she stepped all the way inside, rousing an army of goose bumps. Except, maybe it wasn't the cool air rousing them. Maybe it was something else. Something … *off*. She stopped mid-stride, the floorboards creaking underfoot.

The bench they'd placed in the small foyer was tipped on its side.

Eden considered that fallen piece of furniture—caught by the sight of it like she'd been caught by the black widow spider dangling in her window. Dread seeped into her stomach as she took a hesitant step forward and tried to make sense of the scene in front of her.

The living room. In complete disarray. Every box they had placed there—boxes full of things that didn't fit into any particular room—upended. Smashed and torn. As if someone had ripped them open and dumped the contents. Dad's books lay in splayed, haphazard piles across the floor. And the glass coffee table had been smashed to pieces. Shards of it glinted like splashes of water on the carpet.

Frozen—unable to move—she called for her mom and dad again. Only her voice didn't sound like her voice. It had gone shaky. Uncertain. And there was no response but silence.

The air conditioning unit rattled to life.

Air from the vent sent the sheer, taupe drapes fluttering.

The back of Eden's neck prickled like it did yesterday when she stood in line at the coffee shop. Like someone was watching her.

Dread morphed into fear. Sharp and cold.

She took a step back, stumbling over the bench behind her. She caught herself before falling, stared for one last heart-stopping moment at the carnage in front of her, then turned on her heel and ran. She tore across the lawn, hurdled a shrub, and knocked frantically on the neighbor's door with her heart pounding in her temples, her throat, her knees.

The house erupted with barking. The deep, rumbling kind that made most people back away.

But not Eden.

She punched the doorbell button with her thumb, willing someone to answer—shooting looks at her house as though whoever broke in might step out at any second and smash her next. The barking turned ferocious. Maniacal. But nobody answered. The windows were dark.

Eden ran to the next house.

And the next.

And the next.

But nobody was home.

Like Colbie said, everyone was at the parade.

4

A mile later—filled with adrenaline and urgency—Eden reached the parade route.

Tiny drones circled overhead as little girls in matching sequined leotards shook glittery pompoms, marching in front of a pair of old-fashioned cars honking funny-sounding horns. The drivers tossed handfuls of candy out from opened windows like they had a never-ending supply. Children made a mad scramble for their favorites while adults supervised with varying degrees of vigilance. Behind them, teenagers stood in scattered pockets—watching, laughing, cajoling.

Eden frantically searched the crowd, and just as the two cars passed—horns blaring *ahooga!*—she spotted help. A police officer across the street. In the short gap of distance between those two cars and a Little League team sponsored by Guppy's, Eden made a break for it. On the other side, she wound her way through the throng like a salmon swimming upstream until she reached him. Officer Smith, according to the name badge he wore on his breast pocket.

"Excuse me, sir. I need help."

As soon as his attention swiveled to Eden, his expression went from jovial to alert. His hand moved unconsciously to his baton, as if she, herself were dangerous. "Are you okay?" he asked through the noise.

She shook her head, working to catch her breath. "Someone broke into my house. I-I don't know where my parents are. I can't call them. I don't have my phone."

His eyebrows pulled tight, like a drawstring being cinched together. He escorted her off to the side, beneath the awning of a bicycle shop. "You said your house was burglarized?"

Eden swallowed and nodded. "Yes. I mean—I lost track of time, and when I ran home, my house … somebody must have broken into it. We just moved in yesterday, and there were boxes everywhere. Books, too. Our coffee table was broken, and I-I can't call my parents because I don't have my phone. I must have left it in my bedroom."

"All right," Officer Smith said, holding up his hands in a gesture of calm. "You're going to be okay. Just take some deep breaths."

She tried to obey his orders.

"What's your address?"

"3235 West Buckle Lane."

He pulled a pen and a miniature notebook from his shirt pocket just as the Eagle Bend High School football team came into view, riding in the back of a large trailer, dressed in clean white jerseys with blue lettering. The crowd broke into riotous applause. So loud, it made her want to clamp her hands over her ears.

As if noticing, the officer ushered her inside the bike shop. As soon as the door closed behind them, the noise dulled. But only just. He lifted his hand in a polite salute to the employee behind the counter. "We just need a quiet space for a bit, if that's all right."

"Not a problem."

Officer Smith turned back to Eden. "Could you give me the address again?"

This time, he jotted it down while her heart rate and breathing returned to something closer to normal. She'd found help. Everything was going to be okay. He'd contact her parents, who were most definitely out looking for her. In their worry, they probably forgot to lock up—and then, by dumb luck, someone decided to break in. Her parents would be upset that she'd gone AWOL, upset that some of their things had been ruined, but their overriding emotion would be relief. Everything was going to be okay.

"Was anyone in the house when you arrived?"

"I-I don't know for sure." She recalled the feeling of being watched. Had the burglar been there, hiding in the shadows? The thought sent a shiver down her spine. "As soon as I realized what happened, I left. None of the neighbors were home, so I ran here."

"How far did you get into the house?"

"I walked into the foyer, and I noticed that the bench was tipped over, and then I saw the living room. Please sir, I need to call my parents." For a flash of a second, Eden imagined them at home when it happened. She imagined a burglar barging through the door, wielding a gun. But she quickly banished the thought. If that were the case, the burglar would have told her parents to get down on the ground, and they would have listened. They would have obeyed. They would have let the robber take whatever he wanted, and then as soon as he left, they would have called the police. They wouldn't have abandoned the crime scene. "They're probably out looking for me. I'm sure they're worried."

Officer Smith wrote down Eden's information. Her name. Her parents' names. Their phone numbers. Then he unclipped his walkie-talkie from his belt and radioed dispatch.

"Mercer County, EB. Joe Bravo, 141."

There was a quick burst of white noise, and then, "Go ahead, 141."

"I was just approached by a female juvenile reporting a

burglary, possible burglary in progress. Address is 3235 West Buckle Lane, EB. Juvenile's name is Eden Pruitt. Break."

"Go ahead."

"I need a call to one or both parents to let them know there's been a disturbance at their home, their daughter is okay, and we're headed there now."

"Roger that, 141. Go ahead with the numbers."

Officer Smith gave the dispatcher the two phone numbers, then the dispatcher assigned backup. When he was finished, he clipped his radio to his belt, thanked the bike store employee for the quiet space, and motioned for Eden to follow him outside. He'd parked on a side street. When they reached his squad car, he opened the back door for Eden to climb inside—a déjà vu if ever there was one.

She hesitated.

"I'd let you sit up front with me if it wasn't against protocol."

Eden laughed nervously. What was happening now was not a repeat of what happened in San Diego. Losing track of time wasn't a crime. With that thought firmly in place, she forced herself to climb inside.

Plexiglas separated her from Officer Smith. He slid it open once he situated himself behind the wheel, then began maneuvering around the parade route to get to Eden's new street, asking more questions along the way. Did she have any dogs? How recently did they move? What brought them to Eagle Bend? Eden was fairly certain the majority of his questions were for her benefit—an attempt to distract her. He didn't seem too bothered by a break-in, or by the fact that the dispatcher felt as though back up was necessary. Eden, on the other hand, was having a hard time concentrating on her answers. Why did this have to happen —on *this* day of all days? She balled her hands into fists so tight her fingernails bit into the flesh of her palms. Her knee bounced up and down like a jackhammer as she craned her neck to see if her parents had come home while she went running for help.

Officer Smith pulled up to the curb.

Eden peered at the house. It looked quiet, unthreatening. Like every other house on the block.

Except …

She tilted her head.

The front door was closed.

She hadn't closed the front door, had she? No, she hadn't. She'd been too busy running for her life to close it.

Another squad car pulled up behind them.

"All right." Officer Smith gave her what was probably meant to be an encouraging smile. Only she didn't feel encouraged. She felt off-kilter. Discombobulated. Like she was staring at a beloved painting by Claude Monet that had been subtly altered. "Sit tight."

He climbed out into the humidity and met the other officer— a female officer—at the end of her driveway. She watched them confer, her heart thudding like a dull, pulsing ache in her temples. Eden's attention swiveled from them to the length of the empty street, willing her father's car to appear. The dispatcher would have called them by now. They would know she was okay. They'd be desperate to get to her, and they had to be relatively close. She looked back at the officers. Joe was heading to the porch, when suddenly, the front door swung open.

A man stepped out.

The officers drew their guns and yelled at him to freeze.

The stranger lifted his arms into the air. It was the burglar. He was still there. Which meant he'd been there when Eden was there. She bit the inside of her cheek, waiting for the man to put his hands behind his back so they could cuff him. Waiting for the two police officers to read the man his rights. But the man didn't put his hands behind his back. He was too busy talking. Judging by the severe set of his gunmetal-gray eyebrows, his words weren't happy ones.

Officer Smith and his female counterpart brought down their guns.

Eden pressed her face against the window.

The man gesticulated to the front door behind him.

What was he doing? What was happening? He was the burglar, right? But then, he didn't look so much like a burglar as he did a strict, physically imposing grandfather. Maybe he was one of Eden's neighbors. Maybe he was the owner of the mean, barking dogs. Maybe he realized her house had been broken into, and he was inside looking for the burglar when the police arrived.

She spread her hand flat against the glass, desperate to know.

The man walked back inside. Into *her* house.

Officer Smith turned and squinted at her. He unclipped his radio and spoke again to the dispatcher. Eden rapped on the window to gather his attention. But he turned away and kept speaking on his radio. She twisted in her seat, toward the empty street. Still no sign of her parents. And now the man had returned. He had something in his hand.

Whatever it was, he showed it to them.

They talked some more. There was a lot of nodding. A lot of weight shifting. A lot of brief glances over their shoulders, at her. And then—shockingly—they shook hands. The officers turned around and walked away.

Eden sat with her back ramrod straight, her breathing shallow.

As soon as Officer Smith opened the driver side door, her questions flew—tumbling over one another in a rush. "Who was that guy? What's he doing in my house? Why are you letting him go?"

The officer tugged on the bill of his hat. "Are you positive that's your house?"

Eden leaned back, her chin pulling inward. "What?"

"3235 West Buckle Lane. You're sure that's your address?"

"Of course I'm sure."

He twisted his lips to the side, studying her like she'd gone from victim to suspect. "Ms. Pruitt, do you have any identification?"

She blinked a few times. "Yes, I have ID. But it's inside my house. Along with my phone."

Officer Smith stared at her for a long moment, the corners of his mouth pinched. Then he looked back at the house, sucked on his teeth. "Miss, that gentleman has lived at 3235 West Buckle Lane for the past twenty-three years."

"*What?*" she said again, the word escaping like a yelp.

"And the phone number you gave us for your mother went to a pizza place in Seattle. The other one was disconnected."

"I—I don't understand."

"Have you taken anything recently?"

"No! Of course not. I haven't taken anything. I'm … there's been some sort of mistake. That's my house. I told you, we moved here yesterday."

"My friend there—Officer Tammy? She's familiar with this neighborhood, and she doesn't remember seeing a For Sale sign in the yard recently."

"Th-that's because it happened really fast. My dad was looking for houses, and while he was online, the listing popped up. The lady who sold it to us joked that she didn't even have to put up a sign." Eden cupped her forehead, her mind spinning. He didn't believe her. She could tell he didn't believe her. It was written all over his face. "Please believe me. That's my house. I don't know who that man is, but he's lying. Go inside, and you'll see. You'll see the mess. You'll find my phone and my ID. I swear."

Officer Smith looked down the street, still empty from the parade. "How about we drive to the station, and see if we can't get this all sorted out?"

5

éjà vu. It hounded her as the radio squawked on the otherwise quiet, tense drive. It hounded her as Officer Smith kept one eye on Eden in his rearview mirror. And it hounded her as she followed him inside a back entrance of the police station.

This wasn't her first time.

He brought her to his desk, where there was a framed photograph of a more casual, sunburned Officer Smith. He wore a Hawaiian shirt and cargo shorts and he held a cute, chubby baby in one arm, a paper plate of potluck food in the other.

Next to the framed photograph was a phone.

She had to summon every ounce of strength to keep from lurching at it. Snatching it up. Calling her parents and hearing their voices and shoving the receiver at the man to show him she wasn't crazy. The dispatcher had gotten something wrong. Somehow, in the line of communication that went from Eden to the officer to the lady on the other side of the walkie-talkie, a number lost its place. Like a game of telephone. And with that cleared up, they could get to the bottom of whatever in the world was going on at her new house.

"Can I use that, please?" she asked. "Can I call my parents?"

Officer Smith motioned to a nearby chair. "Why don't you have a seat and sit tight for just a second."

"But—"

"I'm going to talk to that gentleman right over there and then I'll be back."

Eden shot a glance in the direction of his point as Officer Smith set his hat on the desk and walked away. He meandered across the station toward another man in uniform. His supervisor, maybe? The two of them conferred. Smith, with his fist over his mouth, like he didn't want Eden reading his lips. Her leg bounced. The man looked at her over his shoulder, and she quickly looked away—her face hot beneath his scrutiny. She forced her knee into stillness, and clutched the armrests of the chair. Her fingers dug into the upholstery. She would remain calm. She would follow their rules. She would obey protocol, and everything would be okay, just like the officer promised.

The front doors swooshed open, letting in the late evening air. For one hopeful explosion of a second, Eden expected to see her frantic parents rushing inside—their faces clouded with worry—ready to file a missing person's report. Instead, it was a man with leathery skin covered in tattoos. He moved through his retinal scan, then searched the inside of the mostly-empty police station and stopped when he reached her. His gaze lingered for longer than normal, and the same feeling that haunted her in the back of the squad car, the same feeling that followed her here, grabbed hold of her again—*déjà vu*. Somehow, she felt as though she'd looked into those beady eyes before.

"May I help you?" a female officer asked from behind a desk, gathering the man's attention.

He stepped forward, scratching his neck, where there was an inky rendering of a butterfly. "Yes. I'd—uh—like to report a suspicious vehicle."

Eden eyed him, suspicious herself.

Why was he so familiar?

Who was that man at her house?

What was going on?

A voice cleared.

She looked up.

Officer Smith was back. "Let's go ahead and try calling your parents again."

The tension swooshed out of her like the quick release of a breath held much too long. Shifting to the edge of the chair, she gave Officer Smith her mother's number first. She watched him like a hawk as he dialed, and then she pressed her lips together as he brought the receiver to his ear. She could hear the ringing —loud and clear, like the phone was against the side of her face instead of his.

On the third ring, a voice answered, "Good evening, Pizza Palace, how can I help you?"

She reared back as if Officer Smith had slapped her.

He hung up slowly, deliberately. He tried asking for her father's number, but Eden couldn't give it. Confusion had stolen her voice. So he pulled his miniature notebook from his front pocket and showed her the number he'd jotted earlier. She nodded—an affirmative—and Smith dialed again. This time, her father.

Almost immediately, a robotic whistling filled the line, followed by an equally robotic voice alerting the caller that the number was no longer in service.

She shook her head, her brain tying into horrible knots. Her stomach, too. "I don't understand what's happening." Her knee started bouncing again, and the man covered in tattoos was staring—all squinty-eyed and fishy. She flung her hand toward him. "Who is that guy?"

Officer Smith looked in the direction of her gesture.

"He keeps looking at me."

"I don't think he's looking at you."

She jammed her fingers into her hair and squeezed her eyes shut, willing herself to wake up. *Wake up, wake up, wake up!* She was having an anxiety dream. There was no other explanation. This was some horrible, frustrating nightmare, and any second, she would wake up in bed. Preferably in California.

"Let me get you some water," Officer Smith said.

Eden squeezed her eyes tighter.

Officer Smith wasn't real.

None of this was real.

"Miss Pruitt?"

She opened her eyes.

He crouched in front of her, a paper cup held aloft. "Why don't you drink this?"

Her attention flitted to the front desk. The tattooed man was gone.

"Is there anyone else we can call?" Smith asked. "Another family member, perhaps?"

With a shake of her head, Eden took the cup. She drank the water in one gulp.

"No grandparents? Uncles or aunts?"

"I don't have any other family. It's just me and my mom and my dad."

Officer Smith frowned. "You mentioned something about moving into town. What about your old town? Surely you have a friend you can call?"

Erik. She would love to call Erik.

Except she'd never memorized his number.

"All of those numbers are in my phone, and my phone is back at my house. 3235 West Buckle Lane." Her voice rose as she spoke. She sounded unstable. She could hear it with her own ears. She took a deep breath, forcing herself to calm down. Was it possible she'd gotten the address wrong somehow? Were there identical streets and houses in the town of Eagle Bend?

"How about this." He picked up his hat. "How about we get your fingerprints?"

"Why?"

"To see what pops up. We can get an ID and then maybe

we'll find something helpful, like an address or contact information."

Eden scratched her forearm, then fidgeted with the cuff of her jean shorts.

"Is there something you'd like to share?" he asked, head cocked.

"I—it's just ..." Officer Smith would take her fingerprints and she would be in the system. And not because of something benign, like the registration of her fingerprints now that she was old enough to vote. Her fingerprints had been in the system before her eighteenth birthday. Because she'd gotten into trouble. Which meant Officer Smith was going to get the wrong impression.

"Miss Pruitt, honesty is the best policy. Always."

"I got into some trouble back in San Diego."

"Okay."

"Destruction of property. But it's not what it sounds like. I was just ..." Indulging in a moment of reckless abandon? Selfishness? Idiocy? "It was a dumb senior prank. I shouldn't have—"

"It's all right, Miss Pruitt. In fact, this will probably work in our favor. As long as you're in the system, we should have contact information for your parents."

His words might have brought comfort, if not for the fact that her parents' numbers were no longer working.

"Everything is going to be just fine," he said, leading her to a room in the back, where a tired-looking technician with a name-tag that read Dotty took each of her fingers and rolled them across a glass plate.

Eden's hands shook like miniature earthquakes, like there were fault lines in her bones. She kept repeating Officer Smith's words. *Everything was going to be fine.* She would cooperate with these people who were employed to help citizens like her. She would follow the rules and this bizarre, confusing mess would sort itself out.

When they finished, the technician and the police officer stood on the other side of the counter, waiting.

"Here we are," Dotty said, pointing at the monitor.

Officer Smith rubbed his chin, his eyes narrowing as they scrolled down the length of the screen.

Eden's cheeks pooled with heat. She knew what it said. Destruction of Property. Attempted Arson. Although that was never part of the plan. They'd used gasoline to kill the grass in the shape of their graduating year, large and brown on the front lawn of their high school. Nobody was ever going to light anything on fire.

"Do you want to tell me your name again?"

She swallowed. Officer Smith knew her name. He kept calling her Miss Pruitt. "It's Eden. Eden Pruitt."

And just like that, his countenance changed. Like a thundercloud rolling across the sky, gone was the nice cop wearing kid gloves. A no-nonsense officer had taken his place as he swiveled the screen to face her. "If that's true, would you mind explaining this?"

6

She sat in an interrogation room—the kind featured in detective shows. Cold and sparse, with a square table in the center, a pair of chairs on opposite sides, and a mirror on the wall. The mirror—she knew—wasn't actually a mirror, but a window. There were probably people behind the glass, watching her. Observing her as she sat listlessly in one of the chairs. Was it her imagination or could she hear them whispering?

She lied about her name.

She lied about her address.

She lied about everything.

Ellery Forrester.

Somehow, when Officer Smith turned the screen around to face her, this was what she saw. Her mug shot. Her matching fingerprints. And this strange, unfamiliar name.

Ellery Forrester.

She looked at herself in the mirror—a wild-eyed, messy-haired wreck of a girl.

My name, she wanted to say, *is Eden Pruitt!*

She wanted to scream the words. She wanted to lunge at her own reflection and punch through the glass and grab the person on the other side and force them to listen. Something terribly, horribly wrong was happening. But Eden didn't lunge at the mirror. She forced herself to stay in her seat. She would not act like the crazy person they thought her to be. She would follow orders. She would cooperate fully. She would be good. And they would get to the bottom of this. They had to.

The door opened.

Eden looked up.

Officer Smith walked in.

Back in the fingerprinting room—when her identity came up on the screen—he'd morphed from the good cop to the bad. He'd accused her of lying. She'd stuttered and stumbled over her words, with nothing to give him—no explanation, no story other than the one she'd already told. Her name was Eden Pruitt. She lived at 3235 West Buckle Lane. There'd been a horrible mistake. Out of patience, he brought her here, and left her alone and now he was back—his expression changed yet again, only Eden couldn't read what this one meant.

"We got a hold of your parents."

"You did?"

"Yes."

Her breath whooshed free as the upper half of her body collapsed in a heap of relief on the table. If she'd been standing, her knees would have buckled. "They're okay?"

"They're worried about you. But yes. They're fine. Heading here right now, in fact."

Her arms began to shake. Her legs, too. Violent tremors. Aftershocks. The confusion was still there. She had no idea what was going on—who broke into the house, why a man was there claiming it as his own, why their phone numbers didn't work, and most bizarrely of all—why she was in the system under Ellery Forrester. But her parents were okay; they were coming to get her. Right now, that was all that mattered. She scooted the chair back, legs scraping against the cold linoleum.

Officer Smith held out a hand to stop her. "It's okay. You can stay in here and wait. It'll be a few hours yet."

"A few hours?" Her eyebrows pulled together. If a police officer had finally gotten a hold of her parents, they wouldn't wait a few hours to come get her. They'd race here first thing. Straightaway. "Why? What are they doing?"

"Driving."

"From where?"

"Milwaukee."

"What are they doing in Milwaukee?"

With his lips pressed together, he stared at a spot slightly up and left of her face, like he couldn't bring himself to make eye contact.

"Can you please tell me what's going on?"

His weight shifted from one foot to the other. "I'm sure they will explain everything once they get here. You can wait in here until they arrive, as long as you stay calm and cooperative."

"But I don't—"

"Are you hungry?" he interrupted. "I can get you something to eat. Or drink, if you'd like."

It was clear she would be getting no explanations from Officer Smith. It was clear he didn't want to tell her anything. Her stomach growled—long and low and loud. A sound of betrayal. She couldn't imagine eating anything right now—not when everything was so messed up—but there was nothing else to do. So she told Officer Smith yes. Food would be nice. Five minutes later, he brought her a bag of pretzels and a can of Coke from a nearby vending machine. She drank and ate more out of a need for distraction. When she finished, she set the can on the table with a sharp clink and began pacing the room.

For three hours, she paced.

For three hours, her mind spun with questions.

For three hours, she hung on to the only thing keeping her from insanity.

Her parents were okay; her parents were on their way. And

once they arrived, they would explain everything. They would put the pieces of this crazy puzzle together, and then the three of them would go home—wherever home was.

She just had to hold on until then.

At quarter to ten, the door handle twisted.

Her heart jumped.

Officer Smith stepped inside first. He cleared his throat, as though announcing the arrival of her mother and father. Only her parents did not step in behind him. Two strangers did. The man was tall and trim and straight-faced. The woman was short and petite and stepped further inside with immense hesitancy. Like she was afraid to be there.

"What's going on?" Eden asked. "Where are my parents?"

"We're right here," the woman said.

Everything hitched.

The world had a remote and someone pushed pause.

Eden looked from the man and the woman to Officer Smith, and then she laughed—a singular, high-pitched, disbelieving laugh. A laugh nobody joined. They just shifted uncomfortably, nervously, and the laughter died dead in Eden's throat.

"Please, Ellery." The man choked over the name, like the three syllables caused him physical pain.

"Why are you calling me that?"

"Because it's your name, darling." The woman's eyes welled with tears. Her hands wrestled in front of her stomach as she looked from Eden to Officer Smith. "She's not well. She was in an accident two years ago and suffered a traumatic brain injury. Ever since, she's had intermittent bouts of disorientation and—"

"You're lying," Eden said. "I've never been in an accident."

"Ellery, darling. Just come with us. Please."

Eden took a step back. "I'm not going anywhere with you. I don't even know you."

The woman's expression pinched with pain.

Eden took three steps around the perimeter of the room, toward the door. But Officer Smith barred the exit. "Please," she begged him. "Please call my parents. My *real* parents. Ruth and Alexander Pruitt. Or Erik Gaviola. He lives in San Diego. Or … there's a boy at the high school. His name is Colbie. Call him, and he'll tell you. Call Mr. Timmins. Or Ms. Bell. They'll tell you my name is Eden."

"That's enough," the man who wasn't her father said, his words clipped with sharpness. With warning. As though he'd run out of patience a long time ago.

She glared at him. All evening long she'd operated under the assumption that if she cooperated, everything would work itself out. As long as she remained calm, as long as she followed the rules, Officer Smith would help her. This was how life was supposed to work. Only Officer Smith hadn't helped her at all. And nothing was working itself out. Everything kept getting worse.

"Officer, please listen to me. Something really bad is happening right now. You have to believe me. I've never seen either of these people before in my life."

"She does this," the man said. "She does this all the time."

"You're a liar!" Eden shouted.

With a curse, the man removed a syringe from his pocket.

Eden took another step back, a scream building deep in her chest like hot steam in a kettle. "What is that?"

"Nothing I want to use, trust me."

Her heart crashed against her ribcage, pounding to get out as her back met the cool, mirrored wall behind her. She had nowhere to go. She was trapped like a caged animal. She was trapped like her heart. She had no way of escaping, and these people were going to take her. They were going to kidnap her right here, in the middle of a police station. Right in front of a police officer. He was going to watch it all happen. *Let* it all happen.

The man closed the distance between them.

Eden squeezed her eyes shut and crouched into a cowering ball. She plugged her ears and shook her head—a wild monster of a shake. "My name is Eden Pruitt. I live at 3235 West Buckle Lane. My parents are Ruth and Alexander Pruitt."

She heard him take another step closer.

She pinched the inside of her arm—a hard, violent pinch. A command to wake up. Wake up right now. "My name is Eden Pruitt. I live at 3235 West Buckle Lane. My parents are Ruth and Alexander Pruitt."

"Oh, Jack," the woman said on a sob. "Just get it over with."

The scream rent itself loose. It tore up her throat as the sharp needle jabbed into flesh and the world shrunk into a tiny pinprick, then disappeared altogether.

7

Eden emerged from sleep like a deep-sea diver slowly ascending from the murky depths. The closer she got to the surface the more her head ached, as though unable to adjust to the change in pressure despite her careful climb to consciousness. Her eyelids fluttered open, then quickly shut to block the onslaught of light. She groaned, her tongue swollen and dry in her mouth.

Water. She needed water.

With a grimace, she turned her head toward her nightstand where she kept a glass, along with whatever travel book currently held her attention. Over the years, she'd amassed an impressive collection, many of which shared a common setting—Paris. Because of them, she knew every street without ever having been there. Because of them, she could imagine strolling down Champs-Elysees with the sun on her face. A soothing thought as she cracked one eye open. Only instead of finding her nightstand, an imposter stood in its place.

No travel book.

No glass of water.

Just white wicker and a pale pink lamp with a flower petal shade.

This was not her nightstand.

That was not her lamp.

Eden bolted upright, her hand flying to her neck as though remembering the sharp stab of a needle, the nightmare crashing into clarity. Her living room, ransacked. A stranger in her new house. Mom and Dad, missing. Her fingerprints in the system. Ellery Forrester. And that man and woman, coming inside the interrogation room pretending to be her parents. They drugged her inside the police station. They drugged her and they kidnapped her while a police officer stood by and watched.

She scooted back in the bed, blinking down at a comforter that wasn't hers. Flowery pink, like the lamp on the nightstand. Her attention skittered around the room, frantically taking in the sun-yellow walls, the white wicker dresser and the white wicker desk. Light pouring in through a window painted a bright path along the carpet.

Quickly and quietly, she scrambled out of the bed and pressed her nose against the windowpane, looking down into a backyard without a fence, one that sloped into a gully with a row of houses on the other side. Was she still in Eagle Bend? She had no way of knowing. None of her travel books included a mid-sized town in Iowa. She tried to open the window, but it was locked from the outside. And even if it wasn't, there was no easy escape—not two stories up. Even if she held onto the windowsill and let herself dangle, the drop would result in a sprained ankle, at the very least. And then what?

She turned around. The room had three white doors. She walked along the path of sunlight to the door straight ahead. It was locked, like the window. The second door was a walk-in closet filled with clothes. Clothes that wouldn't look out of place in her own closet. She shook the disorienting thought away and opened the third door.

It led into a bathroom with no exit.

She regarded the faucet—desperately thirsty but afraid to turn it on. Afraid the man and the woman might hear. Her thirst won out. She turned it to a trickle and bent over the sink to drink. Handful after handful of bathroom tap water until her tongue no longer felt like swollen cotton. When she finished, she set her hands on the laminate countertop and stared at her reflection.

Smooth skin. Large, hazel eyes. High cheekbones. A straight nose. Thick, honey-blond hair pulled into a bun that was an absolute mess. All of it was familiar. It was her face in that mirror. Eden Pruitt's face. But it wasn't Eden's mirror. It wasn't Eden's bathroom. She didn't recognize the white porcelain tooth-brush cup, or the half-used tube of fluoride-free Toms, or the lime green toothbrush. None of this was hers, including the man and the woman who called her *darling*.

Who were they? Where had they taken her? And what about her parents—where were *they*? What happened to them?

Her heart began beating out of her chest, panic grabbing hold like sharp talons.

She pried them away. She forced the panic down into the pit of her stomach, into a box she could lock up tight. Fear would not serve her now. It wouldn't help her, and it wouldn't help her parents, either. She had to think, and she had to think fast.

The man and the woman had left her alone, but surely not for long. It was only a matter of time before they returned to check on her. She was racing an invisible clock, one that had her turning the room inside out. She searched through the closet and the dresser and the desk drawers—for something, *anything*, that might pick a lock. She refused to be unnerved by the undeniable fact that this was a teenager's room. A girl's room.

In the top desk drawer, she came upon a photograph. Two girls her age. One plain, with pasty skin and thin eyebrows. The other strikingly beautiful with wavy auburn hair, bright green eyes, and a dazzling smile. Who were these girls? Where were they now? The possible answers had her searching harder, more frantically, until the chirping of a phone brought her to a stop— so loud, it seemed to be somewhere in the room.

She quit breathing.

The ringing went silent, and then a voice said hello.

Eden looked down.

The sound was coming up from a vent near her feet.

She sank onto her belly and pressed her ear against the grate.

"You're back?"

It was a woman's voice. The same woman from last night.

"I just got in." The answer belonged to a man—so loud and clear, he must have been on speaker. It wasn't the same man who'd drugged her. This was a different man. But something about his voice was … *familiar*. She'd heard it before. But where? And when? "How is she doing? Is Ellery okay?"

"Ellery is confused. She has no idea what's going on." The woman's voice quavered with emotion. "And she's unconscious at the moment. Asleep upstairs."

Ellery.

Why were they still calling her Ellery?

"That's good. You should keep her sleeping until she gets here."

"She was hysterical. Jack had to tranquilize her."

"I'm sure that was hard."

"It was awful."

"Why don't you and Jack get her in the car and bring her here right away."

"We're going to, as soon as he's back."

"What do you mean—*back*?"

"He had to get more tranquilizer. We had to use all three syringes."

Eden scrambled to her feet. The man—Jack—had left. He left to get more tranquilizer, which meant Eden was alone in the house with the woman. She could overpower the woman. She hurried into the bathroom and rummaged through the vanity, hoping for a bobby pin. Every teenage girl had bobby pins, didn't they? She found nothing but another toothbrush, floss, two folded white towels, and a comb without a single stray hair.

With a jerk of her hand, she swiped at the shower curtain, determined to find something inside.

The metal hangers scraped against the rod.

Eden stopped and looked up. The curtain rod had miniature hangers holding the curtain in place—twelve identical metal hooks attached to small gray rectangles. The metal part reached through twelve evenly spaced slits at the top of the curtain and curved around the rod. The rectangular part acted as a holder, too big to slip through the slits.

She unhooked the closest one and pulled it from the curtain, then turned it over in her hand.

The metal was sturdy, but thin enough to do the job. Gripping the gray rectangle, she looped her pointer and middle fingers under the hook and pulled up. The metal gave way easily. With a surge of hope, she used her thumbs—pressing against the rounded part of the metal until the hook was no longer a hook, but long and straight.

Exactly the sort of thing that could pick a lock.

As quietly as possible, she hurried to the door and slipped the curtain hanger into the keyhole, her hands shaking. She ordered them to stop. Now was not the time for shaking. It took a minute—maybe two, but when it happened, the click came like a choir of angels.

With her heart pounding wildly, she eased open the door and peeked outside.

The hallway was empty. The house, still.

The woman was no longer talking on the phone. Or if she was, Eden couldn't hear her this far from the vent. Holding her breath, she crept out into the hallway, past an opened bedroom door. She made her way to the stairs.

Halfway down, a step creaked beneath her weight.

She froze.

Something buzzed—a loud, vibrating sound. Like a small jackhammer.

With her sight set on the exit straight ahead, she ground her teeth and made a beeline for the door, her socks sliding across polished wood, her heart exploding as she flipped the lock and flung the door open.

Sunlight flooded in.

And there on the other side stood the man—Jack—blocking her exit.

"Whoa," he said, taking her arm. "Where do you think you're going?"

She jerked free and stepped away—her muscles coiled, ready to strike. But the man was bigger. And stronger. And in his hand, he held another syringe.

8

Eden climbed into the back of their Honda Clarity. What other choice did she have? The man named Jack had a syringe full of whatever drug had plunged her into darkness. She couldn't let that happen again. She needed to get away. She needed to find her parents. So, she'd begged. She'd pleaded. She pledged her full cooperation and while he had stood with the needle poised for injection, the woman put her foot down.

Ever since, tension rolled off of them in waves.

Good. Let them be divided.

It could only work in Eden's favor.

Her attention slid to the syringe placed in one of the cup holders. A phone rested in the other. Jack reversed out of the driveway and pulled down the suburban, tree-lined street. If she was quick enough, could she lunge forward, grab the syringe, and plunge the needle into the man's neck? When the car crashed, would she remain uninjured? And what of the woman? Would Eden be able to fight her? Her mind spun with all the potential outcomes—weighing impossible-to-know probabilities—grappling for an escape as Jack eyed her warily in the rearview mirror.

The woman clenched her fist beneath her mouth and stared hard out the window. Jack reached through the mounting tension and took the woman's hand. He rubbed his thumb over her knuckles like a doting husband trying to comfort his distraught wife. It was exactly the kind of gesture a man with a troubled, brain-addled daughter would do.

"Who are you?" Eden demanded, confusion and frustration wrestling inside of her. "Where are you taking me?"

"We're taking you to a doctor," the woman answered.

"*A doctor?*" Eden glared at her in the reflection of the side view mirror. "Why are you keeping up the charade? Your plan worked. You got me away from the police. You don't have to pretend you're my parents."

The woman opened her mouth, but Jack cut her off with a sharp jerk of his head. "Don't engage."

Eden leaned forward, thinking about the phone conversation she'd overhead. A man's familiar voice, calling her Ellery. Only she wasn't Ellery. "Are you taking me to the guy you were speaking with on the phone?"

"His name is Dr. Norton," the woman said.

"*Annette.*" Jack shot her a look of warning.

And the woman called Annette pulled her hand away from his, her lips going thin and tight.

"What does he want with me?" Eden asked.

Her question was met with stony silence.

Outside, the world slid past her window—nigglingly familiar. Every bit as disconcerting as the familiarity of that man's voice on the phone.

Dr. Norton.

Jack flipped his blinker and slowed into a turn.

They passed a green street sign that said Circus Lane.

Eden sat up straighter, sifting through her memories, trying to pinpoint why she knew that name. And then she saw something even more familiar. A gaudy statue of a grinning, plastic clown. On the street corner across from it, sat a rundown building called The Bearded Lady. She had no idea if it was a tattoo parlor or a pancake house, and yet, she was positive she'd seen it before. Eden tried retracing her steps from yesterday. Were they still in Eagle Bend? If so, had she come to this part of town before she ended up in front of Guppy's?

She didn't know.

But how could she not know? Why was such a substantial portion of yesterday blank?

She suffered a traumatic brain injury…

No.

It wasn't true.

The woman was lying.

They were gaslighting her—making her feel crazy when she wasn't.

With her eyes squeezed shut, she ran the truth through in her mind. Her name was Eden Pruitt. She was eighteen years old—a senior at Eagle Bend High School. Her new address was 3235 West Buckle Lane. Her parents were Ruth and Alexander Pruitt. Her mom was an interior designer. Her dad, an accountant. She never got into a car accident. She never suffered a traumatic brain injury. Her best friend was Erik Gaviola. He lived in San Diego. His number was in her phone. Her phone was in her new house. Her new house had been ransacked, and she didn't know where her parents were.

Cold sweat slicked her palms.

She had to get away from these people—these liars. She couldn't go wherever they were taking her. She had to escape. She had to break into her new house and get her phone so she could call Erik. He would know how to help her. Eden glanced at her buckled seatbelt, and over at her locked, passenger-side door as the car slowed to a stop at a traffic light and Jack continued watching her in the rearview mirror.

Eden swallowed. She told herself he couldn't hear the quick pace of her heartbeat. He didn't know what she was thinking.

She leaned back in her seat, forcing her expression into something dull—a look of listless acceptance.

Let him think you've surrendered.

The light turned green. The car started moving again.

Slowly, and what she hoped was imperceptibly, she slid her thumb over the button of her seatbelt and as casually as possible, set her forearm on the arm rest of the door, her finger right next to the lock. She ran her teeth over her bottom lip as the blue digits on the speedometer climbed.

25 … 26 …

She would probably break her legs. Puncture a lung. Or maybe the back tire would run her over and she would die. But it was a risk she needed to take. She had to escape. And when she did, she would run if she could, and scream if she couldn't. She would scream and scream until the window-shopping pedestrians on the sidewalk came to help her. She would scream until someone believed her.

She was not Ellery Forrester.

And these were not her parents.

It was her only option. And she had to do it now, before Jack grew any more suspicious.

27 … 28 …

Her body coursed with adrenaline, and right when the speedometer reached thirty, she undid the seat belt, threw open the door, and hurled herself as far away from the moving vehicle as possible.

There was blinding pain as she hit the pavement and rolled.

A bone crunched.

Tires screeched.

Horns blared.

She came to a stop, sucking at the air like a fish out of water. Searing heat laced through her shoulder, but she didn't have time to assess the injury. To take note of the damage. Cars skidded to a stop all around. One crashed into another, which crashed into another, which crashed into another. Pedestrians gawked, open-mouthed, as she scrambled to her feet.

She had created a pile-up, and there, in the front, was the Honda Clarity.

Jack climbed out from behind the wheel. Their eyes met. And before he could so much as reach for the syringe, she sprinted as far and as fast away as possible.

9

All she could hear was the sound of her own heavy breathing, her own fast and furious heartbeat as she bent over her knees in the shadows of an abandoned alley, bracing herself for the onslaught of pain. As soon as the adrenaline retreated, as soon as the wave withdrew—whatever injuries she sustained when her body crashed and skidded against the pavement would come hissing to the forefront.

But the onslaught didn't come, even after she caught her breath.

She straightened. Her sneakers were scuffed and dirty, but her legs were fine. No gashes or scrapes or swollen joints. Just some debris easily brushed away. Gingerly, she placed her hand over her left shoulder and slowly lifted her arm, steeling herself for a rush of agony. But there was nothing. Her top was ripped at the collar, causing the sleeve to hang at an awkward angle. She slid her fingers inside the tear, touching smooth skin. As far as she could tell, her shoulder was neither broken nor dislocated.

A disbelieving laugh tumbled past her lips.

How was it possible to jump out of a moving vehicle and not get hurt? She'd felt pain. It was there, upon contact. She was certain. But now ...

Eden cupped her forehead.

She sustained a traumatic brain injury …

She brought her other hand into her hair and shook her head just as the sound of a footstep interrupted her rising confusion.

She spun around like a rabbit poised to flee.

Instead, her eyes went round.

It was *him*.

The boy from the coffee shop. The one who'd looked at her like her existence offended him. He stood in front of her now, staring every bit as intensely as he had when she'd bent over to pick up the old woman's change, his attention flicking to her scuffed shoes, then rolling up her body in a way that made her feel naked. "Are you hurt?" he asked, his clipped tone filled with accusation, like getting hurt was as offensive as her existence.

"What are you doing here?" she replied, taking a slow step away. "Are you following me?"

His lips went thin, his eyes filling with the same emotion as before—two cauldrons of dark gold bubbling with contempt. Only she hadn't done anything to warrant his contempt.

She took another step back. "Stay away from me."

"I'm not going to hurt you."

But she didn't believe him. She didn't believe any of them. And he had her backed into a corner—literally—with nowhere to run. Her hands balled into fists. "I will fight you. I'll kick and scream and I won't stop fighting. I'll *never* stop fighting."

He cocked his head, his animosity on hold.

"I'll never make this easy. I'll get away again. I'll find a way to escape. I'm not going with you. I'm not going with them."

"With *who*—the people driving the car you jumped out of?"

"The people you're working with."

"I'm not working with them." He glanced over his shoulder. "I have no idea who they are."

Eden peered at him through the shadows. "Then what are you doing here?"

He ran the underside of his pointer finger across his full

bottom lip, looking as annoyed as she was confused. The longer he delayed, the more her confusion grew. Until she wanted to pull out her hair. She needed answers. She needed them now.

"Does the name Mordecai mean anything to you?" he finally asked.

"Should it?"

"He's involved in Underground Fighting."

Underground Fighting?

She gaped. Somehow, she'd been plucked from her middle-class suburban existence and tossed down Alice's rabbit hole. "Why would I know anyone associated with Underground Fighting?"

Before he could reply, a burst of squawking sounded at the end of the alleyway.

Eden was grabbed. The young man cupped his hand over her mouth, trapping the scream barreling up her throat, and pulled her behind the dumpster. With her nostrils flaring, Eden jerked free just as he slid a gun from his belt. He didn't aim it at her. He held it up and moved his finger to his lips, pinning her beneath a smoldering stare. She looked from him to the weapon—her breathing shallow—as the source of the noise became clear. Two police officers speaking into walkie-talkies.

Eden remained hunched in place, beside this boy with a gun. This boy who'd been following her. He crouched next to her, so close she could see each of his long, dark eyelashes. So close she could see a small white scar on the ridge of his chin.

Dangerous.

The word flashed through her mind—a word she should listen to. But she didn't scream for help. How could she when those officers were probably looking for her? Not Eden Pruitt, but a disturbed runaway named Ellery Forrester. A disturbed runaway with Eden's face and Eden's fingerprints. Somehow, the very people meant to keep her safe had become more dangerous to her than this boy with the gun.

She held her breath, heart pounding into the silence.

She didn't exhale until the two officers were gone. If they were looking for her, they didn't know she was huddled in the back of this alley.

"We have to go," he said, straightening. "I know somewhere safe."

Safe.

It felt like a made-up word.

"Come on," he said.

Eden wanted to protest. She wasn't going anywhere with him. He was a stranger. But the whirr of a drone overhead drew her attention. Every city had them. Practically every street back in San Diego. Until that moment, she hadn't given them a second thought. They were a necessary, relatively unobtrusive part of life. The only people who thought otherwise were those who had something to hide. But now, the sight of this one hovering overhead filled her with panicked paranoia. She felt vulnerable. Watched. Hunted. Like a gazelle in the middle of a wide-open savanna.

Authorities would use the drones to search for her just like authorities were using the drones to search for whoever was sending those pipe bombs. Only Eden wasn't a criminal. She was an upstanding, law-abiding citizen. Barring that one, stupid mistake.

Up ahead, the young man was already more than halfway down the alley. He stopped at the mouth of it, pressed his back against the brick facade of a building, the gun tucked against his right shoulder. She hurried to catch up and surveyed what appeared to be a rundown business district. Not the kind found in mid-sized towns like Eagle Bend.

"Where are we?" she asked.

"Milwaukee."

Milwaukee.

They actually took her to Milwaukee.

The boy lifted the tail of his shirt, revealing the small of his back. The *iliocostalis*, the *longissimus*, and the *spinalis*—a column of defined muscles that ran the length of his spine. She could see it. The diagram from her anatomy class. It was still there in her memory.

He tucked the weapon into his belt and dropped his shirt.

The two police officers were gone.

He stepped out into the open and climbed onto a motorcycle parked along the curb.

"What are you doing?" she hissed, staying in the shadows.

"Hop on," he said.

"*Hop on*? I have no idea who you are."

"You jumped out of a car."

"Because I didn't have a choice. Those people kidnapped me. They kept calling me *Ellery*. They said—"

"They took you from a police station."

"I know." Why was he giving her a recap?

"Any minute, these streets will be crawling with more police officers, and something tells me they're not going to be on your side."

Her stomach turned to rock.

"Stay if you want. Or come with me." He shrugged, like it didn't matter to him either way. But his white-knuckled grip on the handlebars of his motorcycle said otherwise. "If I were you, I'd come."

"Who are you? Why are you following me?"

"My name is Cassian Gray. I'd be happy to answer more of your questions once I get you somewhere safe." He gritted the last few words between his teeth, making it abundantly clear that he would be far from happy to do any such thing. He glanced over his shoulder. "Are you coming or not?"

Her whole life, she tried hard to make the safe choice.

The right choice.

Now?

There was no safe choice to be made. If she stayed, the same thing that happened last night would happen all over again. The police would take her fingerprints, and those would lead to Jack and Annette and possibly a man named Mordecai who was wrapped up in Underground Fighting. If she went, she risked the unknown, and this boy who seemed to resent her. It was a risk that held potential answers. Right then, she wanted answers more than she wanted anything. So she crept out into the open and climbed onto the back of his bike.

With a rev of the engine, he released the throttle.

Reflexively, her arms wrapped around his lean torso.

Dangerous.

There it was again.

The word filled her mind like a foghorn.

The problem was, Eden Pruitt had never been afraid of danger. On the contrary, she'd spent her whole life fighting her attraction to it.

10

Cassian Gray drove like he walked—confidently. He didn't speed. They couldn't afford to get pulled over. But he weaved in and out of traffic without hesitation. If not for the dire situation, Eden would appreciate the thrill. Her brain, however, held no space for appreciation. Just a raw sense of anxiety as sirens wailed in the distance and police officers patrolled street corners and drones circled in the sky.

If only she had a helmet to cover her face. But Cassian Gray didn't have a helmet, a fact that would give her mother heart palpitations. So Eden ducked her head against his side, her heart pounding as the pavement sped by underfoot. She didn't look up until he merged onto an interstate and the expansive blue of Lake Michigan came into view, morning sunlight glinting off the surface of the water.

Ten minutes later, they reached the downtown campus of Marquette. Historic brick buildings with sandstone pillars. Libraries and lecture halls. A large fountain set within an ample green lawn, and students wearing backpacks making their way to early morning classes. This was supposed to be her. Next year. A new adventure all her own—parent-approved—on the cusp of studying abroad, where she would finally experience what she'd dreamed of as a little girl when her mother started reading the *Madeline* books to her before bed. But now? All of it had slid impossibly out of reach.

Her entire life had flipped inside out.

Cassian pulled up to a curbside parking spot and cut the engine, his movements quick and decisive as he climbed off the bike and plugged the digital meter.

Eden barely had time to climb off before he made his way through the current of students. A couple blocks later, they turned up a walk leading to a residence hall. They didn't need to scan their retinas or enter a passcode to enter. The place was awake, alive with kids heading off to classes and breakfast. He only had to snag the door and hold it open for her. She felt conspicuous in her torn top, but looking around at the array of pajama pants and wrinkled t-shirts, she wasn't as noteworthy as she might have thought.

"Keep your head down." He spoke low. Authoritatively. "Cameras to the left."

Eden obeyed. She didn't look up. She hardly even breathed.

They stopped in front of an elevator and waited while three girls stepped behind them. Eden could feel their collective attention sliding from her to him. She dared a subtle glance over her shoulder. They wore brightly patterned leggings and tank tops over sports bras, their hair pulled up into matching messy buns that weren't nearly as messy as Eden's. The girl standing in the middle took a swig from her water bottle, her gaze lingering approvingly on Cassian Gray.

Eden understood.

He was the kind of guy who drew attention—tall and lean with broad shoulders and an athletic build and an attractive face with devastating eyes. He wore a charcoal gray Henley beneath a well-worn leather jacket, black motorcycle pants, and a pair of combat boots. His posture was rigid—almost vigilant—and a muscle ticked in his chiseled jaw, creating a complete package that was as intimidating as it was enticing.

The numbers above the elevator lit up in descending order. When it reached the ground floor, the elevator dinged and the doors opened. They walked inside, and just as he reached for a button on the elevator panel, so did the girl with the water bottle.

Their fingers brushed.

"Oops. Sorry," she said on a breathless laugh as the doors slid shut. "Are you on the ninth, too?"

Cassian stared at her.

Eden had to give the girl points for bravery. She didn't shrink away.

"I feel like I'd know if you were on the ninth floor."

"We're visiting."

"Oh yeah? Who are you visiting? I bet I know him." The girl tucked a strand of hair behind her ear. "Or her."

"Greg," he said.

"Greg? I don't think I know a Greg." The girl looked at her two friends, who both shrugged.

The elevator stopped, dinged.

The doors opened.

Eden stepped toward the exit, but Cassian grabbed her forearm. Then he took a step back—an invitation for the three girls to leave the lift first. They did so hesitantly. The talkative one with the water bottle glanced over her shoulder, as if searching for an excuse to linger. When he gave her none, she continued into the corridor that led off to the left.

Cassian let go of Eden's arm and headed right.

The hallway was mostly empty—just two guys in varying states of undress kicking a hackie-sack to one another at the far end. Music rattled the closed door to their left. A heavy sound— raw and unprocessed, the kind of punk rock familiar to garages. A white board mounted directly under the peephole held several short messages—questions mostly—written out like texts, and above it, a sign that read *Resident Advisor*.

He knocked on the door.

Nobody answered. The person inside probably couldn't hear.

He knocked again, harder this time with the fleshy part of his fist.

There was a moment—maybe two—and then the door swung open, letting out a blast of music so loud, it nearly blew Eden's hair back. A girl stood in front of them dressed in black joggers and a tank top with a silhouette of Big Foot and the words *I Believe* underneath. Her hair was geometrically partitioned into a number of neatly-coiled knots. She had medium brown skin, a skull and crossbones thumb ring on the hand that held the door, and a snakebite lip piercing. She answered with a look of utter annoyance that slid away as soon as she saw the boy.

"*Cass?*" She released a disbelieving laugh. Then she hugged him. "What in the world are you doing here?"

"Can we come in?" he asked, his voice that same low rumble he'd used with Eden downstairs.

The girl stepped to the side and *Cass* swooped past.

Eden followed as the girl shut the door and turned off the music, the silence jarring in the wake of so much noise.

"Eden, this is Cleo. Cleo, this is Eden." With that, he strode to a window and peered down at the street below, as if waiting for an entourage of police officers to show up and take them both away.

Cleo and Eden blinked at one another.

It occurred to the latter that politeness called for some sort of follow-up greeting. *Hi, nice to meet you.* But Cleo didn't seem like she cared that much about politeness, and Eden was grappling with the fact that this stranger-of-a-boy she didn't know had called her by her name. Her actual name. Not Ellery. But Eden. And in the safety of this cluttered, enclosed space, all of her questions rushed to the surface. "Now that we're *safe*, can you please tell me what's going on? Who is Mordecai, and what does he have to do with me?"

Cassian turned away from the window, glancing briefly at

their audience of one—the girl with the Big Foot tank top. Cleo. She stared at them both with raised eyebrows.

"It's a pseudonym," he said.

"*What?*"

"Mordecai. None of the gamblers use their real names. He's one of the biggest."

"Gamblers."

"Yes."

"For Underground Fighting," Eden said.

"Yes."

"And you asked if his name meant anything to me *because* …?"

"He's looking for you."

"Me?"

"Yes."

"Why?"

"I don't know."

"You don't know?" How could he not know? He knew her name. He'd followed her from Eagle Bend to Milwaukee. He had to know plenty. "You were in the coffee shop at Eagle Bend."

He gave her an imperceptible nod.

"And now you're here in Milwaukee."

Another subtle dip of his chin.

"Which means you've been following me."

Cassian set his mouth in a hard line and had the audacity to look irritated—like *he* was the one being violated.

"*Why?*" she demanded.

He looked again at Cleo who was watching the conversation unfold like a spectator at a table tennis match. If she found it bizarre that this boy had pounded on her door on a Friday morning with some random girl in tow—and that the two of them were now talking about outlandish, illegal things like Underground Fighting and high-stakes gambling—she took it impressively in stride.

Cass pushed his hand across his bottom lip. "Mordecai and I have a mutual friend."

"Who?"

"A man named Yukio. He's a bookie. I heard from him that Mordecai was looking for you."

She waited for Cassian to continue, elaborate. When it became obvious that he found his answer sufficient, she turned up her palm. "And?"

"*And* he's not a good guy."

She pressed her fingers against her eyes and released a loud breath. "So let me get this straight. You find out some not-good-guy is after a girl you don't know, and you decide to insert yourself into the situation?"

His eyes flashed like burning gold, as if the combative question struck a nerve.

Eden was undeterred. "I hate to sound like a broken record, but I have to ask it again. *Why?*"

"I don't like when bad things happen to innocent people," he said, his voice measured and low with an undercurrent of warning. Like she had waded into dangerous waters and if she knew what was good for her, she'd turn around.

Eden sank onto the unmade bed strewn with clothes and textbooks and crumpled sheets. The past twenty-four hours had turned her inside out one too many times, and now she just needed to sit. She needed to close her eyes and think. The government of the United States banned the sport of fighting years ago, before Eden was born. According to her parents, it had surged in popularity at the height of the country's division. Her mother said it was indicative of the times—the country was at war with itself, society in a perpetual state of rage. It made sense that people would enjoy watching two opponents step inside a ring and beat the crap out of one another. But then The Attack happened, and everything changed, including the country's lust for blood. Two years after, a prominent fighter took a loaded gun into a bar and opened fire, killing five, and injuring many more. An autopsy revealed significant damage in his brain. Damage that occurred because of fighting. There was a public outcry and this sport that was already waning in popularity was officially banned. Of course, it didn't stop. It moved underground. And now, somehow, a high-stakes gambler wrapped up in that underground world was looking for her.

Eden shook her head. None of this made sense.

Unless …

A few days ago, when she was driving across the country with her parents, they took one final bathroom break at the *World's Largest Truck Stop* on I-80. Even at eighteen, her father had walked Eden to the restroom and stood guard outside, providing a mini lesson on the disturbing connection between sex trafficking and truck stops. If this Mordecai was involved in something as unsavory as Underground Fighting, then it wasn't a stretch to imagine he might be involved in other illegal, financially lucrative endeavors. "Does Mordecai traffic girls? Is that why he's after me?"

Cassian's face went grim. "It's possible."

"The man and the woman who took me—do they work for him?"

"I don't know who else they'd be working for."

The cold fear she'd shoved into the pit of her stomach wiggled its way out, bringing with it a question she didn't want to ask. Was terrified of asking. But she had to know. And so, with every muscle in her body braced for impact, she asked the question out loud. "Do you know what happened to my parents?"

He shook his head.

His response filled her with temporary relief, and a desperate longing to see them—a homesickness so acute, it stole her breath. Wherever they were, they had to be out of their mind with worry. She wanted—more than anything—to find them, communicate with them, let them know that she was alive. She was okay. She'd gotten away. "I need to find them."

She rubbed her eyes, hopelessness sucking her under.

"But how am I supposed to do that? Their phone numbers don't work. I watched the police officer dial them. One went to a pizza place in Seattle and the other was disconnected. We're hours away from Eagle Bend, and even if we weren't, nobody there will help me. Some man is at my house, pretending like it's his, and the police think I'm a deranged girl named Ellery Forrester."

"Ellery Forrester?"

"That's the name that came up when the officer took my fingerprints."

It was probably the same name that would come up had her retinas been scanned upon entrance to this dormitory.

Cassian peered out the window again and rubbed his jaw.

Cleo had sat down in her desk chair. She'd grabbed a box of Hot Tamales, crossed one leg over the other, and ate them like she was part of an audience and they were the show.

Cassian looked at her. "We need a place to lay low for a while."

"Let me guess. You've picked here."

"I'd also like to use your computer."

She rattled a handful of candy into her palm. "And here I thought my return to dorm life would be boring."

11

Cassian Gray watched the girl from the corner of his eye, his entire body vibrating with frustration. She stood behind Cleo, who sat at her desk clearing off the mess to get to the laptop underneath. Cass had told Eden the truth when he said he didn't know the man and the woman. But he hadn't told her the whole truth. Did Mordecai traffic girls? He didn't know because he didn't ask. He never did when it came to assignments like these. Now he was stuck in a college dorm room with this girl he'd been hired to find—his ticket to freedom. She was never supposed to be anything more than that.

So what was he doing? What in the world had compelled him to get involved like this? Deep down, he knew the answer, which led to the most infuriating question of all. Why couldn't Eden Pruitt have simply been like every other person he'd found before?

Aggravation pulled his jaw tight as the girl picked up a folded paper from the desk and read the title out loud. "*The People's Press*." Eden lifted it into the air. "This is a newspaper."

"Early stages," Cleo said, crumpling a loose-leaf sheet of paper and tossing it aside.

"It's not Concordia."

Cleo scoffed. "I prefer reporting truth."

"You don't think Concordia does?"

"Concordia is run by the government."

"So?"

"The press isn't meant to be run by the government. It's meant to be a separate entity."

"We tried that, remember? It didn't go so well."

"You think the solution was to take our freedom away?" Cleo asked.

"It wasn't taken away. The First Amendment changed because we wanted it to change. I'm pretty sure if we could go back in time, people would have changed it sooner."

"*Wow.*" Cleo enunciated the word, then swiveled her chair and raised her eyebrows at Cass, who at the moment, cared very little about Concordia. At the moment, he wanted to know if they were going to be ambushed, and by whom. He peered out the window, at the bustling street ten stories below. As far as he could tell, nobody had followed them.

"What?" Eden snapped, her cheeks going pink.

"You. And everything you're espousing."

Eden frowned.

"They brainwashed you good, little sis."

Cass took off his jacket, tossed it over the back of the futon, and snagged the television remote from Cleo's dresser.

"Look, I get it," Cleo said. "America needed a scapegoat for what happened. The media was an easy target. Whatever. But you tell me what's worse. The media 'starting' the conflict ..." She put air quotes around the word *starting*, then opened her laptop. "Or the government ending it?"

"What are you talking about?" Eden asked.

"Cleo doesn't think Karik Volkova organized The Attack," Cass said, searching for Concordia Local on the small flat screen. Despite Cleo's distaste for the government-owned press conglomerate, he needed to know what was going on outside. He stopped on channel 54—Concordia Milwaukee.

"Then who did?" Eden said.

"The government," Cleo replied.

Eden rolled her eyes. "That's absurd."

"Is it, though?" Cleo typed in her password. "The country was at war. Completely divided with no end in sight. Hemorrhaging money and power by the second. We needed the internal fighting to stop. Say what you will about tragedy, it has a way of uniting people."

"So you think our own government used nuclear weapons to put an end to the fighting? If we were hemorrhaging money and power before, we lost it all after. Almost a million people in New York City and Washington, DC, died. Including our president. Congress was in session—the senate and the house. You think they orchestrated some mass suicide all for the sake of *unity*?"

"When *unity* is code for silencing the oppressed and preserving the power dynamics, that's exactly what I think." Cleo stood and offered her seat to Cassian.

It was an offer he should decline. He shouldn't involve himself any further. He had no business digging for answers. That wasn't part of the job description. But then, curiosity was a powerful thing, and if there was anything this girl stirred in him other than intense feelings of frustration, it was this. Just when he thought he had her figured out, some dueling facet would emerge. Was Eden Pruitt a troubled teen with a record or a sheltered only child in a close-knit family? Was she the high school beauty or the outcast with a best friend who looked like he belonged at a Star Trek convention? Was she the straight-laced student who followed the rules or a girl who tempted fate when she thought nobody was looking?

He'd been looking.

That night on the cliffs—the Pruitt's last night in San Diego—when she stepped so close to the brink, the toes of her bare feet dangled over the edge. For an alarming second, he thought she was going to take one final step forward and plummet eighty feet into the crashing, rock-strewn sea below.

It was not a plunge a person could survive.

Yet she had stood there, eyes closed, moonlight reflecting off her profile, wind tangling with her hair like she had no fear at all. And most recently, she'd jumped out of a moving vehicle. He'd chased after her on his motorcycle, determined not to lose her. And when he finally cornered her in an alley, she'd balled her hands into fists and stared at him with equal parts fear and fierceness.

I will fight you, she'd said.

He didn't doubt she would've tried.

Curiosity won. With a shake of his head, he sat down. What difference would it make if he scratched the itch when he'd already jumped script two weeks ago? He opened the Internet browser and pulled up the Department of Transportation's web page.

It failed to load.

"That happens a lot." Cleo snagged her box of Hot Tamales. It wasn't even breakfast yet. "The service here is diabolical."

He pulled up a list of Wi-Fi networks.

At the top, one appeared in all caps that had Cleo snorting.

"Sex?" Eden read.

"I'm sorry to say that college freshman are no more original than high school boys."

Cass ignored the immature Wi-Fi name and chose the network beneath it. Cleo reached past him to chicken-peck her password as a reporter from Concordia Milwaukee came on the television screen talking about a pile-up on the south side of town.

"The cause of the pile-up can be seen in the following footage." A bird's eye view of moving traffic filled the screen.

Eden set down *The People's Press* as one of the cars—the car Cassian had been following—screeched to a stop and was quickly rear-ended. The reporter rewound the footage and pointed out a figure jumping from the vehicle. Then the screen cut to an eyewitness.

"It was so bizarre," a woman said, her lanyard flapping in the wind. "I was walking to work, and then up ahead, I started hearing horns and that awful crunching sound cars make when they slam into one another. And there was this girl rolling on the ground. I watched her get up and run away."

The screen panned back to the reporter. "The vehicle that caused the crash fled the scene. So far, authorities have been unable to capture an image of the license plate number but we do know it is a blue Honda Clarity, driven by a white male described to be in his mid to late forties. No identification has been made on the young female."

"They fled the scene." Eden turned to Cass. "Why wouldn't they stay and talk to the police?"

He narrowed his eyes, no wiser than she.

Meanwhile, Cleo's jaw had gone slack, her attention zeroing in on Eden's torn top. "You're the young female who jumped out of the car?"

Eden plopped down on Cleo's bed.

Cass tried the DOT's website again and entered in the plate numbers. Surveillance drones might not have had the right angle but he certainly had. He memorized the plate number last night while tailing Eden and the mysterious man and woman from Eagle Bend.

"I recognized his voice," she said, her own sounding faraway.

"Whose?" he asked.

"This man on the phone. He was speaking with the woman. Back at that house they brought me to." She blinked, as if coming out of a trance. "Do you think that was Mordecai?"

"What were they talking about?"

"He wanted them to bring me to him. The woman called him Dr. Norton." Eden shook her head and dropped her face into her hands. "I don't know if I recognize the name, too, or if I'm just imagining things."

Cass frowned, then turned back to the screen, where the

information had finally loaded. Sure enough, the license plate numbers belonged to a Honda Clarity, owned by one Jack Forrester.

Eden came off the bed. "That's him. His name was Jack."

According to the public directory, Jack Forrester was an IT operator for a local tech company in Milwaukee. He was married for the past twenty-three years to a woman named Annette. Maiden name, Carlson. They had one daughter, unnamed with no accompanying photograph.

Cassian opened a search engine, plugged in their names, and quickly came upon two interesting discoveries. Jack Forrester had a criminal record. And the couple had lost a son. Twenty-one years ago, during The Attack. For some reason, this had Eden jerking back, as if the information were fire and she'd accidentally touched it. It was a curious reaction. One Cass didn't understand. A lot of kids died twenty-one years ago.

"Aggravated assault," Cleo read. "Shortly after their son died. He served two years in prison."

Cass ran a search for Norton next. The results were so expansive—the list of possible Norton's so large, even when limiting the search to Milwaukee—they abandoned the effort. Eden didn't know his first name. She didn't know what he looked like. She didn't know what kind of doctor he was, or if he was really a doctor at all. So he abandoned that particular search and went, instead, to the website of Eagle Bend's county auditor. He typed in 3235 West Buckle Lane. The owner listed was Roger *Carlson*, a buyer of the house twenty-three years earlier.

"Carlson," Eden said. "That can't be a coincidence."

It wasn't.

With some uncomplicated digging, he found a connection. Annette Forrester was related to Roger Carlson. He was her older brother by twelve years. He was also ex-military, dishonorably discharged. After that, the trail went cold.

Cass leaned back in Cleo's chair and folded his arms. "You said your parents' numbers don't work?"

"One went to a pizza place. The other was disconnected."

He found himself typing in their names—Alexander and Ruth Pruitt. It was a search he'd run before. A search that led to nothing very interesting. The Pruitts had lived a quiet life. If not for Eden's arrest, he never would have found her at all. He expected the same sparse details to pop up now. But when he hit enter, nothing loaded. Not even when Eden asked him to run a search on California's government website, where he'd first found her. Court records were public, but hers had disappeared. And it had nothing to do with Cleo's diabolical Internet connection.

Eden strode to the window. She leaned against it, rolling her bottom lip between her teeth. Her eyes rose to meet his—big and full of color. Not gray or green or blue, but a mixture of all three. "You've been following me."

The tension in his jaw doubled. Hadn't they already established this?

"I need to know what happened yesterday afternoon when I came home from school. What did you see?"

He narrowed his eyes. "Why?"

"Just tell me what you saw."

"You drove home. You went inside. A few minutes later, you bolted."

"Bolted?"

"You ran."

She kneaded her temples.

"I tried following you but I lost track. So I went to your house again. I looked in one of the windows to see if you'd come back, and that's when I saw the living room. At first, I assumed that was why you took off, but then you returned, and I could tell it was the first time you were seeing it. That's when you ran to the parade and found the police officer."

Eden stood still for a while, as if trying to take his words and make them into tangible memories.

Cass tilted his head. "Do you not remember yesterday?"

"Only parts of it." She squeezed her eyes shut and shook her head—obviously struggling with the lapse in memory, toeing the line between confusion and distress, and that distress had his irritation flaring anew. It shouldn't bother him. She was nothing more than a ticket to freedom. If he acted quickly enough, she still could be. All he had to do was make a phone call and his debt would be paid. He wasn't supposed to be here, looking for answers that had nothing to do with him. He tapped his index finger against the wood of Cleo's desktop, his frustration building. With himself. With her. With Yukio and this entire situation.

He ran his hand down his face and stood.

"Where are you going?" Eden asked.

"Outside" He strode to the door. "I need to make a phone call."

12

Eden stared, jarred by Cassian Gray's abrupt departure. A phone call to whom? And why all the hostility? She'd never asked him to get involved. He volunteered all on his own. And for a guy who said he didn't like when bad things happened to innocent people, he sure was treating her—an innocent person—with a whole lot of contempt.

Her mind spun. This unfriendly stranger had memories of her doing things she couldn't remember herself. He followed her home after school. He watched her leave her house—*run* from her house. What had compelled her to run and why couldn't she remember it?

Cleo opened the miniature fridge next to her desk. She pulled out a can of Diet Dr. Pepper and lifted it into the air—a gesture that said *do you want one?*

Eden held out her hand.

The can sailed through the air. She caught it cleanly, the aluminum cold between her palms. She cracked it open and took a drink that turned into a guzzle, as though she hadn't realized the extent of her thirst until that first swig slid down her throat.

Cleo sipped hers, then set the can beside the newspaper. The *illegal* newspaper. When Eden was seven, a similar one showed up on their doorstep. It wasn't called *The People's Press*, but it wasn't *The Concordia Times* either. Intrigued, she'd brought it inside and showed it to her mother, then watched as all the blood drained from Mom's face. Her hands had trembled when she took it. Her nostrils flared when she fed it to the shredder. Once it was reduced to ruined strips, Mom told Eden that if ever a paper like that showed up on their doorstep again, she shouldn't even touch it. Eden swore she never would.

Now, she didn't know where her mother was, and her safety depended on a girl who was producing illegal newspapers in her spare time. Eden peered at the headline. Random Acts of Terror or Manipulative Fear Tactics? It was too long, as far as headlines went. But it had encouraged Eden to read more—a story about the recent pipe bombs, written from a very bizarre angle. The Attack had paralyzed America and apparently, those in power took advantage. Freedoms were taken. Now, a dissent was rising in the margins. A growing unrest that would soon challenge the country's post-attack status quo. According to an anonymous source, the pipe bombs were a scare tactic to keep the public on its heels. If it didn't work, something bigger was on the way. Cleo said she preferred reporting truth, but the article was completely speculative.

Eden nodded at the paper. "Who's your source?"

"Don't you know what the word anonymous means?"

"Aren't you worried about getting caught?"

Cleo shrugged and popped another Hot Tamale in her mouth.

"You'd get into a lot of trouble." At the very least, she'd lose her RA position. Eden couldn't imagine the administration would be okay with one of their resident advisors circulating illegal contraband.

"I could get in trouble for a lot of things. Like letting you and Cass stay here, for instance." She grabbed her soda and crossed her feet on top of the desk, eyeballing Eden over the can as she twirled the bone and skull ring around her thumb. "What made you jump out of a car?"

"The person driving it drugged me against my will and kidnapped me from a police station."

Cleo ogled Eden for a moment, then lifted her can in a gesture of solidarity.

Eden cast her attention toward the door and decided to take the opportunity to find out more about this stranger-of-a-boy who seemed to hate her. "How do you two know each other?"

"He stayed with me and my mom for a few months when I was …" She pressed her tongue against the inside of her bottom lip, making the snakebite piercing bulge. "Ten, I think? Cass was eleven, maybe twelve."

"Why did he stay with you and your mom?"

"She's a doctor and he was in bad shape, so she took him in."

"Don't most doctors treat patients at clinics or hospitals?"

"Sure, if those patients are 'legal'."

Eden looked at Cleo blankly.

"Cass doesn't exist."

"What do you mean?"

"He lives off the grid."

Off the grid.

Meaning, illegal. Like Cleo's newspaper.

No information in the public directory. No paperwork. No identification. No registered fingerprints or retinas. No social security number. No taxes, either. Eden set her elbows on her knees. "She could have lost her license for that."

Cleo shrugged.

Eden tried to wrap her mind around it. Going through all that work—all of that schooling—then risking it for tax-evaders and outlaws. But then, Cass had been a kid—which meant living off the grid probably wasn't a choice for him. Not back then, at least. She glanced again at the door. "Why was he in bad shape?"

"His dad wasn't a good guy."

The words made Eden's stomach clench into a fist of indignation. Perhaps this explained some of his surliness. Cass was eleven, maybe twelve, and he'd been in rough shape because his father wasn't a good guy. Sometimes, people were truly awful. "It was nice of your mom to take him in."

"She wouldn't call it *nice*. She'd call it right."

Eden considered the statement and decided she agreed. If she was a doctor and an abused kid showed up on her doorstep, she wouldn't care about losing her license either. She'd invite him in. She'd do what she could to make sure he was well. "What happened when he recovered?"

"To Cass?"

"Yeah." Did he go back with his father? What about his mother? And if Cleo's mom was that caring, why not take him in permanently and make him legal? She found herself leaning in, inordinately curious.

Cleo tapped the side of the can with her fingernail. They were painted black. "He went to live with my mom's friend. Mona's always taking in kids like him. But Mona's a pacifist, so when Cass started fighting—"

"Fighting?"

Cleo stared back at her—a pointed gleam in her eye.

"He's a fighter?" Even as Eden said it, she didn't know why she sounded so surprised. How else did he know men like Mordecai and Yukio? And didn't she sense it right away? *Danger.* Just like the newspaper Mom shredded when Eden was seven. Her whole life, her parents had gone out of their way to avoid it. They lived quiet and safe. They followed the rules. They didn't take risks. And they taught Eden to do the same. She tried her best to follow their example, even when the allure of danger did its best to draw her in. Most of the time, Eden could resist it. But she wasn't perfect, and that imperfection led them halfway across the country to Iowa. Now she was with an illegal fighter and a girl who wrote an illegal newspaper, running from a gambler named Mordecai. If danger was an ocean, she was sinking in its depths.

"You're wrong," Cleo finally said.

"About?"

"Cass." She took a drink. "I can tell what you're thinking."

"Can you?"

"Yes. And you're wrong. Cass is a good guy."

"Who beats people up for a living."

"Everybody's gotta eat." With a sigh, Cleo brought her feet to the ground. "And unfortunately, I've got to get to class. I can leave my laptop here. Take notes the old-fashioned way so you two can keep sleuthing for answers. There's a situation I'm monitoring in Madison, but I can have Cass keep an eye on it for me while I'm gone."

"A situation you're monitoring?"

"For my paper." Cleo lifted her eyebrows jauntily, then stepped in front of a hanging mirror on the wall behind the door and gave her coiled knots a cursory primp.

A photograph hung in the upper left corner.

Eden squinted at it. "Is that …?"

"My hero and role model? Yes."

Eden gaped. Cleo's hero and role model was the infamous media mogul—Dayne Johnson, the man with the mega-watt smile. He'd been a big wig for one of the country's major media outlets before they were shut down and taken over by Concordia. He was also an insurrectionist, still at large. At least, according to the FBI's most-wanted list. And here Cleo had a picture of him hanging in her mirror.

She leaned closer to the glass to check her teeth. "People are gonna knock on the door. It usually starts around ten. I swear, the freshman here don't know how to use a microwave without help. Just tell them to write a note on the white board and I'll get to it when I get to it."

Judging by all the notes on the whiteboard already, she wouldn't be getting to it anytime soon.

"Here's my student card. I have an extra. You can use this one to get in and out of the building and get food at the cafeteria if you and Cass are hungry. You might want to change into a shirt that isn't torn in half before you leave. You can borrow one of mine. Just don't ruin it."

"By jumping out of another vehicle?"

"Exactly."

"And if people ask who we are?"

Cleo pulled on a pair of black Converse All-Stars. "Tell them you're friends of mine visiting from home."

"Which is where?"

"Chicago."

The door swung open.

Cass walked inside, his face grim.

"What is it?" Eden asked. "Who did you call?"

"Yukio," he said, a deep furrow dimpling his brow.

"And?"

"He's dead."

13

Eden splashed water on her face. Then she straightened and stared at herself in the mirror—droplets dripping into the basin of the sink. Yukio the Bookie told Cassian the Fighter that Mordecai the Gambler was after her. Cassian the Fighter helped her get away from Mordecai the Gambler, and suddenly, Yukio the Bookie turned up dead. His landlord found him in his apartment with a single bullet hole through his head. A random, unfortunate break-in was the prevailing assumption, but they knew better.

Footsteps sounded behind her.

The girl from the elevator stepped into view—freshly showered with a towel wrapped around her body and another wrapped around her hair. She set a toiletry bag in the sink two over from Eden's and met her eye in the mirror's reflection.

"We met in the elevator, right?" She unzipped her bag and pulled out a small bottle of moisturizer.

Eden moved to the towel dispenser and stuck her hand in front of the sensor. They hadn't exactly *met*.

"You're visiting someone named *Greg*," the girl pressed, her flirtatious tone from earlier long gone.

With a nod, Eden tore off a ream of paper towel and used it to pat her face dry.

The girl rubbed lotion onto her cheeks and chin. "There's nobody named Greg on this floor. I asked around."

"We're friends of Cleo's."

"Why did the guy you were with say you were visiting Greg?"

"He was just … kidding around."

The girl pursed her lips skeptically. Eden didn't blame her. Cassian hardly seemed the type to *kid around*.

"Is he your boyfriend?" the girl asked, examining a blemish on her jawline.

Eden snorted.

"Was that a dumb question or something?"

"No. He's ..." She tried to imagine explaining the nature of their relationship. *He's a total stranger, actually. Apparently, he lives off the grid and fights underground. I jumped on the back of his bike after hurling myself out of a moving car to get away from my kidnappers.*

The girl raised her eyebrows.

"He's not my boyfriend," Eden said.

"Hm."

She wasn't fooled by the indifferent sound. The girl was fishing, and Eden didn't have the mental energy for it. Nor did she want to hand out their names. She threw the crumpled paper towel into the waste bin and left before the girl could finish her inquiry. Cass had taken Cleo's student ID to get them sustenance in the cafeteria. His sleuthing had led to nothing but dead ends and they both needed to eat. Neither thought it wise for Eden to wander around campus, even if her face wasn't being splashed on the news.

Stuck in Cleo's room, Eden flipped between Concordia Milwaukee and Concordia National, as if watching might ease the itchy, helpless feeling in her chest and the physical ache beneath it. In all her eighteen years, she'd never been away from her parents for more than a couple days, and always they were a simple phone call away. Now, not only did she not know where they were, she didn't even know if they were okay. Two facts that made sitting still an impossible feat.

Cassian returned—his mood matching his dark attire as he handed her a pre-wrapped chicken salad sandwich, an apple, and a bottle of water. Eden supposed that this time, his ill temper was warranted. Perhaps Cassian and Yukio were friends. And now his friend was dead. Because of her, one could argue. Something pinched inside her, and for a second—only a second—she forgot about her growing sense of panic. For a second, a softness stirred as she saw through his calloused exterior to an abused, eleven-year-old boy, in rough shape because of *his father*.

"I'm sorry about Yukio," she said.

His attention snapped to her face, as if caught off guard by the apology.

Eden didn't look away. She held his gaze—this hardened fighter who probably intimidated most people he encountered. Well, she refused to be most people. She refused to be intimidated, even if the air in the room was crackling with tension.

He sat down in Cleo's desk chair and awoke the sleeping laptop. Her attention slid from the tanned nape of his neck to the broadness of his back, well-defined even beneath his dark gray Henley. Without his jacket, she could make out the bottom edge of a tattoo on his equally-defined bicep. She pictured him squaring off with an opponent in the ring and her stomach did a funny pirouette. Was he a good fighter? It seemed impossible that he wasn't.

He took a bite of his apple.

The loud crunch pulled her back to the moment. She ate her meal fast, gobbling it up like a woman in need of calories. After she finished, she asked if she could borrow his phone. When he handed it over, it felt odd in her palm—the design and weight of it. Not at all like the phones she was used to. But then, those required a state-issued ID to purchase. All electronic devices did.

Same with vehicles. Cassian lived off the grid, which meant he didn't have a state-issued ID. But he did have a motorcycle. And this strange phone.

"Is there a problem?" he asked.

"No," she said, then excused herself. She wanted to try her parents again on the off chance something had changed.

It hadn't.

One number was disconnected. The other went to the pizza place. Eden tried calling her own number, but that was disconnected, too. With a growl, she returned the phone to Cassian and began a short-routed pace in the small room. With every turn of her heel, the tension grew.

She thought Cassian might snap at her. Tell her to go pace in the hallway. Instead, he dragged his hand down his face and said, "It doesn't make sense."

"None of this does."

"If I were Mordecai, I wouldn't disconnect your phone. I'd wait for you to call it, then I'd trace your location. Government-issued phones are easy to trace."

"Yes, well. You aren't Mordecai, are you?" With a terse sigh, she sat on Cleo's bed as Concordia National replayed an interview with Oswin Brahm on The Colter Show. It was an interview Eden watched with her parents and Erik back in San Diego. Mr. Brahm was good at interviews. They moved naturally from his galactic mining project, which was being funded thanks to the success of his tech company, to the upcoming Prosperity Ball and the lottery that would grant fifty lucky citizens access.

"We could all use some extra fun this time of year, when the memories start to get a little sharper."

"Touché," Colter said, his expression changing into something reflective, slightly somber. "It's hard to believe it will have been twenty-one years."

Oswin shook his head, like he couldn't believe it either. "We've come a long way. And yet all of us who are old enough can put ourselves right back there. The twenty-one years just sort of … disappear, don't they?"

At the time the interview originally aired, Eden had glanced sideways at her parents.

Dad had taken Mom's hand.

And it took everything inside Eden not to grab the remote and turn the television off.

Her parents were Gen Nex'ers. Short for Nexus. A human link between life before and life after. Every person in Generation Nex had a survival story. Where they were and what they were doing when it happened—the day evil saw an opportunity and capitalized on it. It was, and probably always would be the worst attack in world history. And it happened right here, on U.S. soil.

Not an aerial assault with nuclear missiles, but a ground assault with nuclear guns. Crudely constructed weapons of mass destruction that catapulted slugs of uranium through the air, creating flashes of light brighter than the sun—reportedly seen for hundreds of miles, leaving unsuspecting onlookers temporarily blind as two massive fireballs blasted Independence Avenue and midtown Manhattan, carving craters fifty feet deep where the Library of Congress and Times Square used to be, cremating everything and everyone within a hundred-foot radius. Steel, incinerated. Buildings reduced to dust. People instantaneously vaporized. The shockwaves generated winds up to five hundred miles per hour, demolishing statues, flipping cars, snapping power lines, and turning massive debris into deadly projectiles.

All of this happened in a matter of seconds.

Never mind the mushroom cloud of radioactive particles that would fall like rain on the ravaged cities, killing fifty percent of survivors in the days that followed and another ten within the month. It would have happened in Chicago and L.A., too, if not for the fast-acting heroics of their respective police departments.

To Eden, a history lesson.

To her parents, a vivid memory.

That day and the days of hysteria that followed—horror, and fear, and chaos. And when the dust finally settled, a death toll that climbed into the millions. It didn't matter if you were conservative or liberal, rich or poor, black or white, immigrant or citizen, Christian, Muslim, or atheist. All of it fell into the vast ocean of collective lament, and its tide carried away the issues that once so severely divided the nation.

Cleo was right. Tragedy did unite. Eden just wasn't willing to concede that their own government would go to such lengths to do it. The evil of that, she was certain, lay at the feet of one Karik Volkova—leader of Interitus, a terrorist regime that took advantage of the country's weakened state and was thankfully long destroyed.

"Last year you received a fair amount of criticism for naming the ball what you did—*Prosperity*," Colter said. "Some argued, and still argue, that it's an odd name, given the anniversary of such a tragic event."

"Yes, well, I've said it before, and I will say it again. I'm a strong believer in the power of thought. How we speak about a situation—how we frame it—matters. We can be defined by this tragedy that happened to us, or we can be defined by how we've responded to it. I have seen a country that has responded well. That has pressed onward. That has done what's been necessary to survive. I have seen a country that despite all the odds, despite the persistent fear, has put aside our differences for the sake of unity and is determined to prosper. I think that's worth celebrating."

For the sake of unity.

Eden had never thought to question the word before. Unity was a good thing. Especially after such horrible division—the kind that rose to such heights, the country went from civil unrest to civil war. Now, however, Cleo's words were stuck in her head. According to her, *unity* was a tool of manipulation for those in power.

Eden looked over her shoulder, curious about Cassian's thoughts on the matter. But he wasn't watching. Instead, he was staring at video footage on Cleo's computer screen—a birds-eye view of a thoroughfare jam-packed with bodies. There was a large, orange barricade, and police officers directing traffic. At first, Eden thought it was some sort of parade or festival. But when she stepped closer, she spotted signs and deciphered the muted, angry sound of chanting.

"What is this?" she asked.

"A situation Cleo's watching."

"Is that—are they … *protesting*?" Eden had seen one or two in her lifetime. Not in person, but reported on the news. In large part, protests had become a thing of the past, as the government had enacted strict laws after The Attack, and the general public wasn't keen on anyone who started them. The two she had seen fizzled out before they got off the ground. But this one was different. This one was large. "What are they chanting?"

Cass turned up the volume. "Sounds like ... this isn't right, where is Dwight?"

"Who's Dwight?" Eden asked.

Cassian shrugged.

The crowd pushed. Police officers yelled into megaphones, motioning for people to move back. But the people in front didn't listen, or maybe they couldn't listen. The mob pressed closer to the barricade, and one of the officers with a megaphone removed a taser from his belt and jammed it against a woman's neck.

She convulsed, then collapsed.

For one blip of a second, the scene froze.

No chanting. No pushing. No shoving. Even traffic seemed to hiccup as everyone regarded the woman crumpled on the ground.

And then, chaos erupted.

The people surged forward, trampling the barricade. Maybe they trampled the woman, too. The three officers directing traffic joined their comrades and descended upon the rioting crowd. They drew tasers and batons, toppling protestors. A man began a wrestling match with an officer. The unconscious woman on the ground was handcuffed and dragged away. The people who saw it happen hollered and waved their fists.

With a shocked expletive, Eden turned to the television, flipping to Concordia National.

"It's not going to be on the news," Cass said.

"Of course it will." It was *breaking* news. "There hasn't been a riot in years."

"There hasn't been a riot *reported* in years."

Eden shook her head. This was too big to escape the news. Even if reporters didn't want to report it, someone would post about it on social media. Surely, out of all those people, one of them snapped a picture or a video. "You can't keep something like this quiet. It'll end up on Perk."

"Who runs Perk?" Cass asked.

"The—" Eden stopped. "Government."

He gave his eyebrows a sardonic lift, like she was a silly, naive girl.

Heat prickled in her cheeks. "If people are rioting, the public has a right to know."

"Careful," he said. "Those are seditious words."

Eden stared at him, sitting there in front of Cleo's laptop—the pair of them with their farfetched conspiracy theories—when a sudden, jarring thought exploded in her mind. What if they weren't so farfetched?

Her head spun.

This isn't right. Where is Dwight?

Apparently, he'd gone missing.

Like her parents.

Like entire swaths of time.

A traumatic brain injury.

She shook her head. No, there'd been no injury. That didn't happen. But something *did* happen. Yesterday, when her house was ransacked. A period. A *crucial* period. And she couldn't remember it. How was it that she couldn't remember those hours, but somehow, she could remember a diagram from an anatomy book she barely glanced at?

Was she losing her mind?

Her attention returned to Cleo's computer screen when another thought came. Less jarring. More hopeful. "Do towns archive their surveillance footage?"

Cassian looked directly at her. Judging by his expression, he knew what she was asking.

If they could pull up surveillance for Eagle Bend—for her address in particular—they could see who broke into her house. They could see if her parents were home when it happened.

14

By the time Cleo returned from class, Cass had successfully hacked into Eagle Bend's archived surveillance database. Eden had no idea when or why a fighter would have acquired such a skill but acquire it he had. And Eden was too anxious to pry. She stood behind him—her palms clammy, her fingers like ice as he pulled up an index of files and clicked on a folder marked West Buckle Lane 3100-3300.

He scrolled to the very last file—*yesterday's file*—and opened it. An aerial view of Eden's Eagle Bend neighborhood filled the screen, her house dead center. The footage began in the wee hours of the morning. The three of them watched in fast-forward as navy blue sky turned to dusk and the rising sun chased away a layer of fog hovering over green lawns. A cat slinked from the bushes across the street. Next door, a Solterra reversed out of the drive. Then the front door of 3235 West Buckle Lane opened. Eden watched herself step outside, squint up into the sky, then get in her car and drive away while her parents remained behind to continue unpacking.

A long lull of nothing proceeded. West Buckle Lane was a quiet street. The occasional car rolled past. A dog-walker. A jogger. Mom came out once to shake out a rug. Dad a little while later to carry a box to their unattached garage. And then, at half past one, her parents left the house together. Eden watched with shallow, bated breath as Dad's Nissan reversed out of the garage and disappeared down the street.

She hoped they would stay gone. She hoped that lunch and errands—Walmart and Home Depot and the grocery store—would keep them away. But it was a fool's hope. She knew her parents, and although she couldn't remember it, she knew they would be waiting for her when she came home from her first day of school. With a sinking heart, she watched Dad's car return an hour later. Mom and Dad carried bags inside. And at three o'clock, Eden watched herself pull into the drive. With absolutely no recollection, she watched herself get out, sling her backpack over her shoulder, and walk into the house.

A few minutes later, the front door swung open, and Eden ran like something had scared the living daylights out of her. But what? And why would she leave her parents alone and defenseless?

Her heart pounded—great loud thumps, like drumbeats in her ears, her temples, her eyes. Her neck. Even her knees.

Please, her mind begged, as if her parents might be able to hear the plea. *Please, come after me. Leave. Leave before Mordecai or Jack or Annette or whoever it was that tore apart our house shows up.*

But almost immediately after Eden watched herself run, a van pulled into the driveway. A man stepped out and made his way through the front yard. He opened the unlocked door and walked right inside.

Eden cupped her hand over her mouth.

Her parents were in there. Her parents were home. And if this man worked for Mordecai, who'd killed Yukio ... Bile gurgled in her stomach as the seconds tick, tick, ticked and the front door opened again. Only this time, there were two of them. Two men stepped out of her home. Two men who had her parents.

"Where'd the second guy come from?" Cleo asked.

Eden didn't know.

Eden couldn't breathe.

Not when her father and mother were being dragged—bound and gagged—against their will. Her heart contracted painfully beneath her ribcage. *No.* This couldn't be happening. This had to be a nightmare.

Wake up, Eden. Wake up!

She squeezed her eyes shut, but the nightmare pressed on as the two men shoved her parents into the back of the van and drove away.

She stared at the screen, her lungs paralyzed.

Mordecai the Gambler killed Yukio the Bookie—a cold, heartless bullet to the head. And now that same man had taken her mom and dad. Her body began to shake—great, seismic waves. "Why is he doing this?"

If he trafficked girls, if that's what this was about, then why would he take Eden's parents?

But nobody had an answer. Not even a conspiracy theory.

She sat down on Cleo's bed and pressed the heels of her palms against her eyes. She pictured her living room—the shards of glass, the upturned books, the smashed boxes. How hard had they struggled? How badly were they injured? And how was she supposed to find them when they didn't even know Mordecai's real name?

"That second guy," Cleo said. "He must have already been in your house. He must have been the reason you ran."

If that was true, then Eden was a coward.

A pathetic, deplorable coward.

Cass rewound the footage, then paused right when one of the men looked up—straight at the drone—with a twisted sort of smile, like he knew it was there. Like he knew she would be watching later. Cass zoomed in, capturing the man's face. And Eden gasped. She recognized him. Along with the tattoo on his neck.

She came off the bed. "He was at the police station last night.

He was there when I was there, reporting a suspicious vehicle. I thought he was watching me, and I was right."

"Did you see him inside your house?" Cleo asked.

"I don't know. I thought he looked familiar when he was at the station. But I can't remember." Eden tapped her fist against her forehead. "Why can't I remember?"

"Your brain probably repressed it."

"I wouldn't run." Her voice rang with conviction. But inside, doubt crept in. Would she? Was that who she was? No, it wasn't. It couldn't be. "If I saw them being hurt, if I saw that guy at our house, I just … I wouldn't run."

And yet, the footage told them otherwise.

She dug her fingers into her hair. "He was at the police station."

"You … already said that." Cleo shot Cassian a sideways glance.

"He came in through the front. Which means he had to have his retinas scanned. Is it possible to access their retinal data? Because if so, we could get an ID on the guy."

"You'd have to use an illegal browser. It just so happens, I have one downloaded." Cleo reached past Cass and pulled up a browser Eden had never seen before. "Right here."

Cass went to work. In no time at all, he'd made his way into the Eagle Bend Police Department Retinal Scan Database. They went through every single entry from yesterday, but none of the faces matched. Somehow, the guy had either bypassed the retinal scan or erased all evidence of it.

Desperation churned in her gut.

And with it, a possibility took shape in her mind.

Her parents were injured. Taken against their will. Eden had evidence the police couldn't deny. If she took this to the nearest station, would they finally listen to her? Her identity wasn't being reported in the news, and Jack and Annette Forrester fled the scene. They didn't stick around to speak with the police. But then … they drugged her inside a police station. Maybe they were only making it seem as if they hadn't reported her. Maybe the authorities were keeping her identity under wraps so that she'd let her guard down and head to the nearest station. Maybe the second she showed up, Jack Forrester would drug her against her will again, without any opportunity to show the authorities this footage.

A tremble worked its way into Eden's arms and legs. She didn't know what or who was safe anymore. She only knew her parents were in terrible trouble.

"What you need," Cleo said, setting her bag on top of the mini fridge, "is to see inside the house."

Inside the house.

She was right. If Eden could see *inside* the house, she could watch what she couldn't remember. Her eyes locked with Cassian's. Just how far did his skills go? "Can you hack into a private home security system?"

He ran his hand down the side of his face, then curled it around the back of his neck. "Do you know what type of home security system?"

Her mind scrambled. She looked up at the white textured ceiling, rewinding time, trying to pull a name or a logo from memory. Something on the front entry keypad. But she came back completely blank. "I have no idea."

Cass rubbed his jaw, then pulled out his phone and made a short and succinct phone call. He repeated her Eagle Bend address twice, briefly explained what they were looking for, and listened as the guy on the other end said he would see what he could do. And that was that. They couldn't capture the van's license plate; the angle made it impossible. There was nothing left to do but wait. And that made her want to crawl out of her skin. She had to at least try to remember. "Does anybody know how to un-repress memories?"

"You could try hypnotherapy."

Cassian scoffed.

Cleo shot him a look of superiority. "Ignore the skeptic. It's been proven to help people recover memories. Not to mention, a whole host of other benefits. I experienced one of them firsthand. Thanks to Mona, the physical pain I suffered after a car accident completely disappeared."

"Mona lives in Chicago," Cass said.

"Correct. But *I* live right here."

To that, he gave such a severe eye roll, it might as well have been audible.

Eden looked from the skeptic to the believer, whom she might take more seriously if not for the Big Foot on her shirt.

"It's not like it's dangerous," Cleo said. "You wouldn't be unconscious. You wouldn't lose control. All it does is put you into a deep state of relaxation, which gets the memories unstuck. There's no harm in trying."

Eden was fairly sure that in normal circumstances, she would stand confidently in Cassian's camp. Hypnosis felt as hokey to her as voodoo dolls. But these were not normal circumstances, and if there was even a microscopic chance it would help her remember, she had to try.

15

leo turned off the light, closed the sliding curtains, and wrote an impolite version of DO NOT DISTURB on the whiteboard outside her room. She ordered Cassian—who stood by the door leaning against the wall—to keep all derision to himself, and she ordered Eden to relax on the futon—a near impossible feat, given the heat of the skeptic's condescending stare. If looks could talk, his would clearly say, "I can't believe you're doing this." Well, neither could she. But what else was she supposed to do? They'd taken her parents.

Cleo dragged the head of a match along the side of a small matchbox with a sharp *scritch*, followed by a hiss of flame, which she brought to a jar of incense. She lit the end of a stick and almost immediately, the strong smell of juniper and sandalwood filled Eden's nostrils.

Cassian lifted one eyebrow. "Aren't matches and incense against safety protocol?"

"So is your gun," Cleo said. "Now shut it."

She shook out the flame as the incense burned. After a few seconds, she blew that out, too. All that remained was the red glowing ember and smoke that swirled into the air, permeating the room with a scent so cloying it made Eden's head swim.

Cleo sat on her bed and led Eden through a series of breathing exercises, encouraging her to find a focal point—a place to rest her gaze. Eden watched the smoke rising from the wick, curling like gray ribbon caught in a breeze. Cleo started with Eden's toes, commanding each one to relax—then slowly and methodically, she moved up Eden's body, not stopping until she reached the crown of her head. Somehow—perhaps the combination of Cleo's strangely melodic voice and the overpowering aroma—her awareness of Cassian slid away. He drifted into the background as Eden's muscles unwound and her eyelids grew heavy.

"Imagine you're at the top of a staircase," Cleo said.

Eden pictured herself standing barefoot at the top of the staircase leading into the basement of their home in San Diego. It was the only house in the whole neighborhood that had a basement, specially built by the previous owners. Transplants from the Midwest who thought houses ought to have basements.

"I want you to walk down the stairs."

She imagined the cool basement. She imagined sitting in the corner with 12-year old Erik as he swung her pendant necklace —the one with the Eiffel tower charm—back and forth in front of her face.

"You are getting sleeeeeeeepy," he crooned, no longer shy with a whole year of friendship under their belts. "Very, very sleeeeeeeepy."

She played along, feigning a trance-like state.

"Now tell me the truth. How do you really feel about Mr. Bastion's gym shorts?"

Eden had laughed, and grimaced, too, because Mr. Bastion's gym shorts were not a pretty sight.

Cleo's voice cut through the memory. "Keep walking down the stairs. Further, and further."

A warm breeze fluttered the hem of Eden's sundress. It billowed around her feet as she walked back and forth along an aluminum bleacher—the highest one. Much higher than she was supposed to be. But she couldn't help it. She was an acrobat in the circus, and the bleacher was her tightrope, and the height was irresistible, and her dress was a little too big. She tripped on the hem and tumbled head over heels, arms flailing. A rush of wind as the solid ground rose to meet her.

Her mother screamed.

Dad lifted her in his arms and held her close.

"Is she okay?" Mom asked, her voice tinged with hysteria. "Is she hurt?"

"Of course not," he said. "She's fine, Ruth. See?"

Mom crushed Eden against her chest, where her heart thundered.

Cleo's voice broke through again, urging Eden downward.

She stood on a stool in front of a hot griddle at the kitchen counter. Every now and then, Eden got the urge to touch the griddle. Daddy said it was hot. Daddy said it would hurt. Sometimes she wanted to see for herself. How hot was it, really? Once, she might have—when Daddy wasn't looking. But not today. Today, Mommy was sad, and Daddy had flour on his nose, and Eden was extra careful when he let her pour the pancake batter.

"This is a hard day for Mommy," he said.

"But pancakes always help!"

"Yes, sunshine. Pancakes always help."

She ran through the kitchen, through the hall. Into her parents' bedroom, holding a steaming stack of pancakes smothered in butter, thirsty for syrup.

Mom lay in bed, smiling a sad smile.

Eden climbed up next to her and snuggled close, wishing with every wish she could wish that she could take Mommy's sadness away. "Do you want me to sing the happy birthday song?"

"That would be beautiful."

Her small, high-pitched voice sang the familiar lyrics.

"Happy birthday to youuuu. Happy birthday to youuuu. Happy biiiiirthday dear Christopherrrrr. Happy birthday to you."

The scene rolled away like the fluorescent lights rolling overhead.

She lay on a gurney.

It stopped. The squeaking wheels, too. Her mother and father stood over her. They looked worried. She could see it in their eyes.

"The doctor says you won't feel a thing," Dad said.

Mom squeezed her hand. "And we'll be right here as soon as you wake up."

A man in a white coat touched her mother's shoulder reassuringly, then he moved a mask toward Eden's face. She wanted to cower. She wanted to scream. He was going to put that mask over her mouth and her nose, and then maybe she wouldn't be able to breathe. But she didn't cower. She didn't scream. She had to be brave, even if she was scared. She had to be brave for Mommy and Daddy because they were very worried and if she was extra brave maybe some of it would rub off on them.

The man in the white coat must have sensed her fear, because he put the mask next to his mouth. "Nothing to worry about. See?"

With a gasp, Eden's eyes flew open.

Cleo stared through the dimness. "Did it work?"

Eden's heart pounded. "His voice."

"What voice?" Cassian asked, his tone no longer skeptical, but sharp and clear.

"The man who was talking to Annette Forrester on the phone. I couldn't place his voice at the time, but I knew it was familiar. I knew I'd heard it before." Eden looked at him. "I think he put tubes in my ears when I was four."

———

I t was time to find Dr. Norton.

He was real. And somehow, he was connected to all of this. Her parents. Jack and Annette Forrester. Mordecai the Gambler. And now, thanks to Cleo and her hypnotherapy—Eden had his face in her memory. They searched his name and started wading through the pictures. There were several that had Eden questioning—was that him? Fourteen years could do a lot to a person, and there were so many, the faces began to blur together.

She had to stop for a bathroom break.

All three of them stretched their legs.

Cleo didn't bother going to her afternoon Mass Communications lecture.

They stayed in her dorm room, ignoring knocks on her door, pulling up picture after picture, starting with pediatricians and ENTs, the kind of doctors who might actually put tubes in a child's ears. When none turned out to be matches, they moved on to less obvious Dr. Norton's. Until finally, they found him. There was no question about it.

Dr. Benjamin Anthony Norton. Retired *military* doctor.

Roger Carlson—the man who pretended to be the resident of Eden's new home—and Dr. Norton both had connections to the military.

"Why would your parents take you to a military doctor to get tubes in your ears?" Cleo asked.

It was the same question Eden was already asking herself. It didn't make any sense. Kids didn't go to military doctors for that kind of a procedure. She rubbed her face, tired of the mounting questions. There were too many pieces floating inside her head. She grabbed a pen and began jotting them down on a sticky note.

Mordecai. Pseudonym. Gambler. Looking for me.

Jack & Annette Forrester. Criminal record. Dead son—21 years ago.

It was a detail she couldn't escape. For one unhinged second, the sight of it made her feel crazy, like Jack and Annette Forrester were telling the truth. She was their daughter, and they had lost a son. Just like her parents had lost a son. But a lot of parents lost kids twenty-one years ago, she'd told herself. Even so, the detail felt too relevant to be coincidental. Then, and now. So she wrote it down.

Roger Carlson. At my house. Ex-military, Dishonorable discharge.

2 Men — unknown. Tattoos. At police station.

Alexander and Ruth Pruitt — missing.

Dr. Benjamin Norton. Retired Military. Looking for me.

Once she completed the list, she started drawing lines. From Annette to Carlson, because Annette was his little sister. From Dr. Norton to Annette, because Eden overhead the two talking on the phone. From her parents to Jack and Annette Forrester, because they both lost a son twenty-one years ago. From Dr. Norton to her parents, because they knew him. They wouldn't have brought her to him otherwise. And then finally, from Dr. Norton to Mordecai—because both were after her.

She capped the pen. "What are the chances we just found Mordecai's real name?"

Cass no longer sat at the computer. He'd long since abandoned his post, briefly excusing himself to take a phone call. Cleo had taken his spot, and when he'd returned, he hadn't asked for it back, but stood by the window instead, his elbow resting against the wall above his head as he stared broodingly down at the traffic, no longer participating. So it was Cleo who searched the doctor's full name now—Benjamin Anthony Norton. They needed more information. Unfortunately, information was scarce. His presence online, paltry.

They scrolled through several miss hits when Cleo ditched the search and pulled up the browser Cassian had used when accessing the Retinal Scan database for the Eagle Bend Police Department.

"This doctor," she said, typing his name into the new browser. "He's in his what—late sixties? Early seventies?"

"It's a good guess."

"He had a life before The Attack. He was in the military before The Attack. Maybe he's mentioned in articles that were written before The Attack. Articles we're not going to find on the regular web."

Cleo hit enter.

Several results loaded on the screen.

She clicked the one at the top and an article loaded. From a small-town, online paper that wasn't Concordia but wasn't illegal either. Because at the time it was written, Concordia didn't exist. This was America *before*.

"Celebrating a Local Hero," Eden read.

Dr. Benjamin Norton was the local hero. A military doctor who saved half a dozen lives after a roadside bombing in Afghanistan.

Cleo clicked to the second page where there was a photograph of the doctor, his arm slung casually around one of the lives he saved—handsome and young and so achingly familiar, Eden drew back, her mouth going dry. She was staring at a picture of her father. Her impossibly young, handsome father. Dressed in army fatigues. Only … her dad had never been in the army. Had he?

"That's my dad."

"Or someone who looks a lot like him," Cleo said, pointing to the caption.

Sure enough, the name listed underneath was not Alexander Pruitt. But Alaric Taylor.

Eden leaned closer, peering hard at the screen. She saw it, even through the grainy resolution. A small scar near his left temple from a skiing accident when he was fifteen. "The caption has to be wrong. That's absolutely him."

At some point, her father must have been in the military. He was in the military and he'd never told her about it.

Cleo ran another search in the same strange browser.

This time, for Alaric Taylor.

Eden expected another soldier to pop up. Another comrade

saved by Dr. Norton. The writer accidentally attributed the wrong name to her father. They found another article. An engagement announcement in the same small-town newspaper. Between Alaric Taylor and Molly Wick. Cleo clicked on the link and the picture that popped up had Eden's stomach dropping as if the ground had disappeared beneath her feet.

The man was her father. And the woman he'd proposed to—Molly Wick?

It was her mom.

"Why are their names different?" Cass asked, who by now had joined them begrudgingly.

Eden shook her head, in need of sitting but unable to pull herself away from that picture on the screen. Her mom and her dad, with different names.

What in the world was happening?

"The newspaper was based out of Silver Spring, Maryland," Cleo said. "Is that where they used to live?"

"They grew up in Washington. The state. They lived their whole life on the west coast." At least, this was what they'd always told her. Eden cupped her forehead—lightheaded, dizzy, her mind spinning. The world, too. A puff of air pushed up her throat—a short breath of stunned laughter. "Why would they change their names?"

As soon as she said it, a possibility clicked into place.

Witness protection.

People in danger had to go into witness protection. Was that what was going on? Had Dr. Benjamin Norton—otherwise known as Mordecai—pulled her parents into the dangerous, illegal world of Underground Fighting, and they had to go into hiding? But somehow, Dr. Norton had found them. Somehow, their cover was blown.

And then, another click.

Eden, getting arrested.

Eden, with a mug shot.

Her parent's over-the-top worry. Their whispered conversations behind closed doors.

She thought they were overreacting. She chalked it up to residual grief and the exacerbated paranoia after having lost one child. But no. Eden's recklessness had triggered a proverbial floodlight when they'd wanted to remain in the darkness of obscurity. Was this how Dr. Norton found them? Because of a senior prank Eden never should have participated in?

Cleo ran another search—more specific. Alaric Taylor, Silver Spring, Maryland.

New links loaded in the results. They found the wedding announcement, and several years later, a birth announcement. Alaric and Molly Taylor were the new, proud parents of a baby boy. Christopher James Taylor. They found his obituary next. One of nearly a million written during that time, not part of this dark web Cleo had accessed, but fully available to the public. Only Eden had never thought to access it before. Why would she? Eden already knew how he died. A terribly timed asthma attack when the country was on lockdown. Christopher needed medicine they couldn't get. What she didn't know? What she had no reason to even suspect? They'd been living right next door to Washington, DC, when it happened.

She could feel Cassian's invasive stare on the side of her face —but she couldn't meet it. She needed Cleo to keep going. She needed the Band-Aid ripped off, and ripped off fast. Cleo searched on. Alaric served in the military for several years before becoming a business manager in the civilian sector for a tech company called Watt. Cleo jotted the name down to research later. Then clicked on one final article. Like the obituary, this was not found in the small-town newspaper, but in The Concordia Times. An article titled *A Nation Determined to Heal.*

It was about a Fourth of July Festival in Silver Spring, not quite three years after The Attack.

Eden's parents were in the photograph. Her father's strong

arm was wrapped around her mother's small waist as they lifted red plastic cups toward the camera.

Only something was wrong. Something that had the blood draining from Eden's face.

She was born July 10th of that same year.

The picture was taken on July 4th.

And her mother's stomach was unmistakably flat.

16

den ran with her eyes closed—on a high-tech treadmill inside a small, but impressive workout room in the basement of Cleo's residence hall. The room was empty. The room wasn't there at all. She was out in the wide open. Running away, to a place where none of this was real. Not Cassian the Fighter. Not Cleo the Conspiracy Theorist. Not Mordecai the Gambler or Yukio the Dead Bookie, or Alaric and Molly Taylor and her flat stomach on July Fourth.

Hot, acidic betrayal gurgled in the pit of her stomach.

All of Eden's life she'd made two basic assumptions. Assumptions that were such a given, she took them for granted. She'd grown in her mother's womb. She shared her parents' DNA. Now? Those assumptions had been ripped out from under her. Her parents weren't her biological parents. How could they be? They lied. They lied about who they were. They lied about who *she* was.

She squeezed her eyes tighter and pumped her legs harder, trying not to think about Christopher James *Taylor*. Not Christopher James *Pruitt*. Her ghost of a big brother, the one she'd never met but was always there. In every extra tight squeeze her mother gave her, as if hugging two children instead of one. In

102

the empty chair at every table for four. In every birthday, in every anniversary, in every holiday, he came in the form of a melancholy that dug its hooks into her mother—reminding Eden that while she lived like an only child, she was not an only child.

"Where's Christopher's grave?" she'd asked once upon a time, when she was small.

"He didn't like tight spaces," her mother had said, her eyes so sad Eden felt bad for asking.

They told her they spread Christopher's ashes instead—they poured him into the sea because Christopher loved the sea. Eden always assumed the sea he loved had been the Pacific Ocean. Every year, when the country turned solemn with remembering, her mother walked its banks, as if doing so could bring her closer to the child she'd lost. Only Christopher wasn't poured into the Pacific. How could he have been? He died in Silver Spring, Maryland.

The hot, acidic betrayal bubbled.

Eden pushed the up arrow on the treadmill's screen—beep, beep, beep.

Faster.

She needed to go faster.

She needed to outrun the truth nipping at her heels.

But it was too fast to outrun.

There was no birth announcement for Eden Taylor like there'd been for Christopher. Alaric and Molly disappeared off the face of the earth eighteen months after Eden's supposed birthday. Two days later, Ruth and Alexander Pruitt showed up in Seattle, Washington with a little girl. A little girl Ruth or Molly hadn't given birth to. A little girl who, for the next eight years, would sing happy birthday to a ghost.

Eden punched the arrow on the treadmill.

Faster.

Faster.

Her mother's bouts of melancholy—a mere shadow of the

grief she must have felt before Eden came to fill up the sad, empty space Christopher left behind.

"You gave me my breath back," Mom often said. Unaware of the pressure she put on Eden when she said it. Unaware that those shoes were too big to fill for a little girl who just wanted her mother's sadness to go away.

You are her breath, Eden.

Don't mess up, Eden.

Make sure you're good, Eden.

Good enough for two, Eden.

She punched the arrow again—faster and faster. But the questions were impossible to outrun. They chased her down with bared teeth and a snarling growl.

What if her parents didn't change their identities to protect themselves from someone dangerous? What if they changed their identities to cover up something horrible? What if Alaric and Molly Taylor were so overcome with grief, so desperate for another child, they took one for themselves?

What if her parents weren't the good guys?

An ache opened inside her chest, so profound and heavy, she couldn't breathe beneath the crushing weight of it. Eighteen years worth of lies. Lies upon lies.

Faster.

She needed to go faster.

But when she pressed the arrow again, there was no beep.

The treadmill would not go any faster. The treadmill was maxed out.

Eden looked down at the monitor.

Her foot caught.

Her heart careened.

Her arms flailed.

She caught herself before crashing, before tumbling and skidding. With her feet on solid ground and her legs shaking, she stared at the treadmill.

Twenty miles per hour.

The treadmill was going twenty miles per hour.

————

E den's hands squeezed—tighter and tighter—as the person beneath her flailed and choked and spluttered, trying desperately to escape. But the woman couldn't escape. Eden's hands were clamped around her neck like a vice.

"Darling ... stop," she rasped, her face turning from red to violent purple—the life ebbing from her bulging, bloodshot eyes.

White-hot rage boiled. A cauldron full of it, bubbling beneath Eden's ribcage. This woman was a fake. A phony. A liar, and for that, Eden would strangle her. She would strangle her to death. Her fingers bit into bruised flesh. "I am *not* your darling."

"Eden!"

The familiar voice broke through her rage, and relief came like a wave. It crashed over her, dousing the heat into hissing steam. Dad. It was her dad. Not the fake man who jabbed a needle into her neck, but her *father*. He was here, and he was alive, and he was calling her by name.

"Eden, what are you doing?"

She looked down at the woman whose neck she was squeezing, and to her horror, it was not Annette Forrester. It was her mother. Her mother stared up at her, her face etched in frozen terror, her hair tangled, her top torn.

"Let her go," Dad commanded.

She tried to do what he said.

But she couldn't.

It was as if her fingers were possessed. They no longer belonged to herself.

Dad grabbed her wrists and tried to pry Eden away.

"Stop Eden!" he yelled. "She's dying."

A scream opened wide inside of her. A flailing, thrashing scream. Eden looked up at him—her father, her dad—desperate for help. *Help me stop. Make this stop. I don't want to hurt her. I've never wanted to hurt her.* But he was no longer there. She was looking into a mirror. Inside, Eden screamed and screamed and screamed. *Stop, stop, stop!* But in the reflection of that mirror, Eden smiled and squeezed.

With a long, loud gasp, she lurched awake.

Cold sweat trickled down her back. Beaded along her hairline.

Someone crouched in front of her, barely visible through the dark.

She jerked back.

He held up his hands.

It was the young man from the coffee shop. The young man with the devastating eyes and the accusatory stare. The young man who had found her in an alley and taken her to safety on the back of his motorcycle.

Her attention jumped around the room as she grappled for her bearings. She was lying on a futon. There was a soft glow from a bedside clock, revealing a television. A miniature refrigerator. A desk and a laptop. A bed and a heap of comforter and sheets that hid a snoring Cleo beneath, and an abandoned blanket on the floor where Cassian was no longer sleeping.

"You were having a nightmare," he said, his voice extra low in the quiet.

Eden's chest rose and fell with heavy breaths, the cloying remnants of horror digging into her shoulders, refusing to let go. Her father's words reverberated from somewhere deep down inside.

She's dying ...

She's dying ...

She's dying ...

Suddenly, Eden was freezing cold. And horribly, gut-wrenchingly heartsick. Despite everything—the lies, her haunting theory, the questions she couldn't escape—she needed them. She needed her parents to be okay. She needed them to be alive. Even if all of her suspicions were true—even if they were the bad guys who kidnapped a baby and stole her across the country—she could not imagine a world where either of them were dead.

"What if … what if they're …?" She couldn't finish the question. She couldn't say the words out loud. If she did, she was certain her chest would cave in completely.

"They're not," he said—his tone so sure, so filled with authority, it made her want to cry. His eyes bore into hers—golden fire with flecks of ochre. For the first time, they held no spark of animosity. Just pure, unwavering confidence. "Mordecai was looking for you. Not them."

"He killed Yukio. He shot him in the head."

"He's not going to kill your parents."

"You don't know that," she said.

"Yes, I do."

"How?" She stared at him, following the sculpted line of his jaw, taking in the palpable strength of his conviction, as if such earnestness could be absorbed.

"Because he needs them." His gaze traveled from her eyes—one to the next—down to her lips. It dipped further to her throat—where her pulse thrummed—then back up again. "They're his bait."

17

Cassian was no stranger to nightmares. They were like personal demons—cunningly strategic—hiding in the shadows until they could strike at the point of least resistance. In the wake of Eden's, he lay still on the hard floor—aggravatingly awake—with one arm behind his head, staring up into the dark while Cleo slept like the dead, not haunted by anything.

He closed his eyes and pictured Eden's face.

"Do you mind if I ask *why*?" she'd demanded.

Why was he inserting himself into this situation? He'd given her a deceptive truth. He didn't think bad things should happen to innocent people. That was true. But he'd omitted a vital piece of information—he'd been the one to bring the bad thing upon her. Yukio promised Cass this would be the last job he'd have to do. Do this final job, and his debt would be paid—a red flag flapping in the wind. His debt was substantial. But he ignored the flag. He told himself he didn't care.

Then he found her mug shot and the flag went still. The girl was a criminal. Probably an addict, too. Like everyone else who owed Yukio money. A delinquent in exchange for his freedom was a decision he could live with. The two-dimensional face on the screen meant nothing. He gave Yukio, who had given Mordecai, the location of the girl.

Then he went to San Diego, and he didn't find a criminal. He found a girl with two parents who loved her. A girl who seemed to love them in return. He spent the next two weeks watching the family, following them to Iowa—the red flag waving harder and harder, his mother haunting him in his dreams. *Look, son. The Pruitts laugh together. They laugh like you and I used to laugh.* Cassian Gray could ignore many things. But he could never ignore her. Not even her ghost.

On the futon, Eden stirred.

Was she awake? Or had she gone back to sleep? Whatever state she was in, he was annoyingly aware of her—this girl who should have never been more than a picture on a screen. If only she could have been like everyone else he found for Yukio. If only she could have been easier to disregard. It was a despicable thought—one that would have his mother rolling over in her grave. She'd believed nobody should be disregarded, no matter who they were.

He bit back a growl, his body at war with itself.

He pictured her in the nursing home, through the window—smiling and laughing with a frail, old man over a game of checkers. That had been the moment. The tipping point. He could no longer ignore the red flags. With his teeth gritted, he made a phone call to Yukio. What did he want with a girl like Eden Pruitt? And who was the other one—the girl he'd been unable to find?

That's when Yukio told him. Mordecai was looking for them —Mordecai, the notorious gambler—and if Cass knew what was good for him, he would stop asking questions and get on with finding the other one. Yukio hung up and Cass had shouted—a giant war cry of an expletive, causing several people in the vicinity to stop and gape.

Now Yukio was dead. When Cass tried calling him, he was ashamed to admit that he wasn't sure with what goal. To find answers for Eden, or finish the job he'd started and disappear forever. The dark, hardened part of him was more than capable of doing the latter. But Yukio didn't answer. Not the first time, and not the second. Yukio always answered. So Cass called Angelica, and through hiccups and tears, she told him what happened. Yukio had been shot in the head.

Cass had used the same expletive.

He had his freedom. And he didn't. All at the same time.

The death of Yukio was the death of his debt. But the death of Yukio was another death on his conscience. If Cassian hadn't gone rogue—if he'd followed through with the job—Yukio wouldn't have paid the price. But then, what would have happened to the girl? His mind replayed the footage from earlier —Eden's parents dragged from the house. He knew what he told her was true. Mordecai would use them as bait. But Cass knew something else, too. Once Mordecai caught the fish, he would dispose of the bait just like he'd disposed of the bookie.

If Cass bailed now, there would be two more deaths on his conscience. Three if he counted the girl, for she would most likely end up dead, too, after Mordecai got from her whatever it was he wanted. Three more deaths would become an invisible prison he could never escape. Which meant he had only one choice—help Eden find her parents and get all three to safety. Then maybe—just maybe—freedom would finally be his.

So there he remained, lying on the floor in Cleo Ransom's dorm room—running puzzle pieces through his mind. Their research had confirmed one thing. Whatever was going on— Eden Pruitt was innocent. She was completely in the dark. But her parents—Alexander and Ruth Pruitt, previously known as Alaric and Molly Taylor? They weren't who they pretended to be. Upon the discovery, Eden had taken Cleo's badge, borrowed a change of Cleo's clothes, went in search of the fitness facilities, and returned an hour later, freshly showered and white as a sheet. Her misery wrenched something in his chest, bringing to life a compulsion so irritating, so foreign, he didn't recognize it at first. But when she lurched out of sleep—her many-colored eyes frantic and filled with fear—he felt it again.

The urge to comfort her.

It was an urge he had no business feeling.

He would help the girl. He would do what he could to get her out of the danger he'd put her in. He would clear his conscience. But he would not care for her. That—he knew—only ended in pain.

Cass glanced at Cleo's bedside clock.

The digital numbers turned from 4:59 to 5:00.

He wasn't going back to sleep. So why try?

Resigned, he prepared to get up. To check out the workout room Eden had utilized yesterday. He'd spent the last ten years of his life training. Morphing from human to weapon. Unlike most, he relished the pain and exhaustion that came with vigorous physical activity. It was a cathartic release. One he needed now more than ever.

But before his thoughts could turn into actual movement, the girl beat him to it. She silently slipped from the futon. So quiet he had to strain to hear, she took Cleo's badge, the shoes by the door, and left with nothing more than a barely-audible click.

——————

Eden used the restroom. She washed her hands, rinsed her face. Cupped a mouthful of water and gargled. Last night, Cleo grabbed them toothbrushes and other essentials. But she didn't want to wake anyone by rummaging for them at five in the morning. Especially not if Cassian had fallen back to sleep.

She unraveled the tie that kept her hair in a knot on top of her head. Still-damp tresses from last night's shower tumbled around her face, past her shoulders. She touched the tender skin beneath her eyes—bruised with exhaustion—and winced at the sudden memory of her hands around her mother's neck. Squeezing, squeezing, squeezing her dead. She closed her eyes. It wasn't a memory. It was a terrible nightmare. A fact that offered little solace when she couldn't stop seeing them bound and gagged and dragged away.

Were they hurt? Were they hungry? Were they alive?

Eden banished the last question and took hold of Cassian's assurance like a small child clutching a beloved teddy bear in the midst of a storm. She was choosing to believe him. Anything else would drive her mad. She certainly looked the part in the reflection of that mirror—a girl unhinged, in need of a straitjacket. Instead, she wore Cleo's sweats and a black tee that said—of all things—*Anarchy*. This was what Cleo handed her, and Eden didn't have the wherewithal to ask for anything else. Now she was wearing Cleo's badge, too, hanging from a lanyard around her neck.

This was supposed to be her. In a year. A college student waking up early on a Saturday morning while everyone else slept off their hangovers. Because let's be honest, Eden wasn't ever going to run with the wild crowd. Instead of house parties, her scene would be the library. She'd spend Friday nights there with her socially offbeat lab partner from biology. Like Erik, he wouldn't understand why she was hanging out with him, nor would he understand why she preferred his company over the girls on her floor gushing about rush week. But eventually, he'd stop questioning and the two of them would become best friends. Maybe she'd even find someone with an obsession for Paris that matched her own, and together they would walk along the river Seine, explore the Louvre, climb the Eiffel Tower, take in the *Sacré-Cœur* at the top of the Montmartre hill.

Now all of that was out of reach.

Even if they rescued her parents, even *when* they eliminated whatever threat was after her, normalcy was irrevocably lost yesterday, when she found out her parents had been lying to her all her life. She was left with a million questions and a million more confusing, thorny emotions. But at the moment, Maslow's hierarchy proved true. Safety trumped all—safety for her, and safety for them. It was hard to fixate too much on the questions when she didn't know if she'd ever get the opportunity to ask them.

She crept out of the bathroom into the still, silent hallway and shuffled to the elevator. She considered the two buttons—one for up, one for down. She pushed the button for down and waited for the elevator to meet her on the ninth floor. She could hear it moving up the shaft. With a ding, the doors slid open and Eden stepped inside. She pushed another button, as if drawn by some invisible force. Intermingled amongst all of it—the confusion and the turmoil and the unknown—was the idiosyncratic mystery of the treadmill. In all the stress, her mind had played a trick. Most likely, the speed had been set to kilometers per hour instead of miles. She was not a runner. She might be lean, she might even have an athletic build, but she'd never participated in athletics. Or made conditioning a priority.

The elevator stopped.

Eden stepped out into the empty hallway and used Cleo's badge to slip inside the fitness room. She shuffled through the dark, to the treadmill, like a ghost. Like she wasn't real. Like none of this was real. She was still dreaming.

Without getting on, she pressed power on the treadmill's panel.

The tread began to move—a slow, easy start. Eden set her finger over the plus button and continued to press it as the tread picked up speed. Slowly and evenly, she pressed and pressed and pressed, all the way to the max—looking between the numbers on the screen to the black tread cycling past at a mind-boggling speed.

Twenty miles per hour.

With a sharp jab of her thumb, she powered the treadmill off. She didn't wait for it to stop. She spun around and pushed the door open—fast and sudden.

It cracked against something hard.

A loud curse filled the basement hallway.

Eden cupped her hand over her mouth at the sight of Cassian, who was clutching his head.

"I am so sorry," she said, her eyes round and wide.

He pressed his palm against the spot above his left eye.

"What are you doing down here?" she asked.

"I could ask you the same thing."

His biting reply had the muscles pulling tight across her chest. So tight, something snapped. "I didn't ask you to follow me. Not down here. Not to Eagle Bend. And not to Milwaukee either. You volunteered for the position. I'm really sorry about Yukio. I'm sorry if you lost a friend. But stop treating me like I forced you into this."

For a moment, his scowl disappeared. He looked properly chastened. Then a trickle of blood escaped from beneath his palm.

"You're bleeding," she said.

His scowl returned. Only this time, he seemed to direct his annoyance at the blood, which he wiped away with his other hand. "It's fine."

More blood escaped. She could see it lining his left palm, trapped beneath the pressure. "It's bleeding a lot."

"Head wounds usually do."

"Come on. There's a First Aid kit inside." Eden opened the door that had so mercilessly collided with Cassian's head. This time she flipped the switch. Fluorescent light flickered, then flooded the room. She guided him to a bench.

"It's fine," he said again, gritting the words between his teeth.

"Sit down," she replied, her frustration matching his own.

Miraculously, he listened. With his hair tousled from sleep and his hand pressed against his bleeding wound, Cassian sat.

Eden found the white container on the corner shelf, next to a random dumbbell.

"What were you doing in here?" he asked, without the caustic edge.

"I, um … I thought I left something behind last night." The lie turned the back of her neck warm as she opened the kit. Inside on top, a small Ziploc baggie with bandages in assorted sizes grabbed her attention. Band-Aids. A whole bag full of them. She found herself picking it up, turning it over carefully—as though it were something delicate and valuable. Foreign and strange.

"Eden?"

Her trance popped like a soap bubble. She blinked several times in quick succession.

"You okay?" Cassian asked uncertainly behind her.

She gave her head a slight shake, unsure how long she'd been standing there like that, turning the Ziploc bag over in her hands. The bandages weren't foreign or strange. No different from the box her mother kept inside the medicine cabinet in the main level bathroom of their San Diego home. She laughed self-consciously, then tore open a small packet of antiseptic wipes as she returned to Cassian on the bench, his palm still pressed against the injury.

She removed his hand.

The gash oozed.

"This really isn't necessary," he said.

Ignoring him, Eden pressed the wipe against his left eyebrow. As soon as the disinfectant touched the wound, Cassian hissed and drew away.

"I know how to bandage a cut," he growled.

"I'm sure you do," she growled back. "But maybe it wouldn't kill you to let someone help."

His mouth opened, then closed.

She waited a beat to see if he would object. When he didn't, she brought the wipe back to his eyebrow with a gentler touch, then handed him another antiseptic packet so he could clean the mess of blood from his hand. As he finished, he lifted his eyes—

catching her with a stare that was as intense as it was wary, and a current of heat passed between them. An invisible pulse that stirred in her stomach.

"He wasn't a friend."

Her eyelids fluttered. "What?"

"Yukio," he said. "You were sorry I lost a friend. He wasn't one."

"Oh." The same heat in her stomach prickled in her cheeks.

He was sitting at eye level with her midsection, his animosity no longer a guard between them, strikingly close in an empty basement of a college residence hall. The unexpected intimacy of the moment put a tremble in her hands—embarrassingly obvious.

She removed the wipe to look underneath. The gash was deep, but not as bad as it first appeared. "I don't think it will scar."

"I wasn't concerned."

She swallowed. "You have one on your chin."

He rubbed his thumb over the mark—small and white, right where a cleft might be.

Eden blinked, then tore open a third antiseptic packet, handed it over, and went to throw the dirty ones in the waste bin, thankful for the separation. It came like a breath of clarity, like another broken trance. She cleared her throat. "How'd you get it?" she asked with her back to him.

"A fight."

"In the ring?"

The room was quiet. Still.

She turned around.

He was studying her.

"Cleo told me you're a fighter."

"*Used* to be a fighter."

"You quit?"

"Over a year ago."

"Why?"

He broke their gaze first, casting his away—somewhere down and to the right. "I lost my taste for it."

She removed a butterfly bandage from the baggie. Her fingers were still trembling. *Stop it*, she commanded. A no-nonsense, Mary Poppins-inspired reprimand. Remarkably, her fingers listened.

The trembling stopped.

She lifted the disinfectant wipe to the gash.

Cassian hissed again, only not so aggressively.

As gently as possible, she gave the wound a thorough cleaning, then applied the bandage to keep the gash closed. "*Voilà Tout au mieux.*"

"What did you say?"

The sharpness of his tone caught her off guard. She leaned back, startled. She thought they'd gotten past this. But he was glaring up at her with eyes that had gone dark and suspicious, as if she'd said something inappropriate.

"S-sorry," she said. "It was French for *all better.*"

Cassian touched the spot, and with a gruff *thank you*, got up and left.

Eden stood in the room—alone and confused.

18

hen Eden returned to Cleo's room, Cassian wasn't there. And Cleo was awake. With her hair wrapped in a silk scarf, thumbing her skull and bones ring—an opened can of Diet Dr. Pepper and an empty granola bar wrapper by her right elbow, the sticky note Eden started yesterday by her left. Now there was another arrow, from Alexander and Ruth Pruitt to two new names at the bottom of the list—Alaric and Molly Taylor, along with the sparse details they knew.

Silver Spring, MD. Alaric served in Afghanistan with Dr. Benjamin Norton, a third connection to the military. Business Manager for Watt Technologies. Yesterday, they had scoured the internet for hours—including the dark web and deeper still, password-protected portions of the deep web—but found no information about the company, which seemed to drive Cleo crazier than Eden. They followed every trail they could find only to reach dead end after dead end.

"Still searching?" Eden said, setting Cleo's badge on the desk beside the granola bar wrapper.

"I have an obsessive personality." Cleo pulled up a chat room and scrolled through a thread. "When I was a kid, my mother banned mystery books from our household, so I had to smuggle them from the library and read them under my covers at night. Give me a puzzle and I can't rest until it's solved. Especially when I'm supposed to be doing something else."

"Like class work?"

"Sure, if I cared about my courses."

"Don't you?"

"Not nearly as much as I care about that." Cleo nodded toward *The People's Press*, then leaned closer to the screen and highlighted a paragraph. As far as Eden could tell, it didn't contain any information about Watt Technologies. "There's an article I need to write if I'm going to get it out on time."

"About the situation in Madison?"

Cleo turned to Eden with a gleam in her eye. "Cass said you saw the riot."

"Yeah." And he'd been right. So far, there hadn't been a whiff of it anywhere on Concordia or Perk. "Who's Dwight?"

"A guy who decided to speak his mind. On the steps of the Capitol. Police officers took him away and nobody's seen him since."

"So … he's in jail?"

"Authorities aren't saying."

"What do you mean they aren't saying?"

"I mean they aren't saying. His family keeps asking but nobody will give them a straight answer. For all intents and purposes, Dwight's missing."

Eden's brow furrowed.

Cleo studied her, then opened the top drawer of her desk and pulled out a large Atlas. She flipped to a map of the United States. Someone had drawn bright red X's overtop seven cities: Madison, Milwaukee, Detroit, Minneapolis, St. Louis, Seattle, and Fresno.

"Why are these cities marked?" Eden asked.

"Because each of them have had riots."

"What?"

"All within the past year." Cleo pulled a loose, folded piece of parchment from between the pages of the Atlas. She unfolded it. This one had only two Red X's. "This was the year before. Only two. Which means we're seeing a marked uptick."

"How are these kept secret?"

"It's not as hard as you think when the government is controlling communication."

Eden's head swam. Around Cleo's crazy conspiracy theories that maybe weren't that crazy. Around unreported riots and a guy named Dwight who'd gone missing. He disappeared like Alaric and Molly Taylor had disappeared. Had Eden disappeared too? Out there somewhere closer to the east coast, was there a mother and a father searching for their missing baby girl? Last night, Eden couldn't bring herself to investigate. She was too afraid of what she might find. Now, the need to know grabbed her by the throat.

A knock sounded on the door. "Cleo, you awake?"

"Are you kidding me?" she called back.

"My room smells like a joint."

Muttering under her breath, Cleo scooted away from the desk.

"Do you mind if I look something up?" Eden asked.

"Be my guest," Cleo said, marching to the door and swinging it open.

A round-faced kid in flannel pajama pants stood on the other side. "It's wreaking havoc on my allergies."

"It's six in the morning, Chad," Cleo said.

"I know. Which begs the question, why is my roommate smoking weed at six in the morning?"

With a frustrated huff, Cleo excused herself to take care of the problem, leaving Eden in an empty, silent room. She sat down at the computer, her fingers hovering over the keyboard, her heart thudding dully inside her chest. Taking a shaky breath, she brought her fingers to the keys and typed three words.

Missing Kid. Maryland.

Several articles loaded on the page.

At the very top, *Nine Children Missing in Maryland.*

Eden clicked on the link. Every child listed went missing as a teenager.

She returned to the search results and scanned the headings.

A Decade After Vanishing, Her Daughter Returned

Body Found Believed to Be Missing Girl

Missing Children, Baltimore Law

Eden deleted the search and tried a different route.

Missing Kid. 18 Years Ago.

As soon as she hit return, Barrett Barr flooded the page. He hadn't gone missing eighteen years ago. He was an 18-year-old who was making headlines now. His parents adamantly claimed foul play while most assumed he was a runaway.

Like Ellery Forrester.

Eden tried again. This time, *missing babies.*

With her knee bouncing, she clicked on a search engine for missing children. Eden entered in the data she knew.

Gender: female.

Race: white.

State: Maryland

Age range of child when he or she went missing.

Eden considered. She'd seen pictures of herself as a toddler in their Seattle home. She could have been one. Maybe two. She typed in 0-2 years old, then the corresponding years she would have gone missing.

She hit enter.

No results found.

Eden removed Maryland as a data point.

Hit enter again.

No results found.

With a relieved exhale, she leaned back in Cleo's chair.

The door swung open. Cleo was back.

"Did you find what you were looking for?" she asked.

"Sort of." Eden closed her search and pulled up the chat

room Cleo had been perusing. She moved to the futon, very suddenly exhausted. Numb. She leaned her head back against the cushion and let her eyes drift closed. She was just beginning to doze when Cleo's exclamation jolted her awake.

"It never existed!"

"What?"

"Watt Technologies. According to this guy here, it was a cover. One of several used during that time."

"For what?"

"The CIA."

Eden's eyes widened as Cleo's words sank in like a penny tossed into the deep end of a swimming pool. Eden stood up and blinked at the screen, her attention catching on words like *Special Activities Division* and *Covert Operations*, all posted by someone with a creepy avatar and the username T-MoneyBray. "You think my dad was in the CIA?"

"The location fits," Cleo said. "They lived in Silver Spring, Maryland."

Eden rubbed her chin. It was one thing to imagine her father named Alaric. Even serving overseas in Afghanistan. But running covert operations for the CIA? "He's an accountant."

"For who?"

They searched the name of his new firm in Eagle Bend, his old firm in San Diego. Both checked out. Both were real.

The door opened.

Cass entered, his Henley untucked, a towel slung over his shoulder. A bead of water dripped from his wet hair and rolled over the butterfly bandage she'd placed above his eyebrow. For a slip of a second, his eyes found hers, then quickly looked away.

"Eden's dad was in the CIA."

"We don't know that," Eden said.

Cleo showed him the chat room while Eden tried digesting this new possibility. The CIA. But then … was it really so hard to believe? After everything they uncovered yesterday, was this that far of a stretch? Didn't it actually fit? And if true, didn't it spin a better light on her parents? If her father worked for the CIA, he might have gotten wrapped up in something much more dangerous than Underground Fighting. So dangerous, it wasn't enough to simply change their names. They had to change their entire identity, including their birthdays. Something light and fragile blossomed in Eden's chest.

Maybe everything wasn't a lie after all.

"Have you heard anything from your contact?" Eden asked.

"Not yet," Cassian replied.

She dragged her hand down the side of her face. She needed that footage. She needed to see inside her house, to whatever her brain had let slip away. She was increasingly sure that if she could just remember that lost period of time, then something would click into place. A crucial thread that might lead to definitive answers. Maybe even her parents.

But they didn't have that footage. They might not ever get that footage.

And this room was starting to feel claustrophobic.

"I need coffee," she said. "Does anybody else want some?"

"Black Eye, please," Cleo replied. "That's two shots of espresso."

Eden turned to Cass, who was still not meeting her eye.

He lifted his shoulder, as if to say, *I'm good*.

She grabbed Cleo's badge once again and stepped out into the hallway, where there were more stirrings of life. Someone coughing behind a door. Someone yawning as they came out of the boy's bathroom, hair sticking up every which way. The elevator stopped on her way down—fifth floor. A boy stepped inside wearing sweatpants, Buddy Holly glasses, and a sleeveless Bucks jersey.

Eden stepped to one side, avoiding eye contact as determinedly as Cass had avoided hers. Her mind was buzzing—too full to make small talk with strangers. Thankfully, they rode to the ground floor in silence, and when the elevator opened, Eden's heart jumped into her throat.

Straight ahead, on the other side of the lobby, stood a horribly familiar man.

Jack Forrester.

He was showing something to the college student sitting behind the front desk. Something that looked like a photograph.

Buddy Holly had already stepped out. "You coming?"

She shook her head—a singular frantic shake—and jabbed a button on the panel. He gave her a quizzical look as the doors slid shut and her heart pounded like a jackhammer. She punched the round number 9 over and over, begging the elevator not to stop for anyone else who might be awake. Blessedly, she was heading up, not down. Everyone awake was heading down—for coffee, for breakfast.

When the elevator landed on the ninth, Eden rushed out, nearly knocking over Workout Girl from yesterday.

"Oh!" she said, startled. "*Hey.*"

But Eden didn't stop to return the miffed greeting. She didn't stop to apologize. She made a beeline for Cleo's room and burst inside.

"He's here," she blurted.

Cleo swiveled around in her desk chair.

"The man with the needle. Jack Forrester." Eden grabbed her neck. "He's down in the lobby. He was showing the front desk employee something. My picture, I think."

Cass pushed the laptop shut. "It's time to go."

"*What?*" Eden said. "*Where?*"

"Somewhere that's not here." He stuck the sticky note full of names and connected lines into his front pocket and grabbed his motorcycle jacket.

"On your bike?" Eden asked.

"They'll recognize my bike."

"I have a car in the parking garage across the street." Cleo slid her computer into her Camo bag. "We can use it to get away."

"Is there a back way out?" Cassian asked.

Cleo pulled the strap of her bag over her shoulder and snagged her keys. "On the second floor. West side."

This was happening fast—too fast. They were already by the door, ready to leave.

"*Wait*." Eden held up her hands. "What are we doing?"

"Getting away before that psychopath can drug you again," Cleo said. "You and Cass can go out the back. I'll slip out the lobby."

"And if they know you're with us?"

"Then it's the perfect opportunity to lead them away. They see me, they follow me."

"Then they kill you, Cleo. Like they killed Yukio."

This wasn't a game.

"They aren't going to kill me in the middle of a dorm lobby. And no offense or anything, but I'm probably safer apart from you two." She shoved her car keys into Cass's palm. "My car's on the second level, toward the south end. Just hit the key fob, and the lights will flash. Head east on West St. Paul and look for me outside the Greyhound Station. If I'm not out there circle around every half hour until I am. I'll hop in and we'll go."

Where? Eden thought. *Where would they go?*

"We've got to *move*," Cassian said, his tone sharp. Like he had no patience for her hesitation.

Eden dug in her heels. She wasn't a fan of this slapdash plan. It wasn't at all thought-out. But precious seconds were ticking by. And every one of those seconds brought Jack Forrester closer to the ninth floor. They had to go, and they had to go now. So with an uneasy sigh of consent, she pushed open the door and the three of them filed outside. Cleo hit the button for the elevator. Cass opened the door into the stairwell. Eden looked one last time at the girl who'd taken them in with no questions asked and hoped she'd be okay.

The door swung shut behind them.

The empty stairwell reeked of beer and urine. They hurried down seven flights of stairs and stepped out onto the second floor, which was more awake than the ninth. Residents in several of the rooms had already propped open their doors. Music played—not the angry punk rock Cleo had been blasting yesterday, but easy, laid back listening. Perfect for a Saturday morning.

She followed Cass with long, fast strides, their heads down when halfway to the exit, a pair of security guards rounded the corner, talking into their walkie-talkies.

Their sudden appearance made Eden's heart seize. They had nowhere to go. They were in a narrow hallway. Before she could think of what to do—of a way to avoid their fast-approach—Cass took her arm and deftly pressed her against the wall. He set the palm of his right hand on the bulletin board behind her, over a flyer advertising cheap lottery tickets for the Prosperity Ball. He leaned so close, his breath tickled her ear.

"Don't move," he murmured.

She didn't—not even her lungs. Her heart, however? It pounded so fast and so furiously, she was positive he could hear it. Or he could see it in the dip of space between her clavicle. She looked up at him—panic swirling—his face right there, his mouth mere centimeters away. His eyes holding her captive, holding her still. From the outside looking in, they were a couple of college kids on the verge of some serious PDA—nothing particularly noteworthy—and so, the two men in uniform passed without a second glance.

Cass didn't move until they rounded the corner and disappeared from view. Eden didn't exhale until he stepped away, and even then, not properly.

"Come on," he said, and they kept moving.

When they arrived at the door, he held up a hand for her to wait. He reached behind him, took out his gun, pushed open the door and checked outside. After a few seconds, he waved for Eden to follow and returned the weapon to his belt.

She squinted against the morning sun, the air already hot and humid.

With her senses on high alert—her vigilance matching Cassian's—the two hurried across the street to the parking garage. Under its cover, the sun turned into shade. The air grew cool. They hurried to the second level, south end, and just as Cass hit the button on the key fob and a Tesla flashed its headlights, Eden stopped dead.

"C'mon," he said.

But a rush of goose bumps marched across her skin.

He stopped, his teeth gritted. Apparently, Cassian wasn't the type of guy who second-guessed. Nor did he seem to have any patience for people who did. "What is it?"

"I don't know. Something ..." Before she could finish the sentence, a loud hissing sliced through the air. Her eyes caught sight of the small object. It was headed straight for her. She moved out of the way and watched as it sailed past, so close it nearly grazed her nose.

And then, just as suddenly, a man came out of the shadows. Jack Forrester. He surged toward them like a bull seeing red and before Eden could yell or run, Cass pushed her out of the way and spun around with a kick to Forrester's jaw, followed by another, the sole of his combat boot connecting with such power, Forrester flew into the air and landed on his back several feet away as another man—a big, burly, armed man—rushed at him from the other side.

Roger Carlson, supposed owner of 3235 West Buckle Lane.

Cass kicked the weapon from Carlson's hand as his own gun was knocked away. Both clattered to the ground, skidding in opposite directions. Cass dodged a left hook and came back with a hard jab to Carlson's face. It connected with a crunch and a spray of blood. Cass blocked a blow to the side and threw an uppercut that had the ex-military man staggering on his heels.

Behind him, Forrester recovered and closed in.

But not quick enough.

Cassian twisted, caught his fist, and with a pivot, threw the man over his shoulder. He landed hard on the windshield of a parked car, glass shattering as an alarm blared, echoing inside the garage as Eden sat where she'd fallen, frozen in place, her eyes bulging as Forrester grabbed a shard of broken glass and Carlson came back for more.

"Watch out!" she yelled.

But it was too late. Forrester made his swipe, and Eden swore she could hear the glass slicing through fabric and flesh, and the sharp inhale as Cassian was tackled from behind. He bucked Carlson off. Landed his foot hard in Forrester's stomach. Jack doubled over as Carlson shouted and Cass got the upper hand.

"Run!" he yelled at Eden, coming to his feet, shoving Carlson back. "Go!"

It was all the distraction his opponents needed.

There was a loud crack of metal against skull.

Cassian's eyes rolled, then he toppled to the ground as Jack Forrester stood over him with a chest that heaved and a gun in his hand.

Something sharp stabbed the side of Eden's neck.

Carlson limped out from behind the blaring, busted car where he'd been shoved—one eye swollen shut, his nose a fountain of blood, his shirt torn—holding the weapon Cass had knocked away.

Her vision blurred.

The ground wobbled.

Eden collapsed as everything faded into darkness.

19

The world rattled—a loud, clattering sound that shook everything loose inside her head. Something sharp pinched her neck. A mosquito or a fly. She slapped at the spot, but it wasn't a bug. A groan from somewhere deep inside her belly rose up and out. She jerked the foreign object away, dropped it to the ground, and rolled over onto her back, her blurry surroundings sharpening into focus.

There was a metal ceiling above her. The floor vibrated beneath. Rolling shafts of sunlight poured into thin slats, offering dim light in the hot, enclosed space. She blinked—an attempt to clear away the fog in her brain.

A truck.

She seemed to be inside the cargo hold of a moving truck.

Eden pulled a second dart from her shoulder, then sat upright, her stomach lurching as a hazy memory swayed to the front of her mind. They were ambushed. In the parking garage. By Jack Forrester and Roger Carlson. Cassian Gray had fought them.

She twisted around and there he was.

Lying in the cargo hold.

Still as death.

Ice shot through her veins as she scrambled to his side.

He was breathing. And bleeding.

The truck hit a bump.

Eden pounded the metal wall as if the driver might hear—as if the driver might care—trying to recall exactly what happened. She searched for a dart, something that might have tranquilized him, when clarity came gushing forth in a violent wave. He hadn't been tranquilized. He'd been knocked unconscious with the butt of a gun. A sharp crack against his skull. And before that, a shard of glass to his side.

She remembered the way he'd fought—a lethal weapon in human form. He would have beaten them—a pair of full grown men—if not for his concern with her. He had tried to protect her in the parking garage just as he'd protected her in the dormitory hallway. If not for his fast-thinking, she would have been caught by the security guards. He followed her to Milwaukee. He'd driven her to safety on the back of his motorcycle. Because he didn't like when bad things happened to innocent people. This boy who'd been abused by his father. This illegal, underground fighter who claimed to have lost his taste for the profession. There was a story there. And Eden was determined to hear him tell it.

She wiped her brow with the back of her forearm, afraid to move him. Afraid to make anything worse. But she needed to get to the wound. She needed to stop the bleeding.

Carefully, she stripped off his motorcycle jacket. Then she grabbed the collar of his Henley where it gathered in a shallow V and ripped it straight off. Her attention traveled from the half-sleeve of intricate tattoos that wrapped around his shoulder, to the gash below his ribcage, to the right of his well-defined abdomen. She wadded up the torn shirt and applied pressure, her attention frantically traveling over his body as if it might tell her what else to do.

Blood seeped through the cotton of his shirt. The cut was alarmingly deep. Eden pulled Cleo's Anarchy tee over her head, still covered by the camisole she wore beneath. She tore the fabric into thin strips and wrapped them around his torso, over the balled-up Henley, tying each one tight to staunch the flow.

When she finished, she sat back, beads of sweat trickling down her temple, and dug her bloodstained fingers into her hair. What was she supposed to do now? They were trapped in a moving prison.

Think, Eden. Think.

She reached inside his left pocket and pulled out the sticky note. Then she reached into his right and pulled out his phone. The screen was locked. Her phone utilized facial recognition to unlock. This one asked for a passcode. She closed her eyes, trying to remember the movement of his thumb whenever he entered it. She scrunched her face, as if the tighter she could squeeze her eyes, the better she might be able to remember.

Up, down. Up, down. Left, right. Right, left.

"Two, five, two, five. Four, five, six, five," she muttered the numbers under her breath as her thumb followed the same pattern, and the screen unlocked itself.

She released a disbelieving laugh. But now what? Who was she supposed to call? The only numbers she knew by heart belonged to her parents, and both of those were no longer working.

Her thumb hovered over the 9 on the keypad.

She could call 9-1-1. She could tell the operator that her parents had been kidnapped. She'd been taken against her will, along with a boy who'd been knocked unconscious and needed medical attention ASAP. They were locked in the back of a truck, heading where, she had no clue. North or south. East or west. There was no way of knowing. The time told her she'd been unconscious for not more than fifteen minutes, which meant they were still in Milwaukee. They had to be.

Her thumb pressed the number, then moved to the one.

She imagined the operator answering. "9-1-1, what's your emergency?"

Eden would rattle off the scenario, and the operator would ask her name. Without an address to go on, she'd probably look Eden up. Only Eden was no longer in the system. Neither were her parents. She'd been turned into a disturbed runaway named Ellery Forrester. And Jack Forrester was listed as her father. Jack Forrester—the man who was most likely driving this truck. The man who injected her with tranquilizer inside the Eagle Bend police station. And the boy who was injured wasn't in the system either. He lived illegally off the grid. She was calling from his illegal phone.

Eden's eyes welled with frustration.

Calling 9-1-1 would cycle back to this. Being held captive by these people who wanted her for what, she had no idea.

Cassian's phone dinged with an incoming text.

Per your request. ADT footage for 3235 W. Buckle. Aug 22.

Christopher's birthday.

And also, the day everything turned upside down.

The phone dinged again, this time with a link.

He'd done it. Cassian's contact had hacked into her home security system. He'd found the lost hours. The ones she couldn't remember. The ones that were making her crazy. Here they were, at her fingertips. Eden stared at the screen. She licked her dry lips. And then—impossibly compelled—she clicked.

The foyer of 3235 West Buckle Lane filled the screen.

With her heart racing, she fast-forwarded through the day, turning hours into seconds. She watched herself leave for school. She watched her parents—alive and intact and unaware of what was about to happen—speeding from room to room, carrying boxes from one place to the other. She watched them leave for lunch. She watched them return with bags of food and cleaning supplies and random odds and ends. All the while, her heart pounded harder. Blood throbbed in her temples, her breath growing more and more shallow. What was she about to see? Could she handle watching her parents' attack? Wasn't there a reason her brain had blocked it out?

But she'd set this in motion now. Like a train wreck, she couldn't look away. Because there she was, stepping inside the front door, backpack sliding off her shoulders.

Eden stopped fast-forwarding.

She'd reached it—the lost time.

Any minute, clarity would come. Lines and colors and movement would fill the blank space inside her head. The man with the tattoos would appear. He'd sneak in the back—the sliding glass door foolishly unlocked, because this was small-town Iowa. And Eden … what would she do? Run like a coward, leaving her parents behind?

Why would she do that? *How* could she do that?

She watched herself on the screen, waiting. But Eden on the screen didn't move. She just stood there in the foyer with her back to the camera. And then her mother came from the kitchen with a towel in hand. Alone. Unaware of the impending danger. Where was the man with the tattoos? Eden searched the screen, looking for him in the background. Was he headed into the kitchen? Would he go after her father first? Would her mother hear it, and run toward them while Eden ran away? Cold sweat slicked her palms and gathered beneath her arms as she watched her mother stop and tilt her head. Her lips moved—most likely asking if everything was okay. Eden must not have answered, because her mother's brow furrowed. She stepped closer. She reached out and touched Eden's arm.

The Eden in Cassian's phone screen reacted.

She jerked her arm forward. Her hand closed around her mother's neck. Her mother grabbed at Eden's fingers, startled and alarmed, as her daughter pushed her into the living room. Eden switched video feeds with fumbling thumbs and watched herself slam her mother on top of the glass coffee table like Cassian had slammed Jack Forrester.

The table shattered.

Her mother's limbs flailed wildly as Eden's father ran into the room.

She picked her mother up—hand still squeezing her neck—and rammed her against the built-ins. Boxes and books came crashing down as Eden pulled her mother forward and rammed her against the shelves again. Dad jumped on top of her—yelling and yanking, pulling at her arms. But he couldn't pry Eden away. Her grip was like a vice. Her nightmare unfolding in real life. Eden was choking her mother.

Choking her mother to death.

Then she let go.

She turned on her father.

Mom rolled onto the floor, clutching her neck, coughing for breath, crying out as her husband defended himself against their daughter's attack.

And then, as suddenly as it all began, Eden watched herself stop.

The Eden in Cassian's phone screen went still. She stood like a statue inside the wrecked living room. Motionless. Expressionless. Not even out of breath as Dad scrambled over to Mom. He was bleeding. Her mother was still gasping for air. They cowered together on the living room floor, afraid.

Afraid of *her*.

Eden's head snapped up, toward something in the window. A face. The man with the tattoos. Then she turned around and ran straight out the door.

Cassian's phone fell from her hands.

It clattered against the metal floor as the truck jostled over another bump. Eden scooted away from it. As far as possible. She pressed herself against the wall and tried to remember how to breathe.

Cassian Gray was no stranger to pain. He'd felt plenty in his lifetime. Waking up with a splitting skull and a roaring side was nothing new. There was an odd awareness, however. The knowledge that he hadn't stepped into the ring, nor had he completed a relentless training session with Vick. That had not been his reality for over a year now. So why the pain?

The ground shook beneath him.

His left eye cracked open, then his other as the world sharpened into focus.

Eden Pruitt sat in the corner of the metal enclosure—elbows digging into dirty knees, fingers digging into bloodstained hair, rocking back and forth like a woman deranged. She gripped her head like she was trying to crush her own skull and for one confusing second, Cass wondered if this was why his own was splitting in two. He reached up to touch the spot where the worst of the pain radiated, a groan sliding past his lips.

"Don't," Eden said, her face suddenly swimming above his—white as a ghost, her forehead streaked with dirt and blood. She pressed her cool hand against his clammy skin, gently but firmly holding him down. "You're hurt."

He groaned again, his mouth desert dry.

"Stop trying to move," she said. "You'll only make the bleeding worse."

But he didn't listen. Despite Eden's protests, he pushed himself up—movement that shouldn't have required so much blasted effort—and slumped against the wall, lightheaded, his breathing labored, his head splintering. "Are you hurt?" he asked.

"No." She wiped at the sweat on her brow with the back of her forearm.

It was like a sauna inside this rattling box.

He touched the knot behind his ear and winced.

"You were cut," she said again, as if he hadn't understood the first time. "With glass."

"And hit hard with the handle of a gun, if I'm remembering right."

The truck hit a bump.

He grimaced. "How long have we been here?"

"I don't know. Thirty minutes, maybe."

Cass looked down at his naked upper half. Eden had removed his shirt. She'd removed hers too, stripped down to a tank top, her long, lean arms smeared with sweat and grime. She had made his Henley and Cleo's ridiculous Anarchy t-shirt into a bandage.

The truck turned onto rougher terrain. Two small darts vibrated against the metal floor. And something else, too. His phone.

"Did you call anyone?"

She shook her head, her face going paler somehow, like the phone wasn't a phone, but a hissing, venomous snake.

He wanted to tell her to get it for him, but his vision spun and doubled, forcing him to close his eyes. He had a concussion, most likely. He rubbed his head. The pain lacing his temple made it harder to think. Obviously, they were in a bad situation. They were trapped, shoved in the back of a truck. He remembered the plan, and wondered if Cleo was still waiting at the Greyhound Station. Or if she'd been caught, too. He imagined her alone, in a truck like this one. Had he put her life in danger? The thought made him want to swear. Ram his fist into something hard. Instead, he grimaced again as the brakes on the truck groaned.

One of the darts rolled forward and hit Eden's scuffed shoe.

"We're slowing down." Cass pushed himself up straighter. He needed to clear his head and make a plan. Fast. "We know Carlson and Forrester have my gun, and what else—a tranquilizer?"

Eden nodded.

He peeled off Eden's makeshift bandage, wincing as clotted blood pulled at his skin.

"Don't do that," Eden objected.

"Our only shot is catching them off guard. If they think we're still unconscious, we can strike when they're not expecting. Wait for my word. When I say *now*, we go on the offensive."

"I—I don't know how to fight. I can't—"

The truck slowed to a stop.

"Yes, you can," he said, his voice unyielding as he tried salvaging the bloodied, torn-in-two Henley. If they saw that he'd already been bandaged—attended to—his plan was dead in the water before it could begin.

Up front, one of the cab doors opened.

Eden shook her head, her pupils dilated.

She was in shock. He recognized the symptoms.

"Eden, listen to me—"

Shoes hit gravel.

The door slammed shut.

She burst into frantic motion, grabbing the phone she wouldn't touch seconds earlier. She dropped it into her pocket as the back hatch of the truck rolled open with a deep rumble, foiling his plan. Eden was standing. Shielding her eyes, squinting against the onslaught of sun as a darkened figure came into focus.

"She's awake." Roger Carlson, ex-military. His nose crooked, nostrils stuffed with tissue, and a mess of dried blood on his shirtfront.

Next to him, Jack Forrester, ex-convict. One eye swollen shut. His lower lip split wide and a nasty gash along his cheekbone.

Gravel crunched behind them—the fall of approaching footsteps. A man stepped into view, at least fifteen years older than the photograph they'd found online. But he was familiar all the same. Dr. Benjamin Norton. The doctor who'd put tubes in Eden's ears when she was four.

"Who is this?" He looked at Cass, then back at Forrester and Carlson. "What happened to you?"

"*He* happened," Carlson said.

"He was with the girl," Forrester added.

Dr. Norton twisted his lips to the side—as if weighing his options—then sighed a resigned-sounding sigh. Cass didn't know what Mordecai looked like. Fighters weren't privy to a gambler's identity. But Mordecai would know him. And yet this man—their captor—looked at Cass with no hint of recognition. Nor did he look like the people who typically frequented fights. With his tweed flat cap and his silver mustache, he reminded Cass of his own grandfather—a man he'd only seen a few times in his life, a long, long time ago. The memory of him was there, though. Silver hair and kind eyes, always filled with the strangest combination of worry and relief.

Dr. Benjamin Norton was looking at them now in the exact same way.

20

The footage had turned Eden into a spool unraveling. She couldn't unsee it. She couldn't believe it. And yet it seared her memory like a hot branding iron.

Her hands wrapped around her mother's neck.

Her hands making her father bleed.

What was that?

Who was that?

As she stepped out of the truck and took in the sight of the secluded property in front of her, she scrambled to pin down the moment. But time and motion—past and present—flashed like a disjointed strobe light. She could scream. It was right there—swollen on the tip of her tongue. All she had to do was open her mouth and let it out. But who would hear? By the looks of it, the only ears for miles around belonged to Cassian and their captors and the honking geese on the water.

They'd been brought to a cabin on a lake surrounded by woods. Thoreau's Walden Pond, only this wasn't Concord. It was most likely Lake Michigan, and the same niggling familiarity that struck her in the back of Jack and Annette's Honda Clarity when she spotted that green sign for Circus Lane struck her now—the uncanny feeling that she knew this place. It followed her all the way down the stairs into a large, sterile room with fluorescent lighting and equipment and a medical table as Cassian shot off questions.

What did they want?

What were they going to do with them?

Where were they?

She'd ruined his plan. Destroyed any element of surprise they might have had on their side. Now they were inside this basement that looked more like a medical facility as Dr. Norton gathered equipment onto a tray, looking up occasionally to examine Jack and Roger from across the room.

"Why don't you two get yourselves cleaned up?"

Roger didn't budge. He stood with his legs spread, his thick arms crossed, his eyes narrowed at Cassian, watching him like a hawk. Forrester didn't have to be asked twice. He stalked toward Eden, who was standing by the door.

His nearness turned her fear into a visceral, feral thing.

He must have noticed, because he stopped in the doorway and looked down at her—his eyes filled not with contempt or whatever it was a captor's accomplice might feel upon success, but of all things—hurt. "I was never going to harm you."

He swept past, leaving her bewildered. *He was never going to harm her?* He'd drugged her. Taken her against her will. Used a shard of glass to slice Cassian's side. He brought them here, to Mordecai. The man who was hunting her down. The man who had shot Yukio dead. The man who would probably kill her parents now that he had her. The man who was currently … hooking a wounded and uncooperative Cassian to an IV?

Her forehead wrinkled.

If Dr. Norton was going to shoot Cassian like he'd shot Yukio, why was he tending to Cassian's wounds?

The doctor picked up a pair of scissors.

"What are you doing?" Eden asked, taking a step forward.

"I'm treating his injury."

"Why?"

"Because I'm a doctor."

"But—I don't ..." She shook her head. "You're Mordecai. Aren't you?"

He stopped from his work, momentarily distracted. "*Who*?"

Her mind splintered. She thought about the sticky note she'd pulled from Cassian's pocket. All the names and arrows. They'd found Mordecai. His name was Dr. Benjamin Norton. They had to be one and the same. It didn't make sense for two separate men to be after her. "Where are my parents? What have you done with them?"

"I don't know where your parents are. I certainly haven't done anything with them."

Her attention darted around the room, then landed on Cassian—who sat shirtless on the medical table, his eyes no longer ablaze but alert and skeptical. "Who are you, then? What's going on?"

"My name is Benjamin. Your father is one of my oldest friends. I've been trying to help you. Just like I'm trying to help this young man now." He resumed his work, blotting at the blood on Cassian's skin with some sort of disinfectant that made him suck in a sharp breath. "If he would just relax and let me."

Cass glared—all brooding darkness and gritted teeth, his abdomen flexed as Dr. Norton thoroughly cleaned the wound. "It's hard to relax with someone who's holding you captive."

"I'm doing no such thing. You are free to go. I would recommend, however, that you let me treat this first."

He clenched his jaw as Dr. Norton examined the opened gash. He picked up a long, tweezer-like tool from the tray and a package of sutures. Behind him was an empty gurney.

Eden pictured herself laying on it, staring up at the fluorescents, waiting to get tubes in her ears. But for the life of her, she couldn't remember a single ear infection, and Dr. Norton was not a pediatric ENT. So why in the world would they have this man put tubes in her ears?

"What did you do to me?" The disembodied question

hovered in the air like a wraith. "My parents told me I needed tubes in my ears, but that wasn't true, was it?"

"I wondered if you would remember."

"*What* did you do to me?" she asked again.

"I inserted a scrambling device in your inner ear." His voice was even, his hands steady as he threaded a stitch.

"A scrambling device?"

"Something to confuse your location should anyone attempt to track you." He didn't look at her when he said the words. He was too focused on each stitch—carefully sewing Cassian's side back together. He must have put pain medication into the IV, because by the time he finished, Cassian's body had visibly relaxed. Dr. Norton wrapped his torso, then attended to his head injury—flashing a light in each eye.

"It appears you have a mild concussion, and you lost a fair amount of blood. We'll administer some heavy antibiotics to prevent infection. You have soft tissue that will need to heal. But by all accounts, this could have been much worse." He peeled off his gloves and tossed them into a metal waste bin. Then finally, he addressed Eden, who'd been standing there quite stupidly with her mouth agape. "Your father sent me a message."

"When?"

"On Thursday."

"Thursday," she repeated.

August 22.

Christopher's birthday.

The day everything turned inside out.

"When your parents brought you here thirteen and a half years ago, we inserted the scrambling device, and we decided to set up an alarm system—"

"An alarm system?"

He held up his finger and kept going, as though she'd never interrupted. "As a precautionary measure. This past Thursday, the alarm went off on my phone. I accessed your home surveillance and saw two men taking your parents away."

Her heart raced as she tried hard to decode his expression. Was that all he saw? Surely he'd watched the entire footage. Surely he'd seen the same thing she'd seen in the back of that truck. A girl attacking her parents. A girl that could not be her.

"I was overseas when the alert came, which meant I had to improvise. I knew it was imperative to get you somewhere safe. Unfortunately, safety is not always found with the police. The goal was to get you away from the authorities as quickly as possible with as little notice as possible and bring you here."

"So you turned me into Ellery Forrester."

The doctor nodded.

Eden recalled the room she woke up in. A teenager's room. With a closet full of clothes. "Is she a real person?"

"She is who we needed you to be. Jack and Annette are old friends of mine who wanted to help."

"They drugged me."

"A task they were no more fond of than you were, I assure you. But you wouldn't have gone with them any other way."

"You disconnected our phone numbers."

"I didn't want anyone tracing your location should you call the wrong person."

"How can I be traced? You just said I have a scrambling device inside my head."

"I have reason to believe the scrambling device is no longer functioning properly."

She peered at him. Was this the reason she attacked her parents? Was the malfunctioning scrambling device the reason she couldn't remember any of it? Had the technology he put in her brain glitched—making everything go haywire—and now her parents were paying the price? She wanted to know. *Needed* to know. But Dr. Norton couldn't read her mind, and she couldn't ask the questions out loud without admitting what she'd done. And that was something she couldn't bring herself to do.

So instead, she asked the most basic of questions. "Why did you put a scrambling device inside my head when I was four?"

He scratched his mustache, as though deliberating, formulating, censoring.

It made her want to scream.

"Was it because of Mordecai?" she asked.

"Who is this Mordecai?"

"He's a gambler for the Underground," Cassian answered. "And he's looking for her."

"You don't know him?" Eden looked at the doctor suspiciously. If he wasn't Mordecai, then surely he was protecting her from Mordecai. Which meant either way, he had to know Mordecai.

"No."

"Then why did you put the scrambling device in my ear?" She squished the exasperated words between her teeth, all patience wrung dry. His obvious reluctance to elaborate on his answers had a growl building in her chest. "Did it have to do with my father being in the CIA?"

The question seemed to catch the doctor off guard.

Which could only mean Cleo's theory was true.

Her father *had* been in the CIA.

"You've been doing some research," he said.

"We've had a lot of questions."

His cheeks puffed with air. He ran a finger across his right eyebrow. "Your father got wrapped up in a dangerous situation many years ago. The scrambling device was for your protection."

"So people were after him, not me?"

There was the briefest pause—an infinitesimal hesitation. "Yes."

She shot Cass a dark, knowing look. According to him, Mordecai was after *her*. Not her father. Which meant one of two things. Either Cass was misinformed, or the doctor was lying.

"Then why not have your friend, Jack, explain this to me as

soon as I woke up in Milwaukee? Why did they keep pretending like I was Ellery?"

"You weren't supposed to wake up. Not until you got here, wherein I would do the explaining. They were simply trying their best to transport you here as quickly and safely as possible." Dr. Norton looked from Cassian—half-naked with a wrapped torso—to Carlson, whose nose was obviously broken. "I didn't anticipate so much trouble. But you're here now, which is the important thing. And now that you're here, I need to take a look at that scrambling device. I need to see how it's functioning."

She stared at him—this man who *needed* to get inside her head. This man who'd been inside her head once before. He wanted her to believe it was for her protection, but he wasn't telling her the truth. At least not all of it. Parts were missing, leaving her with answers that didn't add up. For all she knew, he was the reason she'd done what she'd seen herself do. "There's just one problem, Dr. Norton."

He raised his eyebrows.

"I don't trust you. So why would I let you inside my head?"

He stared back at her for a long moment, like a game of chicken.

Eden didn't budge. She wouldn't look away. The doctor would have to give first.

"Well," he said on the tail end of a heavy sigh. "For the safety of everyone here, I hope you will reconsider. Now if you'll excuse us." He clapped Roger on the shoulder, whose face was a swollen mess as he continued to stand by like a bodyguard, watching Cassian like he might spring off the medical table to pick up where they left off in the parking garage. "I should attend to my friends."

21

For the safety of everyone here …

His words reverberated inside Eden's skull, bouncing around like a trapped echo. Did he know? Had he seen? And most importantly of all, could she do it again—turn on them like she'd turned on her parents? The questions spun into a tornado of whirling, chaotic thought as the doctor and his henchman left her and Cassian alone in the sterile room.

"Eden."

She took a step back. Away.

For the safety of everyone here …

"Can I have my phone?"

Breath hovered in her throat.

His phone.

The link.

The footage.

He tilted his head. "Eden?"

"I watched it."

"What?"

"The footage. Your contact sent a link when we were in the truck. When you were unconscious." And she wasn't. Despite being shot with two tranquilizer darts. She'd regained consciousness not more than fifteen minutes later. For some reason, the tranquilizer didn't quite work on her. Didn't Annette say so herself? They had to use three doses to keep Eden unconscious through the night, and even then, it wasn't enough. She saw herself strangling her mother. The overpowering way she'd thrown her down on the coffee table, slammed her against the bookshelves. Then turned on her father with a brute strength that had never been hers.

"Was it the man from the police station?" Cass asked. "Was he in your house?"

Eden looked at him—his bandaged torso, the IV in his arm— the past thirty-six hours descending like an apocalyptic storm. The tornado of thought split into two, then three, then four. Swirling faster, pulling up debris that made her stomach revolt. All of it gathered, rising up her throat. She was going to be sick, right there in that sterile, familiar room.

Her legs took over. They carried her away.

"Where are you going?" he called.

But she didn't answer him.

She couldn't answer him.

Her legs kept moving. Down a corridor into a small kitchenette on her left. She walked inside, grabbed both sides of the sink, and leaned over it while everything spun faster. Memories whirling together. Memories resurrected from Cleo's hypnotherapy. She touched a hot griddle when she was five, and while there had been an intense searing sensation, it left as soon as she pulled her finger from the cast iron. There'd been no burn mark left on her skin. She fell off a tall set of bleachers when she was six, and her mother didn't even have to kiss the pain away. She jumped out of a car going thirty miles per hour without sustaining a single injury.

With a gulp of air, she turned on the faucet and began scrubbing the blood from her hands. Cassian's blood. She scrubbed until her skin was pink and raw. Then she turned off the water and grabbed at the towel on the counter, her attention landing on a block of cutting knives.

She stared, transfixed.

She never got ear infections as a kid. Now that she thought about it—*really* thought about it—she hadn't gotten sick at all. While other kids stayed home from school during flu season, Eden hadn't missed a single day. No stomach bugs. No strep throat. Not even a runny nose. What kind of kid didn't get a runny nose? What kind of kid moved through life without ever needing a bandage from the box of Band-Aids her mother kept in their medicine cabinet?

The world spun faster.

Her fingers curled around the handle of a knife. She slid it slowly from the block, her heart careening beneath her ribcage, her mind a cacophony of screaming chaos. She wrapped her hand around the glinting metal, her palm pressed against the blade. And then—quick and decisive—she pulled the blade through.

There was an intense burst of pain.

With a gasp, she unclenched her fist.

The cut was deep. The blood came fast.

But before a single drop could drip into the basin of the sink, the wound she inflicted undid itself. She watched as it closed back up, right in front of her eyes.

The knife clanked to the floor.

"Eden?"

She whirled around.

Dr. Norton stood in the entryway, his attention moving from her hand—outstretched, upturned, bloody but not injured—to the fallen knife.

Her heart pounded in her ears.

"*What am I?*" The low, trembling words came like separate sentences—each ominous syllable whole and complete on its own.

He didn't answer. He just stood there, oozing concern while her body quaked.

"I saw what I did to them. I watched the surveillance." Her voice cracked over the confession. "I don't understand what's happening."

He took a slow, cautious step forward. "I need you to take a deep breath."

"*What am* I?" This time, the question exploded—it burst from her lips and echoed down the hallway.

Dr. Norton lifted his hands into the air, crept an inch closer. "I'm going to get the knife, and then I'll explain everything."

She looked down at the sharp object on the ceramic tile. He was afraid of her. He was afraid because she was dangerous. She hurt them, and she could hurt him. But she couldn't hurt herself. Somehow, that was impossible.

He crouched low—his eyes never leaving hers—picked up the knife and let out a slow, relieved breath.

Eden cracked. Her knees buckled. She collapsed to the ground, put her head between her palms and squeezed, as if she might be able to squeeze it all away.

Dr. Norton crouched beside her and placed his hand on her back. "You need to breathe."

But she didn't breathe. She couldn't breathe. "What did you do to me?"

"I didn't do anything to you."

"Then why did I attack them?" She looked up at him through her tears.

Something sad passed across his face. Something resigned, too. "That wasn't you."

"Yes it was. I saw myself do it."

He took her elbow and pulled her up, unafraid with the knife out of immediate reach. But she didn't understand why. She hadn't needed a knife to attack her parents. She'd used her bare hands. "We're going to sit at the table. I'm going to make us some tea. And I will tell you everything I know."

He pulled out a chair.

Eden sat down, no longer clutching her head, but clenching her fists in her lap.

"First, I'd like to ask you about the boy."

She blinked dumbly.

"Who is he and why is he here with you?"

"His name is Cassian. He's here because he found out a man named Mordecai was after me, and he knows Mordecai isn't good. He helped me after I jumped out of Jack and Annette's car. He brought me to his friend, Cleo. It's where we found out about you."

Dr. Norton rubbed his chin. He glanced toward the hallway, in the direction of the medical room. "What I am about to tell you is extremely confidential. There are very few people who know. Ultimately, I can't force you to secrecy. It's your story, and as such, you have the freedom to share it with whomever you like. Just know that this isn't only your story. I implore you to consider the repercussions before you decide to share."

She swallowed.

Dr. Norton had brought her to the edge of a precipice. Whatever he was about to say would hurl her off the edge and life would never be the same again. No matter what happened—no matter how this shook out—there would be no going back. No way of unknowing. But maybe she'd already been pushed. Because how could she possibly turn away now?

He moved to the stove. Filled a kettle with water and set it on one of the burners. He turned the knob. The gas clicked into flame. Dr. Norton sat across from her and took a deep breath, his expression carefully composed. "Your father first brought you here when you were eighteen months old."

Alaric Taylor. Molly Wick. Her flat stomach on the Fourth of July. "As their own child, or somebody else's?"

She could see it. A glimpse of pity.

And just like that—she was falling, falling, falling.

"A lot of people lost children in The Attack. It was a terrible time for everyone, but especially your mother. She was devastated, Eden. It took them years to get pregnant. Even with treatment and multiple rounds of failed in vitro fertilization. When they finally did, they considered it a miracle."

They considered *him* a miracle.

Christopher.

Her ghost of a big brother.

Never there, but always there.

She closed her eyes. "Their miracle died."

"Yes."

"Did they take me from someone?" Had they stolen her away? Did they bring her to this doctor and turn her into some sort of science experiment—assurance that their second child couldn't die?

"Not exactly."

"What does that mean?"

"Two years after The Attack, an IVF clinic was sued for misplacing frozen embryos."

Eden narrowed her eyes.

"As you can imagine, the story caught your father's attention. He followed the thread."

"And?"

"It led to a cell of terrorists. Members of Interitus."

"Interitus," Eden repeated.

"Followers of Karik Volkova."

The man responsible for The Attack.

What could this possibly have to do with her?

"They were experimenting with weapons," Dr. Norton said.

"What kind of weapons?"

"*Human* weapons."

The hairs on the back of her neck stood on end.

"They were altering DNA by digging deep into the study of Nano science. In particular, they were experimenting with Nano robotics—machines built at the molecular level with the capability of making a person nearly indestructible."

She blinked dumbly. This sounded like one of Erik's science fiction novels. And yet here she was, sitting with this retired military doctor, listening to him talk about things that couldn't really be about her. *Karik Volkova*? He was more infamous than any terrorist who'd lived before him. Somehow, she was supposed to believe that her story intersected with his? "I don't understand."

"Imagine the immune system. It works together to heal a body when it's injured or sick. On its own, let's imagine it possesses the efficiency of a walking pedestrian. Now imagine someone gives that walking pedestrian an S-15 fighter jet."

"The molecular robots are the S-15 fighter jet."

Dr. Norton nodded.

The teakettle began to rattle.

"Now imagine these nanobots not only assist the immune system, but other functions as well—sensory processing, memory, reflexes, speed, strength. If they could successfully inject them into a human being, they could essentially create a superhuman."

Goosebumps marched across her skin.

Dr. Norton took two mugs from a cupboard. "At first, Volkova experimented on adults. But the subjects never survived the injection process. Their bodies saw the nanobots as invaders and their immune systems turned on themselves. He moved on to embryos. It worked. The embryos didn't die. Your father was put in charge of a special ops team sent to dismantle the project and eliminate the threat. Their orders were threefold. Kill the cell of terrorists, destroy the technology used to control the nanobots—"

"*Control?*"

"They are machines, Eden—invisible to the naked eye, yes. But like any other machine, they are programmed, commanded, and controlled."

The pressure gathered. Built.

In the teakettle.

In her.

"Their third order was to extract the nanobots from each of the subjects. There were six in all. Your father followed the first two directives. The last one was more complicated."

"Why?"

"The subjects were babies. And it quickly became evident that they could not survive the extraction process."

Her breathing shallowed. Her mouth went dry.

Dr. Norton dragged his hand down his face, exhaustion pulling at the corners of his eyes. "It was the worst assignment he ever had to carry out. Meanwhile, your mother was at home with empty arms. Desperate for a child."

She squeezed her eyes shut.

"And here was this perfect little girl. No asthma, like Christopher. She couldn't even get sick."

A tear tumbled down Eden's cheek.

"They'd already killed the terrorists. By then, the government had found and executed Volkova. Your father destroyed all the data, all the research, all the technology associated with the project. He believed the threat was eliminated."

"So he took me." She opened her eyes.

Dr. Norton nodded.

This was what she was?

A monster.

A weapon created by terrorists.

Her body teeming with enemies that could make her do things she didn't want to do.

The kettle rattled louder and louder, until the steam screamed free in a high-pitched whistle.

Dr. Norton removed it from the burner.

But the screaming didn't stop—at least not inside Eden's head. "I want them out. I want them out of me right now."

"We tried. It's why your father brought you here sixteen and a half years ago."

"To make sure I couldn't hurt them." The words fell like acid from her tongue.

"To keep you safe."

She laughed a bitter laugh. She *was* safe. She was indestructible. Karik Volkova made sure of that.

"But we couldn't find a way to extract the nanobots without destroying you in the process. So we let them be." Dr. Norton dropped a tea bag into each of the mugs and poured water inside. "A few years later, your father started hearing rumors. Nothing substantial, but enough to make him nervous. If there were any followers of Volkova out there looking for you, he wanted to make sure the technology in your system could not be tracked."

"So you put the scrambling device in my ear."

He nodded.

She could feel her mother's neck beneath her hands. The sinew of muscle and tendon being crushed as she squeezed. The panic. The fading pulse.

You're killing her, Eden. She's dying.

"But I'm not—I'm not superhuman." Even as she said it, experience betrayed her. Her whole life, she'd been normal. Above average, but normal. Lately, however? She'd memorized a diagram in her anatomy class after a single glance. She ran twenty miles per hour on a treadmill without even breaking a sweat. She'd sensed danger in the parking garage before she could see it. She heard that dart slicing through the air and she dodged it before it could hit her. "At least, not until recently."

"That was part of the design. The technology assisting your immune system has been operating since injection. They didn't want one of their subjects falling ill anymore than they would they want a toddler to possess superhuman strength or speed. That particular technology would require activation by an outside source, and only after a pre-determined time."

"So somebody activated me?"

"Yes."

"How do you know all this?"

"Your father's research was extensive. And fascinating. When he brought you here the first time, he left it with me. I've had plenty of time to study it." Steam curled up from Dr. Norton's mug as he sat down across from her.

"Who activated me—Mordecai?"

"I'm not sure, but if you say he's after you, then it seems likely."

"What does he want?"

"I'm afraid I don't know."

Eden remembered the doctor's words from earlier—about the police not always being safe. "Do you think he knows people in law enforcement?"

He held the string of his tea bag, dunking it in and out of the water while Eden's steaming mug remained untouched in front of her. "Roger Carlson is my assistant. I placed him in your home not because I mistrusted the police, per se, but because I couldn't have them walking inside to such a crime scene."

"With my fingerprints everywhere."

"They would have accessed the ADT footage, and they would have seen ..."

"What I saw."

He nodded. "The government can't find out about you, Eden. As far as they know, you were destroyed sixteen and a half years ago. If they discovered you weren't, they wouldn't hesitate to carry out the orders your father couldn't."

The horrible truth of his words seeped deep into her unbreakable bones. "Maybe we should let them."

"Don't say that."

"*Why not?*" she spat.

"Because you matter. You're alive. And that life shouldn't be destroyed."

"My life was created by one of the most vile men to ever live on this earth. He was pure evil, and he ensured that I can be controlled. Made to do things against my will. If it happened once before, what's to stop it from happening again?"

"I think something went wrong."

"What do you mean?"

"You're here. They didn't get you."

"They got my parents."

"Exactly. They tried to control you, Eden. But something went haywire." Dr. Norton's eyes found hers. They were filled with urgency and compassion and a need to fix what was so horribly broken. "If it's all right with you, I'd really like to see if we can figure out what it was."

22

Cass used disinfectant wipes to clean the dried blood from his face, then he clamped the IV tubing and ripped the tape off his arm. The pain was gone, which meant the doctor had given him medication. He preferred a clear mind with pain over a muddled mind without.

Eden had watched the footage. Whatever she saw had disturbed her. Now she'd been gone too long, and the doctor was clearly lying. She suspected it; Cass knew it. Yukio came to him with the job, and the objective had been clear. Find two girls. Nothing was ever said about anyone's father—if that's who Alexander Pruitt or Alaric Taylor was. Now the doctor was with her, and Cass didn't trust him any further than he could throw him. Given the current state of his body, that wasn't very far.

He pulled out the IV catheter as the sound of footsteps approached.

Dr. Norton stepped into the room and frowned. "That was supposed to stay *in* your arm."

Cass tossed it on the medical table, his focus on Eden, who for some suspicious reason, was going through great lengths to avoid eye contact with him.

157

"You should lie down," Dr. Norton said. "The best thing for you right now is rest."

"The best thing for me right now is a shirt."

The doctor opened a nearby closet, pulled a folded white undershirt from a shelf inside, and tossed it across the room.

Cass caught it and pulled the shirt over his head—frustrated with the way his body protested. He never had patience for injuries. An interesting pet peeve, given his former line of work. By the time the shirt was in place, Dr. Norton had moved to a machine in the corner of the room. Cass had been subjected to one before. A long time ago when Cleo's mother wanted to scan his head for injuries. Why was the doctor getting this one ready now? And why was Eden staring so resolutely at the ground?

"You're not letting him inside your head," Cass said.

She folded her arms protectively in front of herself.

He closed the gap between them, needing to see her face, *read* her face, so he could understand what had changed since she left. When she looked up, her forehead was streaked with blood. *His* blood. And fear raged in her eyes, turning them the color of thunderclouds. It was a feeling he knew. A feeling he hated. "I thought you said you don't trust him."

She hugged herself tighter, her attention sliding from the butterfly bandage above his left eye, to the small scar on his chin, to the place where he was stitched beneath the shirt—as if taking each injury into account. "You should go."

"What?"

"Now that your injury has been treated, you should leave."

He narrowed his eyes.

Her cheeks turned pink as she lifted her arm and jabbed her upturned hand toward Dr. Norton. "Whoever Mordecai is, it's not him. I'm safe here."

"Why—because he says so? You don't even know him."

"I don't know you either."

Her words stung. It was irrational. Absurd. But somehow, they did. Like a pinch deep in his chest, followed fast by a wave of hot frustration. She was being foolish. And so was he. Because somehow, this girl had gotten under his skin. Over the past few weeks, while he watched from the shadows. Over the past twenty-four hours, while her world unraveled. She'd gotten under his skin. And now here she was, trying to get rid of him.

"You don't want bad things to happen to innocent people. Cleo is innocent. If you want to help someone, help her. Go find her and make sure she's okay."

He searched her face—exploring every dip, taking in every line. She was giving him an out—a clear exit. He'd done his part and Yukio was dead. There would be no executor collecting debts. Cass could wash his hands—a free man—and disappear. But then, he'd always wonder, wouldn't he? Was she really okay? Were her parents? He'd gotten them into this mess. He couldn't be free—truly free—until he got them out. All of them. He took a step closer. "What did he say to you?"

"Nothing but the truth."

"Which is …?"

In his periphery, Dr. Norton paused from his preparations. Cass could feel him watching from across the room, as if waiting to see what Eden would do or say. She glanced at the doctor, then back at him. Her shoulders trembled. Despite her resolve, she was breaking. Falling apart in front of him.

"I'm dangerous," she said.

He almost laughed. It was a ridiculous statement, especially said to him—a guy who spent the last ten years of his life intentionally turning into something dangerous. "No you're not."

"Yes, I am." She pulled his phone from her pocket. She took his hand—her fingers cold but her touch like fire—turned it palm up and set the phone inside of it. "Watch the footage. See for yourself."

r. Norton handed Eden a towel and a hospital gown. They went upstairs, which was much less like a medical facility and much more like a home. They walked past another kitchen—much larger than the one downstairs—and a high ceilinged, sunlit living room. He showed Eden into a guest room with its own bathroom. The house felt large, especially after being crammed into a dormitory. It was safe and secluded, hidden away from the bad guys chasing her. And yet, she felt the opposite of safe. She felt so unsafe, the feeling of it rattled her bones, fissuring her brain. The only thing keeping her from full-fledged hysteria was Dr. Norton's words in the kitchen.

They tried to control you, but something went haywire.

Nothing more than a theory. But she clutched onto those words like they were valuable pearls. She snatched them up like bricks and built a wall—a barrier between the truth and her sanity. Something went haywire. They couldn't control her. At least not until they fixed whatever was broken.

"Once you're cleaned up, meet me downstairs in the medical room."

Apparently, Dr. Norton didn't want a blood-streaked, sweat-stained girl on his examination table.

She nodded numbly, then closed herself inside. She bolted the door. She turned on the shower. She stripped out of her filthy clothes and she stepped beneath the hard spray as it turned from warm to hot—clear water running reddish brown down the drain. She picked up a bar of soap and scrubbed her skin like being clean on the outside might fix every wrong thing on the inside. She used a washcloth to scrub and scrub until her skin was clean and pink.

Then she turned off the water, stepped onto the mat, and dried herself. She slipped on the gown, tied it securely in the back, and wrapped the towel around her head like a turban. Her reflection was indistinct in the foggy mirror above the sink. She wiped an oval into the condensation as Erik's voice echoed from a past that no longer felt like her own.

"Do you know how obnoxious it is that you never get any zits?" he'd said once while examining his own. In eighth grade, he'd gone through a particularly rough patch of acne.

Her fingers slid across her chin, up her cheek, over her forehead, then down the slope of her nose.

Flawless.

Further evidence that this wasn't a nightmare. This wasn't some horrible mix-up.

A man named Mordecai was after her. He wanted to control her, had already controlled her. Made her do things—horrible things—against her will. He was holding her parents hostage, using them as bait. Because he wanted her. For what purpose—she didn't know. Neither did Dr. Norton.

"You have your mother's heart," her father always said, "and your old man's eyes."

But it was a lie.

He'd made her see what wasn't there.

She didn't have his eyes. She couldn't have his eyes.

She wasn't his.

She removed the towel from her head. She combed trembling fingers through her thick, wet hair, then pulled it up into a high, messy bun. When she returned to the medical room, Cass was gone. There was no sign of Jack Forrester or Roger Carlson either. It was just herself and Dr. Norton, who seemed to be readying the machine in the corner.

"Why do you have all this in your basement?" she asked.

"I served in the military for many years. A fact I'm sure you've discovered on your own." There was a paternal twinkle in his eye. He had a calm, soothing way about him, making her wonder how she could have mistaken him—even briefly—for a man who wanted to hurt anyone. "I learned a lot during that time. About our government. I saw a lot, too. Disturbing things, one of which was how poorly so many of my struggling comrades were treated upon their return home. I decided to retire from the public sector and set up a … private practice, if you will. I treat veterans, mostly. Occasionally I travel outside of the country to provide medical service to those who wouldn't otherwise receive it."

To those who wouldn't otherwise receive it …

The words made her think about young Cassian Gray, and Cleo's mother, the doctor who risked her medical license to treat him.

"Which is where I was a couple days ago, when your father sent a message."

"So you asked an ex-convict and a man who was dishonorably discharged from the military for help?"

Jack Forrester.

Roger Carlson.

A motley crew.

Dr. Norton chuckled. "You've done an impressive amount of digging."

"The information didn't shed the most flattering light." It certainly made the Mordecai connection more plausible.

"Yes, well. It's hard to find work when you've been discharged from service in such a manner. But we all make mistakes. And we all deserve a second chance. Roger has been an excellent employee."

Eden chewed over the words, unsure if she thought they were true. Her attention moved to the staircase, where Cass had disappeared. Had he watched the footage already? And what would he think of her when he did?

Dr. Norton finished his preparations, then explained what would happen. He guided her through each step of the process. He would place a mask over her nose and mouth. It would emit radioactive particles that she would inhale. Once in her system, he would take a series of images that would show him what was happening inside her body.

The whole thing didn't take longer than forty-five minutes.

When he finished, it was time to look at the scrambling device.

"I can put you under, if you'd like," he said. "Another mask. A continuous stream of tranquilizer. As soon as I remove it, you'll wake up."

"No." Her answer came quick, unyielding. The last thing she wanted was more blank space in her mind. She would remain lucid. She would remain in control for as long as possible.

"There will be some discomfort."

"I don't care."

He seemed to understand.

He got out an ominous-looking robotic device with a scope and something that looked like a long needle.

She stared at it sideways.

Dr. Norton asked her to lie back. "There will be a deep pinch."

She winced, squishing up one eye as the pinch moved deeper and deeper—like a needle piercing her brain—until the robotic device let out a small beep, and Dr. Norton pulled it out. At the very end of the needle-like apparatus was something so small, it could be mistaken for a crumb.

"Is that it?" she asked.

Nodding, he brought the minuscule object to his desk.

Eden sat up and watched him examine it carefully beneath a microscope—this scrambling device that had been in her ear since she was four. This reality that had always been hers; she just didn't know about it. He scanned it with something that sent messages to his laptop. When he finished, he sat back with a frown.

"Is it broken?" she asked.

"It seems to be in perfect working order."

"Then how did he find me?"

Dr. Norton sucked on his teeth. "I'm not sure."

He recaptured the crumb and re-inserted it.

The pinch was different this time—less stinging, more pressure.

"There are spare clothes in the closet there. You can find some to change into." Dr. Norton returned to his swivel chair and peered at the images loading on his screen. He clicked the touchpad.

Eden slid off the examination table. "Karik Volkova was executed by the government."

The doctor released a distracted hum of acknowledgement.

"You think he still has followers?" Was this who Mordecai was—some leftover remnant of a terrorist group?

"I'm not sure." He studied the images like a code to decipher —zooming in, clicking, adjusting, highlighting. Eden could see it all clearly from several yards away. And if she closed her eyes, she could recall in perfect detail every measurement on every image. She just didn't know what any of it meant.

"You studied my dad's research."

"Extensively."

"Do you still have it?"

Dr. Norton paused from his examination. He scratched his mustache. Then he stood up and went into the closet with the spare clothes. He punched in a code to a large safe inside and withdrew a thick, manila folder. Written on the tab, in her father's familiar scrawl, were two words: *Subject 006*.

23

Cassian strode into the house with the phone gripped tightly in his hand. He'd watched the footage out front. Multiple times over. While Carlson left with the truck, he watched it. While birds chirped and squirrels chattered and sunlight dappled through the canopy of leaves overhead, he watched it. His body going from hot to cold and back again, like his internal thermostat was no longer working properly.

He spotted Eden through a sliding glass door on the back deck overlooking the water. She took a seat in an Adirondack chair and opened a thick file in her lap as Dr. Norton and Forrester came upstairs, the gash in his cheek no longer split open, but cleaned and stitched shut.

Cass held up the phone. "Where did she learn to fight like this?" He was well acquainted with combat. What he'd seen Eden do to her father—a man at least twice her strength—made no sense apart from intense and meticulous training.

The doctor acknowledged his question with a quick glance from the sliding glass door to the phone in the air but offered no explanation as he opened a closet off the foyer and pulled out a lightweight jacket.

Behind him, Forrester shifted. The man was twitchy. Like a businessman late for an important meeting.

"You're leaving?" Cass asked.

"We have some pressing matters to take care of. If you need a ride somewhere, we'd be happy to drop you off along the way."

"I'm not going anywhere."

"I believe Eden asked you to leave," Norton said.

"And I'm politely declining."

Forrester stepped forward. "You can take your politeness and—"

Norton held up his hand, stopping Forrester mid-sentence. "There's no need to get ugly, Jack."

"He can't stay." Jack pushed the words between his teeth, looking mutinous. This man who'd given Cass the gash in his side.

It made him all the more resolved.

He trusted Twitchy Forrester less than he trusted the doctor.

"You're not actually going to let him?" Forrester said.

Norton stuck his arm through one sleeve of his jacket, studying Cass openly. "You're walking into a dangerous situation."

"Past tense. I've already walked in."

"I suppose you have. The question is, *why?*"

The inquiry scratched like steel-wool. It was the same question Eden had asked. The same question he had yet to answer honestly.

Norton pulled his jacket the rest of the way on and grabbed his flat cap from a hook on the inside of the door. "She told me your name. She said you knew this Mordecai fellow was after her. Which leads me to ask—who are you, exactly? How are you wrapped up in all of this?"

"Why would I answer your questions when you won't answer mine?"

"Because you are asking questions with answers that aren't mine to give." His attention moved again to the sliding glass door. To Eden, bent over the folder. "I wouldn't pressure her to give them to you either."

The unsolicited advice grated.

"I'm not the type to pressure anyone."

"Well, good." He placed the cap over his silver hair. "Now if you'll excuse us, we should be going."

He opened the door, gesturing for Forrester to exit first.

"Wait," Cass said.

The two men stopped, Forrester looking hopeful. Maybe a little desperate. Like he didn't just want Cass to take them up on the offer of a ride but *needed* Cass to take them up on the offer of a ride. Was it simply because of what Cass had done to his face?

Cass considered.

Eden was right; Cleo was innocent. And he'd wrapped her up in this, too. By now, she was probably back in her dorm room, furiously digging for answers. She wouldn't stop until she had them. And then what? "We were staying with a girl named Cleo."

"Eden mentioned her."

"If Mordecai traces our steps to Milwaukee, I'd like to make sure she's safe."

"That can certainly be arranged."

"He knows her address." Cass jerked his head toward Jack. "Cleo Ransom. Room 901."

Norton nodded, his hand on the doorknob. "We'll be gone most of the day. Rest assured, the house is well protected. If you're hungry, feel free to help yourself to food in the pantry." With a tip of his flat cap, he and his angry companion walked out the front door, leaving Cass alone with Eden.

———

ass stood on the other side of the sliding glass door with his hand on the wall, watching Eden sit like a statue in the Adirondack chair, replaying the footage in his mind. She no longer pored over the paperwork in the file. That sat abandoned on the slats of wood by her feet. The pain medicine in his system was long gone, the ache in his head and side considerable. He gritted his teeth against both while the sinking sun turned the surface of Lake Michigan into sparkling diamond and his infuriating confusion grew by the second.

All morning long, all afternoon, he'd given her space. Waiting. Watching. Sure that eventually, she'd come inside. To eat. To use the bathroom.

But the daylight faded and she hadn't moved a muscle.

He clenched his hand into a fist against the wall.

He was done waiting.

Cass pulled open the sliding door. He stepped out into the humidity as loons called hauntingly from the lake and the sky at their back turned a violent pink. The wooden planks groaned as he pulled up a chair and sat down beside her. The breeze caught a loose tendril of hair, sending it into a dance. She didn't sweep it from her eyes or tuck it behind her ear. She didn't move at all. She just sat there with her arms draped across the armrests, her bare feet planted on the deck, staring blankly at the water. She was dressed in a pair of oversized sweatpants and an oversized t-shirt, courtesy of the doctor. Probably taken from the same closet as the shirt Cass wore now.

"I watched the footage," he said.

She closed her eyes. Brought her knees up to her chest and wrapped her arms around her shins.

If he was waiting for her to say something, he waited in vain.

She didn't make a sound.

He shifted. "The doctor is checking on Cleo to make sure she's okay."

Nothing.

He pressed his thumb against his bottom lip and eyeballed the file at her feet, reading its cold, clinical label.

Subject 006.

He took in her profile as she stared at the water, her face expressionless. He tried to imagine what it must have been like for her, watching that footage in the back of a hot truck while he was unconscious and bleeding. The reality of what she'd done sinking in. He knew that feeling well. More than a year later and it still haunted him at night. He wound his hand around the back of his neck, his attention sliding again to the label on the folder.

"I'm a monster," she whispered.

"No you aren't."

She turned her head—her eyes two pools of fury. "You saw what I did."

Right. But he knew all about monsters, and he'd been watching her for weeks. While his first impression left him feeling justified in his search—she was a delinquent with a mug shot—everything that came after contradicted it. There were people in this world who were bad, and there were people in this world who were good. Despite that footage, Eden belonged in the second category.

"I'm a walking grenade. I could go off at any time. And when I do, I will hurt everyone around me."

He stared back at her—this girl who had just described ... *him*. A walking grenade. Only he *had* gone off. He went off just like his father went off all those years ago. And now someone was dead. The monster he'd run from for so long had caught him. Somehow, the monster he'd run from for so long had become him. Cass rubbed his jaw, as though massaging away the tension. He nudged the folder with the toe of his boot. "Is that what this folder says?"

Eden picked it up. And then she did something he didn't expect. Something he would never do. She handed it over, just like that. "Go ahead and look. See for yourself. If you're going to stay, you deserve to know what you're staying with."

———

As the sky outside turned a deep navy, Cassian's phone exploded with messages—short, insistent demands. Somehow, Cleo had gotten a hold of his number. He sent her a brief, singular reply. *Watch your back. Tell no one.* Ignoring the rest, he sat on the living room couch, his elbows on his knees, his left hand holding a fistful of hair, his head throbbing while he pored over every page in the file Eden had given him.

Karik Volkova.

Genetically modified embryos.

Weaponized humans.

One of six.

He flipped to the next page, thinking about the other one— the girl he hadn't found. Was she one of the six, too? Was the notorious Mordecai connected somehow to the infinitely more notorious Volkova? Underground Fighting attracted a sketchy crowd—petty criminals, mostly. A terrorist of that caliber was something else altogether.

The lock on the front door rattled.

Cass stood quickly. On reflex, his hand moved to the small of his back where his gun was normally tucked.

The door opened.

Dr. Norton stepped inside alone. Without the twitchy Forrester or the burly Carlson. His attention slid to the coffee table, where the file lay opened. "She shared it with you."

"Without any pressure from me." A fact that still rankled. She shouldn't be sharing this file. She shouldn't have let the doctor into her head. But then, hadn't he known the second she climbed onto the back of his bike? Eden Pruitt was entirely too trusting.

The older gentleman released a long sigh, then moved to the

kitchen and opened the cabinet above the stove. He pulled out a bottle of pills, shook two onto his palm, filled up a glass of water, and brought them both to the living room.

"I'm not taking pain meds," Cass said.

"If you'd rather feel pain, that's your prerogative. A raging infection, however, won't do us any favors." The doctor handed over the glass of water and the pills. "These are antibiotics. You need to take them."

Without taking his eyes off the man, Cass popped the pills into his mouth and swallowed them down.

With another prolonged sigh, Norton sank into the armchair next to the couch.

"According to this, there were six of them." Cass picked up the file. "What happened to the others?"

The man stroked his mustache. Then finally, he said, "They couldn't survive the extraction process."

Cass narrowed his eyes. The doctor was lying again. He had to be. Why else was Mordecai looking for another girl? The problem was, he couldn't ask that question out loud without incriminating himself.

Norton peered toward the sliding glass door. Eden's hair was just visible over the back of the Adirondack chair. "She hasn't moved?"

Cass shook his head.

"She's in shock," Norton said.

"Can you blame her?"

"No, I suppose I can't." He removed his hat and scratched the top of his hair, where it was thinnest. "Do you want to check on her, or shall I?"

Cass didn't wait for the man to get up.

He found Eden where he'd left her—not expressionless, staring off into the water and the sky beyond. But asleep, the skin beneath her eyes shadowed with exhaustion, her brow slightly crumpled, as though not even slumber could offer an escape from her troubles. The same tendril of hair framed her face. He steeled himself against it—against *her*—and lifted her into his arms, his injured side smarting. His foolish body responding.

I'm dangerous, she'd said.

A ridiculous statement.

But it was true.

The contents of that folder confirmed it.

She looked the opposite now—exhausted and vulnerable, pale and thin.

He brought her inside.

"You really shouldn't be carrying anyone," Norton said.

Cass ignored him. He brought Eden down the hallway, into the guest room. He lay her gently on top of the bed and covered her with a blanket. And then—as though unable to help himself—he captured the tendril of hair between his middle and index finger. It was soft as silk.

It was soft like her own touch when she tended to him in the basement of Cleo's residence hall. The trainers who bandaged him after a fight always did so with uncaring efficiency, just as he preferred. This girl, on the other hand, had cared for him in a way that made every muscle in his core flex against the unexpected gentleness of it.

Voilà. Tout au mieux.

She'd said the words in a perfect French accent after applying the bandage to his brow. She'd said it casually, nonchalantly. Without any clue that he'd heard those words before. A long, long time ago. When he was little and hurt and his mother would gather him into her arms and kiss the pain away. And then she'd whisper those exact same words into his ear.

He'd forgotten.

He'd forgotten, until Eden brought the memory back.

24

Her mother kept calling her name.

"Eden! Eden, where are you?"

They were at the pumpkin patch in Eastmore—the one with the giant maze made out of hay bales.

Eden crouched behind a stack of three, her hand cupped over her mouth to trap a giggle.

But then something in her mother's voice changed. Its playful tone took on a higher pitch. Even though Eden was only seven, she registered the shift. She jumped up like a leapfrog, eager to take the note away. "It's okay, Mommy! I'm just hiding."

Her mother rounded the corner—her eyes bright and filled with frantic relief just as Eden opened her own.

She blinked rapidly—the air heavy in her chest, a fluttering dread in her stomach as her mother's voice echoed from the dream.

Eden! Eden, where are you?

She sat upright in the strange bed, taking in her unfamiliar surroundings—a panicked déjà vu. How did she get here? What was the last thing she could remember? She grappled for clarity, for something solid to grab onto and came up with the file.

Subject 006.

Reality descended like a rock in her empty stomach.

Last night, she'd fallen asleep on the deck, imagining The Attack almost twenty-one years ago. The chaos and the shock of it. The overwhelming fact that the world had been ripped in two —irrevocably altered and impossible to repair. The world as it was had been violently torn from the world as it was now, and there would be no going back. She'd fallen asleep imagining her parents sitting under the weight of all that grief, in Silver Spring, Maryland, wondering if any piece of her present reality reflected their reality back then.

Eden had fallen asleep with her world torn, and she could not get back to the way it was before, when she was the biological daughter of Alexander and Ruth Pruitt. Those weren't even their real names. They changed them and moved across the country, because they'd taken her—*Subject 006*, one of six frozen embryos Karik Volkova had stolen and genetically modified.

The minute hand on the clock by her bedside ticked.

6:26 a.m.

Eden kicked the blanket off her legs and hurried to the door.

It was unlocked.

Someone had moved her in here, and they hadn't even bothered locking her in.

She stepped out into the hallway, heart pounding, ears perked. But all was quiet and still. There was nothing amiss. No splayed books. No torn boxes. No broken glass. Dr. Norton's house was in perfect order, and still, anger flashed like white lightning. At herself, for sleeping away so many precious hours while her parents were being held hostage. At them, for keeping all this from her, for putting themselves in such reckless danger. At Dr. Norton, for doing the same thing. She was a ticking time bomb, and nobody had even attempted to mitigate the threat.

She marched into the living room and ground to a halt as soon as she saw Cassian, asleep on the couch—dressed in fresh clothes, his injuries hidden beneath a cotton shirt.

She couldn't believe he was still here. He'd seen the footage.

He read the truth about what she was. Because of her, he'd been attacked, sliced open, and thrown into the back of a truck. And yet, he decided to stay. A decision that would have filled her with curiosity if she wasn't so consumed with more pressing matters, like the file in front of him on the coffee table.

Subject 006.

With the sticky note stuck to it, on which they'd written all the connections between the players. Eden snatched it up and stared at her own handwriting—somehow unfamiliar. Because this was her handwriting *before*. Before she knew the awful truth. She followed the lines, the connections she'd drawn when she was so desperate for answers. Now they had them—a whole file's worth of answers. But they only came with a pile of new questions, none of which answered the three most important.

Who was Mordecai? What did he want with her? And where were her parents?

She knew now that Mordecai wasn't Dr. Norton. This list of people on that sticky note belonged to two separate teams. Carlson, Annette and Jack Forrester, Dr. Norton, and her parents were on one side. The tattooed man, his accomplice, and Mordecai were on the other. It was these men they knew so little about.

Eden traced the line connecting Jack and Annette Forrester to her parents. Both of them had lost a child—a son—twenty-one years ago. Her thoughts were interrupted by a rhythm—or rather, the sudden lack of one. Like the abrupt absence of ocean waves—a soothing sound she didn't notice until it was gone. It was as if someone had sucked the waves away, and they momentarily stilled on the horizon.

She tilted her head, trying to pinpoint what she was hearing. Or *not* hearing.

And then the waves returned with a whoosh and resumed their lapping.

Breathing.

It was the sound of rhythmic breathing, interrupted by a deep yawn.

She looked at Cassian, still asleep. He hadn't yawned. He hadn't even stirred. But if she tried—cocked her head in just the right way—she could hear the slow, steady *thump-thump* of his heart as clearly as she could if she'd rested her head against his chest.

Her own pounded faster. She kept her head cocked; her ears perked.

There was the sound of moving sheets, and then the *whisper-whisper* of feet shuffling over carpet.

Then louder sounds. More distinct, easily recognizable sounds.

A cough.

A running faucet.

The *swoosh-swoosh-swoosh* of brushing teeth.

Down the length of a hallway and through a closed door, her ears heard all of it—Dr. Norton's entire morning routine. She could hear it because she'd focused her attention on hearing it. She discovered she could do the same with anything in the house, simply by shifting her focus and concentrating. By the time Dr. Norton reached her, neatly dressed in a golf shirt and a pair of slacks —the kind with a sharp crease ironed down the front—Eden held the folder in a white-knuckled grip. "You said he activated me."

Dr. Norton nodded.

"How do we make sure he never does it again?"

Eden examined the images over the doctor's shoulder as coffee percolated in the machine.

Cass poured himself a cup while Dr. Norton pointed at the screen.

"There are differences," he said. "See here—how much

denser they are in the brain and spinal cord than they were before? And that right there—the change of color? They appear to be generating heat."

"What does that mean?" Eden asked.

"I suppose it means they're active."

They were upstairs in the living room. Dr. Norton had his computer open on the coffee table. He'd pulled up the images he took yesterday, along with the second set of images he'd taken when she was four, and the original images he'd taken when she was eighteen months. The differences between the first two sets were negligible. The differences between those and the most recent were significant.

Cassian peered at them like they were a puzzle, a small divot furrowing his brow as he held a steaming cup of coffee below his chin. "There's no way to disable them?"

"Not that I've discovered."

The answer made Eden want to reach inside her own skin and pull them out herself. She had enemies inside of her, and if Dr. Norton's theory was right—if something had gone haywire —then it was only a matter of time until Mordecai fixed the glitch and controlled her again. She ran her hands over her hair and clasped them on top of her head. "You believe that Mordecai can control me remotely?"

"That's the theory," Dr. Norton said.

"Then why did he ever need to locate me geographically?"

"My guess is that the activation process required a geographic location."

A perfunctory knock sounded on the front door. The person on the other side didn't wait for an answer. Jack Forrester let himself in, and almost immediately, Eden's stomach clenched into a fist. Judging by the look on Cassian's face, he wasn't pleased to see him either.

"Did everything go well?" Dr. Norton asked.

The cryptic question had her narrowing her eyes. Roger Carlson was Dr. Norton's employee—in what capacity, Eden wasn't sure. Was Jack an employee, too? And what about the confidentiality the doctor impressed upon her so earnestly yesterday? Sure, everyone deserved a second chance, as Dr. Norton said, but could they really trust an ex-convict and a man kicked out of the military with such a secret? Judging by the way Dr. Norton didn't bother to close the laptop or hide the file, he already had.

Eden scrutinized him. "How are you connected to all of this?"

"I'm a friend of your father's." Jack's answer came quick, almost rehearsed, as if he'd been expecting it. "Our paths crossed a long time ago. I got into some trouble that put me and my wife in a hard spot. Your father helped us."

"How so?"

Jack's attention shifted to Cass, who stared with obvious interest, and something like a shadow fell across Forrester's face. "Let's just say we'll never be able to repay him."

"Where *is* your wife?" Cassian asked.

"That's none of your business."

"Is it mine?" Eden said.

Jack's eyelids fluttered. He cleared his throat. "She's somewhere safe."

The vague answer aroused her suspicion. Perhaps when it came to him, she always would be, given their first encounter. He'd stabbed her with a needle, after all. Drugged her against her will. She'd been helpless. Unable to fight, let alone defend herself.

Eden blinked, her thoughts hiccupping.

"Tranquilizer," she said.

"What's that?"

"Tranquilizer," she said again, louder this time, looking from Jack to Dr. Norton. "He used it on me at the police station."

"He was following *my* orders, Eden. If you're upset, you should be upset with me. At the time, I didn't know any other—"

She held up her hand, interrupting Dr. Norton's apology. "How did that work?"

The three of them stared at her.

"If my body's immune system is like an S-15 Fighter Jet …" She glanced at her palm, where the sharp blade had sliced through flesh. "If I'm able to heal so quickly, how does the tranquilizer work at all?"

"We used a lethal dose. Even then, it only keeps you under for a short amount of time."

But it did keep her under.

She could feel her hands around her mother's neck. Her father trying unsuccessfully to pry them away. Was it the nightmare she remembered, or the reality? Either way, the question pinged inside her brain just the same. What if her father had been armed with a needle like Jack Forrester? "If you can't disable the technology inside of me, can't you just … disable *me*?"

Doubt crept into Dr. Norton's expression.

"I don't mean right now." She didn't want that. She wasn't going to sleep on a gurney, her parents' lives in danger while everyone else worked hard to find and rescue them. "I mean … on demand. Something we can use if Mordecai is able to control me again."

"It would only be a temporary fix. I have a limited amount of sedative."

But Eden was hardly listening. Her thoughts spun. She would probably overpower them should they try to inject her with a needle. She would probably escape them if they tried shooting her with a gun. But if she had something attached to her body, something like … "An insulin pump."

One that attached to the stomach or arm via an infusion set in order to administer insulin. Eden knew all about them because Erik's diabetic sister—Ami with an I—had one.

"Couldn't we use the same technology?"

Dr. Norton's brow crinkled with confusion.

"We could swap out the insulin for a sufficient dose of tranquilizer. Not to be administered continuously, but … on demand. Should the need arise." Her stomach churned with something that wasn't panic, but urgency. Eagerness. Dr. Norton was right. It was only a temporary fix. A guardrail. Eventually, they would run out of tranquilizer and she would wake up again. But if Mordecai controlled her while she was still here, inside Dr. Norton's home, it would buy them time. Life-saving, precious time. The terror of being controlled at any second—forced to hurt or kill these people who were trying to help her—would no longer hang over her head like a rumbling thundercloud.

"Could you design something like that?" she asked.

He pressed his thumb and forefinger beneath his nose and smoothed them over his mustache in opposite directions. "I suppose I could try."

25

r. Norton's quest to diffuse the immediate threat of being controlled muffled the ticking time bomb in Eden's brain, giving her the capacity to zoom in on a problem every bit as dire—her parents. Her lying, non-biological parents—two truths she shoved into a box marked "later" because her brain could only handle so many crises at a time.

First, she had to get the people who raised her to safety.

Then, she could process the fact that everything she believed about their life together was a lie.

Dr. Norton had left—gone to acquire an insulin pump. Before he departed, he'd reached into his pocket and handed her a phone. *Her* phone. It took a second or two before she realized it.

"Cellular service is disabled," he'd said. "Jack wiped it clean in case anyone was trying to gain access. But you should be able to connect to Wi-Fi and use it like an iPad, if you want."

She'd jotted down the Wi-Fi password on the back of the sticky note stuck to her file.

Now, he was gone. Jack Forrester was smoking a cigarette on the back deck. And she and Cass were going over everything they knew about Mordecai.

The list was frustratingly sparse.

He gambled big money in Underground Fighting, which meant he had deep pockets and he probably lived in Chicago. Anyone who was serious about the sport lived there. Somehow, he'd found out about Karik Volkova's failed experiment. And as far as they knew, he had her parents.

"The guy with the tattoos was at the police station Thursday night. He would have followed Jack and Annette when they took me, right? He would look up their license plate numbers just like you did." Eden began to pace. "So what are they doing? If my parents are bait, then why is Mordecai hiding them? Why isn't he reaching out, wriggling the bait in our faces?"

Cass rubbed his bottom lip, studying the sticky note. "When I followed you from the station, I didn't notice anyone else doing the same."

"So you think that guy saw me with the police and just … left?"

"I think something must have happened and they lost track of you."

She filled her cheeks with air.

If that was the case, the two men were probably shot dead like Yukio.

Mordecai didn't strike her as the forgiving type.

She pushed the air out through her lips. "There has to be someone else who knows Mordecai. If he's such a prominent gambler, the trail can't stop with one dead man."

"Guys like Mordecai are very protective of their identity. They work with one bookie. All the big ones worked with Yukio."

And Yukio was dead.

"What about his phone?" she said. "Wouldn't he have had a way to contact Mordecai on his phone?"

Cass stopped rubbing his lip. He pulled his cell from his back pocket and dialed a number.

"Who are you calling?"

He pressed the phone against his ear.

Eden could hear it ringing—loud, like the call was on speaker.

Once.

Twice.

Again, and again.

And then, just when she would have given up on the call, a woman answered.

"Hello?"

"Hey." He was looking down and to the right. All Eden could see was the crown of his dark hair. "It's me."

"Cass?" The woman sounded like Frenchy from Grease, her intonation lilting with an unmistakable note of relief. "Where you been? Your manager came by the other day asking about ya."

"What did he want?"

"He heard ya called. Wanted to know where ya were. It's a mess here, Cass. Yuke's landlord kicked me out. Said I wasn't on the lease. Stuck me with all his stuff, but I got nowhere to put it. Right now I'm crashing on Ruby's couch, but she don't have the room either."

"And Yukio's stuff—what have you done with it?"

"We sold a bunch. Both of us need the money, ya know?"

"Do you still have his phone?"

"The cops took it into evidence."

Cass muttered a curse.

"His computer, too. Everyone's freaking out over here. I mean, if the police get a hold of the wrong information, all of us are in deep trouble."

He wound his hand around the back of his neck. "Could I come by and look through what's left?"

"Well, sure." There was a pause. "Ruby would like that. It's been a while since you two seen each other."

He pushed his fingers into his hair, then told the woman he'd be in touch. He asked her not to say anything to Vick—whoever that was. Then he hung up.

Eden raised her eyebrows.

"That was Angelica. She's a ring girl."

"A *what*?"

"A ring girl. At fights."

She looked at him blankly.

"At the beginning of each round, the ring girl holds up a sign to show everyone what number it is."

"Is it hard to keep track?"

His mouth curved into a ghost of a smile. "Guys like something to look at. She was Yukio's girlfriend. She's the one who found him."

Eden tried to imagine it—walking into an apartment, finding your boyfriend shot through the head.

"If the police took his phone and his computer, it's a long shot. But we can look through any paperwork he has and see if there's something about Mordecai."

"It's better than staring at this sticky note. And it's in the right place. If Mordecai lives in Chicago, my parents are probably there, too." Eden sat down on the couch, pulled her feet up, and sat cross-legged, watching as Cass scooted forward and woke up Dr. Norton's computer by pressing the space bar. The images they'd studied earlier came up on the screen—the color darkest at her brain and spinal cord. She didn't want to look at them. They only made the ticking louder.

She snagged her phone off the table. If she logged into Dr. Norton's Wi-Fi, she could do something normal. Like check her email. She probably had a million from Erik wondering what in the heck was going on, a thought that turned her heart painfully soft inside her chest.

"It's too bad we can't show these to Cleo's mom," Cass said.

Eden's brow furrowed. "Why?"

"It's her area of specialty."

"Nano-robotics?"

"The central nervous system. She's a neurosurgeon."

Eden looked up from her phone. "Cleo's mother is a *neuro-surgeon*?"

"You've probably heard of her."

The furrow in her brow deepened. The general public didn't know many neurosurgeons. Unless … "She's not—you're not talking about … Dr. Beverly Randall-Ransom?"

Cass nodded.

"Wait. She—but you—" Eden closed her mouth. Gave her head a small shake. Dr. Beverly Randall-Ransom was a Nobel Prize winner in medicine. She'd been all over Concordia News for a medical breakthrough that turned a man with paraplegia into a man who could walk again. Erik had written a song about her with his ukulele.

This was the woman who'd taken Cass in when he was eleven? *This* was the woman risking her license for street kids who lived off the grid? Eden tried to make sense of it in her mind. But it was a hard thing to do, especially when she'd been imagining Cleo's mother as a second-rate doctor in some seedy, rundown office. The kind people in desperate situations went to because they had no better option. That kind of a doctor wouldn't mind risking her license on illegals. That kind of a doctor could very well have a daughter who circulated illegal newspapers and owned shirts that said things like *Anarchy* and took on the role of Resident Advisor to help alleviate tuition costs. Never in Eden's wildest imaginings did she picture the sophisticated, highly sought-after professional she'd seen in countless interviews, heard in countless sound bites. Thanks to her father, the news junkie.

Cass seemed slightly entertained by Eden's verbal fumbling.

She gave her head another shake—as if to rattle away the confusion—and opened the settings on her phone. She had the sudden desire to Google the famous neurosurgeon. To look at her picture again in light of this new information. Eden brought up the Wi-Fi networks to click on Dr. Norton's, but something else caught her attention. Something so strange, it pushed all thought of Cleo's mother right out of her head.

"Sex," she said.

Cassian's attention jerked from Norton's computer.

"Look at this." She showed Cass her phone. The list of available networks. Out here in the woods, she expected only one. Instead, there were two. Norton505. And SEX, in all caps. "This was a network back in Cleo's dorm room, remember? And now, somehow, it's here."

It couldn't be a coincidence.

She regarded the folder next to Dr. Norton's computer.

Subject 006.

She took French in high school, but before that, all the way through eighth grade, she'd taken Latin. And in Latin, sex was the number for six.

Her attention caught on Cassian's. And she could see it on his face. He saw the connection, too.

"Do you think I have my own network?"

26

Apparently, Jack Forrester specialized in computer programming and cybersecurity. He could clear a person's phone from a remote location. He'd broken into a government-protected site to change Eden's identity in the system and wipe her parents away altogether. He was no longer smoking cigarettes on the back deck but gathering enough information to hack his way into a highly secure, very sophisticated, password-protected network.

Her own.

It had to be hers.

And it had to be new.

She would have noticed it otherwise, at home whenever storms turned the service spotty. She would have noticed the network while logging back into Pruitt4. Her parents wouldn't have missed it either. Dad would have made some sort of groan-worthy joke—probably in front of Erik—who would have blushed maroon.

But that hadn't been the case.

The first glimpse of it had been in Cleo's dorm room, one day after her mysterious onset of photographic memory. One day after she attacked her parents. One day before she ran twenty miles per hour on a treadmill without trying. All of it proof that she'd been activated—changed in some noticeable way—and despite the fact that there was nothing in her file about networks—no mention of them at all in the notes she'd pored over—she was positive this network had something to do with it.

Maybe once she was activated, the network came online. Or maybe, once the network came online, she was activated. Maybe Mordecai discovered her because he discovered her network. At the end of the day—with the information they had to go on—it was impossible to know, all of it conjecture. But it didn't really matter. What mattered was hacking into it now. If Forrester could do that, they'd have access to vital information—a history's worth of activity and communication.

Unfortunately, hacking required patience. And Forrester proceeded with caution. Aware of the risks involved.

There was a high probability that Mordecai was monitoring her network. They didn't want him to find out they were attempting to break in. If he did, who knew how he might react. This fact alone tied all of Eden's muscles into a million, impossibly tight knots. They needed to find her parents, and they needed to find them now.

The urgency of it pressed against her like a torch pressed against her back.

But what could she do?

They couldn't go to Chicago yet. They couldn't move closer to Mordecai. Not without the safety rail that was the tranquilizer pump. Dr. Norton was working on it now in the basement—a gadget with the ability to render Eden unconscious at the push of a button. All the while Forrester sat hunched over the laptop, typing away, while Cass looked over his shoulder, adding his two cents because he knew his way around networks, too—the tension between them thick.

Eden stood by with nothing to do, so twitchy with helplessness she had to let herself outside into the fresh air. She walked fast—a beeline toward the woods while sunlight squeezed through the leaves and detritus crunched underfoot.

And just as suddenly as she started, she stopped.

Perched on a cluster of milkweed that had sprouted up near the trunk of a large oak was a butterfly—its orange and black patterned wings reminding Eden of the man who dragged her parents into the van.

A monarch.

It lifted off the pink petals, and Eden realized that with a little intentional focus, she could actually hear its wings beating the air. She closed her eyes, taking in the retinue of outdoor noises. Birds and bees and the rustling of leaves, and something else that didn't belong to nature. The clacking of computer keys all the way from inside the house.

Superior sensory processing.

She opened her eyes. Through the green and brown and dappling yellow, she found a spot of bright red—so far away, it was half the size of the butterfly. With the same focus she used to hear, Eden zoomed in with her eyes like a high-powered zoom lens. It worked. Despite the distance, she could see each of the cardinal's feathers in intricate detail.

She peered at a nearby oak, its trunk thick with age. She stepped closer, placed her palms flat against the rough bark, and pushed. She applied steady, even pressure and with a crackling groan, the giant tree shifted like the Leaning Tower of Pisa. Gasping, Eden jerked her hands away. She stared at them with eyes wide, these same hands that almost killed her mother. *Would* have killed her mother, if not for a glitch.

A sour taste bit the back of her tongue.

She stumbled back, then turned around and ran—away from the leaning tree and the cardinal in the distance and the monarch with the flapping wings. She wanted nothing to do with any of it —this evidence of who she was. *Subject 006.* Genetically modified. A weapon of mass destruction. Created by a man who had killed thousands upon thousands of innocent people for no reason other than pure evil. Sadistic pleasure. This was her creator. This was her beginning.

Karik Volkova.

She hurried through the woods, back to the house, no longer wanting the fresh air, but a small, enclosed space—a closet to lock herself inside. Before she could get there, the front door swung open and she nearly collided with Cassian. She inhaled sharply and lurched back, afraid to touch him. Afraid to touch anyone.

He stood in the doorway, scrutinizing her. "Are you okay?"

No.

She wasn't okay.

She was the opposite of okay.

He seemed to study the answer on her face. Then he stepped outside and jerked his head for her to follow. She watched him climb down the steps of the front porch.

"Where are you going?" she called after him.

"Come on," he said, not bothering to look back.

She followed him into the woods, because what else was she going to do? He stopped in a small open patch amongst the trees. He removed a familiar gun from the waist of his jeans. Forrester must have returned it like Dr. Norton had returned Eden's phone. He placed it and his phone on the ground next to a sycamore.

"What are you doing?" she asked.

"Testing your fighting skills."

With the muscles across her chest tightening, she tried to step past him. "No, thank you."

He moved, blocking her way.

"I said, *no thank you.*"

"You stood there while I fought them."

"Who?"

"Forrester and Carlson."

"That's because I didn't—I had no idea … it all happened pretty fast. I didn't know at the time that I could have contributed. And honestly, until you distracted yourself with my wellbeing, you seemed to be handling the situation just fine."

His eyelids drooped, as though bored by her ramblings.

Heat rolled up her neck. "Why are you here?"

"What?"

"Why are you still helping me?"

He opened his mouth.

She cut him off with a lift of her finger. "And don't say it's because you don't like when bad things happen to innocent people. Even if I am *innocent*, Dr. Norton and Jack aren't working with Mordecai. I'm in safe hands now."

"According to who?"

She pulled back her chin. "Are you serious?"

He crossed his arms.

"Dr. Norton was friends with my father. He had my file."

"A file you gave me to read."

"Right."

"Why would you do that?"

She stared at him dumbly, unsure where he was going.

"You said it yourself. You hardly know me."

"So?"

"So you shouldn't be so quick to trust people you don't know."

"If you were going to stay, you deserved to know what you were staying with."

"Who."

"What?"

"*Who* I was staying with. You're not a *what*."

Eden frowned, no longer sure.

Cass exhaled a frustrated breath, then ran his hand down the length of his face. "We're going to Chicago to find a highly dangerous man who has your parents."

"I know."

"You don't think some training would come in handy?"

"I don't want to give myself any more ammunition than I already have."

He quirked his eyebrow.

"I'm the highly dangerous one here. Created by an evil monster who wanted to use me as some kind of weapon."

"Then be a weapon. And use it against him." Without warning, Cass spun so fast Eden didn't have time to register what was happening. One second the heel of his boot rushed toward her face in an expertly executed roundhouse kick, and the next, she was catching his boot in her hand, stopping its momentum in mid-air.

Their eyes caught and held, the small space between them stirring with heat.

Her chest rose and fell, half-shocked, half-angry at his audacity. She shoved his foot to the ground. "What if I wouldn't have caught that?"

"But you did." Then he came at her again, giving her no time to think.

He was crazy fast. Agile and strong.

But somehow, she was faster. And stronger.

She dodged every punch. Blocked every kick. Then she caught his fist the same way he'd caught Forrester's—like watching the move once had taught her everything she needed to know. She spun around and threw him over her shoulder.

He landed hard on his back—a trained fighter, a dangerous weapon in his own right—and instead of looking intimidated or embarrassed or angry at being bested by a girl, his eyes were bright and magnetic—filled with a world's worth of intensity.

With a shaky inhale, she took a step back and tugged on her shirt, and then quite suddenly, remembered the injury beneath his. She crouched down in front of him. "Are you okay?"

"I'm fine." He showed her the clean bandage, and by default, his tan skin around the bandage. No blood. She hadn't opened anything up by tossing him over her shoulder. Cassian sat upright and draped his elbows over his knees, the back of his hair ruffled. "Now let's see how you shoot."

He broke down the different parts of his gun. He showed her how to take it apart and put it back together again. How to load and unload the magazine. How to turn off the safety. He showed her how to hold it properly, how to aim, and how to brace her body against the kick. Then he brought her to the center of the clearing and pointed to a far tree overgrown with ivy.

"Do you see that bare spot of bark in the middle?"

She nodded.

"Hit it."

She pressed her lips together, his command irritating. Part of her wanted to miss on purpose, just to show him he wasn't her boss. The other part of her wanted to hit the target dead in its center.

He moved behind her.

Her breath caught as his hand touched her waist.

A flush rose from the spot as she hugged the cool metal between her palms, straightened her arms, and extended the gun in front of her.

He guided them a fraction of an inch upward.

She swallowed, unable to concentrate. Not with him so close behind her, the definition of his taut muscles making her skin hot. Awakening her senses. She could feel all 98.6 degrees of his heat. She could smell the cotton of his shirt, the musk of his deodorant. The mint of his toothpaste as he brought his lips next to her ear.

"Focus on the target," he said.

She squeezed her eyes shut, commanded the unsteadiness from her arms, the tremble from her breath. Then she peered at the target and pulled the trigger.

There was a loud burst of noise that made her ears ring. An explosion of power between her palms. A hint of a kick that didn't faze her like it probably should have. And a bullet hole, dead center in the bald patch of bark on the faraway tree.

She turned around, adrenaline coursing.

"Nice shot," he said, his attention dipping to her mouth.

Her gaze ran along the strong line of his jaw, then settled on his full bottom lip, the oxygen in her lungs catching fire. He smelled like leather and pine and peppermint.

He leaned closer. Infinitesimally so. But she noticed all the same. And with the noticing came an overwhelming desire that tingled in her wrists, buzzed through her fingers. She wanted to grab him by his shirt and pull him to her until the space between them combusted, until there wasn't any of it at all. Not the space. Not the truth. Not the file or Dr. Norton's cabin or her missing parents. Just this guy who screamed danger. A hardened fighter who seemed impossible to break. Even by someone like her.

Judging by the look in his eye, he wanted to be pulled.

But the sound of her name sliced through the moment.

A call that cut through her thundering heartbeat. She stepped back, away from Cassian and his smoldering eyes. She tucked a loose strand of hair behind her ear and looked toward the cabin.

Dr. Norton stood on his front porch.

He spotted them in the clearing and held up a small device in his hand.

27

Cass leaned against the wall, watching as Eden tore open an alcohol prep pad. She unfolded the wet wipe, lifted her shirt, and cleaned a circular patch of bare skin to the left of her navel.

He looked away.

Eden was not the first attractive girl to come into his life. He'd known his share of attractive girls. Attraction and desire were familiar emotions. Safe emotions. Non-irritating emotions. But the strange something brewing underneath? It wasn't safe. It wasn't familiar. And it wasn't welcome.

He stayed to help her find her parents.

He stayed to undo the damage he'd done so he could walk away with a clear conscience.

That was it.

Dr. Norton showed Eden how to attach the device to her body. The pump was connected to an infusion set—a tube attached to a cannula and a needle. He showed her how to load the tranquilizer, how to prime the tubing, how to insert the needle into the cannula. Then he had her peel off the sticky back and press it against the area she cleaned with the alcohol pad.

"It's spring-loaded," he said. "All you have to do is squeeze these two side buttons."

She squeezed.

The loaded spring released a quick burst of noise like air being shot from a Nerf gun. Eden didn't even flinch. She removed the part with the spring and attached the tubing.

"You did that easily," Norton said.

"My best friend's little sister has diabetes. I've seen her do it a lot." She clipped the pump to her pant waist.

Norton invited her to lie on the medical table.

She hesitated.

Cass didn't blame her.

Once Norton activated that pump with the sleek remote in his hand, she would lose all control. All awareness. Cass would resent such a precautionary measure for himself. He resented it for her. But then—according to that file, according to the footage he'd deleted from his phone—if she didn't do it, she would still lose all control, all awareness. Only instead of lying docile on some medical table, she'd be overtaken. Virtually possessed by a good-for-nothing man named Mordecai. And that was a reality she would doggedly fight. By relinquishing her control to the good side, she was taking it from the bad.

It was an exercise in trust. An exercise in faith. Two things Cass had very little of. Two things Eden Pruitt seemed to have in spades.

"How long will this put me under?" she asked.

"We won't know until we test it."

She climbed onto the table, her eyes—those gray, green, blue eyes—meeting his, and the strange something he'd been shoving down since carrying her to bed last night crackled to life.

"Are you ready?" the doctor asked, holding up the remote.

With her mouth setting in a resolved line, she gave Norton a singular, determined nod.

He pressed the button.

There was a soft beep.

Her eyes went cloudy and faraway. Then they closed and she slumped over on the table.

———

Two hours in, she remained unconscious, and Forrester was still gathering information. Cass stood on the back deck, white knuckling the railing as clouds rolled in from the east and the sun sank in the west.

The door slid open behind him.

He glanced over his shoulder.

Norton came out holding a plate with a sandwich.

"You should eat something," he said, settling into the same Adirondack chair Eden had fallen asleep in the night before.

Cass didn't feel particularly hungry.

The doctor ate behind him as the birds chirped in the trees and Cassian's grip on the railing tightened. He'd had two hours to brood. Two hours to think. While Eden gave over her control, he was grappling with his own. If Mordecai found a way to control Eden while they were looking through Yukio's stuff—if they were ambushed like Forrester and Carlson had ambushed them in the parking garage—the tranquilizer pump would do very little. They'd kill Cass, take Eden, wait until her body burned through the tranquilizer, and then they'd move along with their plans, whatever those plans were. If he wanted to prevent such a fate for her, he would have to master his own. He would have to make sure they didn't kill him.

No pressure, Cass.

He turned around and leaned his back against the railing. This tranquilizer pump didn't fix the problem. Cass wanted to fix it. "You said you can't do an extraction."

"Not without killing her."

"Maybe it's time to let another doctor take a look."

Norton looked at him placatingly, like Cass was a small child offering up a simplistic solution for a problem that was the opposite of simplistic, like world hunger. "Do you happen to know a good one?"

Yes, in fact. He did. "Cleo's mother. Beverly Randall-Ransom."

The man didn't sputter. He didn't fumble over his words like Eden had earlier. But the patronizing expression on his face slid completely away. Cass was no longer the naive child, but a valuable cohort with legitimate ideas. He had Norton's undivided attention. "The young lady Roger's been keeping an eye on. That's Beverly Randall-Ransom's daughter?"

Cass nodded.

Norton stroked his mustache, peering out at the orange sunset.

"She lives in Chicago. Logistically, it makes more sense for us to be in Chicago. Cleo's already involved. Honestly, it'd probably be safer to involve her more."

"How do you figure?"

"Right now, she knows enough to be dangerous. I'm sure she's digging. Who knows what she'll uncover on her own." And what she'd do with it once she did. Cassian had visions of *The People's Press* and a myriad of outlandish headlines. He told her to tell no one, but Cleo didn't take orders any better than he did.

"This is a rather unusual thing to drop on someone's lap," Norton said. "Not to mention highly sensitive."

"She's a doctor. Confidentiality is her middle name. And from personal experience I can tell you, she's well acquainted with the unusual."

———

D r. Beverly Randall-Ransom lived in an 1894 George Maher designed mansion on the Gold Coast of Chicago. All of it was exquisite—the lush landscaping on the oversized lot, the limestone facade, the large sweeping rooms with cathedral ceilings, the roof deck with a garden and a swimming pool and a stunning view of Lake Michigan.

It was the kind of home photographed in magazines, fit for a woman of Beverly Randall-Ransom's caliber—tall and beautiful with an air of unmistakable prestige, a combination that made her presence almost queen-like. She was rich and powerful, living in a home meant for the rich and powerful. And yet Eden knew from Cassian's story that this notable woman welcomed the sick and abused. This opulent house sheltered people living off the grid.

Eden stepped inside the grand foyer where a life-sized portrait of the Randall-Ransoms hung. In it, a young Cleo with a baby-toothed smile and beads in her hair stood between her mother and her father, a white man Eden had seen in photographs. He was killed by a drunk driver over a decade ago, which made the recent surgery his widowed wife performed all the more touching. She'd lost her husband to a drunk driver only to restore a drunk driver's ability to walk after being paralyzed in an accident. It was a story of grace and forgiveness and unde-served second chances. According to Erik, there was already a bidding war over the movie rights.

As Eden walked into the lavishly decorated great room, she tried to imagine eleven-year-old Cassian doing the same. But it was impossible. She couldn't picture him any other way than what he was—strong and brooding and calculatingly observant —even when he allowed the famous doctor to wrap him in a hug.

"Cleo's on her way home now," she said. "Be prepared for a full inquisition."

After brief introductions in which the doctor studied Eden with a look of keen interest, Beverly Randall-Ransom gave them an official tour. Eden got the sense that it was much less about pride in her home—although it was certainly worthy of pride— as it was about practicality. The house was one a person could get lost in. Four whole stories with a guest bedroom on the main level, three on the second, Cleo's room and the master suite on the third, another bedroom on the fourth, and an eighth for extra measure in the basement.

When finished, she turned to Cassian. "I understand you have some business to attend to?"

He nodded.

"Excellent." Her attention shifted to Eden—the interest sparkling in her eyes still very much there. "I look forward to learning more about you soon. I'll send Milly to get you settled."

Her heels clicked on the hardwood as she left them to it.

"What does she know about me already?" Eden asked.

"She knows that we're in need of help," Dr. Norton said.

"And nanotechnology is involved," Cassian added as Milly found them—a Bulgarian housekeeper who greeted Cass with the same warm familiarity as Dr. Beverly Randall-Ransom, only instead of hugging she squeezed his hands. Afterward, he headed downstairs to the basement bedroom while Milly led Jack and Dr. Norton to the second floor. Eden took the one on the fourth.

She had nothing to unpack—no personal items, no clothing. But that didn't seem to matter. Clothes filled the closet—Cleo's perhaps?—and the bathroom was fully stocked with all the necessary essentials and more. Eden sat on the edge of the queen-sized bed, her tranquilizer pump jostling ever so slightly. Under any other circumstances, this would be a delight. A treat. A wonderful, magical getaway from middle-class suburbia. Instead—with the inescapable image of her parents locked in a cold, dank dungeon—all the lavishness made the situation feel extra dire.

She was anxious to get to Angelica's. To search for the bread-crumbs that might lead them to Mordecai. When they got back, she would let the famous neurosurgeon poke and prod and inspect on the off chance she might be able to do what Dr. Norton and her father couldn't—find a way to successfully extract the enemies inside her. Eden searched through the closet and picked out a pair of jeans and a fitted tee, much less conspicuous than the oversized sweatpants and stiff cotton shirt she'd been donning since Saturday. She did a quick reflection check to make sure she looked normal, then descended four flights of stairs and waited for Cass in the entryway.

Outside, they climbed into a black Rolls Royce with an extended cab. The Ransoms had a personal driver named Sam who would take them wherever they needed to go.

Eden pulled the seatbelt across her lap and clicked it into place. "I can't believe I'm inside Dr. Beverly Randall-Ransom's car."

Cassian looked at her with one corner of his mouth quirked.

She brushed her finger under her nose self-consciously, worried she had something on her face. "What?"

"You keep using her full name."

"I'm not going to call her Beverly."

"Why not?"

"She is arguably the most brilliant mind of our time." *He might be on a first name basis with the woman. Eden certainly wasn't.*

"You could call her Dr. Ransom."

She wrinkled her nose. Somehow, that felt as irreverent as *Beverly*. Like greeting the pope with a fist bump.

He shook his head in an amused sort of way, then looked out his window.

Eden looked out her own.

After The Attack, droves of east coast survivors flocked inland searching for something familiar. They made the windy city their home, doubling its size, turning it into the largest in the country. Outside the quiet of their car, the world was loud, bustling and crowded. Honking horns, pedestrians hailing cabs, street vendors selling hotdogs and lottery tickets for the Prosperity Ball, and advertisements everywhere—on trains, on city buses, on digital, brightly-lit billboards. They promoted everything from dental care to virtual reality on Broadway to campaign ads against domestic violence to luxury hotels like The Sapphire, where the ball would take place in several weeks.

Gradually, the flashiness and the glamor faded, deteriorating the further south they drove, until the street vendors turned shady, and bars cropped up on storefront windows and the billboards disappeared altogether and the Rolls Royce stuck out like a sore thumb.

Angelica was staying with a girl named Ruby on the south side.

This was where they were headed, and it struck Eden—as the world morphed from glitz to glum—that this was Cassian's city, too.

"Where do you live?" she asked, interrupting the long stretch of silence between them.

"I have a place nearby."

"Do you think it's being watched?"

"Probably."

"Then if this fails—if we don't find anything about Mordecai —we should make an appearance. Let him know we're here."

"We should probably let Beverly examine you first, don't you think?"

She touched the tranquilizer pump, a Band-Aid when she needed surgery. He was right. As much as she wanted to run headlong into danger so she could rescue her parents, they needed to find a way to keep Mordecai from controlling her. Not just temporarily, but forever. Her fate lay with Dr. Beverly Randall-Ransom. Or Jack Forrester if he could ever hack into her network.

They drove beneath an overpass.

In the brief patch of dark, she peeked at Cassian, her attention traveling the length of his profile, and she was struck with the strong desire to know something significant—something meaningful and true—about this young man who ran in the same circles with criminals like Yukio and Mordecai. This off-the-grid fighter who was on a first-name basis with the most prestigious doctor in the United States. More than a first-name basis. Dr. Beverly Randall-Ransom had hugged him like a mother.

Eden shifted in her seat. "Cleo told me her mom took you in for a while. When you were younger?"

The words made his countenance darken, like storm clouds rolling across the sky.

"She said you were in rough shape and her mom nursed you back to health. That's how the two of you met." Eden captured her bottom lip between her teeth, waiting for a response. He gave her nothing, which only made her more determined to squeeze something out. "What about your mom? Is she—?"

"She's dead." His interruption came curtly. Coldly. With zero emotion.

Eden wasn't fooled. She saw what he was trying to hide. Past the grim set of his mouth and the steady tic of his jaw—buried pain.

"I'm sorry," she said.

"You're not the one who killed her."

Killed.

The potent word came like a thunderclap.

Someone had *killed* Cassian's mother.

She pressed her lips together so as not to repeat the apology. He obviously didn't want it. "My brother's dead."

Her cheeks caught fire the second the confession tumbled out.

What a stupid thing to say.

But Cassian looked at her, and when she looked back, the storm in his eyes had settled into something softer. "Christopher."

Hearing Cass say his name did something strange to her insides. She nodded. "I never met him. He died before I was …"

"Before you were what?"

Born.

But the word stuck in her throat. Christopher had been born.

Eden had been ... what, exactly? Created. Not by two loving parents, but by the world's most infamous villain. A mass murderer. Eden hadn't been placed in her mother's arms in a hospital room. She'd been manufactured in a terrorist's laboratory. She bit the inside of her cheek and looked out the window. "He was two years old. He had really bad asthma. They ran out of medicine when the country was still in lockdown. It was right after The Attack."

She could sense his attention. He was listening carefully.

"When I was younger, I used to spend nights thinking in my bed, imagining what it might be like to have a real big brother instead of a ghost. Someone to play with, talk with, fight with. Share the attention with." She exhaled a puff of breath. "In all my imaginings, I was still there, you know? I was always part of the family. Christopher was the transient one."

It turned out, Christopher was the sure thing.

Eden was transient.

She looked at Cassian.

He stared back at her like her words were riveting. Like the ache they carved in her chest carved something in his, too.

"If what I imagined had been true. If Christopher wouldn't have died ..." She shook her head. "I never would have been there at all."

28

den followed Cassian to the front door of a rundown apartment complex. By the looks of it, the entrance had several bolts once upon a time, but those bolts were now rusted over and broken. She glanced over her shoulder, toward the parked Rolls Royce. Seeing it there reminded her of those primary school worksheets teachers liked to hand out for busy work. *Circle the item that doesn't belong.* Certainly, the Rolls Royce.

The hinges groaned as they stepped into a hallway that smelled like mothballs and cat pee. Cass obviously knew where he was going. Slipping the remote Dr. Norton gave him into his back pocket, he strode down the length of the corridor, past elevator doors with an out-of-order sign, up two flights in a stairwell that smelled even worse than the hallway and stopped in front of apartment number 317.

Cass knocked.

Almost immediately, the door swung open, and the thick smell of cigarette smoke wafted out to greet them.

So did a woman—skinny as a rail with a chest that didn't match. She had platinum blonde hair with dark roots. The tip of her nose was red and except for smudges of black beneath her bloodshot eyes, her mascara had run away. She greeted Cass with an overly bright smile, and then surprise at the sight of Eden. He probably hadn't told her he was bringing a guest.

"Angelica, this is Eden. Eden, Angelica."

A flicker of recognition crossed Angelica's face.

"We've met before." She dropped the R at the end of the word, her east coast accent every bit as thick as it had been over the phone, her voice every bit as nasally.

"I … don't think so."

"Are you sure? Your face is so familiar." She held up her hands, her long nails shellacked in bubblegum pink. "I swear, I'm having one of them déjà vu's."

Unsure how else to respond, Eden shrugged.

"Well, a friend of Cass is a friend of mine." Angelica wrapped Eden in a sudden, unexpected, slightly desperate hug. It was like being wrapped in an ashtray. Her skimpy outfit reeked of cigarettes.

"Come on in," she said when she let Eden go. "Ruby's in the shower."

They stepped inside a living room crammed with furniture and a jumble of boxes shoved into one corner, reminding Eden of her ransacked house back in Eagle Bend. Only none of these boxes were torn.

"It ain't fancy like Yuke's place." Her voice caught over the name. She used the crumpled tissue in her hand to wipe her nose. "He lived in a penthouse on eighth. Didn't think he had so much stuff until we had to cram it in here. The landlord said we had to take all of it. Phone's been ringing off the hook. People wanting to know what the cops got."

She kicked a short filing cabinet in front of her. "This could get all of us into some trouble, you know? But they didn't touch Yuke's files. They took part of the carpet though, where the blood was."

Her eyes welled. She blotted them with the tissue.

Cass's attention wandered around the room—from item to item, as if taking inventory. "Did he leave you with any money?"

Angelica sniffled. Underneath the thick layer of make-up, Eden thought she was probably younger than she appeared. Not much older than Eden herself. "That's goin' to his cousin. A banker on the north side. He ain't want nothing to do with Yuke or his lifestyle when he was living, but he has no problem taking his money now that he's dead. I'd try making one of them appeals if I could, but ain't no fancy pants lawyer gonna work for free."

Cass rubbed his jaw.

Angelica batted her hand in the air. "I'll be fine. We got the money we made from his furniture. Ruby's letting me stay here for a while. We'll sell whatever else we can and burn all the files once you're done looking."

Something in the room went quieter.

A noise had stopped—the shower.

"What are you looking for anyway?"

Cass and Eden answered at the same time.

While he said a vague 'Client information', Eden got right to the point.

"Mordecai."

He shot her a look.

Eden didn't back down. Her parents were taken on Thursday. It was Monday. They didn't have time for vague. "Did he ever talk to you about a man by that name?"

"Was he one of Yuke's clients?"

Eden nodded.

Angelica shook her head. "He ain't ever talk to me about his clients."

The door to the bathroom opened behind them. A woman stepped out in a revealing bathrobe with curves more natural than Angelica's, her lips already formed into a sensual pout as she set her sights on Cass. She looked like a hungry cat, a visual that brought to mind Angelica's words when they'd spoken on the phone.

Ruby would like that. It's been a while since you two seen each other.

Eden had a feeling the two had done more than *see* each other, given Ruby's glare when Cassian introduced them.

"We won't stay long," he said, a comment that only seemed to exacerbate Ruby's irritation. Then he got to work, looking through the files.

Eden joined.

Ruby excused herself to get dressed.

While Eden and Cass searched the boxes, Angelica paced like an addict in need of a fix.

Maybe she was.

"I need to step outside for a smoke," she finally said. "Ruby don't allow it in here."

One point for Ruby.

Angelica paused in front of the window. "I swear, you're familiar."

Eden shrugged again. Because no, she wasn't. In fact, if Yukio were alive and taking bets, Eden would put everything she owned on the fact that her path and Angelica's path had never come close to crossing until this moment right now.

With a shrug of her own, Angelica climbed out onto the fire escape.

Ruby returned—her face carefully done, her outfit every bit as revealing as the robe. She was beautiful, her movements pointedly seductive as she sat on the couch, set her elbow on the armrest, and crossed one long, lithe leg over the other. If her eyes were a predator and Cassian the prey, they were currently eating him for lunch.

He set another box on the already overcrowded coffee table, favoring his left side.

"Are you hurt?" Ruby said.

"I'm fine."

She uncrossed and recrossed her legs—as if trying to pull his attention to them. And for reasons that were probably very stupid, Eden felt incredibly annoyed by all of it. Ruby glanced out the window at smoking Angelica. "Vick won't stop bothering her, you know."

This worked.

She finally had Cass's attention. "What do you mean?"

"He keeps coming by to ask about you."

"Did she tell him I was coming here?"

"She said you didn't want her to say anything."

"I don't."

Eden sat back on her heels. She'd just gone through the last file. All of them had been in alphabetical order, according to first name. Like Mordecai, the majority of Yukio's gamblers didn't have a last name. When she didn't find Mordecai in the M's, she thumbed through the labels on each tab to see if his had been misplaced. But it was nowhere. And why would it be? If Mordecai went to Yukio's apartment to murder him, it made sense that he would have taken his own file. He wouldn't want his information accessible to the cops.

"You know why he's coming around," Ruby said.

"Do I?"

"He wants you back. He's hungry for it. We all are."

Cass scratched the back of his head as he surveyed the room, as if realizing the same thing as Eden. There were no more boxes to look through. This whole thing had been a fool's errand.

"It's been a long enough break," Ruby continued.

"It's not a break," he said.

"You can't quit, Cass. And you have nothing to feel bad about."

This produced a strong reaction. Eden could see it in the tense set of his jaw, the flint-like hardness in his eyes. "I wonder if you'd say the same thing had the tables been turned."

"The tables would never be turned. You're too good." Ruby

practically crooned the words. "Definitely too good to be doing side jobs for a bookie."

Side jobs?

The window opened.

Angelica climbed inside. "I got it!"

They turned to look at her.

"I know why your face is so familiar."

Eden raised her eyebrows.

"You're one of the girls."

"One of the girls?"

"Yeah. One of them girls Yuke was looking for."

"*Yukio* was looking?" Eden's brow furrowed. "You mean Mordecai?"

"No, Yuke. He had a picture of you on his desk. I wanted to know. I mean, what girl likes finding pictures of beautiful women in her boyfriend's stuff? He said it was nothing. Work related." Angelica made her way through the jumble of furniture, toward a desk. She opened the top drawer. "I knew it. Here they are."

She pulled out two photographs and stepped over a few boxes to hold them up.

Eden took them—one in each hand—staring curiously, as if time were suspended. The picture was her. It had to be her. Like a flattering mug shot—only not the one she'd posed for. And something was ever so subtly off. The bridge of her nose, maybe? The arch of her eyebrows? She looked at the other photograph. A girl her age, with wavy, auburn hair.

Like Angelica, the picture gave Eden a strong sense of déjà vu.

She knew this face. Somehow. From somewhere.

"Cass must have found ya," Angelica said.

Eden's attention jerked up.

Clarity came crashing in like a wave.

All of it clicked into place.

Cass, following her.

Cass, taking side jobs for Yukio.

The photographs in Eden's hand.

She shook her head. Took a step back toward the door. Mordecai the Gambler hired Yukio the Bookie who hired *Cass* to find her. The shocking and obvious truth of it had her taking another step back. Cassian was hired by the very people who had taken her parents.

"Eden," he said, his voice low. Even.

Her stomach flooded with nausea and contempt as she turned on her heel and left the apartment. When she got a flight and a half down the stairwell, she heard the door open and shut behind her. He was following her down, hurrying after her. He didn't catch up until she stepped outside into the muggy air.

"Wait." He grabbed her elbow.

She wheeled around, yanking her arm away. She held up the pictures, nostrils flaring. The nausea in her stomach rolling. *"Side jobs for Yukio?"*

He looked at her, his mouth set in a hard line.

"It was you." The scrambling device in her ear was fine. It hadn't malfunctioned. They must have found her some other way. Dr. Norton had said so himself. Well, here was the other way—this boy who pretended to care about her safety when he was the one who put that safety in such jeopardy. "He hired you to find me."

He didn't deny it. He didn't even have the audacity to look regretful. He just looked the same way he had in the coffee shop back in Eagle Bend—angry.

Which made her own anger surge. "Did he also hire you to keep tabs on me until he fixes whatever went haywire? Is that why you're still here?"

"No."

She waited for more. An explanation. An apology. Anything that might quell this hot, visceral betrayal bubbling inside of her.

He dragged his hand down his face. "I stopped working for him two and a half weeks ago."

"After you gave him my location?"

He nodded, his expression grim.

A mirthless laugh tumbled up her throat. "Do you know where he is?"

"I would tell you if I did."

"Just like you told me this?" She crumpled the photographs and threw them in his face.

They fell to the ground at his feet.

"Why?" she demanded, her voice a tremble of rage. Why would he find her for Mordecai, only to help her get away? It didn't make any sense.

"I owed Yukio money."

"You owed him money?" That was it? He'd turned her entire life upside down and inside out because of some debt? She stared, waiting for him to elaborate. When he didn't, the tremble went seismic. "He has my parents because of *you*. He activated me because of *you*. You've been lying to me this whole time. Lying, just like they were lying!" Her voice cracked over *they*.

Her parents.

Liars. All of them.

His flint-like expression softened with what—pity?

She didn't want it.

She didn't want any of it.

He took a step toward her.

Eden held up her hands and backed away, glaring with the full force of her outrage. "Don't. Don't ever come near me again."

She turned around and stalked to the car. Away from him.

Cassian, the betrayer.

29

As soon as Beverly's car drove away, Cass kicked the crumpled pictures and swore. So loud, a bedraggled man digging through a garbage can on the street corner came up for air to gawk.

Cass picked up the photographs and uncrumpled them. He blinked down at Eden's face. An age progression photo. Something he hadn't known at the time but had pieced together recently. If Mordecai had once ran in the same circles as Karik Volkova—if he knew about this failed experiment—then he wouldn't have a recent photo of Eden. All he'd have was a photograph of 18-month-old Eden. He looked down at the face of the other girl—the one he never found. He set his hand on top of his head and fisted his hair, staring at the back end of the shrinking Rolls Royce.

He was just doing a job. Yes, there had been red flags. He wasn't denying that. But if he wouldn't have done it, Yukio would have hired someone else. The girls would have been found. Maybe not as quickly, but eventually. And when he'd accepted the job, Eden was nothing more than a pretty face on a screen. All he'd cared about then was paying his debt and leaving the past behind.

The baggage.

The anger.

The monster he saw in the mirror.

The ghosts that haunted him in this infernal city.

Then he found her mug shot. He gave Yukio her location, then he went to San Diego to see if she might lead him to the other one. The auburn-haired girl he hadn't yet found. The red flags started to wave. What did Yukio want with a girl like Eden Pruitt? It was a question he demanded over the phone after Eden left the nursing home. It was a question Yukio refused to answer.

"Just find the other one," he'd said.

Cass had ground his teeth. This wasn't part of the job description. He found people who owed Yukio money. Not girls who were still in high school with two loving parents.

"Listen," Yukio had said, "if you start asking questions, you're gonna get yourself on the wrong side of trouble. You don't want to cross this guy."

"What guy?" Cass had spat.

There was a pause, and then, "One of the biggest gamblers around."

"Mordecai?"

Yukio's silence had been all the confirmation he'd needed. It was the last time Cass spoke with him. After he hung up, after he raged at the sky, he'd had every intention of disappearing. Forget the other girl. He was out. But then Eden and her father stepped outside their front door in San Diego carrying boxes. Her father had a stack of three. The top one tipped. He made a failed attempt to save it and all three came tumbling down. Eden had laughed, and Cass had braced himself, waiting for the man's wrath. Kids shouldn't laugh at their fathers' mistakes. Instead, he joined her. They laughed together, like he and his mom used to laugh together. Before his father found them. Before his father *hired* someone to find them.

Just like Cass had been hired to find her.

The door opened behind him.

A bashful Angelica peeked her head outside. "I'm sorry, Cass. I didn't mean to cause no trouble."

"It's fine," he said, his words clipped.

He crumpled the pictures into his fist, then turned and walked away.

"Where you goin'?" Angelica called.

Cass didn't answer.

And Cass didn't stop.

He walked with a long, angry stride, needing to vent the steam building inside of him.

Don't ever come near me again.

It was a clear directive. A line he would not cross.

She did for him what he should have done for himself a long time ago.

She'd taken him out of the equation.

So why was he so angry? Wasn't that what he'd wanted—to walk away, unencumbered? Hadn't he resented the fact that he was sticking around to watch after her? He'd put her in danger, but he'd helped her get out of it. Sure, he hadn't helped her find her parents like he'd wanted. But he couldn't have it all, could he? Now he could pack up his stuff and go. Forget about her. Forget about her laughter. Forget about the way she touched him when she tended his wound. Forget about her mom and dad. Forget about what he'd done.

Cassian spit.

The steam continued to build.

And he was being followed.

He could feel it acutely.

The muscles in his back went taut. His fists clenched at his sides.

He vowed never to get back into the ring, but if this was one of Mordecai's men, he would gladly welcome a fight. Cass turned down an alleyway. He walked to the end of it, waited a beat or two, then turned around.

It was his weasel of a manager.

Disappointment grabbed him. Vick might train fighters, but he'd never been in the ring. If it was a fight Cass craved, the man would offer him little satisfaction.

"What do you want?" Cass asked.

Vick's nose twitched nervously. Give him whiskers and a tail and he might as well be a rat. "Where's the girl?"

Cass took an aggressive step forward, glaring down at the man who'd taken a lost and angry twelve-year old kid and turned him into a weapon. "What do you want with her?"

"Mordecai paid me a visit."

"Where is he?"

"Looks like you got yourself into some trouble. I knew you would."

Cass grabbed Vick by the collar and lifted him off the ground. "Tell me where he is."

His beady eyes filled with fear and alarm as he clutched at Cass's hands, dangling precariously. "I don't know. I swear."

"Then why are you here?"

"To deliver something."

"*What?*"

"Put me down and I'll give it to you."

Cass dropped him, pushed him away.

Vick stumbled, nearly tripping over his own feet. When he recovered, he pulled a phone from his pocket and tossed it to Cass, like he didn't want to come any closer.

"If she wants her parents to stay alive, she better answer when he calls."

———

Eden walked into the mansion-of-a-house feeling numb. Wrung out and wrung dry.

"Hey, stranger!" It was Cleo—same hairstyle, same snakebite lip piercing, new graphic tee—standing halfway down the steps with a partially-eaten banana in her hand. She must have arrived home while they'd been out. "I have about a hundred million questions, and I need you to answer all of them. Where's Cass?"

"I don't know."

Cleo came down the rest of the steps with a crinkle in her brow. "What do you mean you don't know?"

A door opened. The bathroom off the foyer.

Jack Forrester stepped out.

And realization dawned for the second time.

The girl.

The familiar redhead in the photograph. Eden recognized her because she'd seen her before, in another picture. Inside Forrester's home the morning she woke up in the strange room. A girl's room. *This* was why he was helping. Not out of good will. Not because he was friends with her father and felt indebted to him for some good thing Dad had done long ago. But because Jack Forrester had skin in the game. Living, breathing skin.

"You have a daughter," Eden said.

He froze, so obviously caught.

"Her name is Ellery." They had turned Eden into someone real. It made sense. It probably took no time at all to switch out Ellery's fingerprints and retinas for Eden's, to swap their photos. Add the bit about the traumatic brain injury and voilà. "That's why you're helping. You have a daughter, and she's like me."

Jack's attention slid uneasily to Cleo.

It made Eden want to scream. To rant and rail until the walls of this giant house came tumbling down. She was sick—*so sick*—of the secrets and lying and being left in the dark. With her jaw clenched, she marched into the great room where the two doctors conferred.

"You said my father destroyed them."

Dr. Norton looked up from his laptop, from the images he was showing Dr. Beverly Randall-Ransom.

"You said it was the worst thing he ever had to do. But it

wasn't true. He didn't destroy them." She jabbed her thumb toward the man behind her, the man who had gone from enemy to ally. The man she still didn't like being around, because her body was quick to remember what her brain had forgiven. "His daughter is one of them."

Dr. Norton gave Eden the same look he'd given her after she'd sliced her hand open and watched it heal before her eyes. One of apology and resignation. "He did destroy them. The first two. After that, he couldn't continue."

The first two.

Which meant …

There were four of them.

Her mind spun. It spun in dizzying circles. There were three others just like her. "Why would you keep this from me? Where are they? Where is *she*?"

"She's with her mother," Jack said.

Annette Forrester.

"Where?"

"Somewhere safe. Far away from here." Jack's attention flitted from Cleo to Dr. Ransom, his face strained and pale. "That's all anyone needs to know."

"As soon as your parents hit the alarm," Dr. Norton said. "I called Jack. I needed to make sure Ellery was okay. That whatever had happened to you wasn't happening to her. Once it was clear that they were fine, they sent Ellery away, on the first flight out of town. And then they worked on getting you safe, too."

"Why keep that from me? Why not just tell me the truth?"

"Because you brought the boy with you." Jack nearly yelled. He wasn't pleased that Cass had been a part of the picture. "We weren't going to tell you about her. Not when you were sharing everything with him."

Eden wanted to argue. But she couldn't.

Jack Forrester's intuition had been stronger than hers. He'd been right to keep it secret. She'd brought in the very boy who'd been hired to find her. Ellery and Eden. He found Eden, but not Ellery. Ellery was safe. Ellery's parents were safe. Worried sick, obviously. But safe. Eden was not. Her parents were not. If Jack would have said something, maybe Cassian would have used it. Maybe he would have finished the job they'd paid him to do.

"Where is he?" Jack asked, as if suddenly registering Cass's absence. "How did you find out about Elle?"

"He had a picture," Eden said, her voice small, faraway.

"What?"

"In Yukio's stuff. There were two pictures. One of me, and one of her. I recognized her from a photograph at your house. Yukio hired Cassian to find us."

Jack's eyes went wide. "Where's the photograph?"

She'd crumpled it up. She'd tossed it at Cass's feet. Was it still there, on the street? If someone picked it up, could it somehow put Ellery in danger?

"Eden, where is the photograph?" he asked again, his tone filled with urgency.

"I—I don't know."

"Does he still have it?"

"I'm not sure. I mean …" Yes, he did. She'd thrown it at him. "I don't know."

Jack swore under his breath. "He knows our location."

"He's not going to rat you out." The confident declaration belonged to Cleo, who'd been listening to the entire exchange. Cleo and her mother, both.

"He gave Mordecai my location, Cleo. Because of him, my parents might be dead." But even as Eden said it—even as she cast the net of blame upon the boy who'd brought this on her doorstep—it offered little relief. Ultimately, no matter how much anger she felt, her parents were in the situation they were in because of what Eden was.

"He must have realized his mistake."

Eden shook her head, closed her eyes. When she opened them again, she turned to Dr. Norton. "If my father only destroyed two, then that means there are two more out there like me and Ellery. Where are they?"

There was a pause. One Eden had no patience for.

"Where are they?" she demanded.

"We lost them."

"What do you mean, *you lost them*?"

"Their parents fell out of contact. By the time your father heard rumors of weaponized humans, we no longer knew how to reach them. We searched, Eden. But they made a point to disappear."

"So, they don't have scrambling devices?"

Dr. Norton shook his head.

"But Ellery does?"

"Of course," Jack said. "We had hers inserted right away."

For the first time, Eden saw him for what he was. A worried-to-death father, desperate to keep his daughter safe. Sympathy swelled inside of her as she turned back to Dr. Norton. "Do you think Mordecai has the other two?"

He exchanged a look with Jack—an infuriating, furtive look.

Eden closed her eyes; took a calming breath. "If you know something, please tell me."

"We believe Subject 004 is Barrett Barr."

Eden's mouth went slack. *Barrett Barr*—the eighteen-year-old kid all over Concordia National because he went missing this past summer.

"Your father recognized his parents as soon as they were interviewed, which happened to be around the same time you got into trouble."

Eden flushed. No wonder her parents were so worried.

"We hoped it was a coincidence. We hoped the public was right and Barrett ran away. But just in case, Carl agreed to be an extra set of eyes and ears. He was in Eagle Bend when your father sounded the alarm."

"And the other one?"

"If Mordecai has Barret, I assume he has her, too."

"Why?"

"We know you have a network. Annette recently discovered that Ellery has one, too. Only she hasn't been activated, which means it wasn't activation that brought these networks online. It leads me to believe that these networks were pre-programmed to come online at a certain point in time. If that's the case, Barrett and the girl would be easily traceable. The only thing that would have kept yours and Ellery's untraceable would be the scrambling devices."

"Which was why he only had the two photographs. Mine and hers."

Mordecai wasn't looking for the other two, because Mordecai most likely had the other two.

And she still had no idea where he was or what he wanted with them.

They found nothing about him, no clue as to his whereabouts. Her parents were still at his mercy. Who knew if they were even alive. The thought tore a hole in Eden's chest, one that made breathing impossible.

But then Dr. Norton asked a question that made everything worse. Infinitely worse.

"Eden, where's the remote?"

The remote.

To her tranquilizer pump.

Her blood went cold.

Cassian.

She'd left it with Cassian.

The safety rail they'd designed to keep the people around Eden safe.

One half of it—the half that made it work should the need arise—was gone. Rendering the whole thing useless.

30

Eden had made it clear. She didn't want to see him again. It was a request Cass would have abided by had not Vick shown up and given him something important to deliver.

He stepped up to the large front door and knocked.

Even through the thick wood, he could hear Cleo's angry music.

Milly answered—the same housekeeper who'd served the Randall-Ransoms when Cass was eleven. A grandmotherly woman with a thick accent who minded her own business and smiled whenever she saw him. She gave him the same smile now as she had back then.

Obviously, Eden hadn't given her the memo.

"You have a lot of nerve, showing up here." The hostile greeting belonged to Jack Forrester, who had just stepped into the foyer.

Milly looked nervously from him to Cass.

He gave her a reassuring look and she hurried away, accustomed to making herself scarce when need be, which was quite often in this particular house.

Forrester came forward, barricading the entrance.

"I need a word with Eden," Cass said.

"She doesn't want to speak with you."

"Then she can tell me herself." He looked past the red-faced Forrester, to the stairs where Eden stood as though she'd heard him over Cleo's loud punk rock. She probably had. She stared at him, hurt and anger waging war in her eyes. And something in him went painfully, piercingly soft. He had acted selfishly. He had acted callously. And now she was paying the price. He pulled the sleek remote from his pocket. "You left this."

Her lips parted. The softest of gasps tumbled free.

She hurried down the rest of the stairs and took it.

"And these," he said, holding out the crumpled photographs.

Those Eden didn't take. But Forrester did. He swiped them out of Cass's hand with a look of pure, unadulterated relief, quickly followed by a skeptical wariness.

"Can I talk to you for a second?" Cass asked her.

She hesitated, her wariness matching Forrester's.

"I'm not working for him anymore, Eden. If I was, I wouldn't have returned the remote or the pictures."

Forrester didn't look convinced.

Cass didn't blame him. He wouldn't be convinced either.

Eden seemed to deliberate.

"I just need a word. And then I'm gone. I swear."

After a second or two, she handed Forrester the remote, asked if he would give it to Norton, and glared at Cass as she walked past him. "A second. That's all."

They stepped outside onto the large front lawn, hemmed in by meticulously groomed privacy hedges.

Above them, the sky was overcast. The clouds hung low, turning the air sticky with heat.

Cass scratched the stubble on his cheek. He needed a good shave. He also needed to pull out the phone Vick had given him and hand it over, something he could have done inside. He was procrastinating. Delaying the inevitable. He didn't actually need a private word. He simply wanted one. And that wanting annoyed the crap out of him.

She crossed her arms, raised her eyebrows.

While she didn't ask for an explanation, he felt compelled to explain. He wrapped his hand around the back of his neck and led with something he'd already told her. "I owed Yukio money."

"Which means what—you were fighting *and* gambling?"

"I was locked into a contract. For four fights. I received a single advance for all of them, but I quit after the first."

"Why?"

"The last guy I fought looked like my father." The statement tasted foul. Cass didn't want it in his mouth. He shook his head, his jaw tight, then walked over to the large fountain in the center of the stone-paved, roundabout driveway and sat on the ledge. The man had looked like Cass's father, and Cass lost control. He unleashed his anger, like he always did. The only place he allowed himself to unleash it. In the ring. Only this time, the anger consumed him. Blinded him. He wailed and wailed on his opponent until all he could see was his beaten, bloodied mother, and the skinny, helpless kid who couldn't protect her. "Turns out, he *was* a father. Just nothing like mine. With two young kids and a pregnant wife. Fighting because he got sacked from his job and he was desperate to feed his family."

Eden didn't move. She stood frozen in place.

"I killed him."

He could hear the small catch of her breath.

He closed his eyes. It was the first time he'd spoken the words. The first time he'd confessed his sin out loud. "I killed him while everybody cheered."

And there hadn't been any repercussions at all.

"What was left of my advance went into an envelope sent straight to the new widow."

Penance for his sin.

It wasn't enough—not even remotely adequate. But it was all Cass had to give.

He stared down at the stone beneath his boots. "After that, I wasn't getting back in the ring. But I'd already been paid, which meant I owed a lot of money."

"So, you found me for Yukio."

"I found a lot of people for Yukio." A year's worth of people. And none of them mattered to him. He was paying off a debt. That's all it was.

Until now.

Until her.

"Why did you intervene?" She cupped her forehead between her palms, then ran them flat against her hair. "I mean, you brought me to Cleo's. You helped me find information. Why would you do that if you were the one who found me?"

"Because you weren't like the rest of them. I should have known better—I *did* know better." He squeezed his eyes, pushed his fingers across his eyebrow.

"So it was guilt, then."

Yes.

No.

He didn't know.

Cass shook his head—aggravated with himself.

It was time to do what he'd come here to do.

He stood up, pulled the phone from his back pocket, and set it in her palm.

"What is this?"

"It's from Mordecai."

Her eyelids fluttered. "What?"

"After you left, my manager showed up. He was watching Ruby's apartment. Mordecai gave this to him to give to you."

"I don't understand. If he knew we were going to be at Ruby's, why wouldn't he just take me?"

"I'm a trained fighter." One of the best around, even a full year after his last fight.

A look of confusion twisted her expression.

Cass thought about their combat in the woods outside Norton's cabin. Without any training at all, Eden had laid Cass flat on his back. "Do you think I could take you?"

Her confusion let go. He could tell she was remembering the same thing.

"Until he can control you, he can't take you. Nobody can." Especially not a weasel like Vick. "He said that you need to answer when he calls if you want your parents to stay alive."

And just like that, her face crumpled. She cupped her hand over her mouth. A single tear raced down her cheek and pooled over the top of her thumb. "They're alive," she said, the relieved words muffled by her palm.

"That's what Vick said."

She swiped beneath her eyes. "Wh-when is he gonna call?"

"If I had to guess, I'd say as soon as he fixes whatever glitched."

Which was only a matter of time.

"Has Forrester hacked into your network yet?" he asked.

She shook her head. "He's working on it."

"Tell him to work faster."

With that, Cass had no more reason to stay. He'd delivered the phone. He'd offered his explanation. It was time for him to do what Eden wanted him to do—leave.

He strode away.

"Wait."

Cass stopped.

Eden stood framed by the fountain, her eyes still wet with relief, looking at him with the strangest mixture of compassion and confusion. As though her emotions were engaged in a wrestling match that was as strenuous as it was perplexing.

"You can't stay."

He gestured toward the street. "I'm not."

"What you did was wrong."

"I know." He bit out the words. Did she think he didn't?

"But I understand."

His breathing stilled.

"I understand why you were working for him. I think it was kind of you to give your money to the widow."

Cass stared at her—befuddled.

She held his gaze for a moment longer—her blue, gray, green eyes fierce—then she turned around and let herself inside, bringing the confusing role he had played in Eden Pruitt's story to an end.

31

Eden sat at the edge of the pool, moving her feet slowly through the cool water. Another day was drawing to a close. Her parents were alive, somewhere with Mordecai. Dr. Norton had her remote. He continued to pore over the images he'd taken of her in his cabin on the lake, scrutinizing them with Dr. Beverly Randall-Ransom, who was riveted. Over the last decade, major advancements had been made in the field of nano science. It was the *now* of medicine. One that was opening doors long closed, offering cures for diseases like Parkinson's and Alzheimer's. And here Eden was, composed of the most sophisticated nanotechnology the doctor had ever seen, right there in her home to study.

Only Dr. Beverly Randall-Ransom couldn't comprehend it.

How could this have been designed eighteen years ago? She knew Volkova was evil. She had no idea he was a genius.

Unsettled by the note of admiration in the doctor's voice, Eden had escaped to the roof, where she sat with Cleo, who had her feet in the water, too. The daughter was every bit as fascinated as the mother, only for Cleo it was less about the science and more about the story. She was poring over the two files Dr. Norton had given Eden after she found out there were more like her. He hadn't shared Ellery's file—Subject 005. That belonged to Jack. But now that the cat was out of the bag, he gave her these. Eden had been looking through them when Cassian showed up.

Now he was gone.

There was no reason for him to come back.

He'd given her the remote. The photographs. The phone she now clasped in her palm. The phone that had the alarm clock in her head returning with a fury—loud and incessant.

Tick.

Tick.

Tick.

How much time was left before it rang? And once it did, would that mean Mordecai had fixed the glitch?

Cleo shut the file she'd been looking through.

Subject 003.

"This is bananas." They were big words coming from the conspiracy theorist.

Big words Eden didn't argue.

This was most certainly bananas.

According to the paperwork, subjects 003 and 004 were returned to their biological parents. Missing embryos from an IVF clinic, now in superhuman form. Her father found the parents, and however it went down, he returned them. Eden and Ellery on the other hand? She had no idea what happened to their biological parents. The files didn't say. She did know this much. Roger Carlson was working for Dr. Norton when her father showed up with four random babies, unsure where else to bring them—aware that Dr. Norton lived in relative seclusion, was disgruntled with the government, and had a medical facility in his basement that could very well come in handy. Apparently, Ruth Pruitt was far from alone in her grief. Carlson had a little sister—Annette Forrester. They'd lost a child, too. They struggled with infertility, too. And thanks to Annette's husband and his stint in prison, they couldn't adopt.

Eden recalled the information they found about Jack and

Annette—the obituary for their son. At the time, it had felt too coincidental to be coincidence. She was right. It wasn't coincidence. It was the reason they were connected.

Two sets of parents desperate for babies.

Two freak babies in need of parents.

It was a nightmare in the making.

Cleo locked her knees so her feet hovered above the surface of the pool. The metal spikes of her black leather anklet dripped in the evening sunlight. She dipped her hand into the water, cupped her palm, and poured the trapped liquid over her shins. "Can you imagine getting a phone call like the one those parents must have gotten? Um, hi, you know that in vitro fertilization you had years ago? Well, it just so happens your missing frozen embryo was stolen by Karik Volkova. He genetically modified it, grew it into a baby, and now it's eighteen months old. Would you like it back?"

Eden blinked slowly—her throat thick. Her insides, blank.

Cleo plunked her feet back into the water. She stretched her arms into the air, twisted her torso to one side, then the other.

"Did Cass tell you he quit fighting?" Eden said.

Cleo brought her arms down. "No."

"Over a year ago."

"That'll make my mother happy."

"He killed his last opponent." Would *that* make her mother happy? Eden turned and looked at Cleo, feeling oddly and fleetingly smug about the declaration. Did she still think Cass was a *good guy*? Eden wanted to ask Cleo the question, but she couldn't say the words. Not when she was so confused herself.

Was Cassian a good guy?

He found her for the bad guys. Then he helped her get away from the bad guys. He killed a man. Then he sent that man's wife all of his money. Bad. Good. Bad. Good. He was an enigma. A *tortured* enigma. She could see that plainly enough on his gorgeous face.

"He said his mother was killed."

Cleo arched one of her eyebrows. "He told you that?"

"Was he lying?"

"No."

"Then why that reaction?"

"I'm just surprised he told you." Cleo leaned in as though sharing something conspiratorially. "In case you haven't noticed, Six, he's not exactly the sharing type."

Six.

It was a jarring nickname.

An unsettling nickname.

A true nickname. Perhaps even truer than her given name. This thing she had always been, even when she didn't know.

Subject 006.

"Was it his father?" Eden asked. "Is he the one who killed her?"

Cleo took a deep breath, then released the air in a slow, steady stream. "They ran away from him when Cass was four. They needed to disappear, so they came here, to Chicago. It's an easy enough place to disappear. The most convenient, anyway."

"Why?"

"Because if you live off the grid, you won't have to do it alone. There's a community here. Plus, there's my mom. Health care is hard to come by when you're not supposed to exist. Especially medicine. Cass and his mom came to Chicago. They met Mona, who introduced them to my mother. They were safe for seven years. And then they weren't."

A lump of sickening dread lodged itself in Eden's throat. For so long, she was led to believe that people who lived off the grid were criminals. Reprobates. Maybe some of them were. But Cass's mother? She was a woman who simply wanted to protect her child. "He found them?"

"And he killed her. He left Cass to die, too. He probably would have if Mona hadn't found him when she did."

Eden's throat tightened. She massaged the thickness away. It was a horrible story. An awful, heartbreaking story.

"Cass, of course, shared none of this with me. I cobbled the facts together via a lot of eavesdropping. I'm glad I did so much of it back then. Because I got it. I understood why he was so angry."

"What do you mean?"

"My dad and I were hit by a drunk driver when I was nine. He was killed. I survived."

This, Eden already knew. She'd heard it plenty of times on Concordia News over the summer. It was, however, more captivating hearing it from the girl herself.

"I was angry for a long time," Cleo said. Then she gave Eden a sideways smile. "My therapist would say I'm still angry."

"His dad never came back into the picture?"

"Not that I know of." Cleo shrugged, like *c'est la vie*. "I think it's why Cass decided to fight, you know? In case his dad ever did come back."

Eden sat with the words, turning the phone over in her hand while Cleo picked up the second file and began reading. Over the years, Eden had taken an interest in psychology. So much so, she had considered studying clinical psychology in college. In the thick of her interest, she'd read a few articles about the impact of trauma on the human brain. There was plenty of it to study given The Attack twenty-one years ago.

The last guy I fought looked like my father.

That had been the trigger. Cassian's *fight or flight* response was activated. His brain chose fight. And he lost control. This didn't make him bad. This made him ... complicated. It made him human.

Beside her, Cleo turned the pages—two, three, four—when Eden heard something far away.

An excited, victorious shout.

She sat up straighter. "Did you hear that?"

"Hear what?"

There it was.

Again.

A whoop. Undeniably triumphant.

Eden could use some triumph.

She clambered up to standing, her bare feet wet.

"What is it?" Cleo asked, looking up at her in alarm.

"Jack." She could hear him now, talking rapidly to Dr. Norton four floors down. "He did it. He hacked into my network."

32

Jack Forrester spent the night plumbing Network 006.

He burned the midnight oil, adding to his matrix of notes while everyone else guzzled coffee and waited for more information. As it stood, they knew a few things. The network was complex. There were several strange components Jack didn't recognize. And hundreds of nodes which amounted to an astounding sum of information.

All of which he needed to wade through.

Eden lasted until four in the morning before her eyelids grew too heavy to keep open. She retired to her fourth-floor bedroom and fell into a deep, hard sleep. When she woke four hours later, it took several seconds to gain her bearings. To catch up with a life that kept changing so drastically. When the haze of sleep dissipated, she bolted upright and checked the phone by her bedside. It had yet to ring. She used the restroom, brushed her teeth, threw an oversized long-sleeve Henley over the tank top she'd worn to bed, and hurried down the stairs.

Jack Forrester was still awake—alone—his eyes impossibly bloodshot as he pecked away on the laptop.

When he saw her, she didn't even have to ask.

He launched into an explanation of what he'd learned while

she sat on the couch across from him. "It's sophisticated. Your network functions in ways I'm familiar with and other ways I'm not. I focused in on the command log, but honestly, it's like trying to read the messages our brain sends on any given day. So much of it is superfluous. So, I started noting the surges, groupings of messages."

Eden pulled her legs up and sat crossed-legged, drinking it all in with eagerness.

"The first grouping occurred at your network's inception. It's the very first signal ever sent. On the first of August. It was a Wednesday."

She rewound the days, trying to pull up that specific one. She was still in San Diego then. A summer Wednesday, probably at the library or the beach with Erik. Only she couldn't remember anything specific or noteworthy about that day at all.

"The nodes were all sending the same message. It was outgoing, like an SOS signal."

"Which means?"

"It's hard to tell on its own, except for the next surge, which was last Thursday. Early in the morning."

The twenty-second of August.

Christopher's birthday.

The day everything turned upside down.

That day, Eden remembered. For as long as she lived, she would remember it. Except for a chunk. A vital, dismaying chunk.

"This time, it was an incoming message. And it came with a massive signal boost."

"What does that mean?"

"It appears as though your network was merged with a larger network, a sort of umbrella network. On the first of August, your network came online. That was the surge of outgoing messages. The 'look at me, look at me' signal. Last Thursday morning, a host from this larger network accessed yours. Unsurprisingly, the IP address is encrypted so I'm unable to find a general location."

"Why the delay?" Eden asked.

Jack blinked at her, confused.

"If my location was handed over when I was still in San Diego, why would they wait so long to plug me in to this larger network?"

"I don't know. Maybe they needed time to get everything in order." Jack scrolled down the screen. There was a mind-boggling amount of data. "Later—on that same day—there was another surge of activity."

"When I attacked my parents."

Jack nodded. "In the middle of all the messaging, there's an error code. A communication glitch. So far, I can't tell what caused it. I can just see that there was an error. Here's where it gets good. When that happened, your network jumped offline. When you came back online, your signal strength reverted to what it was before the connection, and there hasn't been anymore incoming messages since."

When he stopped, his eyes were bright. He looked at her with sleepless frenzy, as if waiting for her to join his enthusiasm.

But she wasn't following.

"Ben was right. Pinpointing your location is a vital piece to the puzzle. Mordecai needed your coordinates to connect you to this larger network, and once that was successful, he used that connection to activate you."

Thank you, Cassian.

"I don't think he can reconnect until he knows where you are. Which means he can't connect my daughter's either."

And he wouldn't be able to.

Because Cassian hadn't found his daughter.

She was somewhere safe. Somewhere far, far away with her mother, Annette.

"Thank God for the scrambling device," she said.

"My thoughts precisely." Dr. Norton walked into the room—

dressed and pressed, as always. He didn't even look tired, and he had stayed up as late as Eden. He carried two mugs of steaming coffee. He handed one to her and kept one for himself.

"What do we do if he calls?" she asked.

The phone was on the coffee table. She'd brought it with her. She would always bring it with her.

"I don't think he will until he's fixed whatever caused that communication error. And by then, I'm hoping I can create a doppelgänger."

"A what?"

"A network that looks identical to yours. If I combine it with the right kind of firewall, I can make your actual network invisible. We can use your original network to boost the decoy's signal, so when Mordecai has your location and attempts to reconnect, he will access the doppelgänger network instead."

All of this was a foreign language. French class without knowing any French. Eden didn't speak computer.

"He's using a host from this larger network to speak to your nanobots. This is how he controlled you. If he accesses the doppelgänger, he'll send commands, but they'll be ineffectual."

"But won't he know? I mean, if I'm not doing what he's commanding, won't it be obvious that something went wrong?" And then what? At what point would Mordecai get angry enough to kill the bait?

"That's where our doctors come in. If I'm right, if this code turns out to be preprogrammed commands that trigger your nanobots to fire in various parts of the brain, then we might be able to establish what behavior would ensue. We could read the commands coming into the doppelgänger network, communicate them to you, and you would act them out accordingly. He'll have no idea you're not under his control."

"And if he commands me to attack my parents again?"

Forrester chewed on his lip—the first sign of uncertainty. "Something in your system already went haywire. I'm hoping he'll assume there's another glitch he can fix later."

Hoping was not a word she wanted to hear.

Hoping was not a guarantee.

But at the moment, it was the best they had.

Eden rubbed her forehead. "So … the first step is creating the doppelgänger network?"

Forrester nodded.

"The first step is sleep," Dr. Norton said.

Eden wanted to object. But Dr. Norton was right. If Jack Forrester didn't stop cranking his brain, it was only a matter of time before it shut down in protest.

"Okay," Jack said, rubbing his eyes. "Only for a little while, though."

Before he left, he put his hand on Eden's shoulder.

Her body did not recoil. Her body was catching up with what her brain had known for several days now. Jack Forrester was not her enemy. Jack Forrester was one hundred percent on her side.

He gave her shoulder a squeeze. "As soon as I'm up, we'll get to work."

33

In all twenty-two years of his life, Cass had never consumed a single drop of alcohol. While most fighters made a habit of drowning their pain in a bottle, he was terrified of who he'd become at the bottom of one. But last night, he sat on a barstool staring down a shot of tequila for the better part of an hour before the exasperated bartender told him to drink up or get out.

Cass had tossed a ten-dollar bill on the bar and did the latter.

He decided to return to his apartment, because *why not*?

If Mordecai was there waiting, so be it.

He'd either get a good fight, or the man would put him out of his misery.

When he arrived, the place was empty. But someone had paid a visit.

Whoever it was had turned his small studio apartment upside down. Every drawer—from the dresser, the nightstand, his desk, the kitchenette—had been removed and overturned, their contents scattered across the floor. Even this reminded him of her and her ransacked living room in Eagle Bend.

When he woke up the next morning after a sleepless night, the mess remained. He didn't bother putting anything back together. Instead, he headed to the same training facility he'd been going to ever since he was twelve. The same training facility that employed him since he left the ring, ensuring Cass could still put his muscles through the brutal workouts to which he'd grown so accustomed. An Italian heavyset man named Lou owned the place. Perhaps a hard workout would chase the worst of Cass's frustration away. He let himself in through the back and got right to work pummeling a hanging punching bag, half-ignoring, half-enraged with the pain in his side where Forrester had sliced him, until sweat soaked his shirt and dripped down his face. But it was no use. No matter how ruthlessly he pushed himself, his mind held onto Eden like a dog with a bone.

He couldn't stop seeing her. Snatches of memory flashed through his mind like images from a film reel.

The carefree laughter she'd shared with her father outside their home in San Diego. The patient way she listened to the old man as they played checkers inside the nursing home. The alarming way she stood on the edge of that cliff the night before they moved, her arms spread wide as the wind whipped her hair. The loneliness that seemed to envelop her when she was leaning against her car in Eagle Bend's U-Haul parking lot. The first time their eyes connected. Inside the coffee shop, when she helped the elderly woman with the fallen change. Jumping out of a Honda Clarity when it was going thirty miles per hour. Clenching her fists when he had her cornered at the end of an abandoned alley. The featherlight touch of her fingers when she tended to his wound in the basement of Cleo's dormitory.

Voilà. Tout au mieux.

The warmth of her body in front of his as she aimed his gun and hit her target dead in its center. The haunting sound of her voice when she told him about Christopher in the back of Beverly's Rolls Royce. The horrified look of betrayal in her eyes when she threw those incriminating photographs in his face. And most confounding of all, her final words before she left him standing dumbly in the Randall-Ransom's front lawn.

It was kind of you to give your money to the widow.

With a growl of frustration, Cass pushed himself harder.

When his body could go no further, he sat against the wall and untied his training shoes as the side door opened and shut, and the lights he hadn't bothered turning on flickered to life.

"Well, well, well, ladies and gents. The MVP is finally back." Lou walked in with a bag full of cleaning supplies and a jaunt in his step. "Where'd you run off to? A family emergency or something?"

"You need a family for that, Lou."

Lou set the bag on top of the front desk. "Hey-ah, Vick came by lookin' for ya a couple times while you was gone."

"I'm sure he did." Cass tossed his shoes in his duffel bag and slipped on a pair of cross-trainers.

"You in trouble, kid?"

"Not any more than usual."

Lou chuckled. "Well, let me know when you're ready to get back to work. I miss the freedom your employment has provided."

Lou owned the facility. For the past year, Cass had run it. His work for Yukio went toward his debt. His work for Lou went toward food and rent and the ability to continue training, a fact that left Vick infuriated. His cash cow was still acting like a fighter but refused to be one. And in Vick's eyes, Lou was the enabler. The place was meant for fighters; Cass was no longer a fighter. So why was Lou still letting him use the facilities?

"He's a gainful employee," Lou liked to say. "One that don't need insurance or benefits. As long as I get to keep more money in my pocket, I ain't got no qualms about who walks in my doors."

Which was true.

Cass saved Lou money.

And Lou liked to double that money by gambling on the very thing Cass refused to do. The man knew people. He had connections. Lots of them.

It was a fact that had him pausing in the doorway. "Hey, Lou?"

"Yeah?"

"You've heard of Mordecai."

"Every gambling man in Chicago's heard of Mordecai."

"You don't happen to know his real name, do you?"

"Aw man, Cass. That's a dangerous question. Not one you oughta be asking."

"I'm asking anyway."

Lou considered him beneath black, bushy eyebrows. "I don't even know what the man looks like."

Whether or not he had spoken the truth, Cass thanked him and headed outside. The forecast called for rain, but the clouds refused to unleash. They hung stubbornly in the sky—dark and low and heavy—a perfect metaphor for his mood.

Back in the apartment, he slammed the door behind him, unable to get the look on Eden's face out of his head. The one she wore when he told her he'd killed a man. He tossed his duffel bag into the corner of the room and jammed all ten of his fingers into his hair. He pushed his hands back, then brought them forward and down the length of his face.

It was kind of you to give your money to the widow.

Kind of him? He was the one who made her a widow.

Voilà. Tout au mieux.

With an irritated groan, Cass tried to shove her voice away.

But it was no use.

The film reel kept running.

He saw her in the dark of Cleo's dorm room, her chest heaving on the cusp of a nightmare that had pulled her out of sleep. He saw her kneeling above him after he regained consciousness in the back of that truck—her face smeared with grime and blood. He saw her sitting wistfully on Norton's deck with her knees tucked to her chest and that incriminating file left on the wooden slats. He could feel her deceptively light weight as he carried her to the guest bedroom in the doctor's cabin. The strength of her when they'd sparred in the woods, and she threw him flat on his back.

A world of depth and contradiction existed in her eyes alone, and all of it had found its way inside his bloodstream like an addicting drug he couldn't shake. Had the phone rung yet? Was Forrester making any progress? Was she doing okay? For a beat of a second, he considered calling Cleo to check. But then he gritted his teeth, stalked into the bathroom, and peeled off his shirt.

He needed to shower.

He needed to shave.

He needed to forget.

A knock sounded on the door.

His arms went still above his head.

The knock came again.

Cass fisted the shirt in his hand and strode through his apartment.

When he swung the door open, Ruby stood on the other side staring approvingly at his bare upper half.

Disappointment cut through him—sharp and profound and utterly foolish. Did he really think it would be Eden?

"Well, hello there," Ruby purred.

"What do you want?"

Her seductive mask slipped. She was taken aback—momentarily knocked off balance by his rude greeting. She recovered quickly enough. "I wanted to come check on you. You disappeared the other day."

"You didn't have what I was looking for." He didn't mean it as a double entendre, but judging by the hurt flashing across her face, this was certainly how she took it.

She opened her mouth to say something, but then her attention slid past him and her eyes went wide. "Oh my goodness, Cass. What happened?"

"Someone broke in." He turned around and helped himself to a glass of water from the faucet.

Ruby stepped in after him. "Who?"

"Nobody's made a confession, but if I had to guess, I'd say the same guy who broke into Yukio's."

She surveyed the mess. "I don't know what you got yourself wrapped up in, but it seems awfully dangerous."

He took a long swig of his drink. This was rich, coming from the girl who so desperately wanted him back in the ring.

"Why don't you pack a bag, come stay at my place?" She bent over—no doubt, strategically—giving him a clear view of her cleavage all in the guise of picking something up. "You know you're always welcome."

He set the empty glass down sharply on the counter behind him and wrapped his fingers beneath the laminate edge.

She came closer, taking in his injured side with eyes that belonged in a bedroom. She touched the bandage he'd applied the night before.

He flinched, his jaw tight.

She ran her cool fingertips along his skin, up his ribcage, then pressed herself against him.

His body was riled—full of restless energy, even after the merciless workout.

"You look like you could use a little TLC."

And she was all too eager to offer it. A fleeting, momentary distraction, like the bottle of tequila last night. He could partake, but afterward, he'd be hungover and longing for the thing he really wanted.

Eden.

Despite himself, his attention dipped to Ruby's mouth.

She trailed her hand up his chest. Around the back of his neck. "If you come over, I can give it to you."

He caught her by the wrist with the same sharpness he'd set down the glass.

She looked at him expectantly, her lips parting.

"You should go."

She blinked—caught off guard. Then her eyes filled with tears.

He wasn't swayed.

As soon as she left, he turned the shower all the way to cold and stepped inside.

34

After the initial examination, the fascinated, albeit stumped Dr. Beverly Randall-Ransom reached the same conclusion as Dr. Norton. She saw no way to extract the nanobots without killing the host. The second opinion was no different than the first. She apologized, then promised to dig deeper once she returned from work, bringing to mind a serious problem Eden's sleep-deprived brain, and perhaps Jack's sleep-deprived brain, hadn't considered. Dr. Beverly Randall-Ransom played a crucial role in Jack's plan. But she already had a job. Not just any job either. An incredibly demanding one. When she wasn't in the operating room, she was doing research, teaching residents, giving lectures, traveling the world to speak at seminars. For goodness sake, the woman owned a private jet and had her own personal hangar at O'Hare. As if that wasn't enough, she provided medical care for illegals in the privacy of her home.

Where in her schedule could she fit translating computer code into human behavior?

The complication tied Eden's stomach into knots.

After a three-hour nap, Forrester had resumed his spot on the couch. He hunched over the computer, conferring with Dr.

Norton and taking strange notes on graph paper. Eden, on the other hand, had nothing to contribute. She found Cleo in the media room on the fourth floor, clutching a controller while she talked smack into a virtual reality headset.

Cleo was a gamer. Interestingly—and oddly—she enjoyed playing regular video games inside the virtual reality meta-verse her friend, Finn, had created. Eden didn't really get it. Most people used the meta-verse to *enter* the game or watch a sporting event or visit some place they couldn't physically visit, like Paris. They didn't use it to sit on a make-believe couch in a make-believe basement, playing old-school video games. But Eden was quickly learning that Cleo was nothing if not atypical.

Eden watched two figures on the viewer screen fight each other in high-definition. One of the players delivered a massive uppercut that knocked the other player temporarily to the floor, making the bar above the avatar's head shrink from green to red.

Cleo laughed.

Eden frowned.

She couldn't help but think of Mordecai with a controller of his own. She couldn't help but think of herself inside that video game, attacking someone she loved. She couldn't help but think of the one who was no longer here, the one she'd told to go. It was stupid to think about him, and yet he kept creeping into her thoughts.

Cleo's opponent jumped to his feet and took revenge.

"No!" she shouted, flicking out her tongue and twisting her upper half as she pounded the buttons on the controller and the bar above her avatar dipped into a dangerous sliver of red.

Eden closed her eyes, but it didn't help.

She couldn't stop seeing Cass, beating his opponent.

Cass, beaten by his father.

Cleo was in a chokehold now, futilely attempting to get herself out.

But the red bar disappeared altogether, and her avatar tapped the mat.

"Finn, you lucky dog!" she shouted into her headset. "I was totally beating you."

Finn said something on the other end about getting to write it now, to which she conceded. Then she lifted the headset from her eyes and looked at Eden with the remote held aloft. "Wanna play?"

Eden shook her head. She absolutely did not.

Cleo shrugged, then said goodbye to Finn and signed off.

"What does he get to write?" Eden asked.

"An article on the Prosperity Ball."

This came as a surprise. The ball didn't fit Cleo's brand. "You wanted to write about it?"

"The ball itself, no. The dark and sinister reason behind it, absolutely." She tossed the headset on the cushion beside her.

"And that dark and sinister reason would be?"

"Smoke and mirrors. A ploy to maintain compliance. Distract the public."

"From?"

Cleo looked at Eden like she was dumb. "Have you seriously forgotten Dwight? The uptick in riots? Decisions are being made behind closed doors. Important decisions. All the while, we've turned into a flock of docile sheep."

"So, the pipe bombs are keeping us in fear. And the Prosperity Ball is an attempt to ...?

"Keep us entertained. It's an effective distraction."

Eden sat down next to Cleo's headset, her mind wandering to the babysitting gig she had back in San Diego. Five-year-old twin brothers who acted like mortal enemies. On several occasions, she'd been tempted to find a cage, throw them in, and let them duke it out. In actuality, she spent the evening distracting them. At the first sign of bickering, ice cream sundaes! The mere whiff of an accusation, Connect Four!

Cleo was right.

It worked.

Was that happening now on a much larger scale?

Her inclination was to say no way. It was too farfetched. But so was her existence and that was absolutely true. Even so, she had a hard time getting on board with Cleo's theories. If they were correct, then who was pulling the strings? And to what end? Eden turned the phone over in her hand. "Did you hear about the plan?"

"Forrester filled me in."

"Do you think your mom is going to be available to help?"

Cleo shrugged. "She's busy; I'll give you that. But I had to get my obsessive personality from somewhere and it wasn't my dad. She loves a new challenge. This definitely fits the bill. I'm sure she'll make more time for it than you think."

For some reason, Cleo's words weren't comforting.

Eden didn't want any distractions at all, even if those distractions were brain surgery.

"Too bad I couldn't give you my photographic memory. You could learn everything your mom knows, and then we could decode all the commands before Mordecai calls."

Cleo pressed her tongue against the inside of her lip piercing. "Photographic memory?"

"It's one of the many oddities I've acquired since activation."

"Right. Along with superhuman strength. Speed. Reflexes." Her eyes were bright. "How fast do you think you can run?"

"I have no idea."

"Want to see? My mom has a brand new treadmill in the basement. It goes up to 30 miles per hour."

With nothing better to do, they headed downstairs. On one side, there was a medical room similar but not identical to the one in Dr. Norton's basement. This was where Eden had been poked and prodded. On the other, there was a small but impressive exercise area across from a bedroom. This was where Cass had stayed. The treadmill was curved, and apparently, self-propelled. Eden put on her sneakers, stepped onto the machine, and began running. Slow at first, then faster. And faster. And faster. Until the high-tech, state-of-the-art machine couldn't keep up. She maxed out at thirty miles per hour—the speed of an Olympic Gold Medalist. And yet, Eden wasn't even tired.

She was positive she could run faster, longer.

A fact that had her stopping and stepping away, suddenly squeamish.

Cleo, on the other hand, looked thrilled. "That was freaking amazing."

More like freaking awful. Because all of it—her speed, her reflexes, her photographic memory, her ability to go toe to toe with a professionally trained fighter—was designed for evil. Destruction. Terror. Built into her very makeup. Further evidence that if Forrester's plan didn't work, Mordecai would have her controller, and nobody would be able to stop her. The pump at her waist was a joke. It might protect the people in this house for a while, but it wouldn't protect them forever. And it wouldn't protect Eden from herself.

The nausea in her stomach rolled.

A clacking sound from upstairs stopped.

There was movement—footsteps overhead.

A refrigerator opened. The bottom of a cup connected with the granite countertop. A drink poured. With the tiniest flare of her nostrils, Eden could smell tomato and ginger. The blend of freshly squeezed vegetables Milly had juiced earlier this morning. Homemade v8. Cleo had wrinkled her nose, but Dr. Beverly Randall-Ransom said it kept her brain sharp. The legs of a chair scraped against ceramic tile. The groan of wood beneath someone's weight.

"You look troubled."

The voice belonged to Dr. Norton.

"Hey." Cleo snapped her fingers. "You okay?"

Eden held up her hand—a sharp request for silence. She cocked her head, drawn to the conversation unfolding above.

"I've been wading through the commands built into her network." A fast-paced, monotonous tapping accompanied

Jack's words, as if he were drumming his finger rapidly against the table.

"And?"

"I came across something disturbing."

There was a pause.

Cleo tried talking again, but Eden shushed her.

"You know how you can use a certain function to shut down a frozen computer?"

Dr. Norton replied with a soft hum of consent.

"Her network has a similar function."

"A command that would shut her down?"

"*All* the way down."

"What do you mean?" Dr. Norton asked.

"Every node within her system would receive the same message and that message would result in a coordinated attack. Right here."

"Her brain stem," Dr. Norton said.

"I don't think we need a neurosurgeon to understand what that would do."

Eden's eyes went wide.

She could hear the soft, rhythmic scratching of Norton's mustache. "I suppose it makes sense. Volkova was making weaponized humans. Of course he'd want to be able to shut those weapons down if one decided to turn on him."

"It's also a convenient threat to hang over someone's head. Obey or die."

Cleo touched Eden's arm, another attempt to gather her attention.

It must look odd, the way she was standing there—her eyes focused but fixed on nothing in particular.

There was a heavy sigh. "Do you see any benefit in telling her about this discovery?"

"No," Jack said.

"Hey," Cleo called. "Where are you going?"

But Eden was already gone, halfway up the stairs—propelled

not by fear, but a wild, euphoric hope. Here was her guardrail. Her ultimate safety net. The thing that kept her hands on the steering wheel, even if Mordecai shoved her out of the driver's seat.

She strode into the kitchen. "If he accesses my network, would that kick you out?"

Dr. Norton and Jack jumped, startled by her sudden entrance. And the abrupt nature of her question. The two exchanged wary looks.

"It shouldn't," Jack said.

"So even if he gets in, you would still maintain the ability to carry out that function?"

Their wariness hurled itself into visible alarm.

Eden shifted impatiently. "If he started controlling me. If he forced me to do something—to hurt someone." Or worse. *Kill* someone. "You could stop it by carrying out that command?"

"Carrying out that command would kill you."

"Then kill me."

Jack shot Dr. Norton a look of horrified bewilderment.

"Eden," the doctor said, his voice carefully measured. "Nobody's going to kill you."

"Being dead is better than the alternative."

The doctor shook his head. "If Jack's plan doesn't work, we'll find another way to get you out from under his control."

"If you find another way, he'll use that function himself. *After* he's already forced me to do whatever horrible things he has in mind."

Her case was strong. She knew it. They had to know it. But neither man budged, making one thing crystal clear. They would never—under any circumstances—use that command. Which meant she would have to find someone who would.

35

Eden feared death. She just didn't fear it more than she feared causing it, especially against her will. There was a monster inside her—made up of hundreds of molecular robots—and she would do everything within her power to keep it caged. Jack discovered a lock so strong, it ensured the monster could never escape, and since he was refusing to use it, Eden had to find someone who would.

She let herself into Ruby's apartment complex, hurried up three flights of stairs, and knocked on the door of apartment 317.

Nobody answered.

But thanks to the monster, she knew someone was home.

She could hear the heartbeat inside.

She knocked again.

There was the sound of clattering, like someone stumbling into something, then the door opened. Ruby stood on the other side, wobbling on her feet. "What are you doing here?" she asked, her words slurring.

"I'm looking for Cass."

"Of course you are." She breathed into Eden's face. Her breath reeked of booze; it wasn't even dinnertime. "Well, I'm sorry to say that he's not here."

"Do you know where he is?"

She leaned on the door, her cheek pressed against the wood. "If I did, why would I tell you?"

"Because I need to talk to him."

"Well, that's *all* you're gonna do." She said it with exaggeration, like some sort of drunken innuendo. Then she hiccupped. "He's in a bad mood. I don't know for certain, but it could be because someone broke into his apartment."

Concern skittered up Eden's spine.

"It's completely wrecked." She hiccupped again, then cupped her fist over her mouth and belched softly. "When I left, I don't even think he turned the bolt."

"Can you tell me where he lives?"

"Cass and I ... we had a thing, you know? I think I was in love with him." Ruby's bleary eyes welled with tears. She turned around and stumbled inside. Grabbed an open bottle of rum off the counter and took a swig straight from its mouth. Then she plopped into a seat at the small, two-person table in the kitchen and slumped over. "I don't understand. I dunno what changed."

Eden stepped inside, her patience wearing thin.

The place was still crammed with Yukio's belongings.

She found a torn, empty envelope on the counter next to where the rum had been. A pen, too. She set the envelope in front of Ruby. "Could you write down Cassian's address for me?"

Ruby slitted her eyes. "I mean ... it's you, right? You're what changed."

"One of us should make sure he's okay. As soon as possible. So, if you would just ..." Eden held out the pen and gave the envelope a tap.

"Sure. Why not? I mean, why wouldn't I give you Cassian's address? He told me to go away, so it's not like I'm gonna use it." Ruby snatched the writing utensil and wrote four numbers, a street name, and an apartment number in a sloppy scrawl.

"Thank you, Ruby."

She lifted the bottle in an inebriated salute. Rum sloshed onto the floor. "Hopefully he's still alive, and not dead like Yukio."

Ruby hiccupped over a sob as Eden hurried away and closed the door behind her.

The address meant very little to her in a city as foreign as Chicago. Thankfully, she had Beverly's driver, Sam. She handed him the envelope and tapped her foot as he drove. Five blocks straight. A left turn. A right turn. Three more blocks, and then he stopped by the curb. She hurried to the front door of his apartment complex, which wasn't busted like the door to Ruby's had been. She buzzed his intercom several times, but there was no response. Eden considered the doorknob. And the large tree on Norton's property. With a simple push, it had gone crooked. She could have toppled it to the ground if she'd kept going. After the briefest hesitation, she gripped the knob, stepped close to the door, twisted, and pushed.

The lock broke.

She stepped inside the dim hallway and didn't stop until she stood in front of his apartment. She knocked once, giving him a chance to answer. When he didn't—when she heard no heartbeat inside—she prepared to do the same thing to his door that she'd done to the front. Only this time, she discovered upon twisting that his door wasn't locked.

Ruby was right. He hadn't bothered.

When she let herself in, she could see why.

His place had been ransacked. Turned upside down. Just like her living room in Eagle Bend.

Cassian wasn't home, so she sat on the edge of his bed and waited.

For forty-five minutes, she didn't move.

Then she found Sam, told him she would have Cass call when they were ready to return to Beverly Randall-Ransom's estate, and headed back inside. This time, as she walked through his ruined apartment, something caught her attention. The backside of a tattered children's book beneath a broken picture frame resting on a pile of clothes, as though the pair had been hidden at the bottom of a dresser drawer, and once that dresser's contents were dumped, it found itself on top. Eden picked them up. She turned the book over in her hand.

It was well loved with an illustration of wolves on the cover. Eden ran her fingers over the title. *When Pup Howled at the Moon.* She set it down, then shook away the busted glass in the frame and found a photograph beneath. Two women. One was older, with a jaunty hat and the kind of wrinkles that looked half from age, half from a life hard lived. The other was younger, with the kind of smile that reached through the two dimensions and begged someone to catch it. And between them, an adorable boy who was missing his two front teeth. He looked up at the smiling woman with a smile of his own.

Eden's breath caught in her throat. Her hand fluttered to her chest.

His eyes were familiar. She recognized the shape and the color.

This was Cassian. *Little-boy Cassian.* Before his father would reenter the picture and steal his smile away. And that woman was his mother. Eden knew because her eyes were the same shape and color. She didn't know who the other one was, but it didn't matter. The other one was superfluous, because right then, the mother-son duo drew every heartrending ounce of Eden's attention.

A floorboard in the hallway creaked.

Eden quickly pulled the photograph out of the broken frame and tucked it into the back pocket of her jean shorts, behind the phone, where she could examine it more later. She stood from her crouched position by the bed as the door handle moved and Cass stepped inside holding a paper grocery bag.

He stopped without looking up, like he could sense her before he could see her. And when he did look, he stared for a frozen moment—his eyes dark and disbelieving. The same boy from the picture, hardened by time and circumstance.

Slowly—like Eden was an apparition that would disappear at the first sudden movement—he set the bag on the counter, casting his attention around his upturned apartment. Then—just as slowly—he removed a jug of milk from the bag and placed it inside a refrigerator that was practically empty.

"Imagine if you couldn't quit," she said.

Cassian stopped—his back to her, the refrigerator opened.

"Imagine if they could force you back into the ring, and make you kill person after person after person."

When he turned around, she could see the pain her words caused him. The confusion, too, because why had she come here to say this?

"Jack Forrester found a kill command," she said.

"A what?"

"A self-destruct function built into my network. A combination of keys someone can press and I'll …"

"Self-destruct."

She nodded.

Cass closed the refrigerator and leaned against the counter.

"Jack has a plan, but it's complicated. There are all kinds of ways it could go wrong. If that happens, if Mordecai controls me … I need someone to take me out of the ring."

He stared at her. Hard.

"Jack and Dr. Norton won't do it and I'm not going to ask Cleo."

"So you're asking me."

Slowly, Eden nodded.

Cassian swore.

"You owe me this," she said, not with accusation, but a steady ferocity. "Please, Cass."

This did it in the end.

She could see the torment in the caramel-colored depths of his eyes.

The concession, too.

Whether it was from the *please* or the sound of her speaking his name—she didn't know. She only knew that with those two words, she had her guardrail. Cassian would do this for her. He would protect her from the worst possible fate.

Should the necessity arise, he would take her out of the ring.

36

It was rush hour. Bumper to bumper traffic.

Eden and Cass sat silently in the back seat while Sam alternated between the gas and the brake—the car creeping forward in stops and starts. Cassian needed space; Eden understood that. Considering the demons that haunted him, her proposition was a ruthless one. He left fighting because he'd taken a life, and now she was asking him to take hers. In an ironic twist of fate, those demons ensured his cooperation. She understood the situation she'd put him in. She wasn't going to force conversation while he processed it.

Twenty minutes into their stop-and-go crawl, he broke the silence.

He wanted to know Forrester's plan.

She filled him in. She told him everything he'd missed, except the part about Ellery—the girl Cassian hadn't found. Eden understood why Dr. Norton didn't say anything about her. It wasn't his information to tell. That belonged to Jack, and Eden had a strong suspicion he wouldn't want this particular boy knowing about his daughter.

Cass listened intently, zeroing in like each word was imperative, like if he missed even one syllable, the whole operation would come crashing down. When she finished, he rubbed his bottom lip, a gesture she came to associate with his furrowed brow—a thing he did when he was chewing over his thoughts. "So, you don't know how to perform the command?"

"Not yet."

But she'd figure it out. She wouldn't stop until she did. Finally, she had a mission. A tangible task. A goal to work toward. The world was no longer spinning into chaos with horrible and limitless possibilities lurking in every shadow. Forrester had his plan, and now—thanks to this unlikely boy beside her—she had hers.

"How's your injury?" she asked.

He gave her an odd look, like she'd asked him an odd question.

"It's fine," he said. "Frustrating, but fine."

Silence settled between them again, different than before. Cass was no longer adjusting beneath the gravity of her request. This silence wasn't one of waiting and patience while her companion processed this significant thing to which he'd agreed. This silence was thick with awareness—of him, of herself, of his knee inches from hers. This was a living, breathing silence that made her skin flush.

She looked at him discreetly—from the corner of her eye— taking in his serious brow, his strong jaw, his straight nose, his broad frame. The definition of his bicep and the black ink of his tattoo peeking out from beneath the sleeve of his heather gray jersey shirt. He wasn't wearing his motorcycle jacket; he no longer had a motorcycle. That was probably towed somewhere in Milwaukee. But she could remember what it felt like to ride behind him—her arms wrapped around his lean torso—this dangerous stranger with answers. And secrets, too.

Her abdomen pooled with warmth.

Somehow, amid such life and death circumstances, the chemistry between them didn't feel silly or frivolous. It felt … vital. Like a tank of oxygen when she was trapped under water.

Did he feel it, too?

Was it possible not to feel something this acute?

The silence simmered.

Eden cleared her throat. Shifted in her seat.

"Chicago traffic is pretty horrible." As soon as the comment escaped, she felt like an idiot. But she pressed onward, determined to slay this sudden bout of reticence. "San Diego was a lot more spread out. Not so claustrophobic."

"Great weather, too."

She shot him a look.

The corner of his mouth quirked subtly, the barest hint of amusement sparkling in his eyes.

She narrowed her own. Cassian Gray was teasing her. For talking about road congestion, given the outlandish state of their situation.

But just as quickly as it came, his amusement dissipated. He cracked the knuckle of his pinkie. "Do you miss it?"

"San Diego?"

Cass nodded.

"I miss aspects of it."

"Like?"

Eden's lips twisted to the side. "The ocean. My best friend."

"Erik."

Hearing him say Erik's name was as discombobulating as hearing him say Christopher's. He knew intimate pieces of her life—pieces she hadn't willingly shared with him. But then, thanks to Cleo, Eden knew intimate pieces of his.

He raised a dark eyebrow at her. "You two seemed like an odd pair."

"Why?"

His attention moved down the length of her body, like this was his answer—a slow, intimate perusal that made her scalp tingle.

She lifted her chin. "I kind of resent the fact that you consider us an odd pair simply because Erik doesn't look the right way."

But that's why she'd chosen him, wasn't it?

Erik didn't look like any of the kids sitting at the popular table. That's why she'd singled him out. If she'd cared about appearances or clothes or any of the other things so many of her classmates seemed to care about, she would have missed out on one of the best friendships of her life. "I was lucky to have him as a friend. He's one of the best humans I've ever met."

"That's high praise," Cass said, annoyance flitting across his brow.

"It's honest praise," she replied, her emotions giving way to melancholy. Eden missed him. Somewhere in San Diego, Erik was most likely missing her, too. Did he think she was ghosting him? As much as she hated the thought of him making such an assumption, it was better than the alternative. A hurt Erik was better than a curious one. If he went looking for her, if he got wrapped up in any of this, he could end up like her parents.

"I saw you on the cliffs."

Eden blinked, emerging from the troubling turn of her thoughts.

"Your last night in San Diego," he said. "I saw you standing on the edge."

Her cheeks burned. She felt like a kid who'd been caught with her hand in the cookie jar. Embarrassed. Ashamed. She thought she'd been alone when she stood on that cliff. Just her and the ocean and the night and the wind blowing through her hair. It was a harmless rush of adrenaline. A thing she did whenever the urge to do something wild grew too big to contain. A secret she didn't tell anyone, not even Erik. And yet, Cass had watched her.

"It looked like you were going to jump."

"I wasn't going to jump."

"Then what were you doing?"

"I don't know." Her cheeks burned hotter. "Sometimes, I—I want to escape. Just for a minute, you know?" She shook her head. "Whenever I would stand on the edge of that cliff, it was like I could—"

"Fly away?"

She poked her finger into the black leather of the seat between her knees. He must have thought she was crazy, seeing her so close to the edge. "I don't know what it is. I guess I've always had this attraction to excitement or ... I don't know. Danger? I've had to work really hard to resist it."

"Why resist?"

She huffed. "My parents already buried one kid. They shouldn't have to worry about burying another." She thought about the picture in her pocket, next to the phone that had yet to ring. Had Cassian's mother spent her short life worrying, too? Did she live with one eye on her son, and one eye over her shoulder, waiting for the other shoe to drop? For her husband to find them?

Sam hit the brake hard and blared his horn at a blue Prius that had cut in front of them.

They were drawing nearer to Cleo's home.

This window of opportunity was closing. Soon, they would open the doors and they would step outside, no longer in this intimate space where Cassian wasn't so closed-off and mysterious. If she was going to ask about the picture in her pocket, it was now or never.

"I found this at your apartment." She slid the photograph free. "I didn't mean to take it, I just ..."

"Took it?"

Eden handed him the photograph. "That woman with the hat —is that Mona?"

He nodded.

"And the other one ... is that your mom?"

Another nod.

"You look like her."

The statement was so simple, and yet it seemed to pierce him straight through. Which pierced her in return. Because hadn't anyone ever told him that before? Couldn't he see the resemblance himself when he looked at this photograph?

"I look more like him," he said.

Him.

His father.

He spoke the word like it was battery acid.

"Cass."

He traced his mother's face with his forefinger.

"Cassian," she said again, her heart breaking. For the boy in that photograph. For the one sitting beside her now. Who would he be if his mother was still alive? If his father had never found them? "You aren't him."

He looked at her like a sailor tossed into the sea. He looked at her like a man drowning and she'd just thrown him a life vest.

———

By the time they reached Dr. Beverly Randall-Ransom's home, it was late. Dr. Norton and Jack Forrester met them at the door like two fathers who'd sat vigil all night long, waiting helplessly for their teenage daughter who had completely disregarded curfew.

Eden hadn't told anyone where she was going—not even Cleo. She'd left with a plan, and she wasn't going to let anyone stop her from executing it. Now she was back with that plan by her side, and Forrester came out of his chair. "What's he doing here?"

"I needed someone on my side."

"*We're* on your side."

"Not completely."

Jack's expression turned mutinous. He was undoubtedly concerned about his daughter. Eden would have to assure him later that she'd said nothing about Ellery nor would she. Now, unfortunately, he was left to stew in his outrage.

Dr. Norton, on the other hand, looked like he was suffering

from a mild case of heartburn. It seemed this was as noticeably upset as the man was ever going to get. "You'd give him this much trust?"

Eden looked at Cass, standing stoically beside her—the only sign of emotion the slight tic of his jaw. He found her, yes. But only because he refused to get back into the ring. He didn't want to lose control. He didn't want to hurt innocent people. When he realized finding her had done exactly that, he did what he could to undo the damage. Even when that undoing was so obviously a burr in his side. All of which meant he understood the necessity of her plan more than anyone else here.

She looked back at Dr. Norton with a slight lift of her chin. "Yes, I guess I would."

Jack glared at Cassian. "You're not staying."

"I'll stay for as long as she asks me to."

"Over my dead body."

"We don't need your permission," Eden shot back. "This isn't your house."

"Exactly." Cleo Ransom descended the stairs like royalty in a punk rock graphic tee, looking quite pleased about Cassian's return. "It's my house. And he can stay as long as he'd like. If either of you have a problem with that, you can go."

37

The phone became a permanent fixture by Eden's side—a countdown clock she couldn't see, but one that ticked nonetheless. They were in a race with an unknown finish line. How long would it take Mordecai to fix whatever had gone wrong? All they had was what they knew. On the first of August, her network came online. Eleven days later, Cassian found her in San Diego and reported her location to Yukio. On the twenty-second, she developed a sudden onset of photographic memory. Then she attacked her parents. Which gave them some inkling of a timeline. Three weeks after discovering her existence—a week and a half after pinpointing her location—Mordecai controlled her. He no longer had her location, but he could get it easily enough with a phone call. And fixing a glitch couldn't be as difficult or as time consuming as getting her entire system up and functioning.

Thursday came and went—marking one week since her parents were taken.

On Sunday, Cleo returned to Milwaukee on her mother's orders. There was nothing for Cleo to do in Chicago but sit around and wait for the phone to ring. Not to mention, she had a responsibility to uphold. Cleo wasn't happy to uphold it. She didn't want to resident advise. Eden expected Cleo to rebel. She seemed like the type of person who would stage a protest. Instead, Cleo reluctantly obeyed.

Dr. Beverly Randall-Ransom's busy schedule remained, although it wasn't as dire of a situation as Eden first worried. The woman thrived on very little sleep. She accomplished more in a day than most people did in the span of several. And Cleo had been right. Her mother's mind refused to let Eden go. She was stumped—an uncomfortable, unfamiliar state for a woman of her intelligence. Which meant that when she wasn't working, she drew vials of Eden's blood to run tests. She attached probes to Eden's head to measure brain waves. She monitored Eden's vitals to chart her heart rate and stress levels. She poked and prodded, x-rayed and examined her newest patient with vigor. All to no avail. If there was a way to safely extract the nanobots from Eden's system, they had yet to find it.

Jack worked obsessively, too. He created the doppelgänger network and the firewall—tweaking and re-tweaking to mitigate the flaws in both. He pored over the data, decoding commands into signals so the doctors could figure out how those signals interacted with the brain. So far, they'd translated several. Flight. Fight. Freeze. Sleep. And another that would most likely put the subject into a highly suggestible state, like a person under hypnosis.

All the while, Eden worked every bit as unremittingly on a goal of her own. One that was proving to be more difficult than she originally anticipated. While Dr. Norton and Jack could do nothing about Cassian's presence in Beverly's home, they certainly didn't cooperate with the reason for it. Eden knew there was a command with the power to override all the others. Eden had someone who was willing to carry that command out if the necessity arose. The problem was, Eden had no idea how it worked, and Jack was holding his notes so close to his chest, he might as well be a professional poker player, leaving her to sneak glances whenever he wasn't looking. He never let her close, but he seemed to forget her superhuman vision. Or the fact that once she zoomed in on a page, she could snap a picture in her mind and recreate it later with pencil and paper. Then she and Cass would study the paper, looking for the series of keystrokes that might solidify her plan.

So far, they hadn't found them.

A reality that made sleep hard to come by.

The little she got was far from peaceful.

Eden inhaled a sharp breath, her eyes flying open as moonlight poured in through the window and spilled across the floor. She'd been having a nightmare. The same one that had plagued her sleep since it arrived that first night in Cleo's dorm. Eden, strangling her mother. Eden, smiling at her reflection as she did.

Waking up didn't make it go away.

It lingered in all its awful truth.

The nightmare was real.

She had strangled her mother. She'd beaten her father. Then she ran and they'd been taken.

She glared at the phone on her nightstand, then flipped on her side. She wanted to turn it off. The phone. Her brain. Her dreams. The constant twisting in her gut whenever she looked at the clock. She turned onto her stomach and dug her hands beneath the pillow, her thoughts turning to Cassian in the ring. Bludgeoning his opponent to death. Eden squeezed her eyes shut. But the visual remained, only this time, it was her. She was in the ring, bludgeoning her parents to death. She buried her face in the pillowcase and let out a muffled groan. It was no use. She grabbed the phone and crept down three flights of stairs—into a kitchen that was dark and quiet.

Eden sat on one of the stools. The digital clock on the oven read 2:12 am. Another Thursday had come, marking two weeks since Eden came home to a ransacked living room. She set her elbows on the marble, pushed her fingers into her hair, and cradled her head between her palms. Was this what torture felt like—the incessant churning of thought? The inability to do anything to make it go away? Were her parents awake? Asleep? Alive? And what was taking Mordecai so long?

"Hey."

Eden jumped.

Cassian stood in the doorway—illuminated by the moonlight streaming in through the windows. He was dressed in a pair of joggers and a Hanes undershirt, his hair slightly disheveled. "Can't sleep?" he asked.

She shook her head.

"Me neither." He glanced at the phone by her elbow, then shuffled inside and grabbed a box of Rice Krispies. He lifted it into the air like a question. When she didn't decline, he retrieved two porcelain bowls from a cabinet, two spoons, and a carton of milk from the refrigerator. He set one of the bowls in front of her and poured the cereal inside, creating a sound so familiar, a lump rose in her throat. The last time had been Fruit Loops. Not here with Cassian, but in San Diego with her father, the night her parents had to post her bail because of a senior prank that started this nightmare-of-a-snowball rolling down the hill.

Cassian poured the milk.

The cereal crackled.

Neither attempted to drum up conversation.

They ate in companionable silence, Cassian with a deep furrow in his brow. When they finished, she took their bowls to the sink to rinse them out.

"Beverly says you're ready for a trial run." He was no longer sitting but leaning against the counter beside her, peering at the phone again.

Eden shut off the water. "It'll give me an opportunity to search for the command."

His expression hardened.

Cass didn't like this project. It was obvious every time they pored over the notes she recreated. Anger rolled off him like it had the very first time their eyes met inside the coffee shop.

But he was there. He was helping her search.

He folded his arms—a movement that drew her attention to the black ink peeking out from beneath his shirt sleeve. She tried to recall what the tattoo looked like, but when she'd seen it in full—an intricate design that wrapped around his shoulder—she'd been too focused on the bleeding gash in his side to pay attention to anything else. Then later, the shocking video footage. And the truth grenade Dr. Norton dropped after she sliced open her hand. Now, however, she was hungry for a distraction. Now, she couldn't look away.

Cassian noticed, his attention traveling from her to his bicep.

"Can I see it?" she finally asked.

He didn't pull up his shirtsleeve but held her gaze with a lift of his eyebrows, granting her permission to see for herself.

Eden hesitated, then slipped her fingers beneath his sleeve and lifted.

His skin was warm.

His muscles, taut.

The tattoo, beautiful.

An intricate pattern seamlessly woven around a central image that was stunning in detail. She traced her thumb over the animal's ear, noticing the small hitch of his breath as she did so.

"A wolf," she said, her voice unsteady.

She ran her finger along the ridge where Cassian's triceps met his deltoid, giving the wolf's fur an added element of dimension. When she looked up, he was staring at her with a deep and unfathomable hunger. She felt consumed—impossibly caught—as fire sparked in the connection of their gaze. She couldn't look away even if she'd wanted to.

"When my mother was little," he said, his tone low and intimate, "she'd fall asleep to the sound of their howls."

"That's a little disconcerting."

"Not to her." He looked away. Far away. The barest hint of a smile toying with one corner of his mouth. "She grew up in Wyoming. Her father was a wildlife biologist who studied wolves for a living. She said it was her favorite lullaby."

It was strange, hearing Cass talk this way. About these people. His mother was dead. Was his grandfather, too? And what of their home in Wyoming?

"He always told her that they were misunderstood. All the fables and fairytales gave them a bad rap."

"Little Red Riding Hood."

"Three Little Pigs."

"Beauty and the Beast."

"The Boy Who Cried Wolf." His hint of a smile went sour. Like his thoughts had shifted course to a different memory. One he didn't want to share.

"So, she told you different stories," Eden said.

His attention darted from the darkened hallway back to her.

"When Pup Howled at the Moon."

The furrow in his brow deepened.

"I saw it in your apartment." Eden imagined them, snuggled up together as she read from the pages, over and over again, until they became tattered and worn. A book he kept hidden at the bottom of a dresser drawer. A memento from his past. She pictured her own ransacked living room. The mess of books strewn across the floor. Had her childhood favorite been among them? If their plan failed—if her mother died—and she got a tattoo, would it be of the little girl in a yellow hat? "My mom used to read the Madeline books to me."

"Madeline?"

"She's a girl who goes to boarding school in Paris." Eden smiled a nostalgic smile. And then suddenly, her chest was caving in. Her heart, crushed beneath the collapse. She didn't want the tattoo or the memento. She wanted her mother. Her living, breathing mother. "I miss them."

"I know."

And he did. He knew what it was like. He'd been here in this very house, missing his mom like she was missing hers. Recovering from a beating by his monster of a father. Cassian thought he looked like him, but when Eden pulled up the photograph in her mind, the resemblance between mother and son was undeniable.

"He used to tell me I have his eyes," she said.

Cassian stared, his gaze as steady as a rock.

"How could he say that?"

"Maybe you do."

"I can't," she spat. "I'm not—"

His.

But she couldn't say the word. Not out loud.

"You are," he said. "In the ways that matter."

Their eyes locked in a fiery gaze, her own brimming with unshed tears. When she thought about her parents—the precarious nature of their fate, the truth that she wasn't really theirs—her chest became an empty cavern of torment. But now, in the dark of Dr. Beverly Randall-Ransom's kitchen, her pounding heart filled the space. She glanced at Cassian's lips—full and perfect—her pulse tapping rapidly against her neck, when a tear spilled over and tumbled down her cheek.

She wiped it and took a rattling breath. She glanced away, at the phone—as silent as ever—and the clock on the oven. It was twenty to four. If she was going to be at her best for the trial run, she needed to get some sleep.

A few hours later, she awoke to a flood of sunlight and a strong sense of urgency. She had to find that command.

Thanks to Beverly's affluence and influence, they had acquired all the right pieces. Like a Bluetooth no bigger than Eden's scrambling device, inserted into her other ear. Not only would this allow Jack and Dr. Norton and Cassian to hear what she was hearing, it emitted the doppelgänger's signal. She also got an eye contact with a camera that could feed video to a large screen in the conference room on the fourth floor of Dr. Beverly Randall-Ransom's home, where Eden stood now, trying not to call attention to the fact that she was taking more mental pictures of Jack's notes as he opened the laptop and began erasing histories and logging out of applications. When he finished, he rebooted the computer and searched for networks.

SEX loaded at the top.

Whether this was her real network or the doppelgänger, they weren't sure. The only way to know was by logging in and trying one of the commands. Sleep would be the most straightforward. The next thing Eden knew, Dr. Norton was hovering above her, shaking her awake. The first attempt was a bust. The doppelgänger hadn't come online, and the firewall had failed.

Eden tried not to panic as Jack did some tweaking and tried again.

The second time was a success. But Eden hardly felt comforted.

"How are you going to make sure this works when it counts?" she asked as he clacked away on his laptop. "If all we can see is one network, and we can't differentiate between the two, how are we supposed to know which one Mordecai has accessed?"

"I'll keep troubleshooting," Jack said. "After we're done here."

The pictures Eden had taken in her mind would have to wait, too.

For now, she went outside. She wandered the grounds of Beverly's estate, carrying out the commands Dr. Norton gave through the Bluetooth—the phone in her hand and the images in her head, urgency nipping at her heels. She needed to examine the latter before the former could ring. Hopefully this time she would find the information she needed.

Cassian swam laps on the roof.

He wasn't participating in the trial run. While he knew his way around computers—while he might actually be able to help—Forrester didn't trust him to do so. And Eden didn't invite him back into her life to help Jack.

Lactic acid throbbed in his muscles as he pushed off the wall, cutting quickly through the water with a front stroke that was both smooth and powerful. His heart pounded in his ears. His lungs screamed for oxygen. Norton had removed the stitches, but the muscle had not completely healed. He should listen to his body. He would pay for this later. Instead, he pushed onward in an attempt to drown his frustration. And the memory of last night.

Her touch. Like fire and ice.

Her words, too.

"I miss them."

He couldn't stop hearing her say those words or seeing the way she looked at him when she did—with eyes so big it was impossible not to get lost. Cass knew what it was like to miss someone like that. He knew what it was like to feel helpless. He knew the pain of failure, too. The profound sense of loss and culpability that turned a heart so bitter and hard, it corrupted all that was good.

Eden was good. And he would do everything in his power to keep the demons that haunted him from haunting her. The problem was, part of that *everything* included a self-destruct command that would destroy this girl who was coming to mean too much to him. She was hunting like a huntress on a mission, intent on finding the right keystrokes that would save her. And kill her. While he helped her pore over the notes she recreated, a piece of him—an increasingly large piece—didn't want her to succeed. Every time they failed to find what she was looking for, he felt relief. And guilt. And a hundred other warring emotions.

It had gotten out of hand—this battle between his heart and his mind. So today, he'd gone through great lengths to avoid her, and all it had done was make him increasingly irritable. He missed the girl he was supposed to destroy. Just like he'd hidden the girl he was hired to find. Making him the world's biggest fool.

He reached the end of the pool, grabbed the ledge, and paused, giving his lungs time to catch up.

"Who are you racing?"

He turned around with his chest heaving, and spotted Eden sitting poolside, her eyes bright, her feet in the water. Her legs long and sexy.

His heart purred. His mind growled.

He shook the wetness from his hair and ran his hand down the length of his face, wiping the water away.

When his palm no longer covered his eyes, he found her attention lingering on his chest. As soon as she realized she'd been caught, she quickly looked away, her cheeks pink. The girls Cass knew wouldn't have looked away. They would have made their desire plain. Eden fumbled with hers, hiding it in a manner that was refreshing, adorable, and ridiculously alluring.

"How'd it go?" he asked.

"Not the greatest. Jack's troubleshooting now."

"You look pretty excited for a trial run that didn't go the greatest." And bright-eyed for someone who'd been sitting in Beverly's kitchen at three in the morning.

She looked over her shoulder—as if checking to make sure the coast was clear—then leaned slightly forward. "Come here."

"Why?"

"Just come here."

He walked through the water until he was standing in front of her, battling the foolish urge to step closer, grab her hips, pull her into the pool, and kiss her until they both forgot who they were and why they were here. Until nothing existed but desire and passion and this girl who was driving him crazy. He rattled the image away, and the longing that accompanied it.

She checked over her shoulder again, then pulled out papers from her pocket and unfolded them. On the front page, she'd circled a combination of keystrokes beneath two ominous letters: SD. Self Destruct.

His heart sank.

"I found it. It's these three keys, right here. You push these three buttons and—"

"You die." His words came out hard and angry.

The brightness in her eyes dimmed.

"It's a weird thing to be excited about," he said.

"I'm not excited. I'm *relieved*. We've been searching and searching. We needed to find it before Mordecai called. And we did. It's right here. We've got it."

"They aren't going to stand aside and give me access to the computer keys."

"Then you'll have to make them."

He turned away, wondering how many more laps he'd have to swim to outrun this.

"Cass?"

He didn't answer.

"You made me a promise," she said, her voice trembling.

"I know."

"Then keep it."

He turned around, his pent-up frustration rising to the surface. "You say that like it's easy."

"It *is* easy. It's three key strokes."

"Three key strokes that stop your heart."

"And ensure I'm still me when it does!"

He ran his hand down his face again.

When he met her eyes, she was glaring. And shaking. "You're a coward."

"Why? Because I don't want you to die?"

"Because you're going back on your word."

"Because I care about you!" His voice thundered, chasing away a pair of birds that had been twittering on a rose bush in the rooftop garden.

Eden sat there, her face white and strained, silence stretching wide in the wake of his outburst. She pressed her lips together and shook her head. "You can't care about me."

"I *can't*?"

"No."

"Why not?"

"You don't even know me."

"I know some of you, and those parts are pretty easy to care about."

"Which ones?" She flung her arms out from her sides, her eyes shining with tears. "The part that attacked my parents? Nearly killed my own mother? The parts that make me so dangerous, I need a tranquilizer pump to keep the people around me safe?"

"Eden—"

"*Don't* care about me, Cass."

"It's too late."

"Then you're a fool."

"I've been called worse."

"I'm not safe!" She clutched her hands to her chest. "I've got these things inside of me. Things that can make me do what I don't want to do."

"You think you're the only one?"

She shook her head. "You weren't created to be a weapon."

"That's exactly what I was created to be. By a vulture named Vick, who saw an angry kid with quick fists and decided to capitalize on it."

"It's not the same thing," she said. "You know it's different. I was created by a terrorist. I was created for evil."

"But *you* aren't evil."

She shook her head again, the shine in her eyes thickening.

He wanted to grab her by the face. Stop the shaking. Force her to listen. "You might not be safe, Eden. But you're good."

Despite what Volkova did to her, his words were true. She

was good. And none of this was fair. But before he could convince her, something happened first.

Something they'd been expecting.

Something he'd been dreading.

The phone by Eden's side began to ring.

38

For a week and a half, Eden had been waiting, watching, staring at the phone she carried with her everywhere she went until it became an extra appendage. And now suddenly, it was ringing. Her heart lurched, her emotions whipping from anger to hope to shock to fear to fury all in a matter of seconds. She'd finally found the key but Cassian was wavering. He didn't think she was a monster, and she wanted to believe him. The phone was actually ringing. Which meant Mordecai fixed the glitch. This man who had possessed her. This man who made her hurt the two people she loved most in the world. This man who was holding them hostage.

She answered after the first ring, adrenaline coursing through her body. She didn't say hello. She didn't wait for him to speak first. She asked her question in a low, ominous growl. "Where are they?"

"Well, hello to you, too," he crooned.

Mordecai.

She was talking to Mordecai.

"Where are they?" she asked again. "What have you done with them?"

He *tsked* in her ear.

She grasped the phone with both hands. "If you let them go, I'll meet you wherever you want."

There was a pause. A consideration. And then, "It seems we're at a bit of an impasse. You want to ensure the safety of your parents. I want to ensure I get what I want. Your parents are my only guarantee that I will. So, no. I won't be letting them go. Not until I have you first."

"How do I know you won't kill them as soon as you have me?"

Cass shifted in the water beside her.

"I suppose you don't. But really, what other choice do you have?"

Dread sank through her, down into the depths of her stomach. He was right. She wasn't the one with the upper hand here. Not when she had too much to lose. "Why are you doing this? What do you want with me?"

"All questions that will be answered. When the time is right."

"Are you a part of Interitus? Are you a follower of Volkova?"

"Volkova is *dead*."

Cass pulled himself out of the water and sat beside her, the phone between them as he leaned closer to listen.

"Here is how this is going to play out. Please listen carefully. I'd rather not repeat myself. I will send two drones to 176th Street in North Allegheny. It's an abandoned power plant just outside the city. If these drones are shot down, hacked into, tampered with in any way—if there is any funny business at all—I will kill your parents without hesitation. Do you understand?"

She swallowed.

"You will arrive by ten tonight."

Ten.

That was only a few hours away.

Jack wouldn't be finished troubleshooting in a few hours.

"And you will arrive alone. If anyone comes with you, I will not hesitate to kill your parents. A car will be there. Your parents will be inside that car. As soon as we have you, they are free to go."

She laughed bitterly.

Free to go?

"Did I say a funny joke?"

"If my parents see me, they aren't going anywhere." Maybe this was the plan all along. Maybe Mordecai was waiting for the first excuse to kill them.

"Do you have a better suggestion?"

"Blindfold them. Don't tell them I'm coming."

There was a soft hum, as though he was taking it under consideration.

"Please," she said. "Please just—"

But it was too late.

The line had gone dead.

———

Eden's worry spun into panic.

There was no time to fix everything that needed fixing, and Cass refused to meet her eye, behavior that pushed Eden to the precipice. He couldn't go back on his word. Not now. She was counting on him. She needed him. A message she would communicate if he would only look at her. But he wouldn't, and everything had turned into a whirlwind of activity.

Dr. Norton removed the scrambling device from her ear. They needed to monitor her location and they were no longer hiding it from Mordecai. Jack was busy double, triple, and quadruple checking the doppelgänger, the firewall, the Bluetooth, the eye contact connection. The location Mordecai gave her was on the opposite side of Chicago. Even without rush hour traffic, it would take Sam the better part of an hour to get her there, and he couldn't get her there all the way. She'd have to finish the last leg of the journey alone.

No funny business.

Mordecai couldn't have been clearer, and Eden was not willing to take a single risk.

Which was why she removed the tranquilizer pump. It fell under the realm of funny business, and it was no longer necessary. This would go down in one of two ways: Jack's plan would work, or Jack's plan would fail. If it failed, the pump would not help her. Mordecai would already have her. Being sedated for a time wasn't going to fix anything. What mattered most was getting her parents to safety. Whatever happened, this point needed to remain. Her parents would get out of the car and she would get in. Mordecai would drive away, giving them enough time to run, and Eden would either be under the man's control or she wouldn't. If the former, Cass had to hold up his end of the bargain. If the latter, she would do what he'd called her to do all those days ago in the woods.

She would be a weapon, and she would use it against him.

She closed her eyes and imagined it—as if enough visualization could make it true.

Mordecai, dead.

The threat, eliminated.

Her parents, safe.

This nightmare, over.

They hadn't had nearly as much practice as she'd hoped, but time was running out.

She needed to go.

Dr. Norton and Jack offered last minute words of encouragement and support, then returned to the house. Cassian turned to follow, like that was it. They might not see each other ever again and he was just going to walk away without saying anything. She grabbed his arm. He stopped and turned and looked at the place her fingers touched, his expression one of pure agony.

Despite everything—who she was, *what* she was—he cared about her. And beneath all of the stress and the anxiety and the worry and the planning and plotting and preparing, she cared about him, too. She cared about him so much, it had become an ache, and who knew if this wasn't the last time they'd see each other. The last time she'd be in full possession of herself. Here, outside this mansion on the Gold Coast of Chicago, beneath a night strewn with stars.

"Cassian," she said, his name a plea on her tongue.

When he looked up at her, a storm of conviction swirled in his eyes. "This is going to work. I know you can—"

She didn't wait to hear what he knew she could do.

Without thinking, without hesitating—while she was still in control, while she was still *her*—she kissed him.

His lips were soft and full and unprepared.

But only for a second.

An infinitesimal blip of surprise quickly replaced by a torrent —of passion and urgency and the heartbreaking possibility of goodbye. Like the flip of a switch, like he'd been waiting right there on the edge with her, he pulled her body all the way to his, dug strong fingers into her hair, and kissed her like she was the last woman on earth, and he'd never get to do it again.

Expertly, achingly, intoxicatingly—he kissed her.

Until her knees were jelly and everything else, aflame.

His thumb slipped under the hem of her top and stroked the bare skin of her hip as all around, the world spun. So fast, so euphoric, she had to grab onto his shirtfront and hold on. And when it was done, her lips were swollen.

Their chests heaved.

The storm in his eyes raged—like his desire wasn't satiated but awakened.

She wanted to kiss him again. She wanted to kiss him forever. She wanted to close her eyes and tilt her head back and let his lips have her throat. Let the sensations he aroused consume her. Consume him. Until nothing else was real.

But the Rolls Royce idled behind them.

Sam was waiting.

With his shirt still clutched in her hands, she looked up into his turbulent eyes and whispered what she needed to say. "Protect me, Cass. *Please*. Protect me from him."

With those words, his agony returned.

It swept in like a violent wave—the kind that meant he would.

39

ass prowled the conference room like a caged lion—his body throbbing, his blood on fire. He flexed his fingers, then clenched them into fists, straining against what little self-control he had left after that kiss. His heart thundered at the memory of her lips, her warmth, the feel of her hair between his fingers. The tiny catch of breath when his thumb found her skin. Skin he might not touch again if this plan didn't work.

He wanted to crawl out of his own.

He wanted to jump into the closest vehicle and follow her to the abandoned power plant. He wanted to grab Mordecai by the neck and squeeze and squeeze until the threat was gone and she was safe. This girl who had torn down the walls he'd erected. Walls that protected his heart from the kind of pain he'd felt once before.

And then she left.

But not before making her final plea.

Protect her.

By destroying her.

Somehow, the two were one and the same, and after his

desire ravaged everything else, he was left with a piercing tenderness that tore his soul.

Jack had his computer open on the table. The video feed was up and running. They could hear what Eden was hearing, see what she was seeing, as Sam drove her to within a mile of their meeting place. They were inside the doppelgänger network. Whether or not that connection would hold remained to be seen.

There was nothing to do but wait until she arrived.

Wait, and pace—with his eyes glued to the screen, watching as rundown neighborhoods grew increasingly dilapidated, then disappeared completely. Sam stopped on an empty street corner. Eden thanked him, then she stepped out into the night.

Forrester cursed.

Cass went still. "What's wrong?"

"We lost the connection." Forrester looked quickly from one screen to the next, pinpricks of sweat forming on his upper lip. Quickly, adroitly—as Eden made her way to the specified location—Forrester pulled up a citywide grid. He used the tracker to pinpoint her location, zoomed in, and seconds later, a single network appeared.

"Is that the right one?" Cass asked.

Forrester didn't answer. He logged in as Eden arrived at a large, deserted lot, where a bright moon gave light to the trees and weeds growing up and around a giant building of crumbling brick and broken window. Eden surveyed her surroundings—looking left, then right—but there was no vehicle anywhere. The place was deserted.

"How do you know you're in the right one?" Cass asked again.

"He doesn't," Norton said, his attention on the monitor that was measuring Eden's vitals.

Eden looked up, giving them a view of the star-strewn sky, where two drones circled like vultures.

One of them dropped lower.

They could hear its mechanic whirr through the Bluetooth.

Another network appeared, sending Jack's fingers into a whirlwind. "It's coming from the drone."

"What is?"

"The signal."

Cass stared hard at the screen. Eleven years old all over again. Locked inside a closet, because his mother wanted to keep him safe. And he didn't know. He didn't know why she forced him inside. Not until the rusty hinges of their apartment door groaned and his father walked in—a man Cass only remembered from his nightmares. A man who was tapping the barrel of a baseball bat against his palm while Cass pressed his against the closet door, staring out from between the slats, his heartbeat thrashing in his ears.

He was back there now. Watching. Helpless. His body crawling with dread as one of the drones dropped lower. Eye-level with Eden. Emitting an infrared light that scanned the length of her body.

"We've got something." Forrester sat up straighter. "From the drone. It's trying to access the network."

Eden stood in place, her breathing steady.

Where was Mordecai? Where were her parents?

Cass gripped the back of the man's chair, trying to make sense of the onslaught of code scrolling down the screen. Forrester followed it with his pointer finger. "He's in."

"*Which network?*" Cass ground the words between his teeth.

But neither the doctor nor the IT specialist could answer.

As Norton already said, they didn't know.

"That's it. Right there." Forrester highlighted a string of code, then put his hand over his ear and spoke into the Bluetooth. "Command Five, Eden."

"What's command five?" Cass asked.

"He's putting her into a highly suggestible state," Norton answered.

"She needs to do whatever he tells her to do," Forrester added.

Eden didn't respond.

She stood there like she was already in a trance as the sound of gravel popped beneath tires.

A black Land Rover with tinted windows approached, turning Cass's stomach to stone.

A hundred yards.

Eighty yards.

Sixty.

Forty.

It stopped at twenty.

Were her parents inside, blindfolded? Or were they banging against the windows, begging Eden to run? Cass didn't know. And Eden didn't move. She stood like a statue as a man stepped out of the driver's side door. A man covered in tattoos.

"Hands in the air," he said.

Eden obeyed.

The guy looked over his shoulder toward the idling SUV and smirked. "Good girl. Now come here."

She walked toward him.

The closer she got, the heavier the weight on Cass's chest became. He was pounding on the closet door. Clawing at the closet door. Screaming through the closet door. Ramming his shoulder into the closet door until bone and lock broke and he scrambled free, desperate to cover her, protect her. But it was too late. By the time he got to his mother, there was too much blood. Her eyes were open and empty. Far away, some place he couldn't go. Then the monster turned the bat on him. But Cassian hadn't felt anything other than the pain in his heart. The pain that was his mother's absence. He would have done anything to go back, to stop it from happening. Just like he would do anything now—beg, steal, barter, get back in the ring. But he was here with no closet door to barrel through, and only one way to help.

Three key strokes.

"Stop," the man said.

She stopped so close the guy's face filled the entirety of the screen. His smirk stretched into a smarmy grin as he pawed her body in what was a thorough and violating search. Her vitals didn't budge. But Cass saw red. Cass saw blood. He wanted to slam the man against a wall, bury his fist in his face. Over and over until he begged for mercy, and even then, he wouldn't stop.

One of the tinted windows rolled open a crack.

The guy stopped his groping. "She's all clear."

The door opened.

Expensive, leather shoes hit the gravel.

A man stood from the back seat—tall and thin and meticulously dressed, his hair slicked back like a mobster.

Mordecai, in the flesh.

He walked slowly—almost reverently—toward Eden, his eyes bright and victorious as he reached out and stroked her cheek.

Cass jerked, as if it were his cheek Mordecai had touched.

"Oh my," he crooned. "You are magnificent."

"And you said she would do … *anything*?" the other one asked.

The cords in Cassian's neck pulled tight. His nostrils flared. His hands clenched tighter. But before the growl in his chest could rumble free, Mordecai removed a gun from the holster beneath his suit jacket and pressed the barrel against the man's neck, right into the orange and black pattern of a butterfly wing.

The man's eyes bulged.

"If you so much as touch her," Mordecai said. "I will kill you."

The guy nodded dumbly, his smirk long gone.

Mordecai put his gun away, walked to the Land Rover, and opened the back door.

Cass braced himself.

He could feel Norton tensing beside him.

This was it.

She was going to see her parents, and if their plan was working, it would take every ounce of her willpower not to react. And if their plan wasn't working …

He swallowed, but the ache in his throat remained. He closed his eyes, Eden's haunted voice reverberating inside his skull. *Imagine if they could force you back into the ring, and make you kill person after person after person.* It would destroy him just like it would destroy her. Until she was no longer Eden, but a monster of Mordecai's making. A fate worse than death. A fate he could stop with three keystrokes.

His heart twisted.

His fingers clenched.

"Please, get in," Mordecai said, his voice smooth as silk.

Norton leaned closer to the screen as Eden obeyed.

She bent to get in the car, but the Land Rover was empty.

Her parents weren't inside.

Like a hiccup, her movement jerked.

Glorious and horrifying—because that tiny reaction meant two things. Eden wasn't under Mordecai's control. And Eden had just given herself away.

Before any of them could respond, there was a burst of static.

The screen scrambled.

And their connection went dead.

———

Eden seized. Her mind. Her lungs. Her muscles. The ligaments and tendons around her bones. Everything except her heart. That careened out of control—so loud and fast, she was positive the whole world could hear it.

Then the whole world went black.

Like a blip in her brain.

When she came to, she was standing in the same place— halfway in, halfway out of the Land Rover with her back to the two men. Only Mordecai was much closer. And one of the drones was beside her with its infrared light scanning the length of her body.

"Are you sure you should take that off?" the man with the rough hands asked.

"The connection is stable," Mordecai replied, only he didn't sound confident.

Eden's eyes darted one way, then the other, trying to gain her bearings. What had just happened? How much time had passed? Why wasn't anyone saying anything in her Bluetooth? And where were her parents?

"You may get in," Mordecai said.

Eden had to keep playing along.

She obeyed.

She moved.

Inside the vehicle, an array of technology blinked. The kind someone might find in the back of a surveillance van. The kind that reminded her of her father, the CIA agent. Her father, still missing. Her fingertips dug into the upholstery. She commanded them to relax. She regulated her breath and her heart rate, too. If she didn't, Mordecai would see it pulsing frantically in her throat, and that could not happen.

Mordecai slid inside. He sat across from her, beside the blinking technology, staring suspiciously while his thumb stroked something small in his hand.

She kept her gaze blank and straight ahead.

He leaned closer, peering into one of her eyes, then the other.

Eden could overpower him. She could overpower them both. She could pin them down and demand to know the location of her parents. But there was no guarantee they would give it, and if they didn't, how would she ever find them? Chicago was enormous; they could be anywhere—locked up, depending on these very men for food and water. If she killed them, she might as well kill her mom and dad.

But what if they were already dead?

And here she was, sitting calmly. Without expression. While inside, her mind screamed.

This wasn't part of the plan.

She didn't know what to do.

And nobody was speaking in her ear.

Not Jack.

Not Dr. Norton.

Not Cassian, either.

Think, Eden. Think.

The man with the tattoos got behind the wheel.

Mordecai pushed a button on the blinking technology. And suddenly, a projection illuminated the back of the Land Rover. A three-dimensional butterfly quickly spun into a large, two-dimensional grid with a pair of blinking dots. One remained stable. The other jumped about erratically. Mordecai swiped the grid away, bringing forth a command log similar to the one Jack had spent days studying. He swiped again, this time to a long list of numbers separated by periods. Then he swiped once more, to a strange image filled with hundreds of different-colored dots —blue, red, and yellow. This, he scrutinized as though searching for something specific. Eden took the opportunity to steal a glance at the object clasped in his hand—a tiny, disc-like gadget with a neon substance floating in its center.

Had that been the reason for her blackout?

Her muscles wound into a million knots as Mordecai zoomed in on a cluster of blue, then swiped the holographic projection away.

"In time, you will realize this isn't necessary." He motioned to the technology. "I mean you no harm."

Eden swallowed a scream. A guttural cry.

Where were her parents?

"I would never hurt you," he said, leaning back in his seat. "Nobody can hurt you."

Inside, Eden raged. He had hurt her. He'd hurt her parents.

Mordecai rubbed his thumb over the disc with an unsettling gleam in his eye.

It was one of admiration.

40

40

As the driver wound through the city at night, Eden couldn't look out the tinted windows. She had no idea where they were headed. She only knew they drove for a long time and the lights grew fewer and farther between. She gazed straight ahead while their driver flicked glances at her in the rearview mirror. The Bluetooth connection might have been severed, but the doppelgänger signal in her ear remained. Which meant Jack could track her. When they stopped—wherever they stopped—they would have Mordecai pinpointed.

And hopefully, her parents, too.

Hopefully, they were still alive.

The probability that they weren't—that Mordecai had killed them weeks ago and she was a fool for believing otherwise—slashed through her chest like a fiery blade. She stuffed the possibility aside. She needed to keep her wits and she wouldn't be able to with the thought of their death spinning in her mind.

The vehicle slowed and turned, tires crunching and popping over gravel. They came to a stop—waited—a red light flashing in the periphery of Eden's vision. There was beeping. A groan as something like machine-operated chain link slid open. The Land Rover crept forward. Eden caught a glimpse of a booth sliding past her window—the kind found at tolls along the highway, and a man dressed like a security guard sitting in the glow of a light overhead.

She wanted to look around, see where they'd taken her. But she couldn't.

She had to wait for several more turns, several more stops and starts, until the vehicle slowly drove past a set of steel doors set into the side of a hill. The night went bright with fluorescent lights as they stopped inside an underground parking lot.

The steel doors shut behind them with a clanging boom.

The tattooed driver got out first.

Mordecai next.

Eden remained, her heart hammering.

Mordecai peeked inside and asked her to join them.

She obeyed, her senses on high alert.

Mordecai's shoes echoed as he walked.

Eden trailed behind, taking in as much as she could while she had the chance.

They'd taken her to some sort of compound—massive, by the looks of it. They walked past several cars and a motorcycle, which made her thoughts flit to Cassian. What would he do, in her situation—keep playing along? At what point would he turn on his captors?

Mordecai stopped in front of a door.

He pressed his thumb against the keypad and the lock buzzed.

They stepped into a small area with a shower and a sink. They walked through another buzzing door, into a cavernous gallery. Framed photographs of former presidents, of the site's construction, of the dreadful attack twenty-one years ago lined the walls. And suddenly, it clicked. Eden knew exactly where she was. A luxury bomb shelter, one of several that made up a project known as SafePad Elite. A plethora of celebrities owned them. Back in San Diego, one of her rich classmates had often bragged about her family's underground property in Utah. Eden thought it was dumb. If another attack happened, how did they plan on getting there?

They passed a rock wall—the kind built for recreational climbing—a dog park made of turf, potted tree after potted tree, along a curved walkway until they reached an elevator lit with red lighting and a female security guard standing sentry outside. Eden could feel the woman's eyes following her as she stepped in. Was she in on it—this security guard and the other one, manning the booth outside? Did they work for Mordecai, or were they employees of SafePad, unaware that a madman— quite possibly a terrorist—was utilizing the famed facilities?

Mordecai pushed a button.

The doors slid shut and they sank through the shaft.

Deeper underground, they walked past maintenance rooms that made a retinue of noises and into a room filled with surveillance monitors. There was another security guard inside. As soon as they entered, he brought his boots off the desk and onto the floor.

"How are they doing?" Mordecai asked sharply.

"Uh ... the same, sir," the young guard replied, his cheeks turning cherry red.

Hope exploded.

They.

Who were *they*? Her parents?

Mordecai scratched his chin as he examined the screens.

Eden wanted to look so badly it hurt. But if she looked, she would give herself away. And she couldn't do that. Not if her parents were here, alive. Not if they were being watched by another security guard, ready to take them out should their plan go awry.

Mordecai's attention slid away from the screens to the side of Eden's face, hot on her skin. Then he turned to his tattooed crony. "Bring her to the examination room. I'll be down after I check on the others. We can run the updates on her first since she's already awake."

The others.

Was he talking about Barrett Barr and Subject 003? Were they here, too? The man grabbed Eden's arm every bit as roughly as he'd searched her outside the abandoned power plant, eliciting an angry hiss from Mordecai.

"What did I say about manhandling her?"

"But—"

"She will do what you say without objection."

"She didn't the last time," the guy muttered.

Mordecai's eyes flashed. "This isn't like last time, is it?" He took a deep breath. Straightened his suit coat like a man trying to inhale composure. "Now please, take her to the examination room."

The guy mumbled an apology and commanded Eden to follow.

"Oh, and Tom?"

He stopped. Looked over his shoulder.

"The parents are no longer needed. Feel free to dispose of them."

Her insides lurched.

Dispose of them.

They were here, somewhere—in this giant, underground facility.

Tom's face twisted with sadistic pleasure—like a little kid who'd been handed a cookie. "Shouldn't they say goodbye first? I'm sure they'd like to know their daughter is in good hands."

"She was never their daughter." Mordecai's words were sharp and biting.

Tom flinched.

Mordecai took a deep breath. Pinching the bridge of his nose, he waved dismissively.

Eden's heart pounded—not with dread, but a great boom-boom of confusion and hope. What did that wave mean? Was Tattooed Tom taking her to the examination room or her parents? As she followed him into the elevator and they sank deeper into the earth, she could no longer control her crashing heartbeat.

The elevator doors slid open.

She followed Tom through a long corridor and stopped when he stopped—at the end of the hallway, in front of a door with a small window.

"Go on," he said. "Take a look. *Mommy* and *Daddy* haven't stopped asking about you. They will be so relieved to see that you're perfectly intact."

With her heart in her throat, Eden obeyed his command. She stepped up to the window. And there—inside a small prison-of-a-room, were the two people she'd been aching to see. Her mother, curled on her side with her head resting on Dad's lap. Her father, slumped against the wall with his eyes closed. His hand stroking his wife's limp hair—one gesture of love, two postures of despair. There was no bed. Not even a bench to sit on. Just cramped space and white walls and the cold, hard ground.

But they were here. They were alive.

With nothing between them but this door.

Behind her, she could hear the quiet whisper of metal sliding against sheath—Tom, drawing a gun.

Faster than a viper, Eden spun. She grabbed the gun with one hand and Tom's neck with the other, her fingers clamping tight around his butterfly tattoo. She aimed the barrel at the cameras mounted in the hallways and shot each one clean through. Tom clawed at her fingers, but his strength was nothing compared to hers. His eyes bulged as she rammed him against the wall. He sputtered as her grip tightened around his throat like it had tightened around her mother's, only this time, she was alert. This time, she was aware. This time, she knew exactly what she was doing as she brought the handle of the gun down against the crown of his head.

His eyes rolled and he sank to the ground in an unconscious heap.

In a sprint against the clock, she didn't bother searching him for a key. If she could knock over a tree, then she could break a steel door. She grabbed the handle and with a shove, the hinges snapped. The door didn't just swing open. It fell to the ground.

Her parents looked up, stunned.

After two weeks in captivity, Eden was suddenly there. The girl who had beaten them, strangled them, was now holding a gun over them. But their expressions held no trace of fear. Only shock. And then, after the short span of time it took for their brains to catch up with their eyes, a flood of unadulterated relief. They scrambled to their feet and wrapped Eden in a tight, fierce hug. She wanted to stay that way forever—sandwiched between the love of her mother and her father—but there was no time.

As if realizing the same thing, Dad took the gun from Eden. He shot through the camera in the upper corner of the room like a man well versed with guns. Her accountant-of-a-father who'd once been in the CIA.

"We need to move." His words were clear, filled with authority.

"What about the other two?" Mom asked. "We can't leave them."

On the tail end of her words, the door at the end of the hallway clanged open.

Eden shoved her mother into the room as guns fired and the world spun into slow motion. She watched the first bullet slice through the air, heading straight toward her. Eden bent backward—dodging its trajectory—as a spray of bullets followed.

Without thought, driven purely by instinct, she jumped and flipped and whirled, evading every single one as she charged forward, straight into the maelstrom, until she was close enough to kick the guns away and engage in hand-to-hand combat with a handful of guards.

Be a weapon. And use it against him.

With Cassian's words ringing in her ears, she fought—spinning and kicking and punching and blocking, until every single guard was on the ground.

Her chest heaved. Blood pounded in her ears as she stood—the sole victor amongst Mordecai's men.

And then …

A wail turned her blood to ice.

She turned around, and there—at the end of the hall she'd just charged down—was her mother, bent over her father, lying in a pool of crimson.

Eden ran to his side.

He was gasping for breath, his face alarmingly pale as her mother searched his body with frantic hands. "Help," she cried. "Oh God, please. He's losing too much blood!"

The second the connection dropped, Cass yelled at Norton and Forrester to move. He grabbed a set of keys hanging by the back door and jumped behind the wheel of the doctor's truck. They used Forrester's phone to track Eden's location. It flashed on his screen as they wound through the city at night, drawing closer as the pit in Cass's stomach grew.

Eden wasn't under Mordecai's control. And she couldn't be hurt. Volkova had ensured it. Except for the self-destruct command. Cass wasn't the only one capable of executing it. A fact that turned his foot to lead.

He ignored every red light.

He ignored Norton telling him to slow down.

When Forrester suggested he cut through a field because it would be quicker, Cass didn't hesitate. He drove onto the curb and over bumpy terrain, not stopping until they reached a chain link fence, and an opened gate, and a deserted booth with an eerie light glowing inside.

"This is it." Jack looked from their surroundings to his phone to a company sticker on the top right window of the booth. "Property of SafePad Elite."

They wound along a gravel road until they reached an entrance in a hillside—its steel doors wide open. It was wrong. All wrong. This place would not be without security. The gates and the doors would be locked. Passcode protected. But Cass drove right in, into a large underground parking lot, and slammed to a stop, tires screeching against pavement.

He didn't bother shutting off the truck.

He jumped out and sprinted further inside, Forrester close behind. Until they were right on top of her. Or at least, where Eden should have been according to the pulsing light on the phone. Cass spun in a circle. "Where is she?"

Forrester hit the button to an elevator. "She must be down."

Urgency pressed at his back.

Unwilling to wait, Cass pushed into a stairwell, taking the stairs three at a time. He stopped at each floor. But Eden was nowhere on the first. Nowhere on the second. Nowhere on the third.

Halfway to the fourth, he heard the sound of crying.

He pushed open the door and nearly stumbled. Over bodies. Five security guards lying unconscious on the floor. And past them, on the other end of the hallway, Eden.

Alive.

Intact.

Still herself.

Relief crashed like a tsunami as he took her in, kneeling beside her mother, the two of them bent over someone on the ground.

Cass ran forward.

The fallen man was Eden's father.

Alexander Pruitt.

Alaric Taylor.

One and the same. Lying in a puddle of blood.

Eden pressed one hand against her father's thigh, the other

below the right side of his chest, using her strength to staunch the flow. Using her strength like a tourniquet.

Cass looked around. "Where's Mordecai?"

"I don't know," she said, her hands covered in red. "If I let go, he'll lose too much blood."

By the looks of it, he'd lost too much already.

They needed to move.

He needed medical attention now.

"I'm going to pick him up." Cass met Eden's eyes. "You keep applying pressure."

She nodded, her face pale. Cass slid one arm under her dad's shoulders, the other beneath his knees, and lifted. Halfway to the elevator, they met Forrester and Norton. Together, they got Eden's father into the back of the truck. Norton climbed in after them. Eden's mother followed.

Cassian shut the hatch.

"I'll stay behind," Forrester said.

Cass nodded.

There were unconscious guards on the ground and Mordecai was missing in action. "If he shows up, don't let him get away."

Forrester nodded as Cass jumped behind the wheel and peeled out of the parking garage.

41

Chaos reigned in the cargo hold of a military truck while Eden's father fought for his life. Blood. Shouting. Tires squealing as Dr. Norton yelled at Eden to keep the pressure on the wounds and Mom grabbed Dad's pallid face between her hands. "Stay with us, Alexander. Please!"

The truck turned a corner.

Dr. Norton fell against the wall, his shoulder hitting metal as he worked to unbuckle the belt at his waist.

Mom shook Dad's head. "Don't you dare fall asleep, do you hear me?"

But Dad's eyes refused to stay open.

They kept sliding shut.

And no matter how hard Eden pressed on the wounds, her father continued to bleed. It pooled beneath him at an alarming rate.

Mom tapped Dad's cheek.

His eyes rolled.

The truck turned another corner.

Norton planted his feet wide and tied the leather belt around her father's upper thigh. "He's bleeding from the exit wound at his back. I need you to apply pressure here and here."

With the bleeding in his thigh staunched, Eden lifted her dad's limp body to a reclined position and did as Dr. Norton commanded, sandwiching his ribcage between her palms. Norton checked her father's pulse with one hand, called someone with his other. He used his shoulder to cradle his phone against his ear as he cinched the belt tighter and notified the person on the other end that they needed emergency medical attention. He used words like multiple gunshot wounds, massive blood loss, unilateral chest rise, and tachycardia.

Outside, a horn blared.

Rubber screeched.

Dad's head lolled in Mom's hands. "Breathe, Alexander!"

Eden pressed harder.

Norton bent his ear to Dad's mouth, using two fingers to monitor the pulse at his wrist. "C'mon Taylor. Stay with us."

Taylor.

The surname Dr. Norton knew best. Before The Attack. Before Eden. Before Dad changed his name. When they were comrades in the military.

The truck ground to a halt.

The back hatch rumbled open.

Cassian stood on the other side, poised for action.

Dr. Beverly Randall-Ransom was already there, outside on her front lawn.

Together with Norton, they lifted her father onto a gurney.

"He needs intubation," Norton said.

Beverly placed a mask over her father's face, listening as Norton briefed her on the situation and they wheeled him up the dark lawn and into her house.

They got him downstairs, into the medical room with a red crash cart ready and waiting.

They worked around Eden, a flurry of commotion as she continued to press her palms hard against the bleeding. They cut off his shirt and stuck electrodes and pads to his chest. They hooked IVs into each of his arms. They yelled orders at her mother and Cassian for gauze and blood and fluids. They shouted vitals.

Blood pressure—eighty-five over sixty and dropping.

Heart rate—one hundred twenty and climbing.

Norton stood by holding a long tube. Dr. Beverly Randall-Ransom removed the mask from Dad's face. Norton quickly slid the tube into his mouth and attached it to a ventilator.

"Airway secured." He moved Eden aside to pack Dad's wounds with gauze as Beverly took a scalpel to her father's ribs. She made a small cut and inserted a tube that filled with blood.

"We need more O Neg, stat!" she shouted.

Cassian handed Beverly another bag.

She hung it beside the IV fluid and used a syringe to inject drugs into his tubing as Eden stared in horror at all the wires and tubes connected to her father in such a short amount of time. All the while, Dad's eyes remained closed. His lips, an alarming blue.

"Heart rate is thirty," Norton said. "Starting compressions."

He pumped Dad's chest with such aggression, Eden could hear his ribs cracking.

The monitor surged with erratic lines and angry beeping.

Mom screamed Dad's name.

And sound escaped into a strange void.

Eden could dodge bullets. She could knock a towering tree over with her bare hands. She could run faster than an Olympic gold medalist. She could hear a whispered conversation from across the length of a football field. She could memorize in perfect detail any graph, any chart, any diagram set in front of her. She could defeat an army of gun-wielding guards. But she could not keep her father alive.

With his blood on her hands and splattered against the white tile at their feet, Eden watched in horror as her mother doubled over and her father's heart went into cardiac arrest. She was back on the staircase Cleo created when she lit incense in her dorm room and tried her hand at hypnotherapy. Eden was walking down the steps—deeper and deeper—to a place she'd never been. A place she'd only imagined, with her mother bent over in pain the same way she was now. Because their baby boy wasn't breathing. He was turning as blue as Dad's lips. Gasping for air with no way to get him the medicine he needed, with no way to breathe for him. Her parents had watched the life slowly seep out of Christopher like Eden watched the life seep from her father.

"Stand clear."

It was the machine that spoke.

Computerized words that had sound returning like a wave through a tunnel.

"Delivering shock."

Her father's upper half lifted into the air, then sank against the gurney as Norton stepped forward and resumed compressions.

———

Cass sat on a metal chair outside the medical room with his elbows on his knees and his jaw clenched tight. He'd just watched two doctors wrench a man from the brink of death. Now that man was in emergency surgery. His wife and daughter looking like warriors after a battle. Or fighters stepping out of the ring.

More than a year later, Cass could still hear the sounds.

The hisses and grunts.

The roar of the crowd.

The thud and crack of pummeling fists.

The spray of blood and sweat.

His chest heaving as the bell rang and the crowd screamed, and Cassian was pulled off the man he'd rendered unconscious, the man he'd rendered dead, as his arm was lifted into the air like a champion.

He squeezed his eyes shut.

But he couldn't stop seeing it.

The blood on his hands.

The blood in the ring.

The blood all around Eden's father.

The blood all around his mother.

He dragged his palm down his face and looked up at the ceiling.

Fluorescent lights blinked above him. Lights he'd looked at once before, when he was the one being wheeled through this room on a gurney. With a fractured skull. Broken ribs. A dead mom. And a shattered heart.

Anger built like steam in a kettle.

At his father.

At Vick.

At himself.

At Mordecai.

He pulled his phone from his pocket. He had a missed call.

He glanced at Eden and her mother, then stood from the chair, walked up the stairs and let himself outside, where he called Forrester.

He answered halfway through the first ring. "How is he?"

"Alive." At least for now. "What about Mordecai?"

"No sign of him. But there is something you need to see."

Cass stopped by the fountain. "What?"

"He has them. Two more."

"What do you mean?"

"A boy and a girl."

Cass's mind shot to the redhead he hadn't been able to find. Had Mordecai located her without him? The muscles in his jaw clenched harder—the need to act, to do something, overwhelming. He was of no use here. But the compound? Perhaps Mordecai would be there by the time Cassian arrived—the perfect outlet for his pent-up rage.

Forrester met him in the underground garage as soon as Cass shifted into park.

Mordecai was still a no-show.

Cass took his gun and followed Forrester along a trail of blood, past security guards who were awake and glaring, tied up and unable to move. He followed him down a hallway, their shoes crunching over broken glass, until they reached a room with the door ajar.

Forrester motioned for Cass to go ahead.

There were two cots inside, both occupied.

There was a girl in one—her hair not red but as dark as a raven's.

And in the other?

A boy Cass recognized.

A boy who had been all over Concordia News.

18-year-old Barrett Barr.

"What's he doing here?" Cass asked.

"He's Subject 004," Forrester said behind him. "And that's 003."

Cass crept forward with his gun. He nudged Barr. The boy didn't respond. But he *was* breathing. That much, Cass could tell. He nudged him again. Nothing.

"Their vitals are strong," Forrester said. "But they aren't waking up. It can't be tranquilizer. It would have worn off by now. Mordecai must have put them in some semi-permanent state of sleep."

Which meant they were under his control.

And highly dangerous.

Cass imagined Eden unconscious in this same way—completely vulnerable to the whims of a psychopath. His blood began to boil. "What does he want with them?"

"It's the same question I asked. But he won't say."

Cass turned. "*Who* won't say?"

"The guy with the tattoos."

The one who had man-handled Eden. His grip tightened around the gun. "Where is he?"

Adrenaline thrummed through Cass's veins as Forrester led

the way. When he reached the room and saw the man slumped in one corner with his hands tied, Cass strode forward, picked him up by the collar of his shirt and slammed him against the wall. "Where is he?"

The man's mouth twisted into a smile.

Cass slammed him against the wall a second time. "What does he want with them?"

"Sadly, not the same thing I want with them."

With a surge of rage, Cass butted his head hard against the man's nose.

There was a sickening crunch. And the sound of sadistic laughter as blood gushed from the guy's nostrils and colored his teeth. Cass shoved the barrel of his gun into the center of the man's forehead.

"Cassian," Forrester reprimanded.

"We need answers," Cass shot back.

"Not like this."

The guy kept laughing.

His blood kept spurting.

Cass pushed him away.

"Have you questioned the other guards?" he asked.

"They don't know anything," the bleeding man answered in a creepy, sing-song voice. He stood slumped against the wall. His neck bruised. His left eye swollen. His hands bound. "They're pawns," he spat, bloody spittle flying from his lips.

"And what are you?" Cass asked.

"The knight."

"Do knights have answers?"

"Of course they do."

"Then I guess we'll have to torture them out of you."

"Can you torture a dead man?"

Cass narrowed his eyes.

The guy lifted his bound hands in a strange salute. "For the Monarch." Then he smiled a wide, toothy grin. It wasn't until he chomped down that Cass saw the capsule between his teeth.

Forrester lurched forward.

But it was too late.

The man's eyes rolled.

His body convulsed, red spit foaming in the corners of his mouth.

Cass got down on his knees like he might be able to stop him. Like he might be able to resuscitate him.

But the man went still, his eyes blank.

With a loud yell, Cass rose to his feet and kicked the wall.

"What's the Monarch?" Forrester asked.

Cass shook his head, staring at the trickle of blood running over the butterfly tattoo on the man's neck.

A Monarch butterfly.

"We have to get Barrett and the girl out of here before Mordecai comes back," Forrester said.

And so they did.

Together, they loaded Subjects 003 and 004 into the back of Norton's truck.

This time, Cass stayed behind, hoping for Mordecai's return.

Until then, he would question the guards.

Even pawns knew their king. If Mordecai was the Monarch, then they should know. On his way to interrogate them, a security room with several screens monitoring the grounds caught his attention. Cass stepped inside, hoping to access the surveillance footage. Maybe that would provide some answers. But every monitor Cass rewound came back blank, their memories fried. And when he returned to the live feed, flashing blue and red lights made his blood go cold.

The police.

And here Cass was, inside a privately-owned, luxury bomb shelter with at least one dead body. He slid his gun from his belt and snuck his way toward the garage. He hid in the shadows as the cops rushed inside with their guns drawn. When the coast was clear, he hot-wired the abandoned motorcycle and fled into the dark.

42

For two days, while Eden's father lingered in a state of unconsciousness—hovering in the mysterious space between life and death—she neither ate nor drank nor slept. The enemies inside her kept her alive while she sat vigil, listening to the rhythmic whirr of the ventilator, hand-in-desperate-hand with her mother, who kept insisting he would be *fine*, as if enough conviction would make it true.

He'd been shot twice. Once in the thigh. Once through his ribcage. Which led to massive blood loss and a collapsed lung. Hypovolemic shock. Cardiac arrest. And a brush so close with death, Eden thought she'd lost him.

The bullet lodged in his leg was gone now. Flesh and bone had been put back together. His lung re-inflated and his blood replenished. But the threat of death still loomed—its presence a cloying, debilitating possibility, chasing away every other worry. Diminishing them into nothing. She couldn't think about Mordecai, or the fact that he was still out there with his sinister plans, whatever they might be. She couldn't think about Subject 003 and Subject 004—a boy named Barrett Barr and a girl without any name at all. Two teenagers like her, one who'd been splashed across Concordia news. One who hadn't. Nor could she think about Cassian, who showed up at the underground compound just when she needed him most, only to leave without a word. Nor could she think about any of the questions she'd wanted to ask her parents upon their reunion.

All that mattered was her father.

So, she sat, and she rocked, and silently she bartered and begged—that this miracle would remain. That it would not slip away. That there would be no takebacks. That her father's heart would keep beating.

At the end of the third day, he opened his eyes and squeezed Eden's hand.

And for the first time since she walked inside her ransacked living room in Eagle Bend, Eden Pruitt took a full and proper breath.

———

Eden's father was taken off the ventilator.

He was terribly weak in its aftermath. The doctors wanted him upright but sitting made his skin clammy, his insides woozy. The simple act of speaking proved to be a Herculean feat. He eked out words like an out-of-shape runner at the end of a long race. Even so, his vitals improved every day. On the sixth, his coloring returned. His nausea relented. He sat wearing a cannula, slowly spooning warm broth into his mouth while Eden filled the silence with chatter.

"Jack is trying to break into their networks." She was talking about Barrett Barr and the girl. They knew her father's name. At least, the name he once had before he took his child and disappeared. They had no idea where that father was now or what name he had given his daughter. Subjects 003 and 004 had been transported to Dr. Norton's cabin in the woods, where they remained unresponsive. Silent. Sleeping. And absolutely lethal. "But he can't even find a signal."

They were tiptoeing around it—the elephant in the room.

At her most optimistic, Eden had imagined—on several occasions—what it would be like when her parents were safe, when they were finally reunited. They would fall into a hug. Then she would pummel them with every question she'd been forced to swallow. Every question that exploded in her mind after seeing a picture of her parents on Cleo's laptop with names that weren't theirs. She hadn't counted on the bullets that nearly took her father away. She hadn't counted on life support. But here they were, six days reunited—the elephant growing bigger by the day as it gorged itself on her unasked questions.

"Jack's getting pretty frustrated, and Cass is searching for Mordecai." At least, according to Dr. Norton. Eden didn't actually know what Cassian was up to, because Cassian had not contacted her. He left when her father was still in surgery and had yet to return.

"*Cass*?" Dad said.

"He saved your life." Dr. Norton had told her this, too. Cass was the one who didn't hesitate when they lost contact. He was the one who grabbed the keys and demanded they go. Eden shuddered to think what might have been had they waited a minute longer.

"Remind me to thank him when he returns."

If he returns ...

The possibility twisted Eden's gut. Now that her dad was out of the woods, thoughts of Cassian had stepped from the shadows and into the light—demanding and incessant and volatile. Her emotions swung on a pendulum from confused hurt to profound gratitude.

"Care to tell me more about him?" Dad said.

Her cheeks flushed.

"I hear he's a fighter."

"*Was* a fighter."

Dad quirked his eyebrow, waiting for her to elaborate.

"He's still connected to people in the world, which is how he found out Mordecai was after me."

"The gambler."

Eden nodded. It was a misleading fraction of the truth, no different from the one Cassian had given her himself in Cleo's dorm room. But Eden couldn't give her father the rest. Even though Cass's absence was causing her turmoil, she felt protective of his reputation.

"Why do I feel like," he said, pausing to catch his breath, "there is more to the story?"

"Isn't there more to most?" Her reply escaped with a bite. A breach in the diplomatic wall they'd built around the elephant.

Dad stopped, the spoon of broth hovering near his mouth.

Eden's hands began to shake—her arms, too—as the wall came crashing down.

Dad set the spoon in the bowl.

"You and Mom lied," Eden said.

"We withheld the truth."

Anger flashed like lightning.

"So you could have a normal life."

"I should never have had a normal life!"

Dad winced.

He'd been through enough pain, but Eden couldn't stop herself. Just like she couldn't stop the security footage from running through her head in a constant loop. Grabbing her mother by the throat. Lifting her into the air. Slamming her down onto the glass coffee table. That's where withholding the truth had got them. "You put yourself in danger."

"As any parent would ... for the sake of their child."

"But I wasn't your child!"

A bloated silence followed the outburst.

Dad closed his eyes.

To hide what—grief? Regret? Exhaustion?

Eden didn't know, and the not knowing fueled her anger. She attacked them. She nearly killed them, and she had no place to hold this information. It was impossible to store in her mind, so it lurked in the open with all its sharp, ugly edges, shredding her from the inside out. Her whole life, she'd gone out of her way not to hurt him. Not to hurt Mom. Now he was weak. Unwell. She shouldn't be pushing him like this. But with this ugly, sharp truth inducing such pain, she wanted to lash out and make him feel it, too. "There was nothing in my file about them."

"Who?"

"My parents."

The coloring he'd regained leaked away.

But Eden couldn't stop. She pressed harder against the wound. "My *real* parents."

Dad set the half-eaten broth on the table beside him and took a deep, labored breath. "I was in the CIA."

"I know."

"Do you also know ... that your mother and I underwent ... in-vitro fertilization?"

Eden nodded.

"They were two separate things. Completely disconnected. Until suddenly they weren't." He looked away, as though haunted by the words. Or maybe the memory.

According to Dr. Norton, it was the worst assignment he ever had to carry out. The subjects were freaks of nature. Karik Volkova's monstrous creations. They were also babies. Her father destroyed two of them.

"I found Barret and the girl's biological father. It was risky. But we made contact. They took their children ... and they disappeared."

Eden pictured Barrett's parents on national television—pleading with the public to help them find their son, all the while knowing what he was.

"I couldn't find Ellery's. Or yours."

Her biological parents. Two people who shared her DNA. Were they out there somewhere, or did they die in The Attack like so many others? She tried to process the possibility—pull it apart, put it back together. But how could she process their death when she still hadn't been able to process their life? Real people

—flesh and blood—who had wanted children like Alaric and Molly Taylor, and in the process of making them, lost her. She was taken and turned into a dangerous weapon.

"What happened?" she asked bitterly. "You and Jack drew straws for the two who were left? Or did he get first pick and you were stuck with the leftovers?"

"Eden."

She bit her lip, shook her head.

He spoke her name again, two syllables filled with all the gentleness in the world.

But she couldn't look at him.

Couldn't face him.

"You have my eyes, kid."

"That's a lie!" The words spewed like lava from a volcano, her chin trembling in the wake of them. Her lungs catching fire. "You told me that, and I believed you. You made me see something that wasn't there. I don't have your eyes. I *can't* have your eyes."

"But you do."

Tears blurred her vision. She swiped at her cheek with the back of her hand, her throat thick and hot.

"Somehow. Miraculously. You do."

Eden shook her head.

But he kept going, despite the difficulty of the prolonged conversation. "The second I saw you ... I couldn't take my eyes off you. It was like ... you were mine." He pressed his fist against his chest. "And because of that, I couldn't finish my assignment. Jack and Annette got Ellery. And Barrett and the girl are alive."

"But we shouldn't be. We were created by a monster."

"You give him too much power. He is not your creator, Eden."

"But—"

"Volkova couldn't create human life. He could only alter it. You existed before him. And all this ..." Dad looked at the monitors and the IV and the tubes that ran to and from his injured body. There were so many of them. "I'd go through it a hundred times more for one day with you, kid."

The tears fell. They dropped from her eyes, too fast to catch.

"You have brought your mother and I so much joy. So much love." Dad took her hand and squeezed it with a strength that belied the weakness of his voice. "Don't ever believe … that you shouldn't exist. That your life … doesn't matter. Do you hear me?"

Eden squeezed back.

She held on.

To him. To his words.

She held on for all she was worth.

43

Cass sat in his ruined apartment on his laptop, safe and secure despite the break-in. Due to its black-market nature, he never took it with him. He kept it hidden behind a loose board of drywall in the back of his linen closet. It had all the software he needed to hack into SafePad's mainframe. Since doing so, he'd spent hours scouring databases, searching through directories, gathering names into a list, then plugging each one into the world wide web, determined to find a photograph that would match Mordecai's face and uncover his real name.

So far, Cass had no luck.

And Mordecai had yet to make a move.

A fact that rankled as much as it confused.

Not only did he not get his hands on Eden, he'd also lost possession of Subject 003 and 004. He had to have plans to retrieve them. So why wasn't he making a move? Mordecai knew Cass was involved. He knew how to get in touch with him. So here Cass remained, inside his ransacked apartment, daring Mordecai to find him. Daring Vick to find him. Daring someone to find him so he could put an end to this once and for all.

The scene that continued to replay whenever he closed his eyes drove him relentlessly onward. The tattooed man pawing her. Mordecai, ogling her. Possibly controlling her. Cass never wanted to be in that position again—forced to rescue Eden by destroying her.

This time, he would rescue her by destroying *him*.

But first, he had to find him.

SafePad Elite had compounds spread throughout the country. Mordecai used the base in Chicago to establish his headquarters, which meant he had to own one or more of those particular units. So, Cass had started there. When he finished with no hits, he broadened his search and broadened again until he'd gone through every owner in the system, along with their spouses.

Not one had Mordecai's face.

With a frustrated jerk of his pencil, he scratched the final name off the list. He rubbed his eyes, then scrubbed his palm down the length of his face—thinking about Eden. Missing Eden. So much it was painful. Over the past seven days, he'd been in touch with Forrester and Norton. But Eden, he left alone. He was giving her space to reunite with her parents, all the while battling a maddening bout of uncertainty. What did he mean to a girl like her?

He wasn't a fool and neither was she. There was a strong chance she'd kissed him to guarantee his cooperation, to ensure he would carry out a task nobody else was willing to carry out. And even if that wasn't the whole truth—even if some part of Eden cared for him—what now? They'd accomplished what they'd set out to do—find and rescue her mom and dad. But with that success came complications. Namely, Eden was a teenager with a set of loving and protective parents. He was an off-the-grid fighter who'd been hired to find her, then agreed to destroy her.

It wasn't exactly a good resume.

Cass folded his hands behind his head and leaned back in his chair, his unfocused attention lingering on the list of crossed off names, then the week-old publication of the Concordia Times beneath it. He didn't usually keep old newspapers, but he kept this one because of the front-page article—a story about the mysterious break-in at SafePad which resulted in four dead guards and a dead John Doe. Authorities had been unable to identify him, which suggested he lived off the grid. The coroner ruled the cause of death poisoning by a high concentration of cyanide. The four guards, however, had been shot cleanly through the head. Like Yukio. But the guards were not dead when Cassian left, which meant an officer must have shot them.

Why?

Did Mordecai have ins with the police? Did he pay off a dirty cop to shoot the pawns to cover his tracks? Cass scratched his chin, rereading the quote provided by SafePad's Head of Security. Then he sat up straighter. These guards were employees of SafePad. Pawns, perhaps. But that didn't mean they hadn't left behind a trail that might lead to Mordecai. Cass leaned forward and pulled up another database. This time, of the compound's security personnel.

He culled together another list.

He started plugging in more names.

Three hours later, he hit pay dirt.

A photograph from an article published over a decade ago in Concordia Chicago, when the compound was first built. In it, the property manager—a woman who didn't own any of the luxury units but oversaw them—was shaking hands with Oswin Brahm, the company's founder. And behind them, was a man listed as SafePad's Chief Investment Specialist.

It was Mordecai.

With a jolt of adrenaline, Cass printed the article. Then he printed several more. He folded them. Shoved them into his back pocket. Returned his computer to the back of his linen closet. Grabbed his gun. And took the stairs two at a time. He jumped on the motorcycle, revved the engine, and peeled away from the curb—fueled by a raging inferno of care and longing and unyielding determination.

He was going to put his tracking skills to good use.

He'd found Mordecai's real name.

Now it was time to find Mordecai.

He wouldn't rest until the threat was eliminated.

He wouldn't stop until Eden was safe.

THE ABERRATION
OF EDEN PRUITT

"A 90 mph start that
doesn't slow down."

- Christy Hall of Fame author
James L. Rubart

K.E. GANSHERT

ABOUT THE AUTHOR

K.E. Ganshert is an award-winning author of clean fiction filled with mystery, adventure, romance, and the fantastical. Her stories are perfect for readers who crave unexpected twists, strange happenings, high stakes, and romance that runs deep but never explicit. She lives in eastern Iowa with her husband and their two children.

TURN THE PAGE FOR MORE

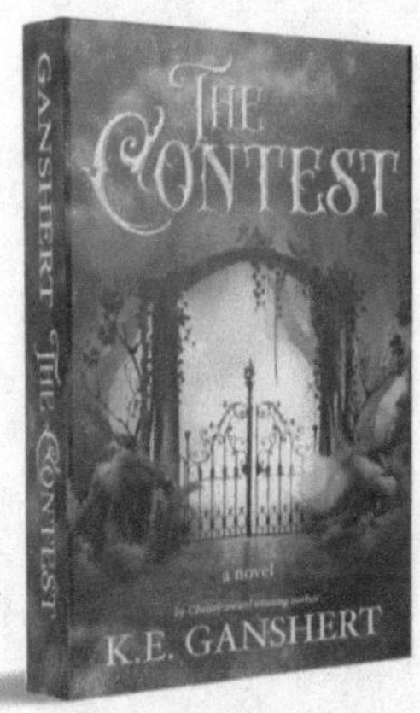

An orphan with no one but her brother.
A prince with everything but his freedom.
A deadly contest only one can win ...

In a world of haves and have nots, where petty crime is punishable by death and magic is forbidden, a deadly contest unfolds in secret. Twelve competitors are mysteriously invited. The winner gets one wish.

For 17-year-old Briar Bishop, this means saving her brother from execution by guillotine, and she's not going to let anything or anyone get in her way. Especially not Leo Davenbrook, the tantalizing High Prince, a mischievous flirt who's grown up with everything she never had and whose very presence threatens her survival.

She has no idea a darker battle wages in secret, one that could lead to a fate far more disastrous than the death of her brother.

**If the world is right, then I am crazy.
And crazy is dangerous.**

In a society that doesn't believe in the supernatural—and punishes those who do—Tess Eckhart is afraid she's losing her mind. After a terrifying incident at a high school party, her family is afraid, too. Enough to pack up their lives and move across the country—right next to a privately owned mental health facility that operates outside government control.

Tess is determined to fit in at her new school, to ignore the whispers and stares. But when it comes to Luka Williams, a reluctantly popular boy in her class, she's unused to a stare that intense. Then the headaches start, and the seemingly prophetic dreams that haunt her at night. As Tess tries to hide them, she becomes increasingly convinced that Luka knows something—that he might somehow be responsible.

But what if she's wrong? What if Luka Williams is the only thing separating her from a madness too terrifying to fathom?